MW00780011

The Lost House

The Lost House

MELISSA LARSEN

MINOTAUR BOOKS
NEW YORK

First published in the United States by Minotaur Books, an imprint of St. Martin's Publishing Group

www.minotaurbooks.com

Designed by Meryl Sussman Levavi

Library of Congress Cataloging-in-Publication Data

Names: Larsen, Melissa, author.
Title: The lost house / Melissa Larsen.
Description: First edition. | New York : Minotaur books, 2025.
Identifiers: LCCN 2024034941 | ISBN 9781250332875 (hardcover) | ISBN 9781250332882 (ebook)
Subjects: LCGFT: Detective and mystery fiction. | Thrillers (Fiction) | Novels.
Classification: LCC PS3612.A7728 L67 2025 | DDC 813/.6—dc23/ eng/20240802
LC record available at https://lccn.loc.gov/2024034941

Our books may be purchased in bulk for promotional, educational, or business use. Please contact your local bookseller or the Macmillan Corporate and Premium Sales Department at 1-800-221-7945, extension 5442, or by email at MacmillanSpecialMarkets@macmillan.com.

First Edition: 2025

10 9 8 7 6 5 4 3 2 1

For my family

Don't you know
I don't believe in letting go?
I don't believe in snow.

Forest Erwin, "Devotion"

Part
One

PROLOGUE

February 3, 2019

I hope I haunt you.

Ása can feel the beat of the music pulsing in her skeleton, but she can't hear it. She can feel Lilja's hot breath on the back of her neck, undoubtedly complaining about something, anything to get Ása's attention back on her, but she can't decipher it. The vodka burns a messy path down her throat and she doesn't know how many she's had, but she can't bring herself to care. There is no party. There is only the high-pitched internal scream that whistles in her ears every time she thinks about him and the words on the screen in her hand. Her fingers hurt from clutching the phone for so long.

I hope I haunt you.

All it takes is a tap, and she'll have sent it. She'll never have to see him again.

She can't do it.

"What's wrong?" Lilja, shouting in her ear.

Ása clicks the button to kill her screen. Lilja will look. She'll search for a gap in Ása's concentration. She can't let things rest. Sometimes Ása thinks Lilja can smell the secrets on her.

Normally, Ása can swallow her irritation. But there's no more room in her stomach. No more patience. The sounds of the party come back in a flood, the music, the laughter, the press of bodies dancing. At her feet, there's a half-empty beer can spinning on its side, vomiting its contents all over the floor. Ása toes it away from her, but it rolls halt-ingly back to her. She kicks it.

The can lands with a satisfying *smack* on a girl's leg, exploding the last of its contents. "*Hey!*" she yells, twisting in place to figure out what's happened.

"Aim higher next time," Lilja says, hoping for a laugh.

Desperate for some air, Ása pushes through the crowd in the living room, into the decrepit kitchen. Lilja follows, as Ása knew she would. They find a corner by the back door, the only open space in the aban-doned house. It's never been this full. Even in the dead of winter, the room is hot with the combined breath and body heat of its inhabi-tants. The smell of sweat and grease and cigarette smoke overwhelms Ása, threatening to choke her. Or maybe it's just Lilja's arm, snaking around her neck. Strands of her hair plaster onto Ása's skin, dragging and sucking like tentacles.

"Is it Óskar?" Lilja asks. "Or is it—"

"Leave it," Ása warns her. She slicks her friend's hair away from her face.

Lilja's eyes are red and unfocused. She asks, "Is it me?" like she's ter-rified to hear the truth that it is, but she can't help herself from asking, just as she can't help herself from snooping.

Ása knows she is equally unsteady, has had even more to drink than Lilja, but the anger roiling inside her props her up. The rage and the desire to run—to him, from him, she doesn't know anymore.

"Does it ever bother you," Ása says, shouting over the music, "how everyone wants everything from you, all the time? No one is happy.

We are all hungry mouths. Opening and closing, opening and closing." She demonstrates with her hand, blinking as her own fingers blur in front of her.

"What?" Lilja aims her ear at Ása's face.

"Nothing," Ása says.

It's true.

It's nothing.

There's another mouth coming toward her. Óskar, cutting through the crowd, shoving at people's shoulders, laughing when he spills someone's drink. He wants Ása to dance.

He wants so much from her.

Ása downs the last remnants of her drink and lets the cup fall to the floor. She's leaving.

"Where are you going?" Lilja asks her, wounded. Hungry.

"I have to piss," Ása lies. She tells Lilja she'll go outside. There's nowhere to go in here, not unless she wants an audience. Lilja starts to follow, but Ása presses a hand against her chest. "I can do it myself. Give me a moment."

She moves before Lilja can voice her hurt, before Óskar can reach her. They came in through the front door, but that's too far away, the crowd too full for her to try. Even if she weren't feeling like this, like her whole world were coming apart and she was the one yanking at each thread, she wouldn't want to be here. It's the big night, the last celebration before they lose access to the house. Everyone's treating it like a great tragedy. But this is just an excuse to drink too much, to dance in the darkness together, screaming into the void.

She nudges the plywood aside from the back door, prepares to throw her body into it to get it free, but the door swings smoothly on its hinges. She slips outside, pulling the door shut behind her. She takes a sharp breath, hoping the frigid air will sober her up. Usually it helps, but tonight, there's no feeling, as though she's walked into a vacuum. There's no light, either. The scant illumination from the lanterns and flashlights inside is nothing against the plywood tacked to the windows. All that's left is a thin line of white leaking through the cracks. The rush of the river, so close, sucks the remaining air from Ása's lungs.

With trembling fingers, she slips her phone from her jacket pocket. There's the message, still waiting to be sent. She's already said so much, but she wants these to be the last words. She wants him to understand. She wants to hurt him, the way he's hurt her.

I hope I haunt you.

She's sick of thinking about it. And staring down at the bright screen is making her feel actually sick.

She presses send.

The relief doesn't come. Ása shoves the phone back into her pocket and steps forward, into the night. She'll go home and sleep this off. It will be better in the morning, when she wakes up new and free and probably so hungover she'll want to die, but at least she'll be alone.

She aims for the trees, for Óskar's car somewhere beyond, but her legs won't cooperate.

She can't find her balance. Her feet sink strangely into the fresh snow, sliding sideways or backward, so that she can't trust each foot-step. That last drink—those last drinks—had been a mistake. She can see it now. Inside, with all the chaos, the unsteadiness had felt normal. Expected.

Everything she has done recently has been a mistake.

Her fingers touch the cold snow and there's pressure in the back of her eyes. When did she fall over? Acid fills her throat, but she swallows it down. If she starts vomiting now, she won't stop.

The world rights itself in slow, blurry stages. She has to get to the car. Óskar left the keys in the cupholder. She'll sit in there, take a min-ute. Warm up with the heater. She can wait for him or Lilja to follow her out. Either one of them can drive her back.

She's in the trees, making her way by feel more than sight, the noise of the party a distant murmur behind her. Here, the quiet throbs against her ears, the snow muffling even the harsh quality of her breathing.

Which is why she doesn't hear it at first.

A voice.

Soft.

She thinks it's her own voice at first, she's whimpering under her breath. But the sound comes again, and it's not her, not her own blurry whisper telling her to move.

It's a man's voice.

Calling her name.

She walks faster, brushing her hands against the rough bark of the tree trunks as she goes. The voice presses closer. Louder.

"What are you doing? Ása?"

There's a catch in her body, hurtling her forward. She's aware of sitting, of both hands freezing in the snow. She doesn't know how long she's been like this. She drank too much tonight. This isn't what she's used to. This is something beyond her body. She's hovering outside of herself, but there's no thought in the outside. Only the trees spinning around her and the vague sense of anger, but even that is draining away.

She looks up into a beam of light.

There are hands in her armpits. Hoisting her back up to standing. She feels safe, because someone who cares about her is here to help her, but there's the whistling again. High-pitched and shrill, a teakettle screaming on the stove. She wonders if he can hear it, too.

CHAPTER ONE

February 5, 2019

The wind rolls over the rental car in a tidal wave so strong Agnes's knuckles turn white on the steering wheel. Snow follows in its wake, swirling against the windshield, packing into small piles on the bottom of the wipers' arc, and she leans forward in her seat, one hand reaching to turn down the volume of the radio, as though that'll help her see. It's seven in the morning, but it's dark enough to be the middle of the night. She's exhausted from the flights, her body cramped and sore.

The GPS that came with the car tells her it's a two-hour drive from the Keflavík airport to the old farmhouse, where she'll be meeting Nora Carver, finally, in person. At the rate she's going, though, it might be closer to four hours. Except for the few cars skidding past her at speeds she can't fathom in this weather, she's alone on the highway.

Agnes has lived in California her entire life, and never the parts that know snow. She can take the turns of the road, the limited visibility, but this snow makes her heart pound in her throat. As do the roundabouts. Every few minutes, it seems, a new oval interrupts the lane, forcing her to slow on the ice, to rub shoulders with the road, and to figure out her next turn. She supposes they're there to maintain the speed limit or to prevent traffic jams, something like that, but they unnerve her.

She tries to relax into the slick motion of the car, into the tunnel of snow pelting toward her. But she can't settle. It's the ache in her joints, her ankle throbbing in time with her too-quick heartbeat, the nausea simmering somewhere in her stomach. Or it's the fact that she's actually here, in Iceland. Or, she thinks, it's the fear of failure.

What will happen to her, if she can't do this?

Her hand reflexively reaches for her phone, propped up in the cup-holder. Her father is the last person she wants to talk to, but he's also the only person who might pick up if she called. She wishes she could call her grandfather. There's so much to tell him, so much to ask. Right now, though, all she wants is to hear him say, as he did at the end of every call, *I love you.*

It's only as her fingers slide over the glossy screen of her phone, though, that she remembers: it's still on airplane mode. She can't afford to roam, and she isn't sure if her phone connecting to the local network will automatically charge her account. She could hardly manage the flights here, booked at the last minute, at the mercy of whatever force makes a plane ticket cost a month's rent because you want to fly the next week. Even with Nora arranging her car and her stay, this trip is beyond Agnes's means. Her medical bills had drained her savings and now she's down to the dregs of what her grandfather had left to her. Her, and only her. Not a penny to her father.

I love you, Agnes. And you love me, don't you?

Her hand drifts back to the steering wheel. No one to call. Fourteen hours of travel. Fourteen hours since she's been online. It's not that long to be disconnected from the world, but right now, it feels like it's all she's known and it's all she'll ever know.

Even though she and Emi had officially broken up six months ago, they've kept in constant contact. Every other day, Agnes manufactures a reason to text Emi. I saw a new way to kill aphids safely with oils. How's the garden coming? And then Emi answers. Emi might have been the one to end it, the one to pack up Agnes's things and carry the boxes one by one out of their apartment and into her father's home, but whenever Agnes texts, Emi answers. And that, Agnes understands now, is the problem. In the early days of the breakup, Emi's generosity had felt like a lifeline. Somewhere along the way, though, it had transformed into a noose. And now even that is gone. Agnes doesn't have service.

She's alone.

Agnes leans into the car's movements, following the signs for Reykjavík. Houses appear out of the darkness, aglow with leftover Christmas lights. She imagines the people sleeping inside, waking up, shuffling through the cozy winter morning, seeking coffee. She pictures herself in this car, zipping past their windows like a dragonfly streaking in a slipstream, and for one brief moment, she can actually relax.

The road gradually takes on more lanes. This place could be California. It's a highway. It's a group of buildings. How different can they be?

The answer is: very different.

This is her first time out of the country, and she's struck, horribly, by a burning self-hatred. She's wasted twenty-seven years patrolling the same highways, absorbing the same colors, the same smells. So much time in one place. What did that get her?

It's not that she hasn't dreamt of traveling. She had long imagined herself in Iceland, coming here with her grandfather. She'd searched out language courses online, but never committed, because she knew that to learn a language, you need to have someone to speak it with, and neither her grandfather nor her father would ever speak it with her. She's settled for listening to the music that comes from there. Here. She's watched the movies. She's fantasized.

But in all the fantasies, it never actually occurred to her that she could just get on a plane and come here. Not until Nora Carver.

Agnes should have come here years ago, before Emi and her grandfather broke her heart. She was a lighter person back then, aimless in a nice way. Not self-destructive. She'd been gainfully employed, coding software for big tech, living with friends, visiting her grandfather every Sunday for either a swim or a long chat in his garden, and she was open to the world. Which is how she met Emi and how she didn't realize how much of herself she'd given to those she loved, not until she'd lost them.

She's supposed to go straight from the airport to Bifröst, to Nora. That had been the plan. But she flicks on her blinker and makes a slow, deliberate turn into the city center.

Now that she's finally here, she's going to see this place on her own terms. Nora can wait.

Signs lead her downtown. She takes turns at random until she's curling around the outskirts of the city, tracing the line of the water to one side, the rise of the city's low buildings to the other. She marvels at the black water, the hint of a mountain just across the way. Warm yellow streetlamps guide her along the unfamiliar roads. She veers away from the water, into the city proper, the streets narrowing. She passes closed shops, dark storefronts. A few figures, fighting the early morning chill. She drives the wrong way down a one-way street, to the astonishment of a car that is, as far as she can tell, two spotlights. She rolls down her window to apologize and receives an ear splitting honk in response. By some miracle, she finds a parking spot on a residential street. And then it takes a monumental effort to get out of the car. Her back creaks and protests, her knee and ankle screaming in collective pain.

Sitting in one set position for the past fourteen hours has sent her back to the early days of her recovery, when her worldview had contracted down to her left leg, and only her left leg. The cold envelops her in a tight, frigid embrace, despite the layers of shirts, a hoodie, and a windbreaker. Her sneakers slide on the snow and ice, her ankle locking up in protest, and she stops in the first open café she sees.

The warmth of the room hits her like a solid wall. The barista, a young woman with too-short bangs and an eyebrow piercing, nods at Agnes, but she doesn't speak. She simply moves about the enormous coffee machine, operating it with an unhurried ease that Agnes admires.

The counter offers an assortment of wrapped chocolates, jars of jam, and bags of coffee beans. Agnes draws a finger over a package of black licorice. Her grandfather's favorite indulgence. Every Sunday, up to the end, featured a bag of this candy, usually thrown onto the table between them. She hasn't eaten any in a year.

Agnes nudges the package forward on the counter to buy it. Her grandfather would want her to. He would've already opened the bag and swallowed a handful.

The barista acknowledges it, Agnes assumes, but continues with her work, unrushed. Agnes turns her attention to the rest of the display. To her left is a corkboard, piled high with what she assumes are the usual offerings at a café bulletin board. Guitar lessons, rooms to rent, flyers to see someone's band play next week.

What catches her by surprise, though, is the photo at the center. A young woman's face stares back at her, her expression bursting with pleasure. There's a cascade of white-blond hair, the flash of a smile, the hint of some shared happiness with the photographer. The surprise comes in stages. First, because at a glance this woman could be Agnes. The hair, the thin eyes. But then the borders of the photograph settle into place. The words, in English, MISSING. And PLEASE HELP.

Agnes leans in to read the text underneath but almost immediately flinches away.

Bifröst.

A student at Bifröst, is what it reads.

Maybe there are two towns named Bifröst. Except there's the university. Agnes thinks of her grandfather, and Nora Carver. It's too much of a coincidence. She finds the barista staring at her, so she orders a coffee and an egg sandwich, trying to ignore the dread settling in her empty stomach.

She chooses a table on the other side of the café, far away from the missing student's smiling face. Next to the fogged-up window, she watches her fingers transform from a troubling white to an even more troubling pink. She'll buy herself a winter jacket before she leaves Reykjavík. She peers down at her frozen, muddy sneakers. And maybe some boots. She'll ask the woman working here for advice on where to go. For now, though, she signs into the café's Wi-Fi, grateful to return to the internet.

No word from Emi.

Nothing from her father.

Nothing in her email inbox except junk.

She took a leave of absence from her job nearly a year ago, and formally quit soon after. Wi-Fi or no, it doesn't matter. She's alone.

She stares out the window to the dark street. It's empty except for a few silhouettes of people walking by, skittering like shadows. A drift of car headlights. Agnes has been holding onto ghosts. The ghost of her relationship with Emi, the ghost of her grandfather superimposed onto her father. What would happen if she let them go? Who would she be?

She scrolls through her latest email exchange with Nora. The last email is nothing more than Nora's directions to the house in Bifröst, in case the GPS fails her, and warnings about the icy roads. *The weather changes fast—and I mean fast. It can be sunny on one side of the road and snowing like a blizzard on the other.* Then, a final word of thanks, before Agnes boarded her plane: *It's an honor to share this place with you. I want you to know how much I appreciate what you're doing here . . . speaking with me.*

Agnes Glin, granddaughter to Einar Pálsson, the suspected murderer in one of Iceland's most notorious unsolved crimes. The first one in the family to break the forty-year silence. The first one in the family to advocate, publicly, for Einar's innocence. Nora Carver has been falling all over herself to make Agnes comfortable. She knows, as they both know, that Agnes could have chosen anyone.

Agnes chose Nora mostly because of the timing, but she'd been impressed by her reputation. As Einar Pálsson's granddaughter, Agnes has spent her life avoiding the true crime genre. She prefers audiobooks, neo-noir detective novels, popcorn action thrillers, anything fictional and completely removed from her life. But she'd heard about Nora's podcast, *The End*, as had everyone else in the past year. Nora Carver, a different kind of true crime podcaster. One who has actually solved a cold case. Or, as Nora demurred in an interview with Rachel Maddow, *contributed* to a solve.

That had been the last season of *The End*, the investigation into the unsolved murder of Adriana Lopez, a twelve-year-old girl found near a playground in Modesto, California, in 1974. Agnes hadn't listened to that season, nor had she followed the case too closely—her grandfather was dying, and she'd had no time for anything else—but she knows enough. With Nora's help, they'd finally pinpointed the murderer. A police officer who had been caught in another, more recent murder of another young girl outside of Stockton, California. He'd never been a suspect, not until Nora found him in some lost paperwork.

When Agnes's father had received the email from Nora a month ago, notifying him of her plans to dedicate her next series to "the Frozen Madonna case," it fractured Agnes's already-tenuous balance with him.

He had recited Nora's email to Agnes, standing over her bed and reading from his phone as though he were a minister in his pulpit raging against the sins of the devil, rather than a reclusive engineer. *You don't have to be on the record, not if you're not comfortable with it. But you could fill in the blanks, color in the details of your mother's life. Your sister's, too, tragically short as it was.* The minister's eyes, startling her.

What are you going to do? Agnes had asked, even though she'd known the answer. She asked because that type of emotion requires an outlet. A storm cloud needs to burst with lightning.

I will tell her no. Her father's shaking hands. *I will sue her. She's turning our family into a spectacle.*

Since Agnes had moved back home, she hadn't experienced her father's anger. She'd expected it, though. She'd needed so much from him. Moving her bedroom from the second floor to the first, so she wouldn't have to contend with the stairs. Helping her to step over the tub, into and out of the shower. She'd waited for the outburst, the exasperation of a man carrying both his own and his daughter's dead weight, but instead he'd borne it all in the same manner he'd raised her. Stoically.

To her surprise, the anger didn't come last week, either, when Agnes told her father she'd reached out to Nora herself. That she'd learned the podcast host would be visiting Iceland—and not just visiting, but exploring the ruins of her grandfather's farmhouse, her father's childhood home—to record her series. To interview those who still live there, who still remember what had happened to her grandmother and her aunt. And that Agnes would be joining her. She would be interviewed, as well.

She'd braced herself for the bolts of lightning. The shouting. But her father had borne that, too, stoically.

The fight had come when she'd left for the airport. Maybe Magnús hadn't believed she'd actually go. Maybe he hadn't even heard her, too lost in the haze of his own inaccessible thoughts, when she'd told him her plans.

Despite her father's rage and disappointment, Agnes is proud of herself. She's doing the right thing. The hospital-appointed psychologist, Dr. Lee, had told her to find something constructive in her life, after her injury. *Humans need to build. To create. That emptiness you feel is the lack of something to strive toward.*

This isn't a hobby, like painting or knitting, as Dr. Lee had suggested. This is something greater. It hits Agnes now, the reality of what she's doing. What she's hoping to do. This is a chance at redemption for her family. Her father doesn't understand it yet. But he will.

She stares down at her phone. Along with the last email, Nora sent the demo she's already recorded, a teaser trailer she's created for the series. Agnes knows she ought to listen to it. She ought to be able to discuss the case using Nora's language, to steel herself for all the details she's successfully avoided all these years. She knows the Wikipedia article. She knows what her father has shared with her—very little—over the years. But there's so much more out there, waiting for her. Archives of blogs and photos. Books. Theories and gory details and photographs.

The Frozen Madonna and Child.

Agnes tells herself to put in her headphones. Hit play. Get it over with.

She can't.

There is no before, her grandfather had said. She'd known not to ask about his late wife and daughter, but if she'd asked any question about his childhood, or his life in Iceland, that was always the answer. *My life began when you were born.*

She's kept her grandfather's silence, and she's respected his privacy. Now she's violating both. Einar, the murderer who went free. Einar, the man who raised her with more affection than her father ever had. Which of these two men was he?

I love you, Agnes. And you love me, don't you?

Her fingers tap at her phone screen, scrolling away from Nora's demo. She sends a note to her father. I'm here, she texts. In Reykjavík. Will be getting there later today. She deliberates. For just a moment, she can hear her grandfather's voice, the soft gravel of his English. Then she adds, Love you.

It's close to midnight in Berkeley. Her father's awake. He's never gone to sleep earlier than three a.m., and even then, he's always somehow online. As a kid, Agnes used to wander into his bedroom whenever she couldn't sleep. She'd inherited his insomnia, just as she'd inherited his square shoulders, his white-blond hair. She'd find her father propped up in bed, glasses reflecting the light of a computer, a cell phone, or a reading light over a book. In her earliest memories, her mother had been there, too, sleeping like a stone on the other side of the bed. After the divorce, after her mother had moved to Maine with her new husband, it was just Agnes and her father. Those stolen moments in the liminal haze of night, those were the times when she felt closest to her stoic father. *Agnes and Magnús,* he'd say, smoothing her hair, his attention mostly focused on his book or his email, *two sides of the same coin.*

There's no response.

He's awake and he's not letting her in.

She doesn't text Emi.

For the first month after her injury, Agnes had been convinced she'd actually died and remained dead. The feeling has since faded over the past year, but it comes back to her in flashes. It washes over her, here in the café in Reykjavík, the tingle of weightlessness, of a secret, the wave lifting her and throwing her around. Nothing can touch her. Nothing can wound. She's above it all.

She drinks three coffees and eats her breakfast. Finally, she puts in her headphones. She presses play.

DEMO

"The Bifröst Murders"—Nora Carver, The End

This time on *The End*, we're entering the world of frozen bodies, of ice and lava fields, and, of course, murder . . . If you have any interest in true crime, you've seen that photo . . . you know the one I'm talking about . . . the Frozen Madonna and Child. The black-and-white portrait of a young woman and her baby, lying together in a blanket of snow. They could be sleeping. Except that the young woman's throat has been slashed, so deeply she was nearly decapitated. And the child? Drowned and frozen solid.

That's right, everyone. On this season of *The End*, in honor of the fortieth anniversary of their discovery, we are going to talk about Marie Hvass and Agnes Einarsdóttir, otherwise known as "the Frozen Madonna and Child."

Oh, and a quick note about names. There are going to be a lot of new names in this series, names and sounds you may never have heard before, or have never tried to pronounce . . . Iceland uses a patronymic system, meaning the last names are derived from the father's first name. Occasionally they're derived from the mother's first name. This is why Marie and Agnes, mother and daughter, don't share a last name. Don't worry, you'll get used to it. I apologize in advance for my pronunciation.

This season, we're traveling to the west coast of Iceland. Bifröst is a small town, home to a local university that hosts a surprising number of students, but it's still quite small, composed only of a handful of streets that bracket the main highway of the island. In summer, the surrounding lava fields are a deep, mossy green. The midnight sun transforms the countryside into a land of light and open skies. We're traveling there in the winter, however, when a thick carpet of snow and ice, hardened by the wind, covers the ground. We're seeing about seven hours of daylight—less with the bad weather, the sharp angle of the earth. We're coming out of the darkest days of the year.

But enough about the weather.

February 13, 1979 is a Tuesday morning. Local schoolteacher Marie and her six-month-old daughter, Agnes, have been missing for four days. There's no note. The family's one car is in possession of her husband. There's no history of Marie leaving her family, not even for an afternoon, not without a note. And with her family back in Denmark, and no connections outside of that small town, there's nowhere she'd go. Her husband, Einar Pálsson, and son, nine-year-old Magnús, are beside themselves with worry.

On this Tuesday, we're going to follow six-year-old Ingvar Karlsson out of the township, into the snow and the wilderness. Ingvar loves his teacher. He insists on joining his parents in the search party, but soon wanders off on his own.

This six-year-old boy struggles in the deep snow. These are untouched fields. The cold stings his face. His fingers hurt. At some point, he'd removed his gloves and now he can't find them.

He stumbles over what feels like a rock, landing clumsily onto his front.

And that's when he sees it . . .

The shape in the snow, the distinct form of a woman's body, lying on her side as though in sleep. He clears the snow away from her, finds the angelic face of his teacher, Marie. He tells her he's frightened. Everyone's looking for her—what's she doing here? Then he looks down.

There's the viscera of an open throat. Frozen in the time of its destruction. It's a blessing that she was left there in winter. In summer, he would've smelled her . . . He would've seen the decomposition and the flies. As it was . . . she was preserved.

That's when the screaming started. From the account of his parents, this little boy's voice could be heard echoing along the valley. They, along with the rest of the search party, found him next to the body of his teacher, his face a mask of terror.

You see, in the uncovering of her neck, he'd noticed the baby in her arms . . .

CHAPTER TWO

February 5, 2019

The jacket and boots cost almost as much as the flights. Agnes hands over her single credit card and prays it won't melt in the polite woman's fingers when she charges it. She hasn't worked in a year, and even after spending the past six months at home not paying rent, she isn't exactly flush with cash. But it goes through, and the woman wishes her luck on her trip. Feeling a little bit foolish, like a five-year-old wearing her new shoes out of the store, Agnes exits onto the street engulfed in the enormous, bright red puffy jacket—a necessity, the woman had assured her, especially if she's traveling farther north—feet clunking in the stiff boots, her old jacket and shoes piled in a bag like dead fish.

In the time it took her to buy her new outfit, the city has finally woken up. A weak ray of sunlight penetrates the dense clouds, its illumination hardly any brighter than the Christmas lights that line nearly every storefront, every tree branch.

Agnes retraces her steps back to the café and the general direction of the rental car, but slowly. She doesn't want to get lost, but she doesn't want to rush out of here. She can hardly believe she's really in Iceland. The language, spoken in the hushed, tired voices of morning commuters, draws her in like a magic spell. It awakens deep memories of her grandfather. Conversations overheard between him and her father. The clipped, gasping rhythm of Einar's voice. She misses him more than she thought she could. Seeing his home country, listening to his language, she feels his absence as a yawning emptiness in the pit of her stomach.

Stuffed in her pockets, her hands shake—not from cold, but from suppressed emotion. Because this isn't just grief tearing her apart. There's anger, too. Anger at her father. She's come all this way to help her grandfather, to reconnect with him after his death, and her father hates her for it.

Is this really who you are? Magnús had asked her, when he'd seen her suitcase by the door. Then, later, when both of their tempers had blown past shouting to a hoarse sort of verbal fistfight, *You're choosing fame over your family.*

She doesn't remember what she said. That's always been her problem—one of her problems. She can remember, vividly, what has been told to her. Shouted at her. But when she loses her temper, there's nothing there. The tape recorder presses pause to give her room to scream. Watching the mix of tourists and locals milling up and down the street, she knows she would have explained to her father that Nora Carver would be recording this series with or without Agnes's help. There would already be a spotlight on their family again. There's always been a fascination with this case. Because it's unsolved. Because it occurred in a country where there's almost no murder, nothing that vicious. Because of the different deaths. And because of that photo. The young white woman, beautiful even in death. Arranged to clutch her baby to her chest. The Icelandic Black Dahlia. The snow-covered *Pietà*.

With Agnes here, she can tell the world how wrong they were about her grandfather.

This is a choice, her father had said, his index finger thrust toward her face. *This isn't out of your control. You are choosing, yet again, to hurt me. Don't forget this. I know I won't be able to.*

A door slamming. His return to his office. Agnes had left without another word. Her father has assumed the worst of her. He's taken the most uncharitable reading of her motivations for coming here. He's made her feel small when she knows she's finally doing something right.

Back in the café, she'd texted her father looking for comfort, a reminder of home. She won't make the same mistake again.

She's on her own.

Agnes retraces her steps to the car, hoping the movement will loosen her stiff joints. She's convinced she can actually feel the bolts in her ankle grinding against the bone, but there's nothing she can do about that, nothing except another pill, and that's the other thing. The other threshold she'd crossed, somewhere over the Atlantic. This past year, the pills have been a blessing, for their oblivion. But she can't prove her grandfather's innocence while she's numb. So she distracts herself by watching the people around her, swathed in their winter gear, and pictures herself as one of them. Some American tourists, traveling as a group, are posing for photos in the middle of a road leading up to a dramatic, pointed church. The cement has been painted in the colors of a bright rainbow, making for the perfect photo op. The Americans take turns posing and laughing, encouraging each other. Agnes is one of them, the tourists, and she isn't. She's happy to be here. Stunned. And yet a part of her is gone. Held back in Berkeley, perhaps, lonely and trapped but ultimately safe.

Now that she's had her moment in the city, it's time to go to Nora Carver. To Bifröst, and to her family's past.

I want to discover the truth, of course, Nora had told her on their one and only phone call last week, when Agnes had finally decided to join her, *but the truth is rare and flexible.* That phrasing has haunted Agnes ever since. *Rare and flexible.* Like a steak, or a woman's body.

What's your definition of truth, then? Agnes had asked.

A laugh. Rich and low, as though they were having a philosophical debate over drinks and not discussing something so very violently real in Agnes's life. *Oh, I like you already. Most people approach cold cases with the mindset that there is one simple answer, just waiting to be uncovered. But life isn't so simple. We all carry our own individual truths, our own stories, our own reasonings for our actions. No one wants to be the bad guy, and so we distort facts to suit our images of ourselves, and we do this so often that eventually, the lie becomes the truth.*

What I'm saying is, don't expect a clean answer about your grandfather's case. Or any answer at all. Forty years is a long time. Memories change every time we access them. How many times have the people who remained in town accessed and changed their memories?

Agnes wonders, suddenly, if Nora has edited the teaser trailer for her, specifically, to remove the rumors about Einar. There hadn't been any mention of potential suspects. Or the prevailing theory, the one Agnes has learned more through osmosis than anything else over the years, that Marie, suffering from postpartum psychosis, drowned her daughter, and her husband, driven by rage, by grief, slit her throat.

Nora had focused purely on the photograph, and the moment when the little boy found the frozen, ravaged bodies of a local woman and her infant daughter in a field. She hadn't said that there were no obvious suspects, other than the woman's husband. A professor at the university, known to be a strict, quiet man, except when it came to his young Danish bride, whom he doted on. There hadn't been any evidence to condemn him in her murder. No witnesses, no mysterious behavior, no unexplained absences. No formal conviction. There had been, however, an informal conviction. The town decided it was him. He was guilty, they just couldn't prove it. Or maybe they didn't need to. Maybe it was enough to know it.

When he took his nine-year-old son and fled for America, that apparently proved his guilt.

Agnes had grown up with the other side of the story. The one given to her by her father, near her thirteenth birthday.

I'm going to tell you this once, he'd said. *And only once.*

On February 9, 1979, Einar had reported his wife and daughter missing. He'd spent that day in his office at the university, staying late to work on a personal project, returning home to find his son alone in the living room, listening to his radio.

Where's your mother? he'd asked his son as soon as he'd stowed his snowy boots, his coat. The house was quiet. There were no signs of dinner, of life outside of the rock music he hated so much.

Why are you asking me? Magnús had countered.

In response, he'd been hit.

Then came the phone calls. To the school where she worked. To her few friends. No one had seen her that day, and she hadn't called in.

There'd been panic. Drives. More calls. Magnús had gone to bed hungry that night, and who knows how many more nights thereafter.

Search parties. A small child discovering the bodies. Conversations with the police. A comprehensive look at their lives. Exoneration—or something like it. Then rumors. Building tension. Kids bullying Magnús until they broke his nose and knocked out a couple of his teeth against the hard earth.

The escape to America.

There was nothing of the devastation of Agnes's family in Nora's teaser trailer, beyond the two deaths. That's what Agnes will give her. A personal account of how her grandfather never recovered, never remarried, never spoke of his wife and daughter again. How her father chose to keep his silence and how he, traumatized in his own right, couldn't get close to anyone, not even his daughter. And how Agnes, the granddaughter, has inherited all of this. Einar's silence. Magnús's secret self.

Agnes settles herself back in the car, contorting her body in awkward positions to remove her new jacket in the safety of the car's heat. The empty jacket rests on the passenger seat like her shadow self, the packet of black licorice from the café weighing down its right side. She places her phone in the cupholder.

It's time, finally, to go.

She nudges the car out of its mini snowbank and grinds her teeth when she feels the wheels slide, momentarily, on a patch of ice. She makes it out of the downtown area easily, turning away from the water and the city, onto the highway that should hopefully guide her north. The sky's opened enough for her to see without her headlights.

They took everything from me, her grandfather had said, close to the end of his life.

She can give everything back to him, even if it's a lifetime too late.

As she drives on, as the landscape changes from the storybook cityscape to something she's never seen before, everywhere white, mountains rising and falling in the distance like mirages, she hopes she's strong enough to do this. This past year has shown her, truly, how weak she is. Too weak to resist the pills. Too weak to fight for Emi. Too weak to speak to her father. And now she has gambled everything on this one trip, and Nora Carver. It's too late to turn back now, but Agnes wonders, suddenly, if she should.

CHAPTER THREE

February 5, 2019

Agnes inches along the highway, waiting until she sees two trucks in her rearview mirror before she slows to a skidding stop on the shoulder to let them pass. And then she can't bring herself to keep driving. She had been too focused on the icy road to take in the view, to appreciate just how beautiful and how foreign this landscape is. Just beyond the highway, mountains after mountains, massive and alive like snow-covered giants, touch their toes to the sea. When yet another truck passes her, she forces herself to move on.

At a certain point, the road curves away from the sea, toward the mountains. Agnes passes through small towns that call to her to stop in. Start over. Forget about her broken life behind her in California, forget about the mission awaiting her. Find some cheap room on this stretch of highway, live off cheese and fresh bread and black licorice, and count the seasons based on their absolute darkness and their absolute sunshine. Maybe she'd be happy here. She thinks she would be.

She keeps going, though, if only because there's a free room await-ing her. And then it becomes just her and the white again.

She hasn't reached Bifröst yet when the GPS alerts her to turn off the highway. There's no difference in the road, no houses visible among the vast fields of snow and rolling hills, nothing but a slight indentation to her right, indicating, perhaps, tire tracks, but the GPS tells her to go, so she goes. And she finds herself on a makeshift road in the snow, dipping down then forward. She threads the car carefully through a vi-brant blue gate that she hadn't noticed from the highway. You wouldn't see it unless you were looking for it.

The GPS chimes with approval. She's here. On the land. Her grandfather's land. Though she's not sure if they'd managed to sell it or not—it's not something that's ever really occurred to her before now. The logistics of picking up the remains of your life and starting over. Her father certainly hadn't told her.

Snow stretches out on either side of her, engulfing her. And there are trees. Agnes had read somewhere that Iceland doesn't have many forests, but these are pines. Tall, towering Christmas trees, inter-spersed with something else that she can't identify, their thin branches bare. The road extends and curves between their trunks. It drops into a small crater, then flattens into a tunnel of pine trees. There's privacy here.

Soon, the tires touch a new kind of road. Agnes pulls up at the edge of a curving driveway, stunned by the elegant house in front of her. Stopping the car at a careful distance from a truck with wheels so rugged they look like they could scale the side of a mountain, Agnes sits back, leaving the engine running. Snowflakes drift onto the wind-shield, soft and relentless. The house before her is large and impossibly modern. This isn't the house of her father's childhood. It's too big, built out of glass and concrete. It's an art museum, not a rural farmhouse.

She's at the wrong address.

A light comes on over the entryway. The front door—an enormous sheet of metal—swings open.

Nora Carver, in the flesh. Agnes recognizes the mass of brown hair, curly and voluminous, a medieval halo surrounding the woman's narrow frame, and the characteristic round glasses with neon-pink rims, from her headshots. She's smaller than Agnes would ever have expected, though. Her hair seems to make up most of her height.

Nora races to the car, not slipping once on the snowy drive. She's in a sweater and jeans, and she doesn't even seem to notice the cold.

Trailing behind Nora is someone Agnes doesn't recognize. A man, lanky with short-cropped white hair, wearing a thin jacket. He takes his time following, hands in his pockets.

"I was just about to call Search and Rescue," Nora says, reaching for the car door. There's that voice. Low and resonant in recordings. In person, it's far more elastic and expressive. "Thor," she calls back, "look who's made it here in one piece!"

The man chuckles. "Yes, I see."

"I didn't know I was on a deadline," Agnes says weakly, thrown by the fanfare. She hadn't expected a welcome wagon. She allows the other woman to pull open the door while she attempts to unfold her aching limbs from their set position. Nora extends a hand in greeting. Agnes grasps it, briefly, then clutches it for balance when her leg, cramped and clumsy, gives out at the knee. Nora, a head shorter than Agnes, catches her.

"Steady?" Nora doesn't release her until Agnes assures her, yes, she can stand on her own. "There's been so much snow this past week, I was worried they'd closed the roads on you. I had all these visions of you, *flipped,* and no one would know where you are and—I'll stop, sorry. I worry easily. It comes with the territory."

"It's an incredible drive," Agnes says. She doesn't apologize for taking her time. She does hear herself say, "Sorry for worrying you," if only to get Nora to stop fussing over her.

Nora laughs. "I was a ball of anxiety before I started this job, and now I feel like putting location tracking devices on all my loved ones."

Now that she's stopped moving, Agnes feels her fatigue settle over her, heavy on her limbs. She swallows, unconsciously and forcefully, her mouth already watering in anticipation of a couple pills. She'd taken her last full dose nearly six hours ago. She's read that symptoms of opioid withdrawal tend to set in six to twenty-four hours after the last use, but that timing depends on the user's habits. Agnes hasn't exactly been tracking her usage. It's more like taking the pills whenever she feels like it, which is often. Which is also why, she thinks, if she were to relax her throat right now, her three coffees and one egg sandwich would slide right out of her, just the same way they came in.

It doesn't help to focus on that, though. *Notice what you're noticing,* is what Dr. Lee told her. There's the rushing sound of the river, somewhere beyond the house. The cool touches of the snow to her cheeks, like chilled fingertips. The coiling and uncoiling of her stomach. The sharp, twisting pain in her ankle, now that it has to accept her full weight without any help from the pills.

There's the man, approaching them so slowly. Too slowly, Agnes thinks. Thor. He's attractive for his odd features, his face so much like a skull. Thin eyes, sunken cheeks, narrow jaw. He's older, perhaps in his fifties, but he carries it lightly. He's saying hello to Agnes, polite and distracted. He starts to look away from her, but he doubles back in an instant.

"*Oh,*" he says.

"You see it, too," Nora says. She's staring at Agnes, her hazel eyes wide open and seemingly counting every pore on Agnes's face.

"What?" Agnes asks, alarmed.

"You look exactly like her," Thor breathes. He opens his mouth to say more, but no words come out. He shakes his head, roughly, as though to clear it. Then he extends a hand to Agnes. "I'm Thor," he says. "Thor Thorsson."

"Agnes Glin," she replies automatically. Then: "I look like who?"

"Sorry to stare," Nora says, "but you didn't mention *this* on the phone." She gestures at the entirety of Agnes. "You're your grandmother's twin. It's uncanny." She waits for Agnes to speak, to laugh, maybe, as she is doing. When Agnes doesn't join in, she apologizes again. "This is inappropriate, isn't it? It's just—I've studied the photographs for so long. I grew up with the Frozen Madonna plastered on my sister's wall. It's wild to meet you. It's like meeting *her*. Isn't it?" She turns to Thor, who appears mostly recovered from the shock of seeing Agnes.

"Grandmother," he echoes. "How strange. Time moves so fast. And it left her behind, preserved like you are now. But no, you are Agnes, not Marie. And I'm Thor. You will be staying in my house." He indicates the fortress behind him. "I hope it's to your liking."

Agnes says, "Right."

Nora hears the discomfort in her tone. "We made it weird, didn't we?"

Agnes aims for a smile. It feels more like a grimace. This isn't what she expected. A welcome wagon and a fangirl of her family's tragedy. "It's just nothing I've heard before."

Nora looks like she's dying to say more, but she holds back, out of respect. And because she's noticed Agnes's shivering. "Let's get you inside before you freeze. Thor, thank you for the help."

"No problem," he tells her, flashing a gap-toothed grin. He checks his phone, taps something on the screen. "I must go," he tells them. "But I hope to see you both again very soon."

"We'll have you over for dinner," Nora offers.

"I am counting the seconds," he says. With one last lingering glance at Agnes, Thor turns and walks away. Not down the driveway. Not to the other truck here. But into the forest.

"Where's he going?" Agnes asks. The tree cover isn't so thick that she can't track his progress, but soon he's nothing more than the suggestion of a man, obscured by the falling snow.

"He's got a place nearby," Nora says. "Incredibly useful on days like today, when the power in the kitchen went out and I couldn't find the breaker box. But come on, you look like a human Popsicle. Let's get you inside. This might sound unbelievable to you, but you get used to the cold. After two months of living here, this is actually warm for me." At Agnes's look, she adds, "I know, I hate me, too."

"Only two months?" Agnes asks, reaching into the car to grab the keys. Nora's reputation is for staying so long on location that she integrates herself into the local community. Two months doesn't seem long enough. Is this time an exception, or is her reputation an exaggeration?

"I celebrated the holidays in Reykjavík," Nora says. "But otherwise yeah, two months here in town. I think it'll be another month or two, in all. I would love to stay longer, but there are other things demanding my attention back in LA."

"Other things?" Agnes leads Nora to the back of the rental car for her suitcase. She regrets, pulling the little rolling bag out, that she only packed two pairs of jeans and not nearly enough socks. She'd packed for a ten-day visit, the length of time she agreed upon with Nora. She hasn't told Nora yet that she didn't buy a return ticket.

"Oh, you know," Nora says, waving a hand through the air, "they're getting ready to start the trial for Adriana Lopez's murderer." She insists on carrying Agnes's suitcase and Agnes, ankle screaming, doesn't fight her for it. Together they hustle through the falling snow to the front door.

"You must be so out of it," Nora says once they're inside. "Jet lag kills me. It'll take you a few extra days to adjust from the West Coast, especially with the minimal daylight here. I've got a lot of melatonin and vitamin D, though, so that should get you through the worst of it. I'm just so excited to have you here. I can't wait to show you around. This is your first time in Iceland, right?"

Agnes nods, but she doesn't elaborate. She can only really focus on the house. The front hall gives way to an expansive view of the land— and the river she'd heard, shockingly close—beyond. The living room's luxurious furnishings, its elegant, plush couches surrounding a free-standing fireplace, seem more suited to the lobby of a four-star hotel than someone's house.

Nora had told Agnes she's *practically* living in the farmhouse. "This," Agnes says, even though it's obvious, "isn't my grandfather's home."

"Yeah, no, it's Thor's," Nora says, arching an eyebrow. "We're on your grandfather's land, of course, but this is a new structure." She beckons for Agnes to remove her boots, then she leads them through the open living room down a long hallway that also has one wall of concrete, the other glass.

"When your grandfather left," Nora explains, "he sold the land to one of the quote-unquote neighbors, and that man's son—Thor, who you just met—built this house a few years ago. He rents it out occasionally as a luxury vacation home. He's given me a very good price. I almost never get an opportunity like this—staying in the place, *near* the place, where it all happened." Close to the end of the hallway, Nora stops in front of a metal door. "This one will be your room."

Overwhelmed, both by Nora's presence, massive for such a small person, and the words *where it all happened,* Agnes steps wordlessly into the bedroom. She's fighting that same sense of unreality that hit her in the café. *Notice what you're noticing.* The room is far quainter than the rest of the house would suggest. The walls aren't glass or concrete, but a soft, grainy wood. Agnes reaches out to test if it's that eighties wallpaper she remembers from friends' homes or real, and of course it's real. The bed, a large twin, wears a thick, inviting duvet. There's a window, a rectangle almost above eye level, the size of a porthole, facing the drive. Behind her is a wooden chest of drawers and a writing desk.

"This is great," Agnes says, feeling distinctly outside of herself. "Thanks."

"I'm happy to have you here," Nora tells her. "For many reasons. One being that it can get kind of quiet, all the way out here by myself, in the dark. Your bathroom's just in there." Nora indicates the door to

Agnes's left. "Why don't I let you shower and get the flight off of you? I know I don't feel like myself until I take a post-plane shower."

Agnes performs, to the best of her ability, the role of someone who is polite and easygoing and not at all freaked out, and assures Nora that she'll be out in a few minutes. "It's the middle of the night for me," she says, even though she doesn't have to. Nora's already leaving, but still, Agnes hears herself making excuses. "I don't know which way is up."

Closing the door behind Nora, Agnes breathes out a shaky sigh. It's been such a long day, and it's not even over yet. She gathers her toiletries and shuts herself in the bathroom. Like the rest of the house, it's luxurious, with a deep bathtub and a separate shower, but Agnes doesn't have the energy right now to enjoy it. She's got to save herself for Nora. She imagines the podcast host will have questions for her, and Agnes has a lifetime of memories to share, most of them unremarkable to her, but maybe fascinating to an outsider. But Agnes worries that Nora will open like a job interview. *So . . . tell me about yourself.*

Should she tell her about how she's spent the past year destroying herself? That if her life were a house, she'd have it down to rubble, and she'd still be hacking away at the foundation?

Or should she tell her she knows nothing about Einar's life in Iceland? That she doesn't even know what Marie looked like, outside of her death mask? That Agnes has only ever seen the famous photograph, but has never noticed the similarities between her face and that of her grandmother's? She's only noted the suggestion of white-blond hair, a slim figure, but that could be anyone.

Under the hot spray of the shower, Agnes scrubs at her skin and tries to swallow her anger. She may not have noticed the similarities between herself and the Frozen Madonna, but her father sure would have. Isn't this something any other father would have mentioned? *You look like my mother.*

Yet another secret. Yet another wall between them.

As much as Agnes has withdrawn from her life, her friends, and him in the past year, that's nothing compared to how he's withdrawn from her. After his father passed away, Magnús seemed to become his own sort of ghost.

She doesn't know why, but she doesn't feel the same anger toward her grandfather. She finds she can't blame him for not mentioning it. *There is no before. My life began when you were born.* Magnús's life had been ruined, of course, just as Einar's had. Both men had chosen to keep their grief locked away from the world. The difference between them is that Einar hadn't held back his affection for her. His pain had transformed into an effusive love.

Agnes pities her father for his pain. And she resents him for it, in equal measure.

There must be photos of Marie somewhere. Her grandfather had to have taken them with him when they left, and her father must have them now. But Marie had never been on display in Agnes's household. Her death portrait had lived on album covers and book jackets and the bedroom walls of countless strangers, but within her own family's home, she'd probably been buried in a box in the basement.

Agnes steps out of the shower. The warm water has done something to ease the throbbing in her knee, the constant electric rumble in that cobbled-together joint, but there's no helping the pain in her ankle. She dresses herself quickly, choosing an oversized sweatshirt to hide the tremors running through her skeleton.

Having something to do helps, that's what Dr. Lee says. Agnes has spent the past year locked inside various rooms, first in Emi's apartment, then her father's home, recovering from the loss of her grandfather, her mobility, her independence. *Your mind is not a bone, or a joint. You can't heal it in stasis. You have to move.* That's what she's doing. Right?

It's time to talk to Nora, but Agnes doesn't make it to the door. Instead, she sits down on the bed and hoists her backpack on her lap. Her hands seem to move of their own accord, unzipping the side pocket, digging down to the bottom, and grabbing for the yellow bottle filled to the brim with small white tablets. NO REFILLS, the expired prescription reads. Agnes wipes the sweat from her forehead, her skin hot and feverish despite the shower.

The withdrawal symptoms are worst at the start, that's what she's read. Not life-threatening, just unpleasant. Back in Berkeley, she'd promised herself she'd go cold turkey. She has to be alert, if she wants to do this, and she can't imagine any other way to separate herself from the pills.

But still, she'd packed the bottle.

For a moment, the enormity of what she's trying to do here overwhelms her, and she doesn't think she'll be able to resist. The empty promises rise up within her. She'll go cold turkey tomorrow. She's in pain. She's overwhelmed. Plans change.

Her mouth's watering. She can practically taste the pills on her tongue.

Her clammy hand slips off the childproof cap, and it's this one pathetic maneuver that brings her back to herself. How many times in the past year has she tried, and failed, to go clean? She's lost count. The empty promises are just that—empty. She's made it this far, hasn't she?

With a tremendous effort, Agnes returns the bottle to her backpack and leaves it behind.

CHAPTER FOUR

February 5, 2019

At the center of the living room, there's the enclosed, freestanding fire-place, its bright orange flames dancing behind the glass. On one side of the fireplace, there's a pair of deep, inviting couches. On the other, there's a table the length of a minivan, half of it covered with gadgets and wires. The technology draws Agnes forward. She spots a couple of handheld cameras, a few GoPros, but the rest is a jumble of machinery and cables. She supposes there must be microphones in the mix, but she can't locate them. There are, however, quite a few expensive laptops. It's a costly operation, and it occurs to her, as she catalogs the many tangles of equipment, that there should be more people here.

Nora's voice echoes down the hallway. "Help yourself to whatever you want from the kitchen. The power went out this morning, so I haven't had time to put any lunch together. Are you hungry?"

Agnes calls back, "No, thanks." She can't remember ever being *less* hungry.

She pulls a seat from the end of the table and falls into it, admiring the lunar landscape outside the living room windows while she waits for Nora. Listening to the rushing flow of the fire, Agnes tries to picture growing up in this country, its foreign magic made ordinary because it's all you've ever known. She wonders how different she'd be if she'd grown up somewhere like here. If she'd know all the names for the plants, the creatures, the constellations in the night sky, if she'd be infused with the lyricism of the language. She wouldn't be this gnarled oak tree born of California's hard, fertile soil. She'd be something much softer, much more elemental. And the anger, the resentment crawling inside her, melts momentarily into regret. Her father had grown up like that. And then he'd left. He has both places inside of him. Or, more likely, he has neither.

Nora enters the living room carrying an armload of folders and loose papers and notebooks. She sets the pile down in front of Agnes.

"My research," she announces. "Thought you'd want to see some behind-the-scenes action."

"You're old-school." Agnes picks up the top folder. It's a plastic envelope, the type she had in sixth grade to organize her homework assignments. Inside are pages and pages of printouts. They look like medical records, but she can't be certain because they're not written in English. "Do you speak Icelandic?"

"No, they didn't have that option at my high school," Nora says dryly. "I have a friend in town who's helping me to translate the bulk of it all."

Agnes replaces the folder on top of the pile, unimpressed.

"I'm picking up some of it," Nora adds. "I try to immerse myself as much as possible in the case, by whatever means necessary. And that's with other, less important cases. I mean, cases less personal to me. This story . . . your grandmother's case . . . it means a lot to me. It was my first exposure to true crime. Did I tell you that? It was my sister. She was seven years older than me, so obviously I worshipped her. Everything she did, I did. She went through a serious Björk phase, and then it became an all-out Iceland mania. She said she'd come here as soon as she had the money to. She had the photo on her wall, like I said. The Frozen Madonna. I always thought, maybe—" Nora stops abruptly.

She must have seen Agnes's skin crawling.

"Is that too much information? Probably, right? I just think it's important for you to know, before we begin any formal interview, before I turn on my microphone and you start thinking of me as Nora Carver, podcast host, that this case is intensely personal to me. I may be a stranger to you and your family, but I don't feel like one." One hand lands close to Agnes's, as though she can't decide if it's appropriate to touch her. It finds the pile of papers again instead. "And not to be too sentimental, but I really do hope you understand how much I appreciate you coming here. This is a gift, one that I can only hope to honor."

She's waiting for Agnes to say something.

"Oh," Agnes says. Then: "I don't—"

"Too sentimental," Nora confirms. "I'll contain myself."

This tears a laugh from Agnes's throat. She can't imagine this woman contained. She should really be thanking Nora in kind, for paying for her car, letting her stay in her place. It's generous. Trusting. It's equally generous to acknowledge the enormity of what she's doing here.

But it's yet another "thank you." Agnes has been so taken care of in the past year. There have been so many meals prepared for her. So many schedules realigned. Hands guiding her in and out of chairs and medical offices and clinical eyes on her body, judging how she's moving, how she's improving. Her father's half-hearted attempts at meals. Bananas, protein shakes, toast. The consideration, every wash day, to guide her in and out of a routine that used to be mindless and private. Part of Agnes feels infantilized, a child impotently reaching for a too-high counter. And part of her feels so unbelievably tired of saying "thank you." Burnt out on the gratitude and the care and the appreciation. Nora's generosity touches Agnes. But it exhausts her, just as much, if not more.

So she says, "Are you really alone here? No one else?"

"I have that contact in town," Nora tells her. "And there's Thor, the owner of the house. He's not too far away. But yeah, I'm flying solo for this project. I've got my assistant and my producers back in LA, but this is largely a one-woman operation. It makes for a leaner, more adaptable machine."

"You don't feel nervous," Agnes says, haltingly, "interviewing all these people, by yourself? Isn't it dangerous?" A woman alone, inviting herself into strangers' houses and lives and poking around the most delicate of subjects. Agnes had thought there would be more people here. Backup for this tiny woman.

Nora wanders up close to the floor-to-ceiling windows. "Even though I'm researching a particularly brutal set of murders," she says, unaware of Agnes's flinch, "Iceland as a whole is a very safe place for me. And even if it weren't, I've been in far worse situations alone, believe me. For most people, the pageantry of an interview, with my official-looking equipment and my reputation, is enough protection. I'm like a security guard at the mall. We've both got Tasers and a veil of authority." She beckons Agnes to join her. "Want to see something cool?"

Agnes closes the distance between them, trying to bend her knee at the right moment, at the very nadir of her stride, straightening it casually, not like she's thinking about it, hard, the way she's become accustomed, but it doesn't work. The limp is there.

Nora points at the glass at an acute angle. "You can see the old farmhouse from here," she says. They crane their necks to catch a glimpse of the corner of a black, rusted roof.

"It's so close," Agnes says, her heart beating faster. That was home. "Can we get there easily from here?"

Nora hesitates, her breath fogging up the glass. "There's no path, so it can be tricky in the snow . . . but no, it's not far."

Translation: easy for me. Not so easy for someone who can hardly manage a concrete floor.

"I'll be fine," Agnes says, her voice stiff. "I shattered my kneecap and my ankle, among other things, but I'm pretty much all healed up. It's not painless to walk on in general, but I can handle a walk in the snow." She hopes.

"If you're sure," Nora says, wincing sympathetically. "How'd you hurt it?"

"Surfing. A wave took me into some rocks, and I hit them, hard."

Nora sucks in air through her teeth. "When was this?"

"About a year ago."

Nora tells Agnes she once tore her shoulder in a car accident. "LA," she says, by way of explanation. "The recovery from the surgery nearly drove me insane. I wasn't sleeping. It was my right arm, and I'm right-handed, so I was useless for a while. Believe me when I tell you, I went *nuts.*"

Agnes pretends to care, but privately she wants to laugh. Nora has no idea what she's talking about. Her recovery probably lasted a couple of months, at the most, during which time she could walk, leave her house, and hell, go to the bathroom by herself. And now she's fine. She doesn't need oxycodone to be able to think about anything other than her ankle.

"I'm okay," Agnes tells her. "Really."

Nora nods and returns to her pile of papers at the table. "There's something else I wanted to show you." She pulls out a printout and brings it back to Agnes. "I thought you'd like it."

What she holds is a Xerox of an old photo. The resolution is grainy, the ink a bit too harsh in places and in others, too light. But this adds to the realism of the portrait, as though the woman were passing under fluorescent bulbs.

It's her. It's Marie. But it's Agnes, too. The woman in the photo has her hair, as far as the printout will allow. It's almost white. There are some notable differences, though—her grandmother's eyes are far more tilted, her cheekbones far more prominent. Her smile is much more open. Agnes's face is closed. Rounder. But Agnes sees the resemblance, just as she recognizes herself in the mirror. Why hadn't she seen herself in the Frozen Madonna before? Had it really been the quality of the photo? Or had it been willful ignorance?

"It's nice to see her alive," Agnes says.

"This was her immigration photo," Nora tells her. "Denmark to Iceland. It was . . . difficult to track down. I thought you'd want to see something new. Or—" She lets out a nervous laugh. "You know what I mean."

"Yeah," Agnes says. She stares down at her reflection. "I'm a year older than her when she died. Can you believe that?"

Her grandmother only reached twenty-six. It's not enough time on earth. Agnes feels like she's hardly begun.

Nora shakes her head. "And she's a kid in this picture. Already married, probably already pregnant. She's got less than a decade to live after this was taken. She was never allowed to be anything but young."

Agnes holds the photograph close to her body, as though she could protect its subject. Nora catches the action, and they share a look. A zap of sudden understanding. Agnes can finally, for this one brief moment, see Nora. Underneath the polished veneer of a crime-solving podcast host, Nora is decent and determined, burning with a righteous passion like Joan of Arc.

"I really am sorry," Nora tells her, "for how I reacted when we first met. I was keyed up, both excited to meet you and worried sick about your drive up. Then, seeing you . . . it was a bit of a shock. It was clear you were uncomfortable, though, and I'm responsible for that."

"I guess it was a shock for me, too," Agnes says. In spite of her fatigue and her skepticism, she finds herself appreciating the other woman's boundless energy. Agnes can feel it propping her own mood up.

"In our defense," Nora says, "not that there is much of one, the resemblance is *so* uncanny. And for someone like Thor, who was eighteen when your grandmother died, he's going to remember her well. When he sees you, the spitting image of her, my god . . . It probably brought up a lot of long-buried memories and feelings."

"That we'll discuss over dinner with him," Agnes says. "Right?"

"That, or something else. Whatever you're comfortable with. I just want the three of us to sit down together. Something interesting's bound to come up." Nora turns back to her pile of research. "You sure you're not hungry?"

Agnes doesn't answer. Instead, she resumes her seat at the dining room table. "Now that we've cleared the air," she says, "I have to ask: my family's case. What do you think happened?" She catches herself before she adds, *Do you think my grandfather's innocent?* She wants the truth, not what Nora thinks she wants to hear.

"It doesn't matter what I think," Nora says. She drags out a chair so they're directly across from each other. "The world believes your grandfather did it. That, at the very least, he killed Marie, after discovering that she killed their daughter. What I believe generally doesn't have any place in the conversation. I follow facts, I trace rumors to their source, and if I have any strong feelings either way, that will create a bias in my reporting. I don't want that."

"That's fine," Agnes says, tamping down a burst of frustration. "But that's not an answer. This is just us, right? Before we get into official business. As a person who grew up with the case, you must have an opinion. You must have your own private thoughts."

"You want to get into it?" Nora asks her, suddenly giddy, like they're playing a game of Truth or Dare. Agnes doesn't blink. "Okay, let's get into it. The signs point to your grandfather. They do. Even without any evidence, his behavior was that of a guilty person. Not speaking up once in his own defense . . . I can understand why people think the way they do. I'm not saying it's right, but the logic is pretty sound. If you were accused of a crime you didn't commit, you'd argue against it, wouldn't you?"

Nora doesn't wait for an answer. "Usually, the most obvious explanation is the right one. Most likely, Einar did it. But if you want my honest opinion? No, I don't think he did. Not because he wasn't arrested, let alone convicted—I've been at this long enough to see many murderers walk free—but because of Magnús, your father. His survival knocks out both parents as the murderer, if you ask me." She holds up a finger. "For Marie: postpartum psychosis tends to have the highest risk associated with the birth of the first child. Nothing I've read has said that Marie suffered from postpartum depression or psychosis when Magnús was born, so it's unlikely that she experienced it with her second child."

Nora holds up another finger. "For Einar: by all accounts, he *adored* Marie. I've never heard of a reason why he would kill her, other than the throes of rage and grief at the death of their daughter—but again, I don't buy that. And if he did have some other reason to kill his family, why spare Magnús? Most fathers who kill their families don't pick and choose. They either annihilate everyone and themselves, or they annihilate everyone but themselves so they can start fresh elsewhere." She waves her hand in the air, as though that settles everything.

Agnes can't find the words to respond. The relief washing through her is too overwhelming.

Nora grins. "Not what you expected, right?"

Agnes shakes her head.

"The job requires me to keep an open mind," Nora warns her, "so I'm going to have to look into him, regardless of what I think. Okay?"

Agnes finds her voice. "Fair enough," she says. She feels herself returning Nora's smile, and the feeling is foreign to her. When was the last time she genuinely smiled? "So, uh, how does this whole thing work? With you and me?"

"Ordinarily," Nora says, "we would sit down together, much like we are doing now, and talk. I have you for ten days, and there's so much I want to know . . . It would be a series of conversations. Ordinarily, these conversations would get less and less formal. Less of an interview and more of a friendly chat. I just want to talk to you about your family . . ." She trails off.

"Ordinarily," Agnes echoes.

Nora runs a hand through her wild hair. "Things have changed."

Agnes waits for her to elaborate, but she seems unable to start. "What's going on?" she asks. "It's still okay for me to be here, right?" Could her father have done something? Followed through on his threat to sue Nora?

In answer, Nora digs into her pocket, dragging out her cell phone. It's an enormous iPhone, one of the latest models that seems closer to a tablet than a cell phone. Nora taps through the screen and passes it to Agnes, having to palm it with both hands so it doesn't fall. On-screen is a brief article, all in Icelandic. Agnes can't decode it. Front and center is a portrait of another young woman with hair so blond it's colorless. Another open smile, but that's where the resemblances end. This isn't her grandmother. This isn't Agnes. This woman has a pointed, narrow face, with eyebrows like semicircles.

"This just happened this weekend," Nora says.

Agnes returns the phone. "I don't know what this is. I don't know Icelandic." She does know, though, that she won't like whatever comes next. The woman looks all too familiar.

"This is Ása Gunnarsdóttir," Nora says. "She's a student at the university here. She was reported missing yesterday, and I have reason to believe it's connected to your grandmother's case."

CHAPTER FIVE

February 5, 2019

Missing. Connected to her grandmother's case. The words hang in the air. Agnes can't grab hold of them. "What?" she asks. She blinks, she's in the humid café in Reykjavík. There's that missing poster, staring back at her. Again, and she's back in Bifröst with Nora, overwarm from the crackling fire.

"This is where things get complicated," Nora says. "How much do you know about the . . . *life* . . . your grandmother's case has taken on in the past forty years?"

"Just tell me."

Nora huffs out a small laugh. "I'm prone to lecturing people," she tells Agnes. "My assistant once told me I'm the only woman who's ever mansplained to her. So I'll try to keep it brief." She sighs. "In essence, within the true crime community there are the casual participants, the fans, the consumers. Then there are the professional participants, like myself. And then . . . there are the extremists. These are the groups who celebrate the macabre, like death metal bands writing songs about the Frozen Madonna and Child, for instance, who use the photograph as album artwork. Or those who get the photograph tattooed on their body. These are the fans who use it as artistic expression and inspiration, even if it's unpalatable to the general public. Some use it for art, some use it for exploitation, violence, what have you."

"And how does this relate to this missing woman?" Agnes asks. "Ása."

"Ow-sa," Nora corrects her, almost unconsciously. "Not Ass-a. Well, your family's case has an enormous draw, for all participants of the community. But something about it really attracts the extremists. The farmhouse is a pilgrimage for some of them. They call it the Bifröst Murder House. And I can kind of understand the draw. Your grandfather's farmhouse still stands, empty, on a stretch of land that for many years had a lot of privacy. Now there's this place, but it's not like it's right on top of the farmhouse. The hardcore people hold a party at the Bifröst Murder House every year around the anniversary of the murders. It's an open invitation to anyone looking for a good time, but as you can imagine, it brings in a lot of extremists. This year's party was this past weekend. They had to do it a few days early, I'm told, because they're losing access to the house this week. Thor, the guy you met? He's closing it, officially, to the public."

Agnes is too hot. Her skin's throbbing from the proximity to the fireplace, sweat gathering at the small of her back. She can't tell if it's the withdrawal or Nora's unrelenting monologue, but it's hard for her to keep Nora in focus. All she can think, clearly, is *I need a pill*. And, somewhere deep in her psyche, *Why the hell are you telling me all this?*

"This woman," Nora continues, "Ása, was last seen at the party. No one knows where she went—or, they're saying they don't know where she went—during or after. She wasn't reported missing until last night. It's been three days since the party. The town has organized search parties, and they're talking to everyone who was there, but so far, nothing has come out of it. The most likely scenario is that she wandered out of the house, drunk, and froze to death. You see this happen all the time, anywhere there's snow and alcohol. If this had happened in any other circumstance, I would say that it's a tragic accident. But it was at a party at the Bifröst Murder House, near the fortieth anniversary of the murders, organized by a group of people who have a certain fascination with said murders. I can't ignore this. Which means, unfortunately, that I'll be somewhat distracted this week. Tomorrow, for instance, I'll have to go in to talk to the police."

Nora leans forward, reaching a hand to Agnes's knee. "I'm still absolutely focused on your grandmother's case, of course, but this is a new element to her story, and it's shifting daily. I won't be able to devote as much time to you as I had planned. There is something here, and it's connected to Marie. Maybe something happened at the party. Maybe she really did wander out on her own. Who knows? People do strange things in the dark. But she's linked herself to Marie, however tenuously. Do you understand?"

Agnes finds she does understand. She's on her own. Entirely on her own.

Nora sits back, sliding her hand off Agnes's knee. "I'm sorry to greet you with such terrible news. There's more pain here to be unearthed, it seems. And it takes time away from you, from what you're doing here. I'm struggling with this, Agnes, to be perfectly honest with you. This is all happening so fast, I've had to scramble. Things are going to have to be . . . looser . . . than I thought."

"You said something might have happened at the party," Agnes says, reluctant to get caught up in anything that takes away from her grandfather's case, but unable to help herself. "What are you thinking happened to her?"

"The majority of people show up just to get drunk. To them, it's just a party. Ása seemed to be of that group. But what if someone, obsessed with the case, suddenly finds themselves in that house, on drugs . . . they see Ása, her passing resemblance to Marie, and . . ." She shows Agnes her open palms in an uncertain gesture. "No matter what, it's a new disappearance on the fortieth anniversary of your grandmother's disappearance, from the exact same house. It would be unprofessional of me to ignore this."

"Are we not talking then?" Agnes asks. "No interview?"

"In a way, we've already started," Nora says. "I've got to warn you, I document literally everything I can. This means wearing a microphone for most conversations—don't worry, I'm not wearing a wire right now. I have legal documents for you to sign before we go down that road. As soon as you sign, though, I'll likely have a microphone on, and I'll ask you to wear one, too. If, for whatever reason, you don't feel comfortable with that, or if you do sign and you change your mind down the road, you are completely within your rights to retract your consent. If someone doesn't wish to be recorded, I can still report what was discussed, or if that leads to dangerous territory, I hint at it. There are many ways to do this. The microphones, though . . . that's the easiest way. For both of us."

Agnes nods. Or she thinks she does.

"Don't let all this extra stuff discourage you," Nora says. "You are still my focus. Your decision to speak with me, to break your family's silence after all these decades, should be acknowledged and celebrated. On that note . . ."

Nora unfolds herself from her chair and searches through her pile of folders. She selects one and passes it to Agnes. "Some more photos you might like. And a timeline of events. I'd love it if you'd be able to fill in some blanks, or if there's anything that seems wrong to you. There's also a cheat sheet with family trees, not only your own but the important players of the town. The names can be hard for some people to get used to. I guess you'd be fine, with a grandfather named Einar and a father named Magnús, but even I need them all straightened out, so I figure I'll be doing a lot of that in the series."

Agnes accepts the folder. "Straighten what out?"

"The generations. There's the first generation of people, including your grandparents, and the other adults involved. There's the second generation, your father, your aunt, and Thor, the house owner, among others. And then there's the third generation. You."

Agnes slips her grandmother's immigration photo inside the folder without peering underneath. She can feel the weight of those unknown photographs on her lap, threatening to drag her down. Something her future self can contend with. "I guess I never thought about the other people involved."

"Now you can," Nora says. "It's strange when you start thinking about the forty-year gap. I'm thirty-six. More than my own lifetime has passed since your grandmother and aunt were killed, which makes it feel immeasurably long and of old times, right? But then you meet the people involved and you realize that forty years is just—nothing. Your father, for example. Nine years old. Now a mere forty-nine. Life can be short and long."

Agnes's stomach lurches, as though the organ were trying to hide from whatever danger lurks outside. She's the third generation. The direct descendant. The only one. She's so involved. And yet. She's just this. She's just her.

"I know this is a lot to drop on you all at once," Nora says, seeming to read her mind. "And I'm sorry our time together will be so disrupted, but please, make yourself at home here. It's still pretty early in the day, not that you'd know it from the looks of it outside." She indicates the softening light outside the living room windows. "If you want to take a nap, a bath, whatever, help yourself. If you're hungry, I can cook us something."

The mention of food does nothing but remind Agnes how nauseous she feels. "Actually," she says, "can you show me the farmhouse? I'd like to see it."

CHAPTER SIX

February 5, 2019

Nora's winter wear is similar to Agnes's, except her jacket and boots are far more lived in. She looks like she skis, like she goes to Tahoe or Aspen every January with her own precious equipment that costs more than Agnes's car. Agnes follows Nora out the front door. They turn left immediately, skirting the side of the house. There's a pathway to a pair of enormous bins—"For ash from the fireplace," Nora tells her. "We'll have to take our trash into town." Then, almost instantly, they're in the indiscriminate snow. Agnes's feet sink clumsily into the powder. It's like walking on a sand dune, except she can't seem to find her balance. She's walking on buried stones and roots and ice patches, so every step is a gamble that twists and grinds her ankle or jolts her knee, keeping her at a snail's pace.

"Are you doing okay?" Nora asks her. She's been quiet so far, but they're moving so slowly, it must be getting to her.

"I'm not used to snow," Agnes says. She slides forward and catches herself with a desperate, Hail Mary wave of one arm. "Or ice."

"Follow me," Nora advises. She pulls ahead, each step deliberate and light. "Put your feet where I put my feet."

Her gait is shorter than Agnes's, which is a blessing. Agnes doesn't look anywhere but at the footwells Nora leaves behind in the white earth. It's normal, she tells herself through a new bout of self-hatred. She's exhausted, she's injured, and she's never done this before. She'll get better at it.

Yeah, right.

It will always be this difficult to walk on unlevel ground with her ankle, so she should get used to it.

The path they take is meandering, cutting along bushes or irregular banks of snow. The trees, which muffle the sound so much more than Agnes thought possible, provide them a natural cover. She feels them give way, with the reentry of the wind's touch on her skin. Nora's footsteps stop. Agnes comes up behind her, breathless and exhausted.

There it is.

The house.

The two-story structure stands in its own clearing, a rock column surrounded by a semicircle of trees. Behind it, Agnes can see the river up close. Can hear the roar of churning water. Her father has told her stories of fishing that river in summer. Falling in and being pulled under. Thinking he would drown, that he would die, only to be yanked out by his father, who then beat him with an open palm for being so careless. Magnús has spent a lifetime since avoiding open water, which is why her grandfather was the one to teach her to swim.

The house has held steady against the elements for forty years and it looks no different from what Agnes had imagined. The small windows, boarded up. The metal roof, black paint mottled with rust.

The only proof that they haven't traveled back into the previous century is a single line of CAUTION tape hanging from the door, drifting in a timid breeze.

"Are we not allowed inside?" Agnes asks. She wipes the sweat from her forehead. She can feel the shivers climbing up her spine, but she's hot. So hot.

"We can go in," Nora says. "Everyone else in town has."

"Isn't that breaking the law?"

Nora shrugs. "I try not to question things that make life easier for me."

Agnes can't tell if she's joking. She hasn't had much, if any, experience with the police or crime scenes, but she's pretty sure this is illegal, or at the very least, unethical. In the end, though, what does a line of police tape matter? Agnes flew all those hours to get here, to see this house. She shouldn't let a piece of plastic, or a vague fear of the police's authority, keep her out.

"The interior is rough," Nora warns her. "Especially after Saturday's party. The house has been left alone for a long time. Thor's started working on it, but it's not looking great in there." She rustles her hands in her deep pockets and produces a thick flashlight. She offers it to Agnes, then takes out one for herself, along with one of the cameras from the house. "Thor's father, of the first generation, bought the house and the land from your grandfather and never touched any of it. Now, our Thor, of the second generation, is fixing it up. He has the best name, by the way. Did you hear it? Thor Thorsson. I love the patronymics here. Why didn't your family follow the tradition?"

"To be Agnes Magnúsdóttir?" Agnes asks. "Well, I was born in the US, so it's different." Her father could have still given her his name. He could also have given her his own—Einarsson. She would've liked that. Instead: "They decided to give me my mother's name."

"And your aunt, Agnes," Nora says, like she can't help herself.

"Yep. No more patriarchy for me."

"Matronymics," Nora quips. She slides a thumb over one edge of the camera, then holds it out in front of her. "Agnes Glin. I like it."

A wave of nausea sets Agnes's head spinning. She has to swallow a mouthful of saliva before she can speak. "Thanks. What's the camera for?"

"I'm a hoarder when it comes to my show. I try to document every possible moment I'm here. Everything I'm doing, I want a solid memory of it. Does the camera bother you?"

Agnes supposes it doesn't. It's part of the agreement, her coming here.

"The walkway's easier here," Nora tells her. "The soil underneath is much more level."

Breathing heavily through her mouth, Agnes heads for the front door. Her feet slide on the back end of her stride, and she's walking over a mess of phantom footprints left in the snow, but Nora is right. The land is much more level here. She's able to cut across to the front door on her own. It's not easy, though.

Agnes takes her time at the front door. The wood ages under her gaze. Reeling, she grips the doorknob for balance, realizing at the same moment that she hadn't thought to buy gloves.

She pushes the door open. It protests, but half-heartedly, swinging back and inviting her inside. Agnes imagines herself as her grandfather when he last crossed this threshold. This had been his home from birth, the center of his universe. Left behind to disintegrate into ruins, into nothing but a monument of tragedy.

The smell of mildew, stale cigarette smoke, and old beer hits Agnes in one fetid gust, obliterating all thought. She can't fight the nausea anymore. One moment, she's standing in the doorway to her grandfather's home. The next, she's trying to walk back to Nora, trying to get away from the smell, but her vision is fuzzy and her legs won't cooperate. She has time to wonder when the gently falling snow had transformed into a blizzard before she feels her body slump to the ground.

CHAPTER SEVEN

February 5, 2019

By the time they return to the house, Agnes's body has stopped working. The frigid air hasn't helped. It's only made the shaking worse. Nora
helps Agnes to the bathroom. "Oh, you poor thing," she's saying, "what's
going on?"

Agnes tries for an "I'm okay," but the words dissolve into another
painful heave.

On the floor next to her, Nora wipes the hair away from Agnes's
sweaty forehead. At some point, she'd brought in some supplies that
she swears will help. Sparkling water, tap water, anti-nausea tablets,
crackers.

"Traveling is a lot of stress on your body," Nora says. "And I probably
haven't helped with the stress, have I? Bombarding you with so much
trauma. I'm sorry, Agnes, I could see it was too much, and I pushed
anyway. Get this out of your system, then we'll get you into bed."

Agnes endures the humiliation, because it's nothing more than
what she's already endured this past year. When she'd come out of sur-

gery, the pain in her leg had caused her first to faint, then to vomit into her lap. The nurses then, too, had been kind. Agnes accepts Nora's anti-nausea remedies, even though she knows the only fix is in her backpack, in her room. Right now, though, her backpack might as well be at the bottom of the sea.

She tries to apologize, but Nora waves her away. "This might sound twisted," she says, "but I kind of like taking care of you. My ex-husband used to get terrible food poisoning every other week—until we finally realized he had an ulcer—so I'm really used to it. He once accused me of poisoning him, like in that Daniel Day-Lewis movie, just so I could mother him." Through the haze, Agnes can only really make out the pink circles of Nora's glasses. "Men, right?"

Eventually, when Agnes is forcing nothing but air from her body, Nora helps her to bed, assuring Agnes she'll be fine in the morning. Nora says so many words that Agnes can't pay attention to, because she's waiting for the woman to leave the room.

With the door finally, miraculously closed, Agnes staggers to her backpack, lying carelessly on the floor in the corner of the room, and claws through it. Here are the pills, here's relief. She opens the bottle and digs out four white tablets. These will make her normal again. She could swallow them and be done with the shakes, the nausea, everything. And the temptation is so strong. Agnes had resolved to get off the pills so she could be alert, not so she could vomit into a toilet all day long.

She steadies herself with a hand on her desk. Her body slides forward, if only because her hand is sliding forward. It's on top of the folder Nora had given her.

Agnes forces herself to look away from the pills to the folder and nudges it open. There's the portrait of her grandmother, staring back at her with her own eyes. Agnes flips it over. Underneath is another Xerox of a photograph, this time in color. It takes a moment for the image to come into focus, and then it takes her breath away.

It's a family portrait, posed outside the farmhouse. They're all standing. The husband straight and proper, the wife holding a bundle in her arms, the son in front and in between. They're all wearing their best clothes. A suit for the man, a floral dress for the woman, slacks and a button-up for the boy. It must be summer, because the earth around them is a rich green, the mountain beyond the river showing a different, happier face.

Agnes bends down for a better look at her grandfather's face. He's not smiling. He's squinting, almost in a grimace, as if he were looking through the camera at her. As if he could see her pain, and it worried him. *I love you, Agnes.* She should have taken more pictures of him. Videos. Audio recordings. So she could hear those words again. She wipes at her cheeks, finding tears now instead of sweat.

The little-boy version of Magnús is staring not at the camera, but up at his father. As though he's noticed the same concern. His mother has one arm around her baby daughter, one hand on her son's shoulder. She's smiling at the camera, radiant in sunshine.

Agnes tosses the folder onto the bed, then she deposits two pills back into the bottle. She pops the remaining two, savoring the bitter, almost rotten flavor as they go down. She has to be smart about this. Going cold turkey had been a crazy idea. She'll just halve her usage. Two pills every few hours isn't enough to ruin her focus. Just enough to stop the worst of her symptoms.

Then, returning to bed, she buries the bottle underneath her mattress. Removing her temptation in theory, but keeping it close by, just in case.

She lies back on top of the quilt, listening to Nora's footsteps padding up and down the halls, weaving in and out of a hazy, fitful blackness. She can't call it sleep. She can only call it the edges of unconsciousness, and she doesn't rest there long. Whenever she comes to, she stares at the portrait.

CHAPTER EIGHT

February 6, 2019

Sometime around five a.m., Agnes surrenders to her jet lag and turns on her light. Her body creaking and protesting, she reaches for Nora's folder and unearths the supposed timeline.

There's a woman named Júlía, mentioned right at the top, her name underlined in ink. *First-generation neighbor*, it reads. *Ingvar Karlsson's mother*. Agnes has never heard of Júlía before. The rest of the timeline, though, matches with the bare bones of what she already knows.

Two bodies found frozen in the snow. The woman had her throat cut, deep and wide, close to the point of decapitation. Bruises dotting her upper arms, as though someone had handled her roughly. The infant, drowned, had bruises, too.

The obvious suspect, the husband, could account for his whereabouts on the day of the ninth. They were the same as every weekday. He woke up before his wife, leaving her to sleep in, and he had witnesses who corroborated that he arrived at the office early, sometime around seven a.m., and had taught his morning classes, had eaten in the common area, had spent the rest of the day in department meetings or student conferences, eventually spending the rest of the afternoon alone in his office, but his coworkers had all confirmed that he'd stayed in there the entire time. It had been on the third floor of the building, so impossible for him to leave from anywhere except the door. He went straight home from work.

As for the evening before, the eighth, he only had his son as his witness. They had had their usual dinner. Father and son played chess after eating, while Marie cleaned and the baby fussed on the carpet next to them. The son went upstairs for bed. Husband and wife soon followed at their normal time—ten p.m. The baby cried throughout the night, as per her routine, as well. She had colic.

The son confirmed that his father had driven him to school the next morning, that he hadn't seen his mother on the morning of the ninth, but that was not unusual.

Most of the town had been interviewed. Júlia and Karl, the neighbors from across the road, with their son, Ingvar, the boy who found the bodies. And the two Thors, father and son, nearby. Everyone had spoken well of the victim and her family. The husband had a reputation for standoffishness, but he clearly loved his wife.

There's a quote from Júlia. *Einar always surprised her with cinnamon buns from the bakery. Sometimes she'd come over smelling of cinnamon, and you know they'd had a good day together.*

And yet everyone had concluded that it could only have been Einar who killed Marie and the baby. There had been rumors of financial trouble, Nora writes, but nothing came from that. No murder weapon found, no blood on the property. No witnesses. Only a feeling. A certainty. The town closed ranks, and there was no further investigation. Then the departure, months later.

There's no DNA evidence, so all Nora has to go on are the crime scene photos, the testimonies. The skeleton of a case.

Agnes reaches the end of the file. There's so little here. So little evidence to accuse someone of murder.

Restless, she pushes herself off the bed. Before the accident, she had never been able to sit still for very long. The recovery time and the pills had all slowed her momentum down to nothing. Now, even through the creaking hell of her body, she can taste the edges of something beyond the inertia. She's had a year of downtime. It's time to move.

She stacks Nora's photographs and bare outlines on the small writing desk. She separates the family portrait from the pile and props it up against the wall so she can admire it. Then she dons layers upon layers of socks and shirts, preparing, this time, for the cold. She leaves the bottle of pills behind, but not without swallowing one more. Just enough, she tells herself, to keep the nausea at bay. She wants to go inside her grandfather's house this time. She knows she's doing what's right. She can't go cold turkey. But still, she's ashamed of herself. She'd promised herself she'd get clean, for her grandfather and for herself. She hadn't even made it twelve hours before she'd given in.

On her way out, Agnes grabs the flashlight Nora gave her yesterday, and she stows her phone in her jacket pocket, even though it'll be useless. It's nice to have a safety net, if a lousy one.

Once outside, she follows the path she and Nora had made yesterday, her feet crunching in the snow. The moonlight illuminates just enough of the white earth for her to go without her flashlight if she wanted to. But she feels better with the flashlight's beam guiding her way. There aren't any predators out here. Just sheep and horses. Or so she thinks. Maybe it's like the forests, though. They say there aren't any, but out here, in the middle of nowhere, the world is on its own. It operates by its own rules.

It's a relief to reach the farmhouse. Until she sees the light, flickering, in one of the windows.

CHAPTER NINE

February 6, 2019

Agnes isn't conscious of turning off her flashlight. She stands in place, in the halfway dark of the blanket of snow and sky, and she tries to think. All she can do is breathe, and even that is a bit of a stretch. There's someone inside the house. It's just one solitary flashlight beam, moving in meandering circles in the second-story windows.

It can't be Nora, can it? She's still asleep, isn't she? Agnes hadn't checked in on her before she'd left, but she'd seen the woman's bedroom door, closed, on her way out. No, Agnes has been awake, restless, for a while now. She would've heard Nora leaving.

The only alternative she can think of is Thor. That must be it. He's the owner of the house now. It can only be him. Hadn't Nora said that he was fixing up the place?

But would he really start work so early in the morning?

Agnes can't quite believe it.

She considers hiding. If whoever is in there decides to peer out the window, they'll no doubt see her and her bright red jacket, standing in the open expanse of the clearing.

But she doesn't move. She doesn't hide.

Instead, she switches her flashlight back on. Aims its beam through the second-story window, jiggling it from side to side. Heart beating in her throat, she fights the urge to laugh, hysterically, at her own stupidity. Ása, the missing student. What if Nora is right? What if someone actually did hurt her? What if they've decided to return here, to the Murder House, to finish her off?

What had Nora said?

People do strange things in the dark.

There's no running away. Literally. Agnes doesn't think she could do it at all, let alone fast enough to outpace whoever lives here.

There's no time to run now, though. They've seen her.

The light inside the house has disappeared.

Agnes waits.

The front door jerks open. From within the darkness emerges a bear of a man. Agnes can only make out his silhouette, but his shoulders fill out the doorframe. He has to duck through the doorway so as not to hit his head. His flashlight is off, tucked away somewhere. Both his hands are empty, held open by his sides.

Agnes shines her light on his legs, as though it were a physical gesture to keep him back.

He speaks and she can discern the word, "Hello," but the rest is an unfathomable jumble of sounds.

"I don't—" she says. Her voice comes out hoarse. She clears her throat. It's still raw from last night. "Do you speak English?"

"Yes," he says. She can see the outline of his face, only through the contrast of his black hair. It frames the circle of his head, both on top and below as a cropped beard, the sharp eyebrows cutting a straight line on his forehead.

She's leaving space for him to elaborate. To translate what he's said before. But he doesn't offer her anything. "What are you doing here?" she asks him belatedly.

"Seems like we could both ask that question," he says.

She bites back a childish response—*I asked you first, asshole*—and tries again. "Who are you?"

"Ingvar."

"Ingvar Karlsson?" she asks. She feels silly asking, but she had just read about him this morning. Ingvar Karlsson, the boy who found her grandmother's and aunt's bodies in the snow. The second-generation neighbor.

To her surprise, he flashes his teeth in a smile. "Yes," he says. "And you are Agnes Magnúsdóttir."

"Agnes Glin, actually," she says. "But, yeah. How do you know that?" She can't slow the beating of her heart.

"Nora," is all the explanation he gives. "Is Magnús here, too?"

"No," she says. "Only me. I guess you knew him?"

He considers this. Or otherwise he's just standing there, inert.

He'd been six, she supposes, when her father was nine. That's an immeasurable distance when you're in it; when you're out of it, it seems impossibly close.

"I knew him," Ingvar says finally. He doesn't elaborate.

"So you know what I'm doing here," she says. "What are you doing here at"—she checks her phone—"six in the morning?"

"There's a missing woman from town," he tells her. "We have been looking for her." He gestures to the abandoned house behind him. "I thought, maybe if she had been running away, she would come back. She might think this is safe."

It strikes Agnes as an odd explanation. Not that this wouldn't be the right place to search for Ása. But the rationale is so specific. *If she had been running away.* And Agnes is painfully aware of how alone she is, right now, with this man. If he's dangerous, she's in serious trouble. She has her phone, but it's on airplane mode, waiting for the next time she's in a Wi-Fi oasis. Nora's inside the house that's built like a fortress. Agnes doubts Nora would hear her screaming for help. And Agnes doesn't imagine she'd get far on foot.

"Is this your first time seeing the house?" Ingvar asks her, interrupting her spiraling panic.

She hesitates. "Yeah."

"Would you like to come inside?" He takes a step backward, inviting her in. "I spent time here as a child. I can show you."

A thrill of fear and, again, horribly, laughter runs through her. She can say no. She knows that. She can just say no and turn around and walk back to the safety of the big house. But she'd hate herself, the minute she got away from him, for her cowardice. This is her chance to see her family's home, with someone who knew it well.

Agnes crosses the distance to the door. She tries to bend her knee naturally, but of course, there's the limp. Ingvar steps aside, indicating Agnes should go first. She braces herself for the smell, but today, with a few pills in her system, she can breathe the stale air without fainting. That's an improvement, at least.

Their boots squeak and grab at the old, beaten-up floors. Tracing her flashlight beam along the floor, Agnes checks behind her to see if she's left a trail of wet boot prints—yes, but they're in good company. The rest of the hallway, as far as she can tell, is a mosaic of them. There are stains on the wood, too. Spilled beer, vomit, she's not sure. If it were something important, there'd be more than one line of police tape on the door, right?

Agnes kicks one foot into the other, trying to clear the snow from her shoes. The wood floors are destroyed, sure, but they're still remarkably beautiful, and she's suddenly certain her grandfather is about to walk out from the kitchen, furious at the sight of water on his precious hardwood. When she was younger, she ran into his apartment in the Oakland Hills in dirty shoes. She'd been searching the garden for his cat, Pip, and had forgotten to take her shoes off at the door. She re-members even now the yank on her shoulder, her grandfather's big fingers twisting her ear, her yell of pain, more at the shock than actual sensation, and then her father's rage. It was the only time she'd ever heard Magnús raise his voice to Einar.

They'd left after that. No visit.

It had taken two weeks for Agnes to convince her father to let her visit Einar again.

I'll be good, she promised.

"Your grandparents had a tapestry on this wall," Ingvar tells her, calling her back to the present. He's indicating the stretch of wall to her left. "This"—he means the wall on her right—"had pegs for coats and boots. But the tapestry, it was handwoven by Marie's mother. It was a fairy-tale scene." He sidles past her, into the living room. "Very beautiful."

"What happened to it? Do you know?" Agnes asks, though she realizes straightaway it probably had been taken by her grandfather. Stored away in the same place where everything related to Iceland, to his wife and daughter, had been buried.

She regrets her frantic kicking. Her grandfather is dead. This home hasn't belonged to him for forty years. There's no point in preserving it for him.

"Not for me to know," Ingvar says. He shines his own flashlight beam down the hallway, mapping out the ground floor for her. There's an enclosed staircase straight ahead. To the left is the living room. To the right, through a doorway with broken hinges but no door, is the kitchen.

Agnes chooses the living room. There's no furniture in it other than a decrepit couch with faded upholstery. Ingvar sketches out the space, where two chairs had been, one for Einar, one for Marie, where they'd arranged the photographs of their wedding on the wall, where the ba-by's toys had been carefully stowed to one corner, where the record player had sat on its own perch for Magnús. Ingvar describes each item with loving detail.

"It sounds like you were here a lot," Agnes says. Actually, it sounds like he has this place memorized. Agnes isn't sure she can remember anything this clearly from when she was six.

"I was," he says. "My mother and Marie were close friends. They traded children, for babysitting."

"Is your mother," she says, uncertain, "Júlía?"

"Yul-ya," he corrects her. He flips his hand between the two of them. "Yes. Neighbors."

"Still?"

"My mother needs the babysitting now." He considers her, his face cast once again in shadow. "You should come visit. She loved Magnús very much. It would make her happy to know you."

This is more than Agnes could have hoped for. The chance to speak to someone from the first generation, her grandfather's neighbor and peer. "I'd like that," she says. "I'm not sure what Nora has planned, but—"

"No," Ingvar says, cutting her off. "Not Nora. Just you."

"Oh." Agnes waits for the man to explain. He doesn't. "Why?"

"My mother is fragile. Better to do these things one at a time."

Agnes says, "All right," because it's just as well. She hasn't quite made up her mind on Nora Carver. Nora's been kind to her—Agnes remembers the woman's care last night and thinks, *Very kind*—but they are strangers still, and Agnes is hyperaware of their roles as interviewer and interviewee. It's in Nora's best interests to keep Agnes happy, for her show.

Ingvar seems pleased. "Today?"

Agnes says, "Yes," without hesitation. She isn't here to create a good show; she's here to find out the truth.

She wanders into the kitchen. The space is shabby, the hub, she supposes, for all the illicit parties. There are beer cans everywhere. There's still the counter, the old rusted sink. The cupboards hang open, messy and vandalized. There's a back door, but it appears to have been boarded up as well.

Agnes tests the plywood against the door. It comes away easily. She tries the doorknob. It doesn't even stick. The door glides open, inviting in a gust of freezing cold air.

Two ways out of the house. One right to the river.

Agnes turns to find Ingvar lingering in the kitchen threshold, observing the room with a distant expression. Seeing it as it was, perhaps, forty years ago, when he was a child.

"Were you there?" she asks him. "At the party?"

"No."

"Why not?"

He doesn't answer. Probably it's an insulting question.

Agnes shuts the back door. "Was Marie a good cook?"

"Yes."

"What did she make you?"

"Soup." A sigh. "Cookies."

Agnes switches hands on her flashlight. The fingers of her right hand sting from the cold. She really should have bought gloves. She'd like to ask Ingvar to tell her more, but she's not sure he's capable of more. Not that his English isn't perfect, but he seems to think one-word answers are sufficient.

She calls out an involuntary *"Hey!"* and throws up a hand to block a searing white glare from her eyes. It's his flashlight, blinding her.

The spotlight drops. "Sorry," he says, but there's a hint of something in his voice. Laughter? "You look like her."

She blinks away the ghost image burned on her retinas. "Yeah, great."

Ingvar ducks out of the room. She follows, only a second behind, irritated but curious. "The staircase is very old," he warns her. "We will have to be careful."

Agnes gestures for him to lead the way. The stairs creak under

Ingvar's weight, but they hold. Behind him, Agnes clutches the railing for support. She's abused her leg these past two days, first on the flights, then with all this walking on uneven ground. Every step upward bears a heavy price on the hardware in her ankle, the tenuous threads holding her kneecap together. She's out of breath already, and there's still more staircase to go.

On the landing, Agnes takes a break. She shifts all her body weight onto her right leg and pretends to consider her options while her left leg throbs. Ingvar waits patiently beside her, flicking his flashlight into each room for her inspection. There are three rooms. Two of them are bedrooms, with sagging mattresses and overturned chairs or dressing tables, and the third is a simple bathroom. Someone, at some point, wrecked the toilet, the sink. Shards of ancient porcelain litter the floor. Black dust shadows the white and blue tiles.

Agnes chooses the room on the far left. The master bedroom, Ingvar tells her. In the corner of the room, underneath the window, stands a small, handmade crib.

The crib draws her forward. She wraps a hand over the rail, feeling the soft, sensitive wood. She doesn't know if her grandfather made this himself. Einar had grown up out here, in the countryside, but he'd been a studious person, not exactly one to work with his hands. He left Iceland to study in Denmark. A high honor, Magnús had told her. Expensive. That's how Einar met Marie, though Agnes realizes she doesn't know if Marie had also been a student or what. All she knew about that story was that Einar, a twenty-six-year-old in Copenhagen with great ambitions, met a seventeen-year-old girl, married her, and less than a year later, brought her back to Iceland, with a child on the way.

Magnús must have been in this crib. His sister, too. Agnes is aware of Ingvar's presence behind her. But she is alone.

She's disconnected. From her father. From his history. Her mother has no family. Her parents died when she was young, leaving her to the foster system. Agnes thinks that's part of the reason why her father fell in love with her, because he craved that blank slate.

Marie, married at seventeen, dead at twenty-six. A kid, like Nora had said.

Maybe that's why her father had Agnes when he was so young. Too young, he'd said. *I wouldn't do it any differently*, he'd assured her, *but we didn't know who we were or what we were doing.*

Agnes runs a finger down the length of the rotted mattress pad. She draws a fingertip through the years and the dust, and something ripples with her, as though in her wake.

For a moment, she's mesmerized.

Then, all at once, she hears the scratching and she feels the distinct movement of a body beneath her fingertip, and she shrieks, jumping backward.

"What?" Ingvar asks her. He's beside her in an instant, grabbing her shoulders roughly and pulling her away from the crib. "What is it?"

Agnes breathes hard.

"What?" Ingvar insists, alarmed.

"Rats," she says, stepping out of his grip. "Or mice. Something's made a home in there."

Ingvar looks down at her, bemused. "Mice," he says.

Agnes exits the room, fast. She wants to see her father's bedroom and she wants distance from whatever creature she'd just been petting.

CHAPTER TEN

February 6, 2019

A battalion of metal army men sprinkle the floor of Magnús's room, next to the bed. An overturned chest of drawers exposes what used to be her father's clothes. There are a couple of moth-eaten sweaters, left behind forty years ago. Agnes feels a moment's gratitude for all the people who have visited this place over the passing years, who have violated her family's privacy yet still left these relics behind. They've allowed her to step inside her father's childhood bedroom and see something of the boy he was. He used to wear tiny, scratchy sweaters and play with army men.

Standing in the center of her father's childhood bedroom, Agnes imagines the little boy—so little, from the size of his clothing—trying to cope with the tragic deaths of his mother and baby sister. Experiencing not only the private devastation within his family, but also the public persecution. The suspicions and accusations leveled against his father, the only family he had left. Then, months later, leaving his entire world behind. Forgetting his metal army men. Thinking, perhaps, that he'd come back to get them soon.

Agnes scoops up a flag-bearer figurine and tucks it into the pocket of her jeans.

The anger and the resentment that's been crawling inside her these past two days drains away, to be replaced with a sudden homesickness. She'd like to tell her father what she's seen, what she's understood.

Of course you don't want me to come here, she might say. *Of course you want to leave all of this in the past. I'm sorry for bringing it back to the present.*

But this doesn't stop her from drinking in her father's bedroom. From scanning every surface in the room, cataloguing every minute detail. She catches a glimpse of ink on the grimy white wall, and she does her best to crouch down to get a better look at the graffiti. Maybe she was wrong, she thinks. People haven't left her father's room alone all these years. As she approaches, though, her mounting irritation dissolves into awe. On the wall, half-hidden in shadow, is the name, written out in cramped cursive, *Magnús.*

Graffiti of a different sort.

The handwriting is so childish, so different from her adult father's steady hand, that it makes her want to cry. This is an entirely separate person from the man she'd grown up with. Left behind, forty years ago. Keeping her flashlight on it, Agnes takes out her phone and snaps a picture of the graffiti.

She straightens up to standing, overwhelmed, suddenly, by the house. By the ghosts of her family populating these rooms, felt but not seen. She stares out the window. This, too, is uncovered. She supposes Thor boarded up the ground-level ones to ward off unwanted visitors—didn't work—figuring no one could reach the second floor. Even old and suffering from decades of neglect, Agnes can see through the dirty glass to the magnificent view of the mountain beyond.

She turns to find Ingvar in the doorway, his attention on his phone. He's tapping out a long message, it seems.

Agnes clears her throat. "Anything else?"

Ingvar takes his time looking up from his phone. "No," he tells her. "I don't know the upstairs well. When I was here, I was always downstairs."

Without another word, Agnes pushes past him, heading straight for the staircase.

Her left leg would give out if she tried to bend it on these stairs, so she takes them one at a time, haltingly, like a child still learning their way around a step. She doesn't stop moving until she's outside, gulping at the fresh air. She hears Ingvar slamming the front door shut behind them, but she doesn't wait for him. She skirts around the back of the house, toward the river.

She doesn't stop until the river is all she can see. For a brief moment, she doesn't think she'll actually stop. Maybe she'll just keep walking until the frigid water engulfs her, cutting her off completely from the world and her own overwhelming thoughts. But self-preservation, this time, wins out. She's at the edge, her toes squeezing painfully in her boots. She shoves her hands and Nora's flashlight in her pockets, and she comes back to herself, slowly.

Ingvar comes up beside her, curious and solicitous, but quiet.

Out from the shadows of the house, Agnes can discern his features more clearly. Blue eyes peek out from beneath heavy, angular eyebrows. Everything on him has been magnified. Big forehead, big cheekbones, big jaw. He's surprisingly handsome, though she doesn't know where that thought comes from. It isn't the features themselves, but the amalgamation of them. The steadiness of his presence. She should be embarrassed for her frank assessment of him, except he's doing the same to her.

"She wasn't in there," she says. "Ása."

"Ow-sa," he corrects her. Again.

She ignores it. "You said in case she was running away," she says, unsure how to phrase the question without it sounding like an accusation.

"They say she was very drunk and probably left on her own. Maybe not. Maybe she—" Ingvar stops, unable to voice the rest. "This would seem like a safe place to hide, if you were upset or in trouble."

"But it's not?"

"The weather changes here. Rain wind snow. You cannot predict it. We haven't been above freezing for weeks. That house can't protect you. In this cold, even in there, you can lose consciousness from hypothermia. And then you're not waking up."

A shiver rattles her body. She tries to imagine staying outside longer than a few minutes at a time. How long has Ása been missing? Four days?

Agnes can't think about it.

"Did you play with my father out here?" she asks, instead.

"No," he says. "I liked to be inside."

"Where it's warm," she agrees. "I don't blame you."

Ingvar rewards her with a smile. She catches a glimpse of the man as he is when he's comfortable. Or rather, when she's comfortable with him. When he isn't a possible threat, but a man kind enough to wake up early to search for a missing woman in the cold, dark morning.

"Even in summer," he says, turning away to survey the river, "I didn't like it out here. I still don't."

"Why? It's so pretty. Like—" She points to the mountain just beyond, the sharp details of its snowy pores.

He seems to consider the question seriously and in his hesitation, she realizes her mistake. Ingvar is the one who found the bodies, nearly forty years ago to the day. Of course he wouldn't like this place.

"I have always felt," he says slowly, "that there was nothing good waiting for me here."

There's an icy fingertip on her ear. Agnes flinches at the touch and discovers only snow. All at once, without warning, without a trickle, the air around them fills with snowflakes. She supposes it's what Ingvar's talking about, how changeable the weather is. She paws at her jacket, flipping the hood up, and screws her eyes shut, the wet snow seeking out her unprotected skin.

"You should get inside," Ingvar tells her. He doesn't seem to mind the snow. He's probably used to it. He's probably wearing more than a couple of pairs of thin ankle socks in his boots.

"Where's your home?" she asks.

He gestures behind them. "Up on that hill, across the road."

"Is it a long walk?"

"I drove."

She hadn't seen his car. He must have parked on the side of the road and wandered in. The driveway most likely has disappeared over the past four decades from lack of use. "What time should I come by?" she asks. "To meet your mom?"

"It's hard to plan," Ingvar tells her. He produces his phone from his jacket pocket and passes it to her. "My mother's moods are like the weather. Unpredictable."

Agnes enters her number into his contacts, her fingers clumsy and numb. "Let me know." She hands the phone back and shoves her fists in her pockets. Then she asks, because it's been waiting for her, this question, since she learned who he was, "Where did you find them? Marie and the baby, I mean."

If it surprises Ingvar that she doesn't know this information, he doesn't let it show. He swings his arm to point beyond Thor's house. "In the lava fields less than a kilometer north of the new house."

He doesn't elaborate, and Agnes likes him for it. He's allowing space, she thinks, for their shared feelings. She imagines the little boy, trudging through this endless snow, cold and wet and scared. Stumbling, then, over the corpses of his beloved teacher and her baby. Agnes stares into those bright blue eyes, and wonders if he's thinking the same thing:

how much trauma like that must shape you. How that shock must live inside you, for the rest of your life.

Finally, when her fingers and toes ache so much she's worried about frostbite, Agnes asks him the other question that has been at the tip of her tongue the entire morning, the entire trip, and frankly, this past year. "Do you think my grandfather killed them?"

There's no hesitation, no softening the blow. Just that unrelenting stare and that voice, unflinching.

"Yes," Ingvar says. "I do."

CHAPTER ELEVEN

February 6, 2019

The house is awake when Agnes returns. The entryway light, now on, illuminates the last stretch of her walk, and when she opens the front door, she's greeted by the overpowering smell of frying eggs and brewing coffee. Agnes struggles out of her boots and walks into the kitchen.

"And where have you been?" Nora, her voice cutting through the pleasant rhythms of domesticity. She has the air of a bemused parent. Not angry, just concerned. When she catches sight of Agnes, she steps away from the stove and brings her a glass of water. "Are you feeling better?"

"Yeah," Agnes says, grateful for the water but embarrassed by Nora's concern. "I just needed some fresh air."

"You like the cold, then? I guess it's in your blood." Nora frowns at her. "How are you feeling, really?"

"Fine," Agnes insists. "Thanks for your help. I think it was just all the traveling, maybe something I ate . . ." She trails off. She doesn't need to explain. She was sick. That's it.

"I made you some dry toast," Nora tells her. "The only food my ex-husband could handle the morning after."

Agnes dutifully accepts the plate of toast and takes a seat at the kitchen island, but she doesn't touch her food. Nora serves herself fried eggs and toast and a large mug of coffee, then sits down at the dining table with a happy sigh.

From across the room, Agnes scans Nora's body, searching for the bulge of a microphone pack, the kind she's seen on reality TV stars, tucked into their bras or the waistbands of their pants, but the soft, well-worn black jeans and billowing sweater hang off Nora's body uninterrupted. For the moment, for whatever it's worth, it's just the two of them. Alone.

Nora catches the stare. Returns it with a smile. "You went to the house by yourself, right, didn't you?" She's quick on the uptake. "How does it feel," she asks, conspiratorially, "to see the things your family kept from you?"

Agnes doesn't deny it. "It's not like they kept it from me to exclude me," she says, hearing the defensive note in her voice, unable to help it. "My grandfather couldn't ever come back here, not without being treated like Jeffrey Dahmer. This was his home. He wasn't allowed to go home. That's what I'm feeling, when I look at this place. It isn't that I'm seeing something my family kept from me. I'm seeing what was kept from them." She hadn't realized this was how she felt, not until she said it aloud. She looks at Nora, almost startled by the force of her emotion.

"You're in a lot of pain," Nora says. "Aren't you?"

"I miss my grandfather. That's all."

"That's what I meant," she says gently. "This is real to you, in a way it can never be to me. I'm so glad you're here."

Agnes turns away, suddenly self-conscious. Nora takes the hint and focuses on her breakfast. She pulls out her phone, flipping through her emails and texts while she chews.

With Nora preoccupied, Agnes slips the metal army man she'd stolen from her father's room out of her pocket. She hadn't been able to make it out clearly in the dark, abandoned house. Now, under the kitchen's bright lights, she can see the little flag-bearer's paint has chipped away, either from time or heavy use, she can't be sure. The man is no longer wearing a uniform, and his flag is nothing but a thin sheet of rust. There's something on the flag, though, that compels Agnes to look more closely. A splash of something red.

Blood?

Agnes fumbles with the figurine, and it drops to the floor, bouncing underneath the table.

"What was that?" Nora asks, through a mouthful of eggs.

"Nothing," Agnes says quickly. She slips off the stool and crouches to see where the figurine went. "One second." She has to crawl, painfully, on hands and knees, to get to it.

"You need some help?" Nora leans over, awkwardly, in her chair, her hair spilling almost to the floor.

"It's fine," Agnes says from the shadows.

Nora's phone chimes, and she straightens up to check it. "That's my alarm," she says. "I have to get going."

It's there, underneath the table, where Agnes can only see Nora's socked feet, that she remembers what's been bothering her. "You said the police want to talk to you."

The toes curl inward, forming a strange fist. "In twenty minutes," Nora says. The toes relax, then flatten, as she comes to standing. There's the clatter of silverware. A loud gulp as she finishes her coffee.

"Why do they want to talk to you?"

"They're talking to everyone who was at the party," Nora says. "Well, everyone who was at the party and is still in town. Most of the out-of-towners are long gone."

Agnes grabs the flag-bearer and crawls back out from the table. It's an effort to stand, her knee popping extravagantly when she straightens it. Her joints ache, but that's nothing new for her. No, the strain she feels today is muscular. She hasn't asked so much of her body in a year.

"You were at the party?" she asks Nora, belatedly. Had Nora told her this yesterday and she'd just forgotten? Somehow Agnes doesn't think so.

"Of course. Can't miss an opportunity like that. The police want to know if I saw anything suspicious. No one knows what happened to Ása after she left—apparently, no one even noticed her leaving. So that's the focal point of the investigation."

"Did you?" Agnes asks. "See anything suspicious?"

Nora shrugs. "Nothing that comes to mind."

"Do you know her?"

"Who? Ása?"

Agnes waves the hand that isn't holding the metal figurine. *Obviously.*

"No," Nora says. "I noticed her at the party, but I noticed everyone who was there. I haven't had much of a chance to talk to the students yet."

"You didn't talk to her at all?" Agnes doesn't know why this bothers her. Maybe it's the way Nora's focusing more on Ása's disappearance than her grandfather's case. Nora seems to care about this missing woman.

"Hardly," Nora says. "She stopped me when I walked in. She said something in Icelandic, and when it was clear that I didn't understand, she said, *You're the American.* I said yes, I am, and she warned me not to let a guy named Óskar know. Then she brushed me off. That was the only time we spoke. Not much in the grand scheme of things, but significant in a murder investigation."

"Do you really think it's a murder investigation?" Agnes asks. She thinks of Ingvar's desperate search for the missing woman. Meanwhile, Nora has already resigned her to death.

"It's tricky," Nora says. "The feeling in town—you'll see—it's as though people are afraid to say it. Murder. They'd rather it be anything else. I can't say I blame them, but suicide is violent, too."

Agnes recoils. "Those are the only two options?"

"The two most likely, I'd say. It's all a guessing game until we know more."

"*We?* Are you working with the police?"

"Nope. The police haven't exactly been forthcoming with me. I can't really blame them for that. I'm running my own investigation." Nora eyes Agnes's full plate on the kitchen island. "What will you do while I'm gone? Rest?"

Agnes checks her phone. No messages from Ingvar, not even one to give her his number so she can contact him. She considers her options, while the fact of the day spreads out in front of her. She pictures the bottle of pills, nestled safely in her bed.

She can't stay in the house. Not alone.

"Are you going into town?" she asks Nora. "To the police station?"

"Technically the closest station is in Borgarnes," Nora says. "You passed it on your way up. They're about thirty minutes away by car. But they've set themselves up temporarily on campus for the interviews."

"I'll follow you into town," Agnes says. "Look around. Do you have a spare set of keys for me? Or can we leave the door unlocked all the way out here?"

"I'd say yes," Nora says, "except I'm a true crime podcaster. Never leave the door unlocked, no matter how isolated you think you are. The Vampire of Sacramento said he only murdered people whose doors were unlocked, because he thought they were inviting him inside." She takes her plate, cleared, to the sink. "What will you do in town?"

"I'm not sure yet," Agnes says, sickened by the moniker *Vampire of Sacramento*. Did her grandfather ever get such a nickname? *The Butcher of Bifröst*, maybe? She shudders.

"I wish you'd wait for me."

Agnes doesn't know how to answer that, not without displeasing Nora. This is her life. Her family. She's not waiting around. And she can't stay in here all day. Not when she's trying, desperately, not to backslide into the bottle of pills.

Nora concedes with a sigh. "Just keep all your impressions of the town fresh, okay?"

With breakfast done, they move quickly. Or rather, Nora moves quickly. Agnes sits by the front door, her puffy jacket hanging over her shoulders, while Nora fusses with her folders and her hair and her layers of warm clothing. Agnes takes the opportunity to examine the flag-bearer. The red splash on the flag is too luridly red, she decides, to be blood. She slips it into her jacket pocket, next to her phone. That was the last chip of paint from the flag, she tells herself. Nothing else.

"Ready?" Nora's holding out a spare set of keys for Agnes.

Finally, they're outside. Nora in the gargantuan truck, and Agnes in the rental car.

The drive off the property is meandering, the winding path through the snowy woods somehow longer than yesterday, and then the highway, empty, is a breeze. It's a short commute to town, but Agnes tries to absorb every second of it. The lava fields to either side of the road, the great expanse of craggy black rock interrupting a soft blanket of white. Where Ingvar says he found her grandmother and her aunt.

Is this missing woman, Ása, there, too?

CHAPTER TWELVE

February 6, 2019

The town's few streets line the highway. The truck ahead signals a left turn off the main road, and Agnes follows. The truck pulls up to a stop in the middle of the street. Agnes stops, too. Looks around. They're in front of a row of residential buildings. Something that looks like a school. Perhaps the primary school where her grandmother worked. Nothing like a university campus.

The truck door opens, and Nora hops out, jogging to the car and speaking before Agnes has the presence of mind to roll down her window.

"... where I'll leave you," Nora's saying.

"What?"

"The campus is a few blocks away," Nora says. "So this is where I'll break away. Okay?"

"Right."

"It's not that I don't want you seeing it," Nora says, reading Agnes's every objection in that one word. "I'm actually protecting you, believe it or not. There's someone there who wants to interview you more than I do, which is saying something."

"The police?" Agnes huffs out a laugh. "Nora, I think I'll be okay. I have a pretty strong alibi."

Nora's sigh is visible in the icy air. "No, it's Hildur. My local source? She wrote a book about your family, and when I told her that you were coming . . . she practically tore me apart begging for details. She's on campus most days, and I just know you'll run into her when I'm not there and you'll give her everything you're supposed to give me." The look on her face is so baldly desperate, Agnes feels herself relenting.

"I'll stay away," she promises. She would like to see where her grandfather had worked, but it's been forty years, and he was practically run out of town by an angry mob. There's not going to be a tribute to him on campus. She can live without seeing it for a day.

"Call me if you need anything," Nora says. "And don't stray too far, okay? For all we know, there's a killer on the loose."

"I'll keep the door locked," Agnes assures her.

Satisfied, Nora trots back to the truck. The engine comes back to life and she's off, driving straight to the end of the road and disappearing on another left turn.

Agnes should probably have told Nora that she can't call her if she's not connected to Wi-Fi. But it doesn't feel urgent. She isn't going to need help. She's here to take a quick look around town and then she'll find her way to Ingvar's, with or without an invitation. She nudges the car to the side of the road and parks. She could drive through town and be done in five minutes, but that's no way to experience a place. Even if there might be a killer on the loose.

Bundling herself into her jacket, Agnes stands by her car, uncertain of where to go. There's the primary school across the street. Snow-covered swings hang frozen in its playground. The building itself is modern, with fresh paint and long, low windows that allow her a picture-perfect glimpse of many small, round faces. Agnes doesn't quite believe that this is the same building where her grandmother worked, forty years ago. Besides, what is there for her to see, if it were? She didn't know her grandmother.

She feels a jolt of shame. She hasn't thought much about the murdered women. Marie and Baby Agnes. She's only thought of her grandfather, proving his innocence, and secretly, her father, proving him wrong. She's prioritized the men, the ones who survived. The ones she knew and loved.

The grandfather who taught her how to swim in the Pacific, who listened to her work through her complicated feelings, the ones she couldn't understand herself, not without help. She'd come out to her father first, at twelve years old, in a terrified, random burst at the dinner table. It was a problem she couldn't find a solution for, and that's what Magnús was good at, solutions. She couldn't stop thinking about her friend, Claire. Claire kept talking about boys and Agnes, well, Agnes didn't give a shit about boys. *Dad*, she'd said, *I think I'm a lesbian.*

Her father's solution had come quick. *You're too young to be a lesbian.*

She hadn't known how to respond to that, so that's where that conversation ended.

He'd been right, in his own way. There had been more girls. But there had also, eventually, been boys.

She finally told her grandfather when she was sixteen, on one of their Sundays, when she couldn't hide the truth any longer. He hadn't known what "bisexual" meant. After she'd explained, he'd grabbed her hand in a tight grip.

Great, he'd said. *But if you want my advice, only date women. Men are animals.* He'd made a sound of disgust that had her laughing.

She'd tried again with her father after that, on one of the rare occasions when the three of them were together. Christmas Eve. She'd needed her grandfather beside her to work up the courage to tell her father.

That's none of my business, Magnús had said.

Einar hadn't left Agnes room to respond. He'd exploded in Icelandic. The two of them argued, back and forth, in their shared secret language, with Einar concluding, in English, *You have no idea how lucky you are to have a daughter like her.*

Her father's eyes on her. Agnes can still remember the look on his face. So distant, like he was staring at her through the wrong end of a pair of binoculars. Then, finally, he'd apologized.

Magnús had met Emi once, on the day she'd helped move Agnes back into his home. They'd exchanged a polite hello, nothing more.

Agnes walks up the street, careful to avoid the ice that's grown on the concrete like moss. It's not that her father cared about her sexuality, one way or another. His discomfort with his daughter is not bigotry; it's his innate myopia. His inability to connect with someone else on their terms.

At the intersection, the apartment buildings give way to a row of shops. A café, a convenience store, what looks to be a thrift shop. Each storefront window has been stamped with a row of papers.

Agnes crosses the road to confirm her suspicions. The storefronts all display the same missing poster she saw in that café in Reykjavík. MISSING PLEASE HELP. The smiling face of the probably-dead woman. Ow-sa, not Ass-a. Agnes finds herself in front of the café window, transfixed by the photograph. The beaming face, the white-blond hair so much like her own. Suicide, murder, kidnapping. Drunken mistake. Whatever has happened to Ása, it isn't pleasant. Agnes hopes that, for her sake, it was fast. She fell asleep in the snow and froze, unaware.

A touch on her arm gives Agnes a tremendous jolt, her heart leaping into her throat at the man's voice. Calling her by name. She yanks her arm out of the grip and turns, protesting, but the man is already apologizing.

"Oh, no," he says. "I'm sorry."

Ingvar, the boy who found the bodies, the man from the farmhouse.

He's different in daylight—or in what passes for daylight here. More real, somehow. The blue eyes, set deep, glitter. Now she sees the shape of his stomach through his heavy sweater. The drooping slope of his shoulders. He's more of a person, and less of a dream.

"I thought you saw me," he's saying. In the clarity of day, out from the shadow of the farmhouse, there's more humor in him, a shy smile. He points to the window. "I waved."

She follows the gesture, through the glass to the busy café. There are eyes staring back at her, white faces and empty curiosity. Agnes hadn't noticed. But this doesn't shock her. Emi used to accuse her of having extreme tunnel vision, of seeing only what she wanted to. These jokes started out teasing. By the end of the relationship, though, they'd become yet another reason to break it off.

"Sorry," Agnes says. "I was checking out the poster."

"Yes," Ingvar says. "She is everywhere." The good humor drains from his expression. "But apparently also nowhere."

"Do you know her?" He seems to be taking this woman's disappearance hard, searching for her early in the morning, losing all happiness at the sight of her missing poster.

"No," Ingvar says, and it's a complete sentence. "Where is Nora?"

"Talking to the police," Agnes says. "I'm on my own for the time being. I was going to look around town and then stop by your place, if that's still okay." A gust of wind picks her hair up and away from her face, exposing the back of her neck to the cold. "To meet Júlía."

"Yul-ya," he corrects her again. "Have you seen the view?"

Agnes takes in the small town. "This?"

He flashes her a smile, his teeth so white against his dark beard. "No. Come with me." He stows a small wax paper bag into his jacket pocket, explaining that it's a treat for his mother.

Agnes follows Ingvar down the street, trying to picture him as a small child. She can see big cheeks and big round eyes. Not much different from now. Forty years probably hasn't changed him much. But still, the image throws her off. The man beside her is forty-six. Only three years younger than her father. But they seem remarkably different. Her father feels older to her, of course. With Ingvar, maybe it's the fact that she thinks of him as the boy who found the bodies. He's infantilized, because he's been immortalized in that moment from his childhood.

Agnes asks, without thought, "Do you have kids?" They'd be a bit younger than her.

This startles him. "No. Do you?"

"No," she says with a laugh. She's about to say *I'm too young*, but that's not true, at least not in the case of her family. Marie had Magnús before twenty. Magnús had her when he was not much older.

"Okay," Ingvar says.

Agnes struggles to keep up with his long stride. Each step is a debt owed to her body, unable to be repaid.

"This," he tells her, "is the main road of town." He points out the shops she'd already noticed. The school. Most of the town is housing, it seems, with a couple of hotels.

"No grocery store?"

"Not here," he says. "In Borgarnes."

"With the police station." He looks surprised. "Nora," she explains.

He nods. "She says you are here to talk about your grandfather. She says you were very close." At this, she catches an odd expression on his face. A darting look, like he's suddenly noticing what a freak she is, to be very close to a murderer. "But you don't speak Icelandic."

"Right on all counts," Agnes says. She doesn't elaborate. Instead, she asks, "What do you think happened to this woman? Ow-sa?"

Ingvar doesn't answer. He doesn't even seem to hear her. They just keep walking forward, through the parking lot at the end of the road, crowded with cars. Ingvar tells her he'll show her the town from up high. At the end of the lot, there's a sudden rise of a hill. From a distance, it looks like a steep incline, but to Agnes's relief, as they approach, the slope flattens. Agnes steps off the trusted concrete and into the snow, following Ingvar's lead.

She's forgotten her question when Ingvar finally deigns to answer. "I don't know," he says. "But it was no accident."

"How do you mean?" Agnes is out of breath, her ankle locking up and making her toes squeeze into a bear claw. She'll be damned, though, if she lets herself admit she's in pain.

"We would have found her," Ingvar says. "If she had made a mistake, she wouldn't have gotten far on her own."

At the top of the ridge, they stop. The wind tears at their hair, scraping at their clothing. Agnes turns in a circle, surveying the town, the tight cluster of buildings, the highway she drove in on.

"There's the university," Ingvar tells her, unnecessarily. He has to raise his voice to be heard over the pitch of the wind.

The university is another ecosystem all on its own, attached to the town by one spare road. There's this brief glimmer of civilization, the campus and the town, and then there's the expanse of snow hemming them in.

Agnes finds a modicum of shelter next to the big man. "Is that it?" she shouts.

In answer, he just points beyond them, away from town.

There are bodies dotting the static white landscape. Widespread groups of figures, all wearing the same reflective gear that catches flickers of the wan sunlight, pacing out slowly into the fields. Calling out in hoarse sounds that the wind carries back to them.

Ása.

They've found the search party.

"Why are they going so far?" Agnes asks.

Ingvar hunkers down, so he doesn't have to raise his voice. "They are looking for Ása."

"No, I know that," she says, exasperated. "But the farmhouse is way over there. This is nowhere near it."

"Ah." The dancing blue eyes. There's a measure of humor again, but the smile on his face is bitter. "Because we don't think it's an accident. Someone may have taken her."

"Taken her all the way out here?" Agnes asks, incredulous, even though she knows, deep down, this makes sense. Her grandmother's body, too, had been found far away from home. The town remembers.

"There's the crater." Ingvar gestures with one arm into the distance, toward the horizon. There are endless rolling hills. He seems to be indicating the biggest hill, separate from the others. "The Grábrók Crater," he tells her, as though that name will mean anything to her. "Many people hike into it. She may have been taken there."

Agnes considers the lone hill, desolate in winter. She stares back up at Ingvar, using his bulk to protect her from the wind. "My grandfather wasn't a killer," she tells him.

Ingvar doesn't reply. His jaw is set tight against the cold.

The wind presses at their backs, escorting them away from the search party, away from the present, into the past. With an awkward maneuver, Ingvar pats Agnes on the shoulder. "Let's go see if my mother's awake."

CHAPTER THIRTEEN

February 6, 2019

The entrance to Ingvar's driveway is nearly exactly opposite to her own. But instead of a mostly flat road through a tunnel of trees, this is a leisurely climb in the open air, skirting the edge of a long, rolling hill. Ingvar's truck handles the incline easily. Agnes's rental car skids, only once, on the last sharp turn to level ground. There, in the middle of this plateau between two hills, stands a low, wide home. Lights blaze from the windows. It's cozy, a beacon of life in an otherwise empty place.

Ingvar's already parked his truck and reached the front door by the time Agnes has struggled out of her car. "I will check on her," he calls out to Agnes, before disappearing inside.

It's somewhat rude to race in before her, but Agnes appreciates the privacy while she limps across the icy drive. Her left leg feels like it's composed of broken glass, grinding with every step, and the rest of her body is cramping. She hasn't walked so much in a year. And while the nausea has left her, in its place is a sharp ache at the back of her skull, sending lightning bolts through her brain whenever she turns her head too quickly. She needs a pill. Just one more. To dampen some of the pain. As soon as she gets back, she promises herself.

When Agnes reaches the front door, she pauses in the threshold to catch her breath. She doesn't think she'll faint. But she might need to lie down, all the same.

She removes her boots and her jacket, and she waits, panting, for Ingvar to return.

He finds her a moment later. "My mother is in the living room," he tells her, beckoning for her to follow.

He leads them out of the entryway, through a warm kitchen. The setup is minimal, outdated. There's an old stove, a behemoth iron thing, at the center of the kitchen, which overshadows the rest of the narrow appliances, the thin cabinetry, and a breakfast table, upon which there are piles of newspapers and plastic utensils designed to feed teething children. A cold hand squeezes Agnes's heart. Those forks and spoons must be for Júlía. Ingvar doesn't have kids.

"Wait," Agnes says, stopping in the kitchen. Ingvar turns to her, curious and slightly furtive. "Is she—are you sure your mother is able to handle this?" Those final visits with her grandfather had been difficult. She remembers his fatigue, his soft skin. Einar had been so proud. There had been a period of weeks when he hadn't allowed her to spend time with him. He hadn't wanted her to see him that way, he'd said. Love had won out, though. *You must only remember the Before-Me*, he'd told her. She'd promised. Now, remembering him in those last days, the slightness of his shoulders, the weakness in his voice, she feels a sense of betrayal. Both to that man, to that promise, and because he'd made her promise something impossible.

She doesn't want to intrude on this woman's privacy. Or Ingvar's, for that matter.

"My mother loved Magnús," Ingvar tells her. "This will make her happy. If it doesn't, then you can go."

Agnes huffs out a nervous laugh, and follows him into the living room.

It, too, is a cozy space, filled with craft supplies and piles of books. There's a well-loved couch against one wall, with two simple recliners to either side of it. Nestled into one of the recliners is a small, straight-backed woman. She's focused on a ball of yarn in her lap, ignoring the pastry set out on the coffee table in front of her. She doesn't look up when they enter, only mumbles something in Icelandic.

"Don't cut it," Ingvar tells his mother, in English. "I'll untangle it for you." Then, when she doesn't look up, Ingvar prompts her again, but this time, it's in Icelandic.

Whatever he says has his mother's head whipping up. Her eyes are her son's, but they don't glimmer with humor. They glint like steel. She reminds Agnes, suddenly and totally, of a vulture on its perch, surveying its territory closely. When she finally takes in the entirety of Agnes, the yarn falls from her gnarled hands, bouncing off her lap and falling to the floor, forgotten. The eyes, narrowed before in suspicion, widen in surprise.

Agnes is too slow. The jet lag, the long day, the half doses, it's all slowed her down. She's supposedly her grandmother's twin. What must this poor old woman think, forty years later, seeing the mirror image of her murdered neighbor walking into her living room?

"She speaks English," Ingvar says, switching back himself. "Agnes is from America. Magnús's daughter."

The old woman doesn't seem to hear him. She appears to have stopped breathing. "Marie," she rasps. There's more in Icelandic.

"No," Ingvar insists. "English. This is Agnes, Magnús's daughter."

Agnes steps forward, uncomfortable, caught between mother and son. She offers the old woman a smile. "Hi, Júlía. I'm—"

"Agnes," Júlía concludes for her. "I know." She looks to her son, pointedly, and asks for something in Icelandic.

He answers in English. "Yes. I'll get you both some tea." Ingvar offers Agnes an encouraging smile on his way back into the kitchen.

"Come here," Júlía orders Agnes. She indicates the seat closest to her on the couch. She watches Agnes from her perch, and Agnes wonders if the old woman can sense the weakness in her. Júlía waits until Agnes is settled, and then she leans farther in. "It's you." Her voice is barely higher than a whisper. "Marie."

The old woman reaches a hand to Agnes's arm, taking her wrist in a surprisingly strong grip. She says something in Icelandic. The sentence seems to go on forever.

"I'm sorry," Agnes says, out of her depth. "I don't speak Icelandic. What?"

"Marie," Júlía says again. She shakes her head, her face screwed up in a mixture of confusion and some high emotion Agnes can't identify. "I hate what I've done."

"What?" Agnes asks, drawn in despite herself.

"I told him to go," Júlía says, squeezing her wrist tighter. "I told Einar to take his boy and run."

Dread pools in Agnes's stomach, settling like a heavy weight. "Why did you do that?"

A tear slides down the old woman's cheek. "I thought he killed you. He killed you. We all knew. But here you are." She switches to Icelandic, overcome once again with confusion and, Agnes recognizes it now, regret.

Agnes casts a look to the hallway. No Ingvar. She turns back to the old woman. "I'm glad you did," she says, and that's true. She wouldn't be here if her grandfather hadn't run to California. But . . . "What do you mean, you thought he killed me?"

Júlía doesn't answer. She stares back at Agnes, her piercing gaze turning cloudy. "I don't know you," she says. The grip on Agnes's wrist slackens. "Do I?"

"Yes, you do," Agnes says. She tries to give the woman a reassuring smile. She knows, without having to see it herself, that it's come out more like a desperate leer. "I'm Marie's granddaughter. Agnes. You said you thought Einar killed Marie. What makes you so sure?"

"No," the old woman mutters. The hand slips away, back to her own lap, fretting absentmindedly with the material of her pants. She speaks, but again it's in Icelandic. A short, declarative statement, the rasping voice suddenly unsteady. She won't meet Agnes's eye.

"What is it?" Agnes presses. "What do you know?"

"*Nei*," the old woman says, and it comes out sharp and loud. Loud enough for her son to hear.

Ingvar appears in the doorway, concern etched into his face. Spotting his mother's distress, he hurries into the room.

"Should I leave?" Agnes asks, already standing to go.

Ingvar's whispering something to his mother. Agnes edges toward the hallway, apologies on her lips. Ingvar comes to standing, his expression grim. Without another word, he escorts Agnes to the front door.

Shoving her feet back into her boots, Agnes apologizes again. "She thought I was Marie," she explains, unnecessarily. Agnes hadn't exactly corrected the old woman, though, had she? She'd terrorized her.

"Maybe we will try another time," Ingvar tells her, no hint of good humor left in his expression.

CHAPTER FOURTEEN

February 6, 2019

Once she's safe inside Thor's house, Agnes peels off her jacket and removes her boots with trembling fingers. *He killed you. We all knew.* There it is. The certainty with which everyone who knew her grandfather best labeled him a murderer. Agnes feels rubbed raw, her nerves chafing and frayed. She'll have to talk to Júlía again. She'll have to find a better way to ask the old woman what she knows. What did they all know, that they didn't bring forward to the police all those years ago?

Drained, Agnes staggers back into her room. She drops onto the side of her bed with a groan, her leg almost not bending at the knee. She unfolds herself in stages, grunting with the effort.

She hadn't reached for the bottle consciously, but the pills rattle in her left hand. She can't seem to let go of the bottle, even though she's telling herself she won't open it. She's gotten this far on just one. In her right hand is her phone.

She logs in to the Wi-Fi. No messages.

She finds her way to Emi's Instagram, out of habit. The last time she checked, Emi still had photos of them together on her profile. Selfies posing in the garden, sun soaked and dirty, scenes of Agnes draped on their couch in their apartment. A portrait of Agnes surfing in Bolinas, her grandfather in the foreground, hands on his hips, watching her. The caption reads: *tfw Kate Bosworth in Blue Crush was your sexual awakening and now you're dating her.* That had been a day so wonderful it had wounded Agnes. The drive into Bolinas, all three of them carsick from the curving roads, her grandfather's booming laughter at Emi's jokes. When they got home, Emi had thanked Agnes for sharing her family with her.

Her heart squeezes. She had to scroll for a while to find these photos.

Her family's gone. Grandfather dead, Emi reduced to the occasional polite text, her father no longer speaking to her, and her mother—well, her mother's in Maine.

She dials Emi's number.

What time is it in Berkeley? Seven a.m.? Eight?

Agnes listens to each ring, the line staticky and different, and pops the pill bottle open. She digs out one tiny white pill. Not to swallow. Just to look at. They'd given her so many of these after the operation. Her surgeon had lamented, over and over, what bad luck she had. *This is going to be a long road,* he'd warned her. In addition to destroying her kneecap and tearing the ligaments surrounding it, she'd shattered the bottom of her shinbone, right at the root of the ankle. At first, the pills were what kept her from screaming. But somewhere in the third month, when her leg had wasted away to skin and bone, she understood them for their true effects.

That, unsurprisingly, was around the time when Emi broke up with her. She wouldn't kick Agnes out of their apartment for another two months, when Agnes started to get the pills not from the pharmacy but from a man she met through a mutual acquaintance.

The line picks up. There's a burst of something on the other end—a laugh, maybe. Then there's Emi's hushed, concerned voice. "Hey, baby. What's going on?"

"I—" Agnes stutters, thrown by Emi's tenderness. Does Emi know that she was just collateral damage? Does that make their breakup better or worse for her? Agnes is afraid to ask. And what a way to start a phone call. So she hears herself say, stupidly, "I made it. I'm in Iceland."

"Oh, *good*. How is it?"

Agnes searches the room for something to look at, something to distract herself, but there's nothing. She is held captive by the silence on the line. By how much she's left unsaid.

"It's okay," Emi tells her. "You're okay. Have you eaten anything today?"

Agnes lets out a hoarse laugh. "No."

A harsh sigh. "I will fly out there and force you to eat, don't tempt me."

The confession spills out of Agnes. "I'm so lonely, Em."

There's a pause, unbearably long, long enough for Agnes's gaze to finally snag on something. The writing desk. It's where she'd arranged Nora's notes and the photos of her family. She had placed them in a pile, the family portrait propped up on the table.

It's gone.

Agnes scans the floor. Stands to get a better look at the table. It could have slipped back down onto the pile.

"...honey," Emi's saying.

"What?" Agnes shuffles through the pages. No sign of the portrait.

"Oh, I'm sorry, am I interrupting you?" The snap in Emi's voice brings Agnes back to attention. "You called me. You're the one putting this on me."

"I'm not putting it on you," Agnes says. She drops back onto the mattress, rubbing her eyes. Maybe she put the portrait in her bag for safekeeping and forgot about it. She isn't exactly operating at full capacity right now. "Or if I am, I don't mean to. I just—I need—I need a friend right now, Em. That's it."

Another sigh. "I know."

Agnes waits for more, but it doesn't come. "I'm sorry," she says, even though it's not enough. She fidgets with the tiny white pill in her hand. She's never been any good at resisting temptation. "Are you—have you—I mean, have you been seeing anyone?"

A long inhale.

"That's great," Agnes says quickly. "Don't tell me."

The conversation ends abruptly. Emi has to get ready for work. She reminds Agnes to take care of herself. "Find a friend," she tells her. And then the line goes dead.

Agnes returns to Emi's profile, to the more recent photos she'd ignored on her quest to find herself in Emi's life. There's a new photo of her, sitting in someone's backyard. There's someone else with her, cradling her body from behind, tucking their face into her neck. The caption reads, *Soft launch.*

She had known Emi would find someone else. Would tell anyone honestly that she'd hope she'd move on, be happy. But still it's a blow. It's a reminder of the before. Before Agnes became this shell of herself. Before she discovered the pleasure that comes in skirting around the edge of something completely, vastly unknown. Something that consumes you not because it's seeking you out, but because it simply is there and it is so much bigger. A black hole.

Sickened, suddenly, by herself, Agnes drops the pill back into the bottle. She seals it shut and stashes it back under the mattress.

She checks her bags, both the backpack and the suitcase, for the family portrait. Nothing. She hobbles out into the hallway. Considers Nora's closed door. She's opening it before she can second-guess herself. She's not snooping, she tells herself, she's looking for something Nora gave her. Maybe Nora took it back, without Agnes knowing, for reasons known only to herself. Agnes skims the surfaces of the expansive room.

No Xeroxes, no loose papers. Nora's tidy. There's a pile of plastic storage boxes in the corner of the room, filled with folders. Agnes gets lightheaded just imagining pilfering through those files.

She returns to the living room. She might have dragged it out here. It doesn't make any sense, the desperation she feels, but she wants to see her grandfather again. The Before-Him, as he'd called it. She's so close to him, but she feels so far away. *He killed her. We all knew.* Agnes is searching between the couch cushions when the front door opens.

"Perfect timing," Nora says. She beams at Agnes and throws her arms wide open. "I have a lead."

CHAPTER FIFTEEN

February 6, 2019

"I know who I need to talk to," Nora says, dropping onto the couch opposite Agnes. "Finally."

"Finally?" Agnes can't hide her skepticism. "Hasn't it only been a day since she was reported missing?"

Nora tosses her hair over her shoulder. "An eternity for someone as impatient as I am."

Agnes feels herself relaxing. She hadn't thought she would, hadn't even given it a second thought, but she likes Nora. That had never been part of her considerations, when she'd decided to come here. As a person, Nora was irrelevant. All that mattered was what she could do for Agnes. But now, listening to Nora's plotting, Agnes has to admit to herself: she likes Nora and that does matter.

Find a friend.

"You have no idea how much I *hate* not knowing," Nora's telling her. "It's been excruciating waiting to know what they're looking for, what they're thinking, and now . . . I know more than they do." She barks out a triumphant laugh. "This means I'll be out again tomorrow, though. So I have a proposition for you. It's unorthodox, but I'd like for you to join me when I talk to Ása's friends. I don't love the idea of you here all by yourself when you've come all this way. And when, frankly, it does sound like something happened to Ása. I'd feel better if you weren't roaming the woods by yourself. What do you say?"

"Yeah," Agnes says. "Cool."

This isn't what she came here to do, but she might as well join Nora. She's curious about this missing woman. And she doesn't think she could handle another day to herself, alone with all her temptations.

"What's the lead you've got?" Agnes asks. "You said you know who to talk to?"

"It's something I overheard when I walked in. I passed a couple of the kids who had been at the party, just as they were leaving. They were arguing about a phone. The girl said, 'We have to tell them about the phone.' And the guy told her to be quiet. He was furious."

Agnes waits. When Nora doesn't elaborate, only looks at her like, *See?* she asks, "That's it?"

"Are you kidding?" Nora asks. "I know who Ása's friends are. I know that, for whatever reason, her friends are keeping something from the police, something about a phone. It's so much information."

"Did you tell this to the police?" Agnes wonders, watching Nora's mind work, if she should tell her about Júlía. *He killed her. We all knew.* What would Nora do with that information?

"Not yet. I'd like to talk to these students first. Hildur's helping to find a time for us all to talk tomorrow. She's an adviser at the school. She knows these kids."

"She's the one who wrote the book on my family, right?"

"Exactly." Nora eyes Agnes. "You sure you're up for it? You're still looking a bit clammy."

"I just need some sleep tonight, I think." Agnes wipes her forehead, whisking away a fine mist of sweat. She probably has a fever. She hasn't taken her usual handful of pills, hasn't eaten properly for days, hasn't slept, and she's walked more today than she has in a year. She's lucky to be speaking in full sentences.

"If you're sure . . ."

"I am," Agnes says, and it comes out more harshly than intended. "It's just jet lag," she says.

"Understandable," Nora says. Then, stretching her back, she gets that same daring look from yesterday. "How would you feel about an interview? A bit more official, this time."

"Right now?" Agnes's stomach lurches. She knows this is why she's here, but she can't help but feel a knee-jerk burst of stage fright.

Nora repeats, "Only if you're up for it," but she doesn't wait for Agnes's answer. She's up and at the dining table in a heartbeat, digging through the pile of machinery, searching for a microphone. "You signed the consent form, right?"

"Yeah," Agnes lies.

As Nora clips the microphone to her sweatshirt, Agnes comes to a decision—or, she realizes that she's already decided and has only just now noticed. She's not going to tell Nora about her talk with Júlia. For all that Agnes likes Nora, this isn't Nora's family. This is only a show to her.

"Oh, hey," Agnes says, "you know that family portrait you gave me? The one where they're all standing outside? Did you take it from my room?"

"No," Nora says. She returns to the dining table to set something up on one of her expensive laptops. "I have my own copy."

Agnes pinches the bridge of her nose, trying to remember what she did with it. "Maybe I really did misplace it."

"I'll make you another copy," Nora offers, "if you can't find it."

Agnes rebuffs her offer, for now. She had the printout this morning. It didn't disappear into thin air.

By the time they're finally sitting across from each other, both wearing their respective microphones, the sun has set again. The world outside the windows is a uniform black. Nora has flicked on the lights, started a fire, and even set them out a bunch of "pre-dinner snacks." The atmosphere in the room is intimate, but there's too much darkness, too quickly. Agnes is upside down, not even confident what day it is anymore.

"In my more 'official' interviews," Nora begins, "I use a bigger, more impressive microphone. It's a lot of pageantry. You'll see it tomorrow. But between you and me, I want you to try to forget, as much as you're able, what we're doing here. This isn't me asking you a series of leading questions, hoping to get one particular answer. I just want to know what your grandfather was like. Who was he to you? Not, *Is he a murderer or isn't he?* That's not helpful to anyone. I mean, unless he said it explicitly to you, unless there's something you want to tell me." She waits. When Agnes doesn't speak, she adds, "Does this sound fair?"

Agnes isn't listening. She's too distracted by the weight of the microphone, the touch of its plastic to her skin. She imagines the comments on Nora's podcast. The thousands of ratings. The reviews that treat the real people involved like characters in one of Agnes's murder mystery shows. *He's guilty and the granddaughter knows it. She's lying when she says she doesn't know anything.*

"He's innocent," Agnes hears herself say. "I don't have proof. I know that's not what you want to hear. He's gone, and he can't say it for himself anymore. He never could. It was too huge. But he wasn't a murderer."

Nora asks, "What was too huge?"

"The truth," Agnes says. "His grief. His sadness. My grandfather led a very solitary life in California. I spent every Sunday with him—that was our day—but I don't think he went out much during the week. He read. He tended to his garden. He went swimming. But he never remarried and he only had me for company, which isn't much. He died alone."

At the very end, Agnes's father had arranged for a daytime nurse to take care of her grandfather's needs. Agnes had been living with

Emi then, had been too busy with work. Einar died sometime in the night, alone in his apartment. He'd been young. Too young for how he looked. *He lived a hard life,* her father had told Agnes, after. *Stress has a way of ruining a body.* Stress, and a nasty bout of meningitis from which he never fully recovered.

Her grandfather had been found by the nurse in the morning. Agnes had been too busy to help him, and so a stranger had been the one to tend to him. This fact haunts Agnes, the loneliness of it threatening to swallow her whole.

Nora nods. "Sundays were your day. Was this religious? Was your father present?"

"Not religious," Agnes says, feeling her face relax. Her grandfather, a staunch atheist, would have been insulted by the question. "And no, it was just me. The visits started when I was in elementary school. My parents' marriage was falling apart, and I wasn't taking it well, so I think they thought I needed something more stable. Or maybe they just needed time to themselves, to figure things out. We kept up the tradition, though, after the divorce. Up until the end, actually. We would try to see each other more often throughout the week, too, but we always ensured we had that time together. I loved those days. He was like my second father."

More than that, Agnes thinks. Her real father. But she holds back from saying this, if only because Magnús might listen to this. She's angry with him. They have a complicated relationship, which is probably downplaying it by a lot. But she's never wanted to hurt her father. Especially not now, when he's the only ally she's got left.

"It doesn't sound like he was close with your first father," Nora says, calling Agnes back to the present.

"I don't know." The answer is no, Magnús and Einar hadn't been close. They hadn't known how to speak to each other, not for much longer than a short visit. But they'd loved each other, Agnes had felt it. "My dad would never have left me alone with him, though, if he thought his father was a murderer. If he thought his father had killed his own wife and child. That has to be worth something, right?"

"Can I give you some advice?" Nora asks. "Recalibrate your expectations. You aren't here as the sole advocate for your family. I know that's what it feels like, but I'm not out to *get* anyone. And you also aren't here to prove your grandfather's innocence. Frankly, you can't. I just want to know about your life with him, and without him. It sounds like you two were very close, and that's valuable. Far more valuable than your opinion on the case."

Agnes says, "Right," if only to keep the conversation moving forward. She has to be able to prove his innocence. She doesn't know what she would do, if she couldn't.

"Besides," Nora says, "you say Einar never spoke to you about his wife and daughter at all. Right?"

Agnes hesitates. "Yeah," she says, finally. "I don't speak the language. I've never been here before. My family never talks about Iceland. It's not a casual topic in our household. I don't blame my grandfather for his silence. I know what people think, that if you're innocent, you'd scream about it. I know that they say silence is complicit admission, or whatever. But that's not fair. That's not human. What my grandfather went through—what my father went through—I don't think people understand what that must have been like, for them. I don't think they understand how much grief changes you."

"Trauma," Nora says.

Agnes doesn't hear her. She sees her grandfather's hands, the skin mottled and papery thin, as they were in those last months. She had grown up with his strength, with the power of his arms vaulting her through the waves in Bolinas, the unshakable grip. She'd grown up watching that power transform from something external to something entirely internal. And then it had waned, until he was something delicate. She sees him suddenly as a man, not a source of comfort. A man who had been born in another country, who had endured many lifetimes of tragedy in one, and who had held his tongue. Who had contained the world in his body, until that, too, failed him.

I love you, Agnes. And you love me, don't you?

Nora's speaking still, prompting her, but Agnes isn't listening.

"I don't want to talk about it anymore," she says.

"You're doing great," Nora assures her. "It's always messy at the start, but—"

"I can't," Agnes says. "Not right now."

"All right," Nora says, and there's so much tenderness in her voice Agnes could cry.

Agnes runs a hand through her hair, but her fingers don't get far. Her hair is tangled, windswept and unbrushed. She wants nothing more right now than the oblivion of sleep. "Can I have a melatonin?" she asks Nora. It's like asking for cucumber water when what she needs is vodka, but it'll have to do.

Nora agrees. She digs through her stash in the kitchen and returns, putting a handful into Agnes's waiting palm. "This ought to last you a few days," she says. "Are you going to sleep now?" She checks the time. "I was about to make dinner."

"I'm sorry," Agnes says, "but yeah."

Nora touches her shoulder. Just lightly. "You should rest, then. Tomorrow's a big day." The touch disappears. "You aren't alone, Agnes. I'm right here with you."

CHAPTER SIXTEEN

February 7, 2019

This time, Agnes rides into town in Nora's truck. They might as well be flying for all they feel of the road, and Agnes, hazy and strange from a fitful night of half sleep, sips at the to-go cup of coffee Nora fixed for her. "You take good care of me," Agnes says.

"What can I say? I'm a nurturer." Nora guides the truck into town and finds the right apartment building without any help from the GPS. She parallel parks in front of the building as though she's done it a thousand times before.

"This," Nora announces, "is where Ása and her friends live."

The morning is predictably dark, but the streets are lit up well, allowing Agnes a good view of the building. She likes it. Not for its anonymous modern design, but the personalities of those living inside. Each windowsill features some type of light, either an upside-down triangle of electric candles or stars or even a warm salt lamp. They're fighting off the darkness. As though everyone were holding hands, shoring each other up against a strong current.

Nora hops out of the truck and Agnes follows, more carefully. Before they'd left, she'd swallowed two pills, not because she'd been thinking about it all night, she'd convinced herself, but to curb the pain rocketing up her leg. It's not enough, not nearly enough, to ease her cravings. Just enough, she tells herself, to be a person. She waits on the sidewalk while Nora grabs her equipment from the trunk. Her equipment turns out to be an oversized backpack and a tote bag. It surprises Agnes, again, how little Nora needs for this award-winning podcast. No crew, no huge cases of machinery. One woman with a backpack.

"Listen," Nora says, coming around the side of the truck, "I think it's best if you don't speak in there. Of course you can say hi, whatever, you're allowed to be you, but you aren't technically part of the show. Right?"

Agnes agrees easily. She hadn't expected otherwise. This is Nora's domain and, frankly, beyond a burgeoning curiosity to find out what happened to this student, Agnes doesn't really care. She's here for Einar, not Ása.

"Great," Nora says. She fiddles with her belt. It takes Agnes a moment to figure it out, but it's her microphone pack. She's turning it on. This gives Agnes a jolt of pleasure. They hadn't spoken much this morning over breakfast, but they had spoken. And it hadn't been recorded.

Nora leads her to the front door, but a voice, loud and cheerful, stops them in their tracks. "Nora! Agnes!" It's Thor, wearing the same thin snowsuit as before. He rushes up to them, grinning.

Nora's delighted. "What are you doing here?"

"I have to help the search however I can." He claps Nora on the back and nods a friendly hello to Agnes. "How are you liking the house?" he asks her.

"It's fantastic," Agnes says honestly. "That view."

"Oh, yes." Thor's pleased. "That stretch of the river is something your grandparents and I shared and cherished."

"So you really knew them well?" Agnes asks.

"I knew Marie best," he tells her. "She spent more time in town. Einar, he kept to the university and his office." He shakes his head, smiling at a distant memory. "I was so in love with Marie. But so was everyone. She was a bright presence in town, walking with her little students. She was an angel in charge of all the cherubim."

Agnes hears herself laugh.

Nora interjects, "You said you're helping with the search today? Did you not get the permission to restart work on the farmhouse?"

Thor clicks his lips in a dismissive gesture. "That was easy. They are eager for me to rebuild. I have restarted, so please, do *not* go in there. It won't be safe to walk through while I work." He pulls out his phone to check the time and groans. "Busy, busy, busy," he says. He offers them both an apology. "I hate to keep running away from you two. When are we having dinner?"

"Soon," Nora says. "I'll get in touch with you later today or tomorrow, see what your schedule's like."

"Wonderful," he says. He rushes through his goodbyes, then he's off, racing down the street.

Satisfied, Nora returns to the apartment building, searching for the correct number on the buzzer to ring. "You don't mind a dinner, right?" she asks Agnes, distracted.

Agnes doesn't answer. She asks, because it's been bothering her, "He's fixing up the farmhouse, right? Why?" After all these years, why now?

This gets Nora's attention. "Well, you know how he rents out the house we're staying in? He's restoring the farmhouse to rent it out, too, as a vacation home. He says he wants to build a series of cabins on the land. Bring some tourism dollars into the town and his own pockets, I guess."

Agnes imagines staying in her family's home, living among all the ghosts. For a moment, the image, though morbid, appeals to her. Until the other shoe drops. According to Nora, the farmhouse is already a pilgrimage for some true crime fans. Now they'll be encouraged to visit. To stay.

The Bifröst Murder House will become a tourist attraction, after all.

If Nora notices Agnes's horror, she doesn't comment on it. She focuses again on the task at hand, finding the correct buzzer for Ása's friends. She jams her thumb into one of the buttons and waits, tapping her foot impatiently.

With an effort, Agnes brings herself back into the present moment. "Do these students know I'm with you? Like, who I am?"

The door clicks open and Nora shoves her body into it. She doesn't cross the threshold, though, not yet. "Do you want me to tell them?"

"I don't know," Agnes says. "No."

"I haven't," Nora admits. "I might, though. In this conversation, your identity might be pertinent, it might not. In others, it absolutely will be. But you're not going to be able to go incognito much longer. This is a small town. Word will get out that you're here, and places like this . . . they have a long memory."

CHAPTER SEVENTEEN

February 7, 2019

The staircase is wide, carpeted. They have to walk up three flights, and by the time they reach the top, Agnes's left leg is shaking uncontrollably. Whatever relief the pills had afforded her is gone, metabolized in this one painful activity.

The door that awaits them sits ajar. Nora, ahead of Agnes, knocks on the wall before entering. Agnes trails in behind her, breathing harshly through her nose. The apartment is little more than a single room, with a kitchenette on one side of the rectangle, and a bed and chair on the other. The walls are bare, except for a few posters of bands Agnes has never heard of. There's a desk in the corner by the bed, its surface overrun with books and papers. This is unmistakably the studio apartment of a student.

And there are the students. Just two of them. A woman and a man. The man, a redhead with dark circles beneath his eyes, lounges on the bed. The woman, a brunette, straightens up in a chair beside the bed. She'd been curled over something, a notebook. Agnes can see the sharp lines of a woman's face etched in black ink before the brunette clutches the notebook to her chest.

Agnes scans the room for a chair. Her knee's throbbing, and she's not confident it won't buckle underneath her. But the redhead and the brunette have all the seats in the house.

Nora starts to introduce herself, but she's interrupted by the sound of a flushing toilet. A second later, an older woman emerges from the bathroom. She greets Nora like an old friend, swooping in for a hug. Her skin's lined, her straw-colored hair bundled into a messy bun. She reminds Agnes of the wealthy women in the Bay Area who drive white Range Rovers and have abs of steel. Everything they wear and own is a bit scuffed up and anonymous, but their outfit would cost you more than a month's salary.

"Thank you so much for arranging this," Nora's saying, her body absorbed into the older woman's thick sweater.

The woman's eyes light on Agnes. It's obvious she recognizes Agnes as Marie's doppelgänger. Agnes braces herself for the cry—*You look exactly like her!*—but the woman recovers herself.

"I'm Hildur," she says, disengaging from Nora and extending a hand to Agnes.

Agnes grips the woman's unwashed hand and mutters her name in response. There have been so many meetings, so many new names. Under this woman's scrutiny, Agnes has an overwhelming desire to go home, where she can swallow her pills in peace, where she doesn't have so much responsibility, where no one stares at her like she's a dead woman.

The man on the bed clears his throat loudly. He directs something to Nora in Icelandic.

"I'm sorry?" Nora says.

He groans dramatically. "How can you expect to help us if you don't speak our language? If you don't know anything?"

Hildur chastises him, but in Icelandic. Her gaze begins on the redhead, but it slowly drifts back to Agnes. Then, in English, she says, "Óskar, this is Einar Pálsson's granddaughter. These women may be Americans, but they know more than you think."

The spotlight, sudden and bright, lands on Agnes. The redhead's lip curls in disgust. "Einar Pálsson's granddaughter," he says. He might as well be uttering a curse. "What are you doing here?"

This earns him another reprimand from Hildur, but he's not paying her any attention.

Part of Agnes would like to leave, right now. The other part of her, the part of her that thinks this man doesn't even deserve to say her grandfather's name aloud, would like to tell him as much. She compromises by saying nothing.

This doesn't impress the redhead. He turns to Nora. "Hildur said you wanted to interview us for your show. She said you want to help us find Ása. How does bringing the murderer's child back to Bifröst help anyone?"

Nora ignores his question. "You're Óskar, right?"

He grunts. He gestures to the brunette woman beside him. "Lilja," he calls her. Then: "What do you want? How can you find Ása by talking to us?"

Nora introduces herself, formally. She's Nora Carver, the host of the popular true crime podcast, *The End*, here to document the 1979 murders of Marie Hvass and Agnes Einarsdóttir. She heard about the disappearance of their friend and has decided to offer her considerable skills to help find Ása. She tells them about her podcast in depth. It's an effective tool, Agnes thinks, as she loses focus. Nora's bombarding the students with her credentials, taking control of the conversation.

Agnes finds herself staring at the brunette. Lilja. She can't figure out her relationship with this man, the odd push and pull of their bodies, as though they were opposite poles of magnets. They must be friends. But Agnes can't imagine choosing this man as her friend. There's a familiarity in the way they're situated, so close, but the woman, to her credit, seems to flinch away from him. Maybe they aren't friends when they aren't with Ása. Maybe she's the glue.

There's something more about Lilja, though. She's beautiful. Stunning, even. She's cropped her dark brown hair close to her jaw, the tips of her ears poking out of the curtain of hair. Her eyes, also dark, track Nora's movements, but she has what Agnes's grandfather would call "ceiling eyes." Always staring slightly too far up, dreamy and sleepy.

Nora concludes her speech by handing the students waivers to sign. "Agnes," she says, "is just as concerned as I am about Ása. She's here because she cares. Is that fair to you, Óskar?"

The man grunts again. From the sound of it, Agnes understands he's not conceding. The argument just isn't worth his time. He signs his waiver. He tries to give Lilja the pen, but she doesn't take it. She's holding her own waiver, but like a spiderweb. It's connected to her, but she's not aware of it. Óskar pesters her in Icelandic until she seems to come back to them all.

"No," she says, finally, in English. Her voice is fuller than her ethereal presence would suggest. Firm. "I am not participating in a film."

"It's a podcast," Nora corrects her. "And that's absolutely fine. Would you still be comfortable speaking with me if it were off the record, though? Your name would never be released, nor your voice. I'm well-versed in investigations. I can help you. I want to find Ása. Like you do."

Lilja stares at Nora's forehead, as hard as her soft gaze will allow. "You were there," she says. "I recognize you. You saw what I saw."

"But I didn't know Ása," Nora says. "I wasn't with her at the party, like you were. I wasn't with her before the party. I don't know who she knows or what she might have been dealing with in the weeks leading up to this party. Only you and Óskar can provide valuable information like that."

"It's a waste of time," Lilja says, "to be talking when we could be looking for her."

There's a new voice now. Hildur's. She keeps it in Icelandic, among the three of them. Whatever she says, it has a marked effect on Lilja. She lets out a deep, long breath. "Off the record," she says.

"Of course," Nora says. She sends Hildur a subtle, questioning look.

Hildur shakes her head, her expression grim. "Ása is in trouble," she says in English. "She would want us to do anything we could to find her."

CHAPTER EIGHTEEN

February 7, 2019

Óskar leads them to Ása's room. He has a key, he tells them, just as she
has one of his, in case they lock themselves out, which has apparently
happened quite a few times. "Ása isn't good with details," he says, pushing the door open.

Lilja will wait her turn in Óskar's room. If it had been Agnes's decision, she would have interviewed the two students together, getting
to know their dynamic and their story as a pair. Singling them out like
this makes it feel like an interrogation—which, she supposes, noticing
Óskar's snide smirk as he watches her limp up the stairs, it probably is.
He's too hostile to interview.

Then they're inside the missing woman's apartment. Evidently, the
police haven't cordoned this room off, either. Suicide or murder, Nora
said. It seems like everyone has decided it's suicide.

Ása's apartment is much more of a home than Óskar's place, with
plush pillows, photos on the walls, knickknacks lining the windowsill,

and a jumble of chocolate bars on the kitchenette counter. Óskar grabs one of the candy bars and asks Nora what she wants from him.

Nora ignores him, taking her time studying the space. There's Ása's bed, close to the window, then a small table separating the living space from the kitchen. There are again only two places to sit—a swiveling desk chair and a simpler one meant for a dining room table which is currently being used as a clothes rack. Nora directs Óskar to position one of the chairs in front of the photo wall.

"I'll record this interview," Nora tells him, "both on microphone and on camera. I like to have multiple records, if you don't mind."

Óskar doesn't mind. He deposits the clothes on the floor and plops into the seat, staring at Nora, then Agnes, sizing them both up.

Agnes admires Nora for her poise. The lines around her have solidified, like she's made herself denser. She has two other women in the room with her, just in case, but she doesn't seem to need them. She doesn't seem to even remember they're there. It's all about Óskar.

Suffering now, Agnes seeks out the one other place to sit that isn't the missing woman's bed: the edge of the windowsill. There's a salt lamp in one corner of the windowsill, now off, and a tiny figurine of a rocket ship in the other. Agnes nudges the rocket ship to the side so she can sit. She takes some of the weight off her leg while Nora disassembles her backpack, pulling out a fancy microphone with its own tripod stand. She sets it up in a practiced maneuver, placing it between Óskar and her, and tilting the bulbous head toward Óskar. With that complete, she digs into the tote bag, unveiling a camcorder, thick and squat and somehow low-tech. She flicks it on and positions it on the table to capture Óskar in full. Agnes wonders if Nora's planning to add visuals to this season. Perhaps turn it into a television series. Or maybe it's just prudent, when you're talking to so many people, to have as many failsafes as possible.

"Einar Pálsson's granddaughter," Óskar calls, catching Agnes's attention. "Tell me something. Is he here, too?"

Agnes tries to train her expression to neutral, but she can feel her cheeks heating. "No," she manages.

"He knows better," Óskar says. "You should have stayed with him."

"Are you from Bifröst?" Agnes asks, floating somewhere above her body. She's aware of Hildur's attention on her. Aware of Nora's, too, but she doesn't see them. "Do you have family here?"

"No. I'm from Kópavogur."

"Then leave me alone," Agnes tells him. "You have no—"

"Enough," Nora interrupts. Óskar's grinning, like he has something choice to say. Nora steps closer to Agnes. "Maybe you should wait outside," she says softly. "Until we're done?"

"No." It's Óskar. "Let her stay. Better here where we can watch her, hey?"

Frustration flares, hot and bright, through Agnes's limbs. She should leave. She has no reason to stay here and listen to this man. But she doesn't want him to feel like he's won, like he's run her out of this room or this town. She resumes her seat at the windowsill, not meeting Nora's eye. "I'll stay," she says.

Nora returns to her own chair with a sigh. "Right," she says. To Óskar, with no preamble: "Tell me about Ása. What is your relationship with her like?"

Óskar tilts his head, as though he were considering his answer carefully. "Close," he says. "Like a sibling you can fuck."

Nora doesn't flinch. "So you're together?"

"No," Óskar says. "We're friends."

It says a lot about Ása, Agnes thinks, that she'd be friends with this person.

Nora's skeptical. "Comparing your relationship to incest ... that isn't exactly how I would describe my relationship to my friends. Even my closest friend."

Óskar spreads his hands. He's enjoying himself. "You need a better social life."

"Do you have any siblings?"

"No."

"So what compels you to describe your relationship this way? Why not say 'friends with benefits'?"

Óskar sighs. "It was a joke. Okay? We're friends. We fuck. Who cares?"

"Speaking of family," Nora says, "Ása's been missing for days now, and her parents aren't here. They're still in Seyðisfjörður, across the country." It's clear from Óskar's expression that Nora has butchered the pronunciation, but he doesn't correct her and Nora doesn't let it slow her down. "Do you know why that is?"

"That's obvious."

Nora gestures for him to elaborate.

"They don't love her."

"Did Ása say that?" Nora persists. "They don't love her?"

"No."

"So how do you know?"

"Some things are understood. Not everything has to be said. Ása doesn't want to talk about her family. She doesn't want to talk about her feelings. That's not what defines her. Her parents aren't here. They don't care."

Nora changes tack. "Why aren't you in a relationship with her?"

"She's taken."

"By who?"

"She never said."

"You don't know?" Nora is incredulous.

This gets a grimace. A sore spot.

Nora doesn't press too hard on it. "Do you have any guesses?"

"She grew up with all those brothers and sisters," he says. "She knows how to keep a secret, when she wants to."

"Why aren't those siblings here?"

Óskar lifts his hands in an exasperated gesture. "I told you. They aren't close. And she is the oldest. Most can't travel all the way here on their own to see her."

"Walk me through the night," Nora says, pivoting again. "The party. Whose idea was it to go?"

Óskar looks to Hildur. It seems to be a question for her.

"Everyone in town knows," Hildur says. "It isn't a secret. I told them to go."

"You told who?" Nora asks. This appears to be new information to her, and Agnes is insulted on her behalf. Isn't Hildur supposed to be her friend? Why hadn't she told Nora about the party? She'd said she'd had to crash it, that she hadn't known about it until it was already happening, right outside her door.

"I told Ása," Hildur says, "and Óskar. I heard them talking about the party, outside my office. Ása said she was busy. All I said was that it's Saturday, she's young, she should enjoy herself."

"Right," Nora says. She turns back to Óskar. "So walk me through the night."

"Ása brought a bottle of vodka to my place. Lilja came after."

"At what time?"

"Ahh, around nine."

"Was it just you three the whole time?"

"Yes. I have told this to the police, if you want the interview from them."

"I'd rather hear it directly from you," Nora says, flashing her teeth in a smile that doesn't reach her eyes. "Ása brought a bottle of vodka to your room at nine and you, what? Stay there? Pre-game? Or do you head straight to the house?"

"We drank. We played music. I'm in a band. I play the guitar and I sing. Ása sings, too—not for the band, but when she's drunk, she sings. We drove there in my car. We got to the party sometime after midnight, I don't know when. We were there for hours. You saw. Then Ása tells Lilja she has to piss. She doesn't come back. Now we're here."

"When did you notice she hadn't come back?"

"I don't know. It was a party. I wasn't looking at the time."

"What did you do when you noticed she hadn't come back?"

"The place was crowded. I forgot to look for her until I was ready to go. I thought she might have gotten a ride home. She wasn't having fun."

"Why not?"

"She doesn't like crowds," Óskar says, clearly bored now. "She wasn't feeling well. She doesn't like being in the Murder House. Choose one. Or go talk to the police."

Nora ignores him. "Would she really leave without telling you?"

He doesn't have an answer for that.

"What about when you and Lilja left?" Nora continues. "You drove in together, and now suddenly one of the three is nowhere to be found. What did you do?"

Agnes searches the man's face for guilt. For the *what ifs*. What if he had looked for her sooner? What if he could have protected her? There isn't anything except his usual smirk.

"Lilja came home with me," Óskar says finally. "I thought Ása left with her boyfriend."

"You think he was at the party? Wouldn't you have seen her with him?"

There's no answer.

"Why keep her boyfriend a secret?" Nora persists.

"Ása doesn't like to talk about her feelings," Óskar says. "She is private. I respect her privacy."

"So you just left without her. Without even checking for her."

"Do you assume the worst when your friends don't answer their phones?" Óskar counters.

"You called her?"

"Yes."

"Is there anything you didn't tell the police?" Nora asks, and Agnes feels a thrill of something like giddiness run through her. The phone. Finally.

"Like what?" Óskar asks. "That I murdered Ása and hid her body in the lava fields like she's the new Frozen Madonna?" He smirks at Agnes.

Nora doesn't take the bait. And, to Agnes's disappointment, she doesn't pursue the point further. Instead she asks, "How did you know about this boyfriend if she was so good at keeping secrets?"

Óskar's smile dies. "She would disappear."

"What do you mean?"

"Her car," he says. "We park in the lot outside the building. Her car would be gone for days. This is a big open space. The highway can take you anywhere. No one would know where you're going, if you leave at the right times. Which Ása did. And she'd come back a little different each time. Sweeter. And sad, like she missed whoever it was."

"Could she have been visiting her family?"

"They are on the other side of the country. I thought maybe she met someone in Reykjavík."

"How often would she disappear?"

"Not much at first, then a lot more."

"When did that start?"

"Since midsummer."

"So—six months? A bit more?"

A shrug.

"Is it possible that this is what's happened now? She's gone off with her boyfriend?"

"Her car is still here."

"That's not an answer."

"No, then."

"But this mystery man could have been at the party," Nora insists. "You said it yourself. Who do you think he is?"

Óskar doesn't answer. He doesn't even blink.

"What do you think has happened to your friend, Óskar?"

The veil of Óskar's bravado shifts, visibly. Beneath it, he's frightened. Or, that's wrong. Agnes struggles to identify the emotion.

Nora presses on. "What makes you think this isn't the boyfriend? You said you thought she left the party with this guy, but now you're saying she isn't with him. She could be in Reykjavík with him, but you don't think so. Where is she? What makes you think this is something else?"

When Óskar says, "I just do," Agnes understands. It's not fear he's feeling. It's grief.

He thinks his friend is dead.

Or maybe he even knows that she is.

"This doesn't make sense to me," Nora says. "She didn't have her car with her. You drove her there. She'd been drinking since nine o'clock and was likely too drunk to go anywhere on foot—not that there is anywhere to go, really, from there. It tracks that either she'd call her boyfriend to come get her or he was at the party and able to leave with her. Don't you agree? Unless she didn't have her phone with her? Unless she wasn't with her boyfriend? Or unless she didn't leave alone?"

Óskar looks his age. Young and tired and out of his depth.

"Óskar," Nora says. "You love her. That's obvious. You love her and you look out for her. You have a spare key to her apartment, you call her a sibling you can fuck. You watch her, you know enough to know that she has a secret boyfriend—someone she's likely keeping secret *from you*, because you love her. Isn't that right? I saw you at the party. I saw you with her. You watched her in the room. You wouldn't have lost track of her, not for that many hours. And you certainly wouldn't *not* check in with her after the party. She wasn't reported missing until Monday night, so, what, you didn't try to see her for a full two days? What are you not telling me?"

"Lilja was right," Óskar says, coming to standing. "This is a waste of time."

"Wait," Nora says. She stands, too. "I'm not trying to accuse you of anything. I'm just trying to understand. You must be worried sick for her. Aren't you? Thinking that she's with her boyfriend would be so much more comforting than thinking she's somewhere out in the cold, or worse. But you don't think that. Why is that?"

Something within him collapses. "Stop."

"Stop what?"

"Stop talking to me like I'm lying."

"Then tell me the truth."

Óskar's eyes, Agnes notices with a start, are bloodshot. "You want the truth?" he asks her, his rough voice now guttural. "Ása's dead."

"*What?*" It's Hildur. She looks stricken.

Óskar doesn't look away from Nora. "Ása was diagnosed a year ago. Bipolar. She stopped taking her medication a couple of weeks ago. She was depressed. She went into the snow on purpose. She had a death wish."

CHAPTER NINETEEN

February 7, 2019

Refusing to speak another word, Óskar slinks out of the apartment. Hildur accompanies him, ostensibly to summon Lilja, but Agnes guesses she's going to try to get more information from Óskar along the way. Has he been this forthcoming with the police? Do they know about Ása's secret boyfriend? Or her supposed death wish?

Nora doesn't waste a second of her time alone in Ása's apartment. She drags the camcorder's gaze slowly along every corner of the room. She brushes past Agnes, gives her arm a squeeze on the way.

"Sorry that was so unpleasant," she says. "He's an asshole."

"I—" Agnes begins, unsure of what to say. What almost comes out is, *I admire you.* She hadn't realized what this all entailed. Nora has interviewed her, but not like this. Nora had somehow gotten information from someone who had decided not to tell her anything. In the end, he had trusted her enough to betray his closest friend's privacy. Instead, though, Agnes hears herself ask, "Do you think he hurt Ása? There's something weird there, right?"

"Define 'weird,'" Nora says, disappearing into the bathroom. Agnes follows close behind. Nora's nudging the medicine cabinet open, her sleeve protecting her fingerprints. There, among a plethora of makeup tools and containers, are a few pill boxes. Each prescribed to Ása Gunnarsdóttir. Nora records it all.

"Just," Agnes says, searching for the right words, but finding only, "off." When Nora doesn't answer, she asks, "Why did he talk to you, if he thinks Ása killed herself? What's the point of doing this, if he thinks he knows the truth already? I mean, doesn't it make you nervous? Like maybe he hurt her? And he's covering his tracks?"

Nora settles her hip against the bathroom tiles, turning to face Agnes. She places the camcorder on the counter. "You've been watching too many crime shows," she says. "I can't speak to his motivations. I don't know him well enough. But, in my opinion, that kid is devastated. He tried to hide it with all that asshole bullshit, but he's grieving, hard. I think he'd talk to me because he's hoping he's wrong."

"What do you think happened to her?" Agnes asks, pitching her voice low. She can hear Hildur coming up the stairs. This can't wait, though. Not when she's seen Nora in action. Agnes has suddenly figured out what it is about the woman that she likes. They both observe from behind their outer shell. There's a hypervigilance, an acute awareness of what everyone else is doing.

Agnes knows she's got the tunnel vision Emi resented so much. She knows she's self-absorbed. In the past year, with her injuries, she's had to be.

What Emi never understood, what Agnes is only coming to understand about herself, is that this self-absorption is a defense mechanism, a suit of armor protecting her from the constant assault of other people's expectations, thoughts, and feelings. She recognizes the same suit of armor around Nora. Only Nora hasn't withdrawn behind her shell to protect herself from her hypervigilance.

She's withdrawn to weaponize it.

"I don't know what happened to Ása," Nora says, shaking her head.

"Do you have a guess?"

"Do you?" Nora counters. She indicates that they should get out of the bathroom. She's heard the other two women coming, too.

Agnes doesn't move. "The river. I think she jumped in the river."

There's no time to gauge Nora's reaction. She's pushed past Agnes, back to her starting position to welcome Hildur and Lilja to the apartment. Agnes reclaims her spot by the window, disappointed and a little bit stung by the brush-off. This is Nora's job, she tells herself. She's busy. *But*, another voice whispers, *what if she's doing the same thing to you?* What if Nora's handling her, just as skillfully as she's handled Óskar?

Agnes's paranoia and hurt feelings fade into the background when she hears Lilja's voice, dismissing Nora's thanks. "I want to help Ása," she's saying. She takes Óskar's vacated seat without prompting.

Lilja doesn't have her sketchbook anymore. She's squared her shoulders, prepared herself. She scans the room. Agnes wonders how she must feel, sitting in the apartment of her missing friend with two strangers and their recording equipment. And Hildur. Hildur, who Agnes can't help but dislike. It's a visceral repulsion, in the same way that she has a visceral attraction to Lilja.

The ceiling eyes are on her. Electricity sparks at the base of Agnes's spine. A short frisson of awareness. Agnes waits for Lilja to move on, but she doesn't. She's frowning slightly, staring at Agnes intently. Not angrily, as Óskar did, but curiously.

It's been so long since Agnes felt like a person. She breaks the stare to assess her own body. The leg she's spent the past year resenting and treating like something alien to her. She's become a jumble of separate, malfunctioning parts. She hasn't thought of someone else, let alone herself, as desirable in so many months. She can't fathom what Lilja sees, when she looks at her.

Nora says, briskly, "Off the record, right?"

Lilja nods.

"Okay." Nora flicks both the camcorder and the microphone off. "Tell me about Ása."

"She's everything," Lilja says, and Agnes feels a burst of envy. Envy for these two women, for their friendship. For the conviction with which this woman described her friend as complete.

"What does that mean?" Nora asks.

Lilja doesn't answer.

"Is she everything to you?" Nora asks. "Or just—everything?"

"How does this help find her?" Lilja asks. "How I feel about her?"

"I didn't ask you how you felt about her," Nora says. "I said 'Tell me about her' and you're the one who took it to your feelings. 'She's everything' is a loaded, emotional statement. That's what you think, when you think about her. What would she say about you, if I asked her that same question?"

Lilja appears arrested. Then she flushes with color. "She's everything to me," she says. "But I am not everything to her."

"She has a boyfriend she's kept secret from Óskar," Nora says. "Do you know who he is?"

A deep inhale, then nothing.

"You're her closest friend, right? Best friends?"

"Yes." It comes out small, but defiant.

"Why would your best friend keep her boyfriend secret from you?"

"She's private," Lilja says. The words are rote, like it's something she's had to repeat often in the past few days. "She's a private person."

"So this is not the only secret she keeps?"

"'You don't need to know everything about someone to love them.' That's what she says. We are more than what we think of ourselves. More than our histories. We are whatever we choose to be in the present moment. You can love someone easier that way. That is what Ása wants."

"Does she love easily?"

Lilja's eyes hover somewhere above Nora's head. "Men use her," she says. The words are harsh. "She had a difficult home life. The only attention she understands is sexual. That's why she—" She stops herself.

"Why she loves easily," Nora finishes for her. "She loves Óskar, doesn't she?"

There's no answer, but obviously it's a yes.

"Does Óskar want more from her? A relationship?"

A shrug.

"I saw you three at the party. Not for long, but I saw the way you moved around each other. Óskar's jealous, isn't he?"

"Ask him."

"I did," Nora says. "But there's the problem of the secret boyfriend. Do you have a guess of who he is?"

Lilja gnaws on her lower lip. She doesn't even seem to have heard the question.

"*You don't have to know everything about another person to love them,*" Nora quotes to her. "But this isn't the past. This is her present-day romantic life. She's keeping it a secret from her closest friends. I understand being private. I consider myself to be a private person. But this . . . I can't help but wonder if there's another reason for the secrecy. If maybe she's trying to spare someone's feelings."

"Mine or Óskar's."

"Exactly. And you don't strike me as a violent person."

Agnes shifts in her seat. Her foot's falling asleep. When she looks up, it's to find Lilja's eyes on her again.

"Would Óskar ever hurt Ása?" It's Nora.

Lilja flinches away. The moment's over. "No," she says. "He loves her."

"That doesn't mean he wouldn't hurt her," Nora says. "It's never so simple as we think."

"I don't want to do this," Lilja says.

"I know it can be—" Nora begins, but Lilja cuts her off.

"No," she says. "This isn't finding Ása. You're asking me if I've hurt her. If Óskar has. You aren't trying to help her. You're looking for some-one to blame. I have to go." She comes to standing, and even though Nora and Hildur entreat her to stop, she doesn't wait. "I have to find my friend," she insists. "I didn't hurt her. I don't know where she is. If you want to help, go into the fields. Look for her. But don't ask about things you know nothing about."

Then she's out the door, slamming it shut behind her, leaving the three women behind in a sudden, pregnant silence.

"This is hitting all of us hard," Hildur says. "Ása, gone like this. The town remembers your family's tragedy." This, to Agnes. "It is our trag-edy, too. I'm sorry they didn't participate." This last to Nora.

"Oh, no," Nora says. "They participated. Thank you for arranging this. That was so useful." She pulls a notebook and pen from her tote bag and starts jotting down notes. "I'd like to talk to them again, actu-ally, if I can. Soon."

"I will see if they want to," Hildur says. She's turning to Agnes, anticipation clear on her face.

"Excuse me," Agnes says, pushing herself up to standing. "I have to make a call."

She takes the stairs faster than her knee can comfortably allow, and catches the front door as it's closing. Then she's out in the cold air, calling the woman's name.

Lilja.

CHAPTER TWENTY

February 7, 2019

Bundled up now, Lilja slows her stride, but she doesn't stop until she reaches a compact car, parked halfway down the block. She watches Agnes's approach warily, as though expecting her to thrust a camera or a microphone in her face.

"Sorry," Agnes says, feeling self-conscious, "for shouting. Can I talk to you for a second? Just person to person."

"What do you want to talk about?"

A gust of wind yanks away the last of Agnes's warmth. Lilja gestures for her to get in the car. She settles into the driver's seat while Agnes gratefully takes the passenger side. In a moment, hot air filters through the vents.

"Thanks," Agnes says.

Lilja turns as much as the little space in the car will allow, the better to take Agnes in. "So?" she asks. "What do you want?"

Agnes hesitates, thrown. She likes Lilja. There's something luminous about her, on her own, but there's also something of Emi in her.

Not their physicality. Emi's curvier, her skin a radiant umber, where Lilja is a jumble of angles, a white shadow. But the dreaminess. Emi volunteers for a community garden near UC Berkeley, and even though Agnes can't stand the texture of dirt on her fingers, she used to join her, just to observe the way Emi communicated with the sentience of the plants around her. This woman has that same ethereal, almost alien kindness.

"I didn't know about Ása," Agnes says, clearing her throat, "until I got here the day before yesterday. I'm sorry this is happening to you. I'm sorry about your friend. You're going to the search party?"

Lilja makes a soft noise. Agnes takes this for a yes.

"Without Óskar?"

"Like he's ever joined the search party before," Lilja says. Some of her earlier viciousness returns to her. "He cares more about his show in Reykjavík than finding Ása."

"What show?"

"He's in a band," Lilja says. "They're playing in a bar this Saturday in Reykjavík. He's going, even though Ása needs him."

"You think she's out there," Agnes says. "Alive."

"She is not dead," is all Lilja can say.

"Do you think she's with her boyfriend?"

"I don't know."

"This has been bothering me," Agnes says, warmth flooding through her. The car's heating flows over her skin, soothing her. "I don't really understand how you know about him, if he's a secret."

There's no answer.

"Did you see her with him?"

"No."

Agnes asks, "Are you in love with her?" and Lilja's expression doesn't change. The question doesn't register. She's staring at something Agnes can't see.

When she speaks, her voice is resigned. "I have to go," she says.

"But—"

"I'm not in love with her," Lilja snaps. "I love her. That's why I have to go. I have to find her."

"Where do you think she is?" Agnes asks. When the other woman doesn't answer, she brings up the medication. "Óskar says she's stopped taking it. He's an asshole, but he's observant, especially when it comes to Ása, right? Is there part of you that thinks she's done all this on purpose?"

She's gone too far. Lilja tells her to get out. She has to go.

"Wait," Agnes says. She searches her backpack for a pen, not quite knowing why she's doing this, other than this is the most she's felt like a person in a year. She tears a corner off the book she'd read on the plane, scribbles her name and number on the scrap of paper and hands it to Lilja. "If you—" She stutters, losing her courage. "If you need to talk. Or need help finding your friend."

Agnes doesn't wait for Lilja to reject her. She steps out into the wind, watches it play with Lilja's short hair, obscuring her face. Then she slams the door shut and walks away, back to the apartment building, cheeks burning.

CHAPTER TWENTY-ONE

February 7, 2019

The front door of Ása's building is locked. Agnes leans against the side of the recessed entrance, grateful at least for the shelter from the wind. She supposes she'll have to ring for Nora, except she doesn't know what the apartment number is and her phone is on airplane mode. She should feel panicked, out in the cold, alone, but for now, all she can feel is a general sense of relief.

Two people in uniform pass her by. A man and a woman, both shrouded in their official police costuming—stab-proof vests, hats, utility belts. Agnes wonders if they'll recognize her, but they keep moving past, distracted by their own conversation.

In their wake, she hears a woman's laugh. She tracks the sound to the opposite end of the street. Another pair. Again a man and a woman, but in the costumes of winter, not police. The man, so much larger than the woman. The woman, unknown to Agnes, anonymous in her wool coat and tight pants, runs a hand through her hair. She uses the movement to tilt into the man's personal space, laughing harder. Agnes recognizes the man's black hair, his sloping shoulders.

Ingvar.

He's everywhere.

Agnes jolts. Ingvar's lifted a hand to her. A mute wave.

She nods back, unwilling to expose more bare skin to the cold, and turns away, embarrassed to be caught spying. She moves in time to find Nora and Hildur descending the stairs to the lobby. Nora seems energized, bouncing ahead to open the door.

"Everything okay?" she asks Agnes, giving her a once-over that lets her know that she, in fact, does not look okay.

"Fine," she says. "Chilly."

"You should be careful." It's Hildur. "The cold eats girls here."

"What's that?" Agnes asks.

"We don't need two girls missing," Hildur says, unrepentant. For all her talk about the town's collective trauma, she doesn't appear traumatized.

Nora cuts in before Agnes can bite Hildur's head off. "Truly," she says, "thank you for setting this up. I'll get in touch with you later today about the next round, yes?"

"Of course," Hildur says. Her gaze snaps to something high above Agnes's head. "Ingvar," she says, followed by a question in Icelandic.

Ingvar steps into their makeshift circle and says, "Yesterday. It's my fault." He shows them all his right hand. The fingers, white stained pink from the cold, wiggle out from a massive cast. The plaster extends beyond his jacket sleeve.

Nora hisses through her teeth. "What happened?"

He gives her a rueful smile. "I slipped on the ice. I was looking for Ása and my legs were suddenly up here." He raises his injured hand to his eyeline.

"You've spent too long in the city," Hildur admonishes him. "You've gone soft."

"Where'd you fall?" Agnes asks. She's been so careful of the ice, but this is a reminder for her to go even slower. She can't afford to hurt herself again.

Nora's hands are on Agnes's shoulder. "I'm sorry to interrupt," she says, "but the timing is exquisite." She introduces the two of them. The bright blue eyes meet Agnes's. Sparkling, it seems, at their private joke. They've danced this dance already.

"Nice to meet you," Agnes says. The lie slips out of her before she can decide what to do. She had already resolved not to tell Nora about her meeting with Júlía, but she hadn't thought about Ingvar. At this point, to explain how she knows Ingvar would require so much effort and so many carefully worded lies. It's just easier this way.

"You, too," Ingvar says, playing along.

"So where did you fall?" Agnes asks, aware of their audience.

"Out in the fields," is the vague reply. Then a sigh. "It aches in this weather. I will have to go home."

"Are you going now?" Nora asks.

"To my mother, yes," Ingvar says. He gives Agnes a significant look. "You should come by. I am sure it would make my mother very happy to meet Magnús's daughter."

Agnes does her best to conceal her surprise. She's lying to Nora because this is her own business. She has no idea why Ingvar's lying to Nora, though.

"Whenever works for you," Nora says, inordinately pleased. "So long as it is before the fifteenth. That's when Agnes has to leave us."

Another lie. Agnes hasn't felt like telling Nora she didn't buy her return ticket. Nora had suggested ten days, and Agnes had pretended to agree. But ten days in Iceland hadn't felt long enough. She'd rather decide when it gets closer to the date. She supposes she'll have to tell Nora this eventually. When the time is right.

"Come with me now," Ingvar suggests. "My mother should be awake from her nap. She is usually happy when she wakes."

Nora coordinates with Ingvar, whose truck is parked farther down the street. They'll follow him down the road, just as Agnes did yesterday. Hildur, watching the entire conversation with interest, seems ready to join them, but Nora heads her off with a friendly "We'll talk soon."

Hildur accepts the dismissal. She waits for Nora and Agnes to pile back into the enormous truck, and she's still standing there, watching, when Nora pulls out. It's only as they're turning out of sight that the woman moves. Back into the apartment building, back to Ása's friends? Agnes can't tell.

"Hildur bothers you," Nora says, with no preamble. She looks comically small in the driver's seat, with it pressed as far forward as it can possibly go so her feet can reach the pedals. It's a miracle she can drive this truck.

Agnes doesn't know how to describe the visceral repulsion without sounding petulant. "I don't like the way she talks," she says, finally. *The cold eats girls here.*

"To be fair," Nora says, accelerating on the highway, "there is a linguistic barrier."

"She outed me to Óskar and Lilja," Agnes counters. "You have to admit, that was rude."

"Again," Nora says, "to be fair, she did it in your defense. But I know what you mean. She rubs people the wrong way."

"Why didn't she tell you about the party?"

Nora's smile disappears. "That is a very good question. It doesn't matter, really, though, does it? I made it there." To Agnes's silence: "I'm going to ask her about that. One of these days. She's a tremendous resource, for all her faults. She got me in the room with those kids."

"Why didn't you ask them about the phone?" Agnes asks. She shouldn't care about any of this. It has nothing to do with her grandfather. But still, she's drawn in, in spite of herself.

"It's too soon," Nora tells her. "They both stormed out of the room today, and I wasn't even pressing them that hard. I have to build a little bit of trust, or at the very least, familiarity, first, before I pounce on them. I'm not the police. I can't detain them, and they don't have to talk to me. It's a delicate process."

Agnes concedes the point. Again, though, there's that paranoid voice whispering in her head. *What if Nora's handling you, too?*

But of course Nora's handling her. She's interviewing Agnes along with everyone else.

Agnes knows this. She just doesn't know why this disappoints her.

"They'll talk to you again," she says to Nora. She stares out the window blindly. "Or Óskar will. He has to, if he's going to get you to promote his band."

"How do you know about his band? Did he ask you to promote his show, too?"

She's been caught. Agnes tells Nora about running into Lilja outside. "She said he's still going to do the show, even though his friend's probably dead."

Nora isn't surprised. "Yeah. Isn't he delightful? He gave me a flyer on my way out. Are you interested in a little field trip? Want to see Maidenhead play in Reykjavík?"

"Maidenhead? What, are they an Iron Maiden cover band?"

"Or he's just a creep. It's ye olde slang for a woman's virginity."

Agnes grimaces. "Doesn't it frustrate you? How he's using you?"

"Everyone uses me," Nora tells her, unbothered. "That's why I don't get attached to anyone or any one theory. Everyone has a motive. Everyone wants something when they tell a story. My job is to sift through it all, figure out what they want, and see what that reveals. Often the truth is hiding in a lie. And . . . I would have to say . . . I'm using them right back."

They're already turning off the highway, climbing into the snow in pursuit of Ingvar's truck.

Agnes rubs her forehead, as though that could ease her headache. How can Nora stand this? She pictures Óskar and Lilja, their awkward friendship. She tries to fit Ása in there. She can see Óskar hurting Ása. He never appeared overly violent—hostile, sure, but not violent. But he's an aggressive, possessive man. It's easy to sketch him into a scenario. It's standard. Man hurts woman. Agnes tries to imagine Lilja hurting Ása, and she balks at the thought. Lilja seems to worship Ása and their friendship. But when she spoke of Ása, she, too, was possessive. A love like that, it's unwieldy. Everything that doesn't conform to the person's image of the other is a betrayal. And there had been a betrayal, hadn't there? Ása had been spending time with someone else, someone she wouldn't share with Lilja.

As they trace the long line of Ingvar's driveway, Agnes tries to peel herself away from the sudden certainty that both Lilja and Óskar are somehow responsible for Ása's disappearance. This is the trap, the same one that damned her grandfather. That a lie, that a suspicion, is enough to accuse. To condemn.

CHAPTER TWENTY-TWO

February 7, 2019

Before Agnes can even unbuckle her seat belt, Nora's stopping her. "We have to be careful in there," she warns her. "I haven't met Júlía the whole time I've been here. She's not well. Early onset dementia, Hildur told me, combined with a few strokes. We're going to have to tread lightly."

"What about Ingvar's father?" Agnes hadn't seen him yesterday, and Ingvar hasn't mentioned him.

"Karl passed away a while ago. According to Hildur, Júlía was fine on her own until she suddenly wasn't. Ingvar moved home about six months ago to take care of his mother. We're walking into some delicate territory."

She lets Agnes unbuckle her seat belt. They hop out of the truck, careful on the ice.

Like yesterday, Ingvar's gone inside without them. Nora rounds the back of the truck to retrieve her equipment from the trunk. Agnes doesn't wait for her. She starts for the door, slow on the ice and snow. She has no idea what will happen when Júlía sees her. Will she remember their last meeting? Will she experience the same horror? The same desire to apologize?

He killed her. We all knew.

When they reach the front door, Ingvar is there, waiting for them. He has removed his outer layer, but he hasn't had time to wake his mother. He'll show them to the living room, he says. There's no twinkle in his eye now. No shared joke with Agnes. And Agnes finds herself wondering, yet again, what he wants out of this visit. This is twice now he's insisted she meet his mother, even after yesterday's spectacular failure. And what happened to her being too fragile to speak to Nora?

"I'm honored to meet your mother," Nora says, following close behind as they make their way into the living room.

"She has been talking about Magnús," Ingvar says, distracted. "This will make her happy." Without another word, he disappears in search of his mother.

Nora and Agnes choose the couch. Nora unpacks her microphone, her camcorder. She sweeps the room with the camcorder, swiping the lens across Agnes's profile.

"Are you hoping to turn this into a show?" Agnes asks. "With all the footage you've taken, it seems like you could make a documentary."

There's a low rumble of voices through the walls. Ingvar's, mostly, but with a feminine moan occasionally thrown in. His mother.

"I've thought about it," Nora admits. "But that would distract from the process. The interviews, what people say, that's far more vital than getting a good shot of someone."

Ingvar appears at the doorway, alone. "She's tired," he says.

"Should we go?" Agnes asks, eager, suddenly, to get out of here. She doesn't know what she'll do if Júlía remembers her. If she will have to come clean to Nora about meeting her and Ingvar. And, she thinks with a guilty pang, if the old woman remembers how poorly Agnes had treated her.

"I will check on her again in a minute," Ingvar says, "when she's had more time to get used to the idea." He hunkers down to his knees and starts a fire in the hearth. It's a clumsy, laborious procedure with his cast, but he refuses help from Nora. The job finished, he collapses onto one of the chairs.

"How long do you have that on for?" Agnes asks him, meaning the cast.

"They say five weeks. Maybe six."

Nora groans in sympathy.

Practically a dream, Agnes thinks. Easy.

Ingvar dismisses their concern with a wave of his uninjured hand. "Not important," he says. He leans forward in his seat and takes Agnes in with somber eyes. "I would like to apologize to you."

"For what?" Agnes asks, startled. What has he done to her?

"I am sorry that I found your grandmother," he says. "It shouldn't be that my name is wrapped in hers. Ingvar, the boy who found them. Her death, and the baby's, they should not be my story."

Agnes doesn't consider her next words carefully. She hears herself speak, and she assumes she knows what she's doing. "They are, though," she says. "Part of your story. You were a child when you found them. That's your life, too."

He nods, but Agnes can tell that she's missed his meaning.

"It's okay," she offers.

"Could we—" Nora says, looking between the two. "Would you mind if I recorded this conversation?"

Ingvar asks, "For your radio show?"

"Podcast, yes."

He shrugs. "That is all I wanted to say."

"Agnes knows very little about her family's history," Nora persists. "Her grandfather never spoke of his wife and daughter to her, right, Agnes? I think it would be meaningful for her to hear about her family from you. In the same way that it is meaningful for you to apologize to her."

Ingvar lifts his eyebrow in question. *Would it really?*

"Sure," Agnes says. She regrets Nora's presence, and that of the microphones, but this is exactly what she's wanted. When Nora sets up that same bulbous microphone on the coffee table and beckons for Agnes to sit closer to Ingvar, she feels the anticipation building in her spine, quick and hot.

He killed her. We all knew.

CHAPTER TWENTY-THREE

February 7, 2019

The fireplace flickers to their sides. Agnes pulls off her hoodie, leaving herself bare in shirtsleeves. Ingvar, in a sweater, seems unconcerned. Nora and Agnes have switched roles. Earlier, Agnes had been the one to melt into the background, watching, while Nora had been running the show. Now, Agnes does her best to emulate Nora's strength. "Do you want to tell me," she begins, "about the day you found them? The bodies?"

Ingvar scratches his beard with the hand of his injured arm, his fingers poking out from the white cast. "I was six years old," he says. "At the time, I knew Marie as well as my own mother. I must have spent every day with her, in school or at her home. My mother and Marie, they supported each other."

"They took turns, though, right?" Agnes asks. "Your mom watched you and Magnús here, right?"

"Yes," he says. "My mother says she raised Marie's babies more than Marie did. I don't remember much time spent with Magnús, though.

He was old enough to be on his own. But I remember the baby girl."
There's more underneath the surface, something Agnes can't quite see.

"Were you and Magnús friends?"

"No."

"Why not?"

A shrug. "Magnús didn't like me."

Agnes thinks of her father. The stories of his isolated childhood.
The time spent alone, playing in the fields. She had never thought it
had been by choice. "Why is that?"

"He didn't say."

"Did something happen between you two?"

"Some people," Ingvar says, "you just don't like. To me, he was a wild
hero. He would explore the fields on his own for hours. Return with stories of capturing fish with his bare hands, of going out until he couldn't
see any sign of civilization. He told me he climbed the crater by himself.
Now, as an adult, I wonder if he really did go that far on his own, or if he
was telling those stories to scare me. But as a child, I envied him, and I
think he envied me, for his mother's affection."

"She doted on you?"

"Yes."

"Someone told me that everyone was in love with Marie. Is that
true?"

"She was beautiful," Ingvar says, as though it were that simple, as
though *beautiful* were an objective term everyone can understand in
the same exact way. "She was the brightest thing in the room. Every
room."

"You loved her."

"Very much. She wasn't my mother, but she was."

"A second mother," Agnes says, thinking of her grandfather, the way
she referred to him as such only a handful of hours ago. The parent
who isn't a parent. The parent who you feel more freedom loving because they are further removed, because they aren't the ones who shout

at you for breaking a glass, who ask you if you're pretending not to understand long division to punish them. Who, perhaps for that same distance, feels more freedom to love you.

Agnes focuses on Ingvar. "How would Marie care for you that was different from her relationship with her son?"

"She would send Magnús out," Ingvar says. "He was driving her crazy. With me, though, she wanted me there. She brought me treats. Made sure I was comfortable in the living room with cookies and Magnús's record player. Later, when the baby came, she would ask me to watch the baby for her. Marie said I was her best friend." There's an edge of understanding in his voice, the adult recognizing the hyperbolic praise, but it's a faint outline to a child's heady pleasure, the gratification of a special relationship with an adult who isn't a parent.

"It was a big shock when she disappeared," Ingvar continues. "I cried to my mother for a day, because I thought it was my fault that I couldn't see her. I begged my mother to let me join the search party." He recounts the day. The fear of being lost, discovering the woman buried in the snow. The throat. The silent, blue baby, the one he had cared for all those many months. His voice cracks only when he speaks of the baby.

"My mother," he says, collecting himself with a long inhale, "she took me home. The police came soon after. They asked me how I found Marie. They asked about my days alone with her. They asked if I ever saw anything suspicious. I told them about my time with the baby. That Magnús ran wild. That sometimes he had bruises on his arm, from his father's hands."

"You saw Einar hit him?" Agnes cuts in. She's heard this before, straight from her father. Mostly in comparison to how gentle Einar was with Agnes. How he'd softened over time. That Magnús used to be punished, harshly, for childish mistakes.

She'd heard of sharp words. The occasional strike of an open palm. She'd never heard of bruises on her father's arms.

"No," Ingvar says. "When Einar came home, my mother would get me, or Marie would take me. I wasn't supposed to be there when he was home. I was always told it was because he worked so hard. He wanted to eat dinner with his family. But Marie worked just as hard. Harder. And the only time alone she had was when I would watch the baby—or if my mother could take us both."

"How did the police react to your testimony?"

"How much influence does a six-year-old boy have?"

"What do you think happened?"

"Your grandfather killed them."

It hits her, yet again, like a fist to the stomach. It's the intimacy of the accusation—*your grandfather*—that winds her. Luckily, Nora takes over. "Why?" she asks. "Why are you so certain?"

"Because Marie was afraid of him," Ingvar says. "His own son was afraid of him. Children understand fear, even if they don't understand the complexity of a marriage, or death. I understood that he frightened them."

"But why would he kill her?" Still Nora.

"I don't know."

"If you had to guess."

"I don't know of any reason why someone would kill a baby, let alone their own. I don't know why someone would want to kill that woman." There's an undercurrent of rage in his voice now, a rising red hue along his cheeks. "But you would have to be a dangerous person to do it."

"He has an alibi," Nora says. "He was at the university most of the day."

"He left. He said nothing."

One of the logs in the fireplace crumbles on itself, sending a shower of sparks into the air. Agnes, startled, shifts out of its reach. "There's now another woman missing," she says.

"Yes," he says. "A tragedy."

"Is it bringing up old feelings?"

"I don't know her," Ingvar says, "so it's different. But I worry for her."

"What do you think happened now?" There's an undercurrent of rage in her voice, too, but she can't help it. She enjoys its taste on her tongue.

"I can't say."

"And you don't know her."

He shrugs.

"It's a small town," she says. "Very small. Wouldn't you run into practically everyone here?"

"I recognize her," he says. "But no, I do not spend time with the students. Either I am here or in Reykjavík."

"What are you doing in Reykjavík?"

"Going into the office. I used to work full-time. But now . . ." He trails off, meaning his mother's condition has changed everything.

"Do you have a girlfriend?"

Her anger has the opposite effect on him. He chuckles. "Not anymore," he says. "When I moved here, I lost her. I don't have time now to go looking."

Agnes thinks of the woman she saw him with in town, just outside Ása's building. How old was that woman? Agnes can't remember. But she'd heard the tenor of their conversation. The flirtation. Ingvar doesn't have to go looking—the women find him. Agnes opens her mouth to say more, but she hears her name. She finds Nora standing at her side, one hand on her shoulder.

"Sorry to interrupt," Nora says to Ingvar. "But I think your mother's calling for you?"

He is up and out of the room before Nora finishes her sentence. Leaving her to stare down at Agnes, clearly debating saying something.

"What?" Agnes asks.

"You went into crime show detective mode," Nora says. "I could see it. You were like a shark. You had the bloodlust."

"He goes into Reykjavík," Agnes says, casting her voice to an angry whisper. "That's where Óskar thinks Ása was going with her secret boyfriend. It would make sense that they'd keep this relationship a secret, wouldn't it? He's twice her age."

"Bloodlust," Nora teases.

"You did the same thing with Óskar," Agnes says. "You treated him like a suspect. That was you in crime show detective mode, too, right?"

Nora surprises her with a laugh. "Because he is one," she says. "He's lying to the police. Of course I'm going to have to manhandle him to get him to talk to me. But Ingvar wasn't at the party, and he's never met Ása. It's different."

"So he says," Agnes counters.

"I know it hurts to hear people accuse your grandfather of murder," Nora says. "But that's the name of the game. Right? This is just a conversation. Be soft."

CHAPTER TWENTY-FOUR

February 7, 2019

Ingvar escorts his mother into the room, leading her with his unin-jured hand on her elbow. Today, Júlía's wearing an overly large sweater and a pair of slacks, but she takes small, uncertain steps as though she were wearing a narrow skirt. Despite her son's solicitousness, she seems stronger today. There's something in her expression that straightens Agnes's posture, as she and Nora come to standing for the woman's inspection. Júlía scans Nora first, mouth set grimly. She lingers on the younger woman's neon-pink glasses, whether out of disapproval or in-terest, Agnes can't tell.

Agnes braces herself, waiting for the recognition to dawn in the old woman's eyes.

But when Júlía turns to Agnes, she doesn't jump in surprise. She doesn't say, *You again,* and she doesn't lose her composure. Something in her expression softens.

"Marie," she says. Then, frowning: "No."

Ingvar nods. "Magnús's daughter," he tells her. "She's from America."

"Yes," Júlía says. She appraises Agnes with a keener eye, with no indication that she remembers yesterday's conversation. Instead, she pushes past her son, past Nora, the better to see Agnes. "Where is he?"

"Magnús?" Agnes asks, relieved. "California."

"So far away," Júlía marvels, though again, Agnes isn't sure if she's approving or criticizing. "Good. Go back there and tell him hello from Júlía. He was a crazy boy, but always kind. Is he a kind man?"

"Yes," Agnes says. When he isn't raging against his daughter's choices, yes.

Júlía nods once, hard, as though physically storing that information somewhere important. "Einar?" she asks.

"He passed away. A year ago."

"He lived longer than Marie," Júlía says. "Every day was borrowed against hers."

He killed her. We all knew.

Ingvar takes advantage of Agnes's silence to beckon his mother to sit. She chooses the chair closest to Agnes's position at the couch. Agnes sits, too. Nora cuts in between them, giving Júlía her most dazzling smile while she introduces herself. "I don't want to interfere," she says, "but with your son's permission, I would love the chance to hear more about your memories of Marie and Einar."

"You don't need his permission," Júlía rasps. "You need mine."

"Of course," Nora says. She's blushing—that's a first. "I misspoke. Can you tell me more about Marie, as you knew her?"

"Her husband murdered her and her child."

Agnes can't help her reaction. The reflexive flinch, like she's been hit. She's here to find out more, she knows that. She's tougher than this, isn't she? But no one in this town, other than Nora, has expressed even the slightest bit of doubt about her grandfather's guilt. It's a common fact that he killed his wife and child, described in brutal nonchalance.

Júlía notices Agnes's discomfort. "This upsets you? It should."

Agnes takes a deep breath to steady herself. "What makes you so certain?" she asks, trying to keep her tone polite, measured.

There's no answer. There's only that flinty gaze, impenetrable and faintly disapproving.

Nora persists, "What was Marie like?"

"A fine woman," Júlía says. "But she had no spine. She had this way about her." A swipe of one gnarled hand, left to right, as though she were clearing the air of a foul stench.

"What way is that?" Nora asks.

"Silly," Júlía says. "Passive."

"Why do you say that?"

"She was so young," Júlía laments. "She didn't know how to take care of Magnús. Karl and I tried for so many years. I wanted a child, she didn't. Magnús became my own boy, until Ingvar. Then I had two boys. I showed her how to be a mother. It was okay until the baby came, and then she became funny."

"Funny?"

"She gives birth to Agnes in August," Júlía says. She turns to Agnes on the couch beside her, squinting, trying to keep the two names straight. She says, "Not you. You are Magnús's daughter. This was Marie's daughter." She touches a finger to the wrinkles between her eyebrows, eyes fluttering closed. She takes a long beat to sort through her thoughts. Ingvar prompts her gently, and although Agnes can't speak a lick of Icelandic, she can imagine he's getting his mother back on track.

When Júlía opens her eyes again, though, there's something fuzzy in her expression. "Agnes was a healthy baby," she says. "A sweet thing, like a kitten. Einar, he was so proud of Magnús. Always bragging about how smart he is. But with this beautiful baby girl, he says nothing. Marie gives her to me, almost the same day she gives birth. 'Can you take her?' she asks me. 'The crying bothers Einar.' Babies cry. I tell her this. She knows this. Magnús wasn't a quiet baby. She says, 'No, no, take her. I just need some time. Please.' She and Einar, they hated the child. I had Agnes in my arms. Marie's telling me she can't stand it. Not her life. Not with this baby. I tell her to calm down. To look at her baby." Júlía's hands lift from her lap, curled underneath the armpits of a phantom child. "'Look at her,' I tell her. 'Find your peace in her.' Marie can't do it. She says she sees her and feels a sense of hatred. There's something wrong with her." Júlía's hands sink back to her lap, the child gone.

"Something wrong with the baby?" Nora asks. "Or with Marie?"

In answer, Júlía shakes her head. Either, neither, both.

"Did she say what she hated about the baby?" Nora persists.

"I told her to go home and sleep. I would take the baby that night, like she wants. She says no. She takes the baby and she goes." Those hard eyes, unforgiving. Agnes pities her grandmother. Seeking help and finding only judgment. This, she knows all too well.

Nora asks, "Why do you think she felt this way?"

"Einar," Júlía says, as though it were obvious. "The baby cried at night. Babies cry. But he was losing sleep and they were fighting. Always fighting. He hates the baby, so Marie must hate her, too."

"Have you heard of postpartum depression?" Nora's leaning forward, hardly sitting on the cushions anymore. "After giving birth, often the mother will suffer from depression, a new sense of anxiety. It's chemical. Hormonal. Sometimes this can be dangerous, to the mother or the child. Especially if it goes untreated."

Agnes bites the inside of her lip. She knows what Nora is doing. Covering all her bases. Following rumors to their sources. It would be irresponsible, Agnes tells herself, if Nora didn't investigate the postpartum psychosis theory.

Still, it makes her sick.

"I had this," Júlía says, and this gives her son a jolt. "No matter how much I wanted my baby, after he came, there was no happiness left in the world. It took months, but I made it through, and I didn't blame my baby. This was not that. I saw Marie at the fishmonger's, laughing with the boys working. In town, taking care of the other children. This was not depression. This was hatred."

"Tell me about Einar. Her husband."

"Soulless."

The sun takes its last breath, then vanishes behind the hills, leaving the room in a sudden, incomplete darkness. The fireplace casts the room in what should be a cozy haze, but it seems like all the color has drained from the room. *Soulless.* The man who raised her. Agnes should be demanding answers from this woman who seems to know everything about her grandparents' marriage. But she's incapable of speech.

She sees her grandfather's hand, reaching for her own. Weeks to the end. He'd said he could feel it coming. *It'll be okay*, he'd told her. He was the one who was dying, and he was comforting her.

"When you spoke to Hildur," Nora continues, as though Agnes's heart wasn't breaking next to her, "you said he doted on Marie. He brought her cinnamon buns from the bakery. You said it was obvious he loved his wife."

"After they fight," Júlía says, "he brings her gifts to keep her happy. To keep her. Any man would take her in a second. He knows this." She considers the women in front of her. Then she turns to her son, speaking in a whisper.

"This visit is over," Ingvar tells Nora. There's a hint of a smile on his face. "The mention of cinnamon buns has made my mother hungry."

Júlía watches closely as Agnes comes to standing, as she thanks her for her time and promises to tell Magnús hello. The old woman says, "Goodbye, Marie," and no one corrects her.

CHAPTER TWENTY-FIVE

February 7, 2019

"Finally," Nora says, hoisting up her glass, "we can have dinner together."

Agnes, seated across from her at the dining room table, lifts her wineglass in a half-hearted salute. She has hardly eaten. Her appetite hasn't returned, not at all. Instead, she's focused on the wine, trying to dull the pounding in her skull, the aches in her joints. She's done it. She's made it a couple of days now without getting stoned. She's earned this.

Nora's drinking Icelandic gin. She says she likes to integrate herself into a place. "Taste everything, smell everything," she says, leaning back in her seat. "Enjoy myself, you know?"

The gin tempts Agnes. The sides of Nora's tall glass glisten with cold sweat. But the wine, at room temperature, seems to be soothing her stomach. The icy drink will only complicate things.

"Tell me something," Agnes says, taking courage from the alcohol. "Ingvar. How come you're so sure he isn't Ása's secret boyfriend?"

"I'm not sure," Nora says. "Not at all. But I just don't really see it. The guy's practically a saint. He left his job and his girlfriend and his place in the city to move back home and care for his dying mother. You couldn't pay me to do that with my own mother. Not that I have anyone to leave at the moment, but the point still stands." Nora finishes her drink. "I don't see him dating a student at the same time."

Agnes raises her eyebrows. "Maybe that's exactly why he's dating her. No one's a saint. He might need some excitement in all his martyrdom."

Nora laughs.

"What?" Agnes asks, feeling defensive.

"Nothing," Nora says. She tosses back her mane of hair. "I like you."

Agnes huffs, secretly pleased. Then, more seriously: "Speaking of Ingvar's mother . . . What about this story she told us? Do you think there's any truth to it?"

"That Marie hated her daughter?" Nora asks. She pours herself more gin, then tops up Agnes's wine. Agnes hasn't had much to drink in the past year, not with her focus on other, more pleasurable pursuits, but this is helping. "I don't know. This is all forty years in the past. Júlía's got memory issues, but with stuff like that, it's short-term memory that's the problem. Long-term memory tends to take over. I think Marie probably said it, or something similar."

"And?" Agnes prompts.

"And what?"

"And what about the theory?" Agnes doesn't want to have to say it. *Tell me you still think he's innocent.* "Marie's postpartum psychosis."

"Well," Nora says, dragging out the word. She looks uncharacteristically uncomfortable. "From what Júlía told us, it sounds like Marie may have experienced postpartum depression with her firstborn. Magnús. Of course, she was still a teenager when she had him, so she could really just have been overwhelmed by the sudden responsibility. I wouldn't be surprised, though, if it was also PPD. That gives more weight to the idea that she might have experienced it again, with her second child, and this time . . . without her support network . . ." She doesn't complete the thought. And she heads off Agnes's objections with a raised palm. "It's not what you want to hear, I know. But I'm not going to sugarcoat this for you. I want us to be on the same page. Square. You're trusting me with your memories of your grandfather. The least I can do is make sure you know where I'm at. Right?"

Agnes sits back. "What," she says. It's not a question.

"I'm going to try to talk to Júlía again, because she is the one who called the police. Originally." Nora says it as though this is supposed to shock Agnes.

"So?"

"So," Nora says, "I've lived in small towns. They take care of their own. With something like this, you'd think that they'd at least spend a day or two figuring things out on their own, before calling for help. That's just the way it works, especially when the nearest police station is not in the town proper. But Einar calls Júlía to ask if she's seen Marie, she says no, they hang up, and she immediately calls the police. That's suspicious. What did she know about their relationship that made one day's absence worthy of a call to the police?"

Agnes pushes her chair away from the table. "I have to sleep," she says. "It's the jet lag."

"Wait," Nora says. She stands, too. She's wobbly, but in control. She grabs for Agnes's shoulders. "If it were me, I would want to know everything. So I'm telling you everything. You have to let me know where your limit is. Did we hit it?"

Agnes takes a deep breath. "No," she says. "I want to know everything." She can see the relief, visible, on Nora's face. She wishes she felt the same.

"Tell me," Nora repeats, "where your limit is. It can change at any time. Just tell me. I like to think we're friends. Or we're getting there, right?"

Agnes says, "Yes," and is surprised by the truth of it.

"Friends tell each other things." Nora gives her a tiny shake, then releases her. "Now go to bed, you're starting to look like a zombie."

Once she's safely hidden in the dark shadows of her room, Agnes folds herself onto the floor, leaning her back against her bedframe. She should shower before she gets into bed, but that requires much more effort than she can afford at the moment. She checks her phone.

There's a text from an unknown number.

Lilja.

So Agnes now has her number, too.

Agnes stares at the screen, trying to see through it to the woman's face. Had she sent this message happily? Nervously? Why hadn't she said more? Agnes slides her right foot into her body, hugging herself tight. She considers her options. Leave it? Let the message sit until she's somewhat sober? Somewhat rested?

She's never been the type to wait.

Hi, she types.

Restless now, almost giddy, she dials her father's number. She doesn't think of the time when she calls, but she figures it must be early for him. With the phone pressed to her ear, it's all just a matter of leaning over to one side, to grab the pill bottle from beneath the mattress.

He answers on the second ring. "Yes?"

She squeezes the bottle in one hand. "Am I interrupting you?"

"Yes, but what is it? Are you okay?"

Agnes remembers her father standing at the foot of her hospital bed, after the accident. One hand wrapped around her right ankle. She can still feel the tremor in his fingers. He hadn't been able to look at her left leg, encased in gauze and metal and smelling of disinfectant.

What did you do? he'd asked her, as though the doctors hadn't told him.

Hot tears poured down her temples. There was nothing to say. He knew it all, already.

And still, though, he'd asked. *Why would you do this?*

Now, her body aching and her mind fuzzy, she wants to tell her father she's glad she came here. *You were wrong about everything,* she could say. *About Nora, about me.* Even with all the hurt. She's doing the right thing. Instead, she says, "I'm really tired," because that is also true.

"You should sleep." There are the familiar clunks and shuffling noises of him rearranging himself in his office chair. "What's it like?"

"So cold," she says. "How did you ever survive the winter?"

"Out of necessity," he says. She imagines him at his desk, a mug of coffee cooling next to his keyboard. Forgotten, as it frequently is. Long tracks of the liquid delineating the sides of the mug, from when he spills on his walk from the kitchen to his office. "I hated it. All that relentless darkness. It was awful. In summer, I could camp out on my own. In winter, I would've died. It's like living in two different places."

"I've been hearing stories of you going outside on your own," she says. "Júlía says hi, by the way."

There's a horrible, thick silence.

"Júlía," he says, finally. Agnes wishes she could see his face, so she could read his mood, but there is only the faint echo on the line, his wooden voice. "She's still there."

"Yeah," Agnes says. "I think she's dying, though. We could only talk to her for a few minutes. Sometimes she thought we were in the seventies." She considers telling her father more. *She thought I was your mother.* She keeps quiet, if only because she doesn't want to have that particular argument. *Why didn't you tell me?* she could ask. *Why didn't you ever tell me how much I look like her?*

Talking to her father has never been easy. Now, at this distance, it's next to impossible.

"You know, Agnes," her father says, breaking the silence, "you're an adult and you're entitled to do whatever you want. But what you are doing is making a terrible mistake."

"Dad—" she begins, but he interrupts her.

"No," he says. "No *Dad*. You have no idea what you are doing. You have no idea what this Nora Carver is capable of. How are you going to feel when she proves that your grandfather killed his wife? His child? How are you going to feel when you've helped her destroy our family?"

"That's not fair," she says. The world spins around her. "He didn't—"

"He *did*, Agnes."

She disappears inside herself, her father's words echoing down the hollow halls of her body. She imagines she says, "What?" but she can't be certain she's actually said it aloud.

"Come home," her father says.

"No," she says. "What do you mean, he did? Dad? What are you saying?"

"Why do you think we left, Agnes?" Her father's sigh is harsh in her ear. "Why do you think we moved halfway across the world? Just because it was difficult?"

She comes back to herself, all at once. The searing pain in her chest won't let her dissociate into the ether. Her fingers strain around the pill bottle. "Why didn't you tell me?" she asks. Then, the incredulity: "Why would you let me near him? Why would you ever leave me alone with him, if you thought he'd slaughtered his wife and daughter? What's wrong with you? Why did you wait until I—"

Her father cuts her off. "Because he's my father." The words reverberate between them. "He was the only family I had. For whatever reason, he did what he did. And he didn't hurt me. I had to trust him, Agnes, because he was all I had left."

She ends the call before she's aware of what she's done.

The phone is in one hand. The other has the bottle of pills. She places her phone on the mattress, then doles herself out two pills. Then, without another thought, three more.

Agnes, her father had said, standing over her hospital bed, the large hand encircling her ankle like a cuff, *what did you do this time?*

CHAPTER TWENTY-SIX

February 8, 2019

The conversation happened on one of their Sunday visits. Einar had less than two weeks to live, though neither of them knew that at the time. They were just going through their routine as usual, or as best as they could. Einar hadn't been able to leave his bed. The living room was too far for him, the garden practically a galaxy away. Agnes had brought tea to his bedroom and opened the window, so they could smell the sun-warmed magnolia tree.

I have been thinking, Einar had said.

Good stuff? Agnes had tried for a joke. It didn't land.

Some of that, he said. *But mostly the regret. I have made so many mistakes in my life. I hope you can live without so many regrets. Nothing is clear, when it's happening. You try to control the outcome. But life has a way of playing with you, doesn't it?*

Agnes, still madly in love with Emi, agreed with him. She was losing her grandfather, she understood that intellectually, and she'd been able, so far, to comfort herself with the idea of Emi. Einar had reached for her hand, squeezing it as tight as he could. It wasn't much, but she felt it, felt the pressure squeeze her heart.

I love you, Agnes, he'd said. *And you love me, don't you?*

I love you so much, she'd said.

You know what they say I've done, he said. *My life—before.*

Yes.

You never believed it, did you?

No. Of course not. That had been true.

Because you love me.

Yes.

A strange smile, then. A twist of his eyebrows. *Would you still love me,* he said, *if it were true?*

When Agnes finally emerges from her bedroom, haggard and hollow, it's to find the house empty. There's a note from Nora on the kitchen counter, telling her that she'd tried to wake her, but she'd had to go. Something to do with the police, or Ása's friends. Agnes finds she can't bring herself to care.

Standing in the kitchen, Agnes lets Nora's note drop back to the counter. She pulls up her phone, squinting at the screen.

Hi, she'd sent to Lilja.

Hi, she'd answered. Late last night, after Agnes had finally slipped into sleep.

It's not much, but right now, it feels like enough. Something bright and different. Agnes types, What are you doing today? Can we talk? Not for the podcast, just us?

The response comes back almost instantly. I'm home all evening.

Great, Agnes types.

She is still learning who she is, she's still finding out so much about herself, but she knows that she can't be alone today. She's about two seconds away from swallowing a handful of pills in one gulp, just to start. Seeing Lilja is one way to stop herself from doing that. Until then, though, she can't be here. So she returns to her room, bundling herself into her many layers, and she marches out the front door.

She has only a vague formulation of a plan. She'll join one of the search parties looking for Ása, out in the snow. She used to process her feelings physically, used to swim or paddle or run through the feeling until she was out the other side.

Agnes is afraid of what she'll do if she stays inside today.

She's almost to her car when she hears someone calling her name. She turns in place, but she can't see who called her. There are the trees, the snow, the house. The shadow of the space where Nora's truck had been parked. Agnes looks for color. The day is overcast and dark, the ground and the sky the same shade of gray. She's starting to think she imagined the voice, when she sees the man emerge from the trees.

It's Thor. He's dressed in a khaki-green snowsuit. In the forest, it had been like camouflage. He pushes his hood away, revealing a bright orange beanie.

"Hello!" he calls, raising a hand. He reaches her quickly, moving confidently and powerfully through the snow. "I hope I didn't frighten you."

"I'm fine," Agnes says. "If you're looking for Nora, though, she's not here. She's—"

"—in town," Thor finishes for her. "I know. She tells me that she has business there. Interrogating Ása's friends, like the Hollywood detectives. I thought I might come and ask you for company while I searched the fields. We didn't get much chance to meet each other. But if you're busy, too . . ."

"No," she says. "I was actually just going to try to join the search."

"Wonderful," he exclaims. "We'll go this way." With a gentle touch to her lower back, Thor guides her to the right side of the house, in the direction of Bifröst. All Agnes can see are the trees surrounding them, the backdrop of the river below. There's no easy way to walk through the thick, frozen blanket of snow. Each step is a crunch and then a drop, about six inches deep, in the unmarked snow. Thor has more grace, or perhaps practice, but Agnes soldiers on, gritting her teeth against the grind of her joints.

"Where have you been searching so far?" Agnes asks, already out of breath.

"We have looked in the radius of the house and her apartment building," Thor tells her, indicating that they should turn right again. The earth pulls downward, and they stop at what appears to be a staircase, embedded in the rock, snaking a path to the riverbanks. "We will walk along the water," he tells her, "then cross up and over. Now that we've exhausted the usual places, we are having to expand away from where she might have taken herself. Go where she might have been taken."

Agnes says, "Okay," while hoping desperately they aren't going too far.

Thor insists on descending the staircase first, to which Agnes readily agrees. She follows his steps slowly. "No one wants to say it," he tells her, "but this is no longer a rescue mission."

"I'm sorry," Agnes says, and it's true. "Do you know her?"

Her foot slides out from beneath her, but Thor's hands are right there. He keeps her upright. "Careful," he says. Then: "I see everyone. I know everyone. But it's not about her. It's about the town. We are a connected, living thing. Losing someone, after Marie and Agnes—" At this, he gives Agnes an odd look. A frowning smile. "—your namesake, I am guessing. We all remember, and we can't have this happen. Not again."

What had Nora said? *They're all afraid to say it. Murder.* Thor's not afraid. She supposes it's because he's already dealt with this before. She sneaks a glance at him. He was eighteen when it happened. This makes him nearly sixty. He looks closer to her father's age, maybe just a bit more lived-in.

Thor catches her staring. "I apologize," he says. "I shouldn't speak of this. It makes it real, when you speak of it."

"Yeah," she says. "Sometimes, though, it helps to talk about it." She thinks of her sessions with Dr. Lee. At first, it had felt like she was lying. Like she was coming up with things to say, because that's what the woman expected of her. Then, the more she spoke, the more she understood that everything she'd said was true. They'd felt like lies because Agnes had alienated herself from those thoughts.

She'd alienated herself from herself. Or so Dr. Lee had told her, when she'd confessed to this experience, much later in their sessions.

She can feel it happening again. Swift and complete, like she's shutting a door within herself.

This walk was supposed to help her work through the feelings. But instead it's just helping her to shove them away. She focuses on Thor. On the beautiful landscape around her. She is nothing but this Agnes right now. The tired woman walking in the snow, searching for a missing student. Soon, the other Agnes, the one who had never doubted her grandfather's innocence, not once in twenty-six years, not until he himself had planted that seed within her mind, disappears from view entirely.

Once they reach the riverbank, though, Agnes loses some of her calm. The chill of the rushing water overwhelms her. It hurts, physically, to breathe. There's no air. There's only cold. Has anyone choked on cold before?

Intuiting her distress, Thor stops. He pulls at his neck, producing a thin woolen scarf, and holds it up to her face. "This will keep you warm," he tells her. "Trust me."

Desperate to keep moving, she relents. Thor wraps the scarf over her nose and mouth, around the back of her head, crisscrossing and pulling it tight. He tucks the ends into the neck of her jacket. "Secure this," he instructs her. While she fumbles with it with her numb fingers, he yanks her hood over her head.

It works. The scarf retains the heat of her breath, warming the tip of her nose. "What about you?" she asks.

"I'm used to it."

They continue forward, skating the edge of the rushing water. Ice extends far into the stream, but still an unimaginable amount of water flows underneath, fighting against the rocks strewn about the middle, billowing like silk scarves in a strong wind.

Here, though she believes—hopes—that they're walking over solid earth, there's a layer of ice on top that slows her steps to what could be considered a crawl. Thor graciously doesn't comment on their speed. He just matches her pace, wrapping a hand around her elbow to keep her upright. They make it to a land bridge that crests over a narrow portion of the river. Thor tells her to hold his hand. Hers is bare, aching, in his gloved fist. To follow each of his steps exactly. He won't let her fall, but—

"Pour your weight down into each foot," he tells her, miming the motion. "*Straight* down."

Nodding, terrified, she tells him to go. She grips his hand through his glove, hard, and feels the breath leaving her in a rush. There, to either side of her, is the water. The silk scarves surging beneath, beckoning her down.

Over too many agonizing moments for her to catalog, they reach solid land again. Out of an impulse born of pure exhilaration, Agnes throws her arms around Thor's shoulders.

"There, there," he says, squeezing her in return. "That was easy, wasn't it? You're your father's daughter."

She pulls out of the hug. "I guess you knew him well, right?"

"Not *well*," Thor says. "He was a little boy, and I was a man. But he was Magnús! The little goat. He used to tell stories about climbing that hill, you know." He means the mountain they're standing underneath. "He had a big mouth. I thought he was lying, trying to impress me. But then one day I saw him from the house. This tiny body, against the sky."

"From the house?"

In answer, Thor points to the trees across the river. Agnes turns, scanning the line of the forest. There's a glint of metal not too far away. "Is that the house you grew up in?" she asks.

"Yes."

She revolves in place to take in the rest of the river. There, almost laughably close, is the new house. It feels like they've been walking for hours, but they're still within shouting distance.

"Close neighbors," she says.

"My father and your grandfather had a lot of . . ." Thor says, choosing the words carefully, "disputes over that. The land, you know. We weren't as close as we should have been." At her questioning look: "It's one of those boring arguments people have when it comes to property ownership. There was a common ancestor, not too far back. Different sides of the family had different parts of the land. It fell down to your grandfather and my father."

"But then Einar sold his side to your father," she says, "when he and Magnús left."

"Now I have everything, yes."

Agnes tries to block it out. *Why do you think we left, Agnes?* But it's there, it's inescapable. She shoves her hands deeper into her pockets, trying to warm her frozen fingers. "Does that mean we're related?" she asks Thor.

He huffs. "The joke is that everyone in Iceland is related."

"But we go back, don't we?"

"We do," he says. For a moment, he doesn't seem too happy to follow that train of thought. She wonders if he's worried she will try to lay claim to her part of the land. But he shows her his gap teeth in a wide smile. "You could be my daughter. My Californian daughter. Tell me about it. Is it sunny?"

While they continue up the river on this side, she describes the Bay Area. She expects some kind of homesickness to take her down, to cut her at the knees. But it feels so far away. This place, it's reducing

Agnes's life there, and her grandfather, to a distant memory. Even her own emotions, she watches them drift away, until it feels like she's describing dreams she's had, ones that she can hardly remember.

Dr. Lee would say she's alienating herself.

Agnes would say she's handling things as best as she can.

"Do you miss it?" Thor asks her. "Home?"

"The sunshine, yes," Agnes says. "But I like it here a lot. More than I thought I would, and I always thought I would like it here."

"Here, Iceland? Or here, Bifröst?"

"Both," she says. "Right now, though, mostly here, Bifröst. It's a special place."

"You feel it, too," he says, beaming. "The gravity." He stops her again. They're on a ridge now, overlooking the river, the trees, the valley beyond. The sun, as though summoned, peeks its face out of the clouds. She feels the tendrils of its light on her skin—the small bit left to the air—and warms. Thor's face has brightened, the glitter of his eyes taking on color again.

"My ex-wife used to talk about this Swedish concept called smultronställe. Have you heard of this before?" Thor chuckles. "No, I suppose not. It means, literally, the place where wild strawberries grow. But it can also mean a special place. A place that belongs only to you, that you return to, again and again, because it's yours and it's safe. You share it with only those you love, with only those you can trust. This is what Bifröst is to me. Maybe it can be this to you. You have returned here, after all. And you should. You are Marie's twin, and you are named for her daughter. You belong here."

"Thank you," Agnes says. He couldn't know how much she needed to hear that. "That's very kind."

"It's not kind," Thor says. "It's just true."

The rush of the river lightens. Up here, it's nearly completely frozen over. They turn again, away from the river. Now they're walking into the vast, blank fields, keeping their steps careful and light on the uncertain ground. The open world, so alien, momentarily steals her focus. There's no sign of life out here, other than trails of some type of animal footprint. They're small, clearly paw prints. Foxes? Otters?

Thor stops them, not to look at anything in particular, just to enjoy the view. "It took me so many years to understand that I belonged here. I left when I was eighteen. I moved to study in Copenhagen, and I stayed there, until my father moved out and I realized, this place is who I am."

"When was this?"

"Three years ago."

"Where did your father go?" The first-generation Thor. Thor Senior.

"It doesn't matter," Thor says, his expression hardening. He guides them forward again. "It's better that he is gone."

"I'm sorry," Agnes offers.

"No," Thor tells her. "He wasn't a good man, my father. He took great pleasure in your grandfather's loss. We should only mourn those who we love."

Agnes closes her eyes.

Would you still love me, if it were true?

She'd said yes. Of course she had. Of course she would.

But not in the same way. Not anymore.

Thor guides them in a wide, meandering circle through the fields of snow. Stopping, now and then, to examine a lump of snow, peeling away the layers of frozen water to discover yet another rock, yet another hibernating bush. No bodies. No faces in the snow. There are no footsteps but for their own, and those of the foxes. In the silence, in the cold that threatens to solidify Agnes from the inside out, she wonders what it means about her, to belong to this place.

CHAPTER TWENTY-SEVEN

February 8, 2019

They're almost home. Agnes can see the structure, the glint of glass, the gray concrete. But she doesn't know if she can make it. It feels like her left leg is held together by barbed wire. She tries to keep up with the conversation—Thor's telling her about his life in Denmark, she thinks—but she can only focus on the creaking in her joints, the grind of her skeleton.

"Do you need assistance?" he asks her, finally. He offers her his arm.

"No," she says, her voice harsh. She tries to soften it with a "thank you," but she'd rather crawl right now than have him drag her back to the house.

Which is why it takes them so long to reach the driveway. When they crest that hidden staircase, he pulls away from her with a sigh of exasperation. Agnes flinches, certain that he's sick of keeping pace with her, but then he's calling out, and it's not to her.

There's a group of townspeople, she assumes, spread out in the trees. Shouting for Ása.

"They've already looked here," Thor tells her, shaking his head. "Not very organized. They shouldn't be wasting time. I need to talk to them. Will you be okay?"

"Fine," she lies.

Thor takes off with an athletic jog through the snow. He gathers the group around him. Agnes doesn't stop to watch or listen. Every step sends a lightning bolt of pain up her leg, straight to her jaw, making the last few steps to the front door a tremendous feat of pure will and blind rage.

Which is why she doesn't hear her name until the door's already open.

"Agnes?"

Steeling herself, Agnes stops. Turns around.

Lilja, right there. Uncertain.

"What are you doing here?" Agnes asks, leaning her weight on the doorknob.

"I'm looking for Ása," Lilja tells her.

"So was I," Agnes says. "Up that way." She notes the woman's chapped skin, the strain in her eyes. Considers how much longer she can stand without her leg collapsing underneath her like a crumbling sandcastle. "Do you want to come inside?"

"In there?" Lilja asks. "You're staying *here?*"

"Technically, Nora is. But yeah. Why?"

"It's expensive," is all Lilja can say. But then she shrugs. "I will come inside, yes."

Agnes nearly groans with relief. The temperature inside is offensively hot, her face and fingers almost catching flame. She sheds her many layers to the floor, only half aware of Lilja doing the same. In shirtsleeves and jeans, Agnes feels something closer to human. She notices Lilja's eyes on her. Lilja looks away, fast.

"Do you want coffee?" Agnes asks.

"Yes," the woman says. "Please."

The journey to the kitchen is a long one. Agnes can't stifle her limp, and she senses Lilja behind her, senses her eyes on her again. "Thor said they're wasting their time looking here," she says. "Everyone's already searched the house."

"That's assuming she's a body to be discovered. Not a person, conscious, not wanting to be found."

"Why do you think she doesn't want to be found?" Agnes asks, reaching the kitchen counter. She fiddles with the fancy coffee machine. She doesn't need coffee. What she honestly needs are her pills, but she can't exactly take them right now, in front of Lilja, so coffee and sitting on a couch will have to do. "Why would she run away like this? And wouldn't she take her car, if she was going to run?"

Lilja comes up beside her. Her face is broad, her ceiling eyes set deep, veiled behind roughhewn cheekbones. She's severe, and almost too beautiful to look at directly. She doesn't have any trouble staring at Agnes, though. "Who are you?" she asks.

"What?" Agnes can't mask her surprise. "You know, I'm—"

"The murderer's granddaughter," Lilja says dismissively. "That's not what I mean. Who are you?"

The coffee bubbles away, hot, fragrant steam making curlicues in the air between them. It takes Agnes a second to catch up to this moment. She had gotten a feeling yesterday, in Ása's apartment. She'd tested it in Lilja's car. *Are you in love with her?*

She's getting the feeling again, stronger now.

"I'm a software designer from Berkeley," Agnes says. "Or, I used to be, until I hurt myself." She gestures to her leg. "You might have noticed. It's been almost a year, but they had to do a lot to fix it. I've been in recovery mode for a long time. I . . . There's . . ." She searches for what else she can tell this woman. Who is Agnes Glin? What has her life become? "Yeah. That's who I am now, or who I've been until now. It's a relief to be here and to be someone else. So—This. I'm this."

In this light, Lilja's eyes are black. "And what do you want with Ása?"

"Nothing. I told you, I didn't even know about her until I got here. Now that I have, I want to help." She doesn't say that she feels she understands Ása, or that she's starting to admire her. Not in a way that she could name. But Ása disappeared. She made it out.

Agnes pours them both a coffee. She normally takes hers with a splash of milk, but she doesn't have the energy to walk to the fridge and back and then make it to the couches. She falls into the cushions with a sigh. She watches Lilja follow, folding herself next to Agnes. Not close enough to touch. But close enough that they have to turn their bodies to the side to see the other in full.

"Who are *you?*" Agnes counters.

This makes Lilja smile. It might be the first hint of humor Agnes has seen in her. It's a stolen glimpse of an entirely separate person, one more lighthearted and impish. But the smile dies as fast as it comes. "I'm afraid," she says.

Agnes falters. She's never been good at giving comfort, not when she can hardly handle receiving it.

Lilja tries again. "When I am not afraid," she says, "I'm studying law. Ása's working in business, like Óskar. We spend so much time working, each of us needs our own outlet. Óskar has his music, Ása has her boys, and I have my drawings."

"Can I see some of your drawings? Do you have a page?"

Lilja pulls out her phone, taps into her Instagram profile. She hands the phone to Agnes, their fingers grazing at the edges. Mostly she works in black ink, it seems. There are some watercolors, though, experiments with landscapes.

"This looks familiar," Agnes says, meaning a reproduction of the river outside.

Lilja snatches the phone away from her, her expression softening only when she sees which image Agnes has pointed to. "Yes," she says. "This place is an easy subject."

Agnes sips at her coffee, impressed. She's always expressed herself through movement. Surfing, running, hiking. She had spent so many days sitting still for work, losing herself in screens, but she'd balanced this with physical exertion. She misses that most of all, the burning in her lungs, pushing past the boundaries of her being.

Maybe this is why Dr. Lee had been so adamant she should take up a new hobby. Painting, knitting, something distracting. But nothing could replace that feeling.

So she'd chosen nothing.

"Are you okay?" Lilja asks her. "You look sad. You look afraid, actually. Like me. What do you have to be afraid of?"

Agnes hears herself laugh. Knows that it's humorless, but she can't stop it. "That's too hard for me to answer," she says truthfully. "I don't know. And that might be it."

It's nonsense, but Lilja seems to understand the nonsense, because she's nodding. "Okay," she says. She stares down at her phone. Pulls up a portrait and shows it to Agnes. Ása. "No one cares," Lilja says.

"I'm sorry," Agnes says. "I don't know Ása, but I—" She stops. She doesn't want to say, *I envy her*, but that's a horrible thing to say, and not entirely true, anyway. "I want to help you," she says finally.

Lilja abandons her mug on the coffee table. "They act like she's dead," she says. "They're planning her funeral."

Agnes scoots forward. Slowly, haltingly, she wraps an arm around the woman's shoulders. She feels the shudder run through Lilja's body. Agnes hates this part of knowing someone. Letting them cry. She forces herself to weather the storm.

Lilja's arms come around her middle, seeking support. Agnes marvels, dumbfounded, at the pleasure of being held. She'd become a clinical being, every part of her body touched for surgery, for examinations. She'd discovered, after she'd been sent home from the hospital, a leftover heart rate monitor stickered to the underside of her breast. The intimacy of this embrace shocks her. She doesn't want it to end.

When Lilja pulls away, it's with an apology. "I shouldn't do this," she says. "I don't know you."

"We know each other a little better now," Agnes offers.

The black eyes find her own. They're bloodshot, yes, but they're still stunning. Lilja is stunning. Maybe it's her vulnerability, the way she's opened herself up to Agnes so readily, that appeals to her, but Agnes thinks it's something more.

She's so distracted, she almost springs back when Lilja thrusts a phone into her hand. It's a different phone than before. An earlier model. Not Lilja's iPhone. A Samsung.

"What's this?" Agnes asks.

"It's her phone," Lilja tells her. "Ása's. Her secret phone."

"What do you mean?" Agnes asks, resisting the urge to drop it. The idea of it, of holding a dead woman's phone, sends a thrill of fear crawling up her spine. She shouldn't have this.

"She had two phones," Lilja says. "One normal. And one she would try to hide from us." She comes to standing and paces away from Agnes. "The police have the normal one. And I have this one."

Agnes stares at the phone in her hand, shock slowing her down. The screen lights up. The background picture is a selfie of Lilja and Ása, with identical smiles, their faces pressed tightly together. "Why would she need a secret phone?"

Lilja doesn't answer. She just waits for Agnes's brain to catch up.

"Oh. The secret boyfriend."

Lilja nods.

"But that's—" Agnes can't find the right word for it. *Overkill?* Lilja paces to the windows. Then back to Agnes. Agnes watches the woman's expression become more haggard with every step she takes. Like the weight of whatever she's holding inside is killing her. "Why," Agnes asks carefully, "do you have this?"

"She dropped it," Lilja says, as though that explained everything. "Now I don't know what to do with it."

"Why are you giving it to me?"

"Because I lied," Lilja tells her, her voice low and strange. "Óskar and I lied. About that night."

"Okay." Agnes wishes she could say anything else except "Okay."

"You don't understand," Lilja cries. "I didn't know it was so bad. Ása was upset at the party, but she's always upset these days. Stressed. With"—she makes an angry gesture to the secret phone, still clutched in Agnes's hand—"whoever that was who gave her that phone. At the party, she was angry. So angry, and so drunk. She left to take a piss, she said, but she walked out so far. Óskar went to get her. He found her sitting in the snow, in the trees, crying.

"He put her in his car. He came back to get me. He told me he needed help with Ása. We drove back to their apartment building.

"Ása wouldn't tell us what was wrong. All she said was, 'Everyone wants everything all the time.' She was babbling. We got her into her room. I wanted to stay with her. But she told us to leave. She shouted at me. She's one person, she said. She's not the solution to all our problems. So we left her alone, to cool off. Óskar went to his place downstairs. I walked home.

"I was hurt," Lilja says, tears spilling down her cheeks again. "She hasn't wanted to see me in weeks. So after that night, I didn't call her. Didn't text. Didn't try to see her. Óskar said he did the same. We all needed space. We thought she was with her boyfriend. But then . . ." Lilja trails off, losing steam. She slumps onto the couch beside Agnes again. Closer now. Seeking comfort.

Agnes wraps an arm around the woman's shoulders, more out of reflex than the desire for intimacy. She can smell the fear, sharp and feral, on the woman's skin.

"But how," she asks again, more softly now, "do you have her phone?"

"Óskar," Lilja says. "I saw it in his room yesterday. He said Ása dropped it in the snow that night, and he picked it up and forgot about it. To him, it doesn't matter. He thinks she's dead. He thinks she's killed herself. I took the phone from him, but I don't know what to do with it. I can't give it to the police. Not with Óskar . . . They'll think we've hurt her, when all we tried to do was help her."

Agnes starts to lean away from Lilja, but the woman tightens her hold.

"I didn't hurt her," Lilja insists. "I want to help her. But I don't know what to do."

Agnes should call the police. She knows this is what she should do. But there's the broken note in Lilja's voice. "Do you think Óskar hurt her?"

The answer comes just a touch too quickly. "*No.*"

"But—"

"He *loves* her."

It's the same as yesterday. Like love can't be destructive.

Agnes smooths a hand over Lilja's arm and considers the phone. There are so few avenues for privacy in this world, let alone in this small town. She asks, as it finally occurs to her: "What do you want me to do with this? Why are you telling me all this?"

Now Lilja pulls away. "I can't have it," she cries. "I don't know what to do with it. But I know I can't have it. I lied to the police, because I thought I was protecting her privacy. They asked me about her phone. They found her normal one on her nightstand. They asked why she would go to a party without her phone. I'd seen her at the party with *this* phone. I said she wouldn't need her phone. At the time, I didn't think she was hurt. I thought she was with her boyfriend. I didn't know Óskar had this. By the time we knew she was actually missing, it was too late to tell the truth." Lilja sucks in a shaky breath. "Something's happened to her. I have to find her."

With a visible effort, Lilja pushes herself to standing and walks to the front door.

Bones creaking, Agnes follows. "Where are you going?"

"To look for her," Lilja says, jamming her feet into her boots.

"The phone," Agnes insists. It's still in her hand.

"Keep it," Lilja says, backing away from Agnes. She's already opening the front door. "Tell them you found it," she says. "Tell them anything you want. Just don't tell them I gave it to you. They won't believe me." When she smiles this time, it comes out crooked and pathetic. "You said you wanted to help me."

CHAPTER TWENTY-EIGHT

February 8, 2019

Agnes stands at the front door, frozen. She's holding a missing woman's secret phone. She's holding it because Ása's friends took it from her, the night she disappeared. She's holding it because those same friends lied to the police. And now Agnes is responsible for it. She puts it in her jacket pocket.

She'll give the phone to Nora. That's the only course of action she can take. Nora's probably handled sensitive evidence like this before. She'll know what to do, what to tell the police. Agnes can only hope she'll keep Lilja out of it.

Lilja, who's lied. Who's caught in a web of lies. Agnes understands. God, does she understand. She's stuck in her own web, too.

Once again, though, she is on her own. Once again, she's faced with an opportunity. The pills. Take the pills. Swallow a handful. Stop thinking.

She thinks of Ása, drunk and desperate. *Everyone wants everything all the time.* Maybe Óskar did hurt her. Maybe the secret boyfriend did. But somehow, Agnes doesn't believe it. She can only imagine the young woman, her brain chemistry out of balance, leaving behind her phones, all ties to her life, in search of some peace. Finding it, somewhere in the snow.

Agnes forces herself to go outside. The rental car has been waiting for her in the driveway. She scrapes away the ice from the windshield, and it feels as though she's scraping away the surface of her skull.

She doesn't let herself think about it. She just goes, her frozen hands locked on the wheel, until she's pulling up in Ingvar's driveway. There's no smoke coming from the chimney, no truck in sight, but there are lights on inside. Júlía, alone. Perfect. Her heart in her throat, Agnes knocks on the front door. There's no doorbell. Nothing but her frozen knuckles against the thick wood. She waits, counting to fifteen in her head. If this doesn't work, she'll drive into town. Find Nora, give her the phone.

Just as she's turning to leave, though, the door opens, revealing the tiny old woman.

"Marie," Júlía says, then there's more Icelandic than Agnes could ever dream of following. Are there separate words? Or is everything just one long descriptive word?

It's a precipice. Does Agnes correct the old woman, or does she deceive her? She wavers on the edge. If she does this, she's crossing a line. Betraying a moral code she never before had to articulate to herself.

But when has she ever let the fear of falling stop her from leaping?

"Can I come in?" Agnes asks.

The old woman steps aside. She switches over to English, following Agnes's lead. "No baby for me today?"

"No. Just me."

"This way." Júlía leads Agnes into the sitting room. "I am knitting a sweater for Karl."

The old woman resumes her knitting—as far as Agnes can tell, she's just begun, because all there is on the needles is a thin tube of blue yarn—and watches as Agnes folds herself onto the couch. "Out with it," she commands, her hands flicking laboriously on the needles. "What has happened now?"

Agnes doesn't hesitate. "It's Einar."

"What did he do?"

"Have I ever told you that he's hurt me?"

"He tells Karl that he only wants two things in this world: his work and you. But he gets so angry."

"Do we fight often?"

"I am not your husband."

How does Nora do this? How does she find the right questions to ask, to get the other person talking?

Agnes tries another way. "Why did you call the police? When you heard I wasn't home, why did you call them?"

Júlía considers her answer carefully. She threads the yarn over and over, a repetitive motion that makes Agnes a little seasick to watch. "I was afraid for the baby," she says finally.

"Why?"

Over and over, the blue yarn.

Agnes asks, "Did you think I would hurt her?"

A mistake in the needles. "Did you?"

"Have I ever?"

No answer.

"Do you really think I hate my child?" she asks. "Is that why you think I hurt her?"

"You hate both of them," the old woman says. "Magnús and Agnes. You don't want them. You take care of all the children. You take in my Ingvar, but now he tells me he watches over your baby, while you rest. I see it. You are mother to all, but you hate it. You don't want this."

"I don't?"

"I see it," Júlía insists. "When you think no one sees, I see the emptiness in you."

"Why am I empty?"

The needles drop to the old woman's lap. "Because it was all taken from you," she says, her voice tough and unforgiving. "Everything inside of you. That man, he loves you more than anything. But sometimes love takes, and he took everything from you. You were a child in another country about to start your life. Your paintings. Now you are a child with two children in an unknown place. You have been *ravaged*. But you cannot punish your children for this. You have to find a way to live."

"Thank you," Agnes says, and she means it. She's grateful for the old woman's brusque comfort.

"Don't thank me," Júlía snaps. "You are so close to ruining your life, Marie, and you will have no one to blame but yourself. You are not allowed to use your pain as a weapon against your family. Einar has tolerated your humiliations enough."

"Humiliations," Agnes echoes, stunned.

Júlía looks angry enough to spit. "Running around with the neighbor," she says. "You ask for so much trouble. You're lucky you still have a bed to sleep in." The rest of her vitriol dissolves into Icelandic.

"The neighbor," Agnes says. Before she can ask who he was, there's a knock on the door. The sound startles both women in their seats.

There, standing in the threshold of the sitting room, is Ingvar. Agnes jumps to her feet, guilty and desperate. She doesn't know how long Ingvar was listening for, but she's been caught. Caught abusing the kindness of a sick, elderly woman. And stopped, just at the wrong moment.

Júlía beams at her son. "Look who's here," she says. "It's your other mother."

Ingvar's expression, unreadable, softens when he considers his mother. "Yes," he says. "How lucky I am."

CHAPTER TWENTY-NINE

February 8, 2019

"I'm sorry," Agnes says, as soon as they are out of earshot. She hesitates at the front door, afraid Ingvar will kick her out before she can explain herself. "She thinks I'm—and I just wanted—there's no way to rationalize it. I'm ashamed."

Ingvar looms over her, arms folded.

"I shouldn't have done it," she continues. There's no way to ask him how long he'd listened for. What he'd heard. If his world has been rocked, as hers has. Agnes needs Nora. She needs help.

"My mother doesn't know what she's saying," Ingvar tells her. "She's not well."

"I just—" She deflates. "Yeah."

He nods. But there's so much disappointment.

It's the withdrawals. It's this place, so beautiful but so full of ghosts. It's Lilja asking *Who are you?* and only being able to talk about her goddamned leg. It's sitting in front of someone with dementia and pretending to be her dead grandmother. It's learning that her grandfather did, in fact, have a reason to kill his wife and daughter. Agnes isn't shocked, not really, but she is horrified to find herself crying. Tears course down her cheeks, and she buries her face in her hands, apologizing through the sob.

She hasn't cried like this in a year.

After a long moment, in which Agnes tries with all her will to shove the emotion back into her mouth with her fingers, she feels a pressure on the top of her head. A hand encompassing her skull.

And that is it. That is the only comfort Ingvar offers.

Still, though, she sobs. For her grandfather, a stranger. For her grandmother, the empty woman. For her aunt, just an infant, resented all her too-short life. For herself, alone and unmoored.

When the tears dry up, she lifts her head and the hand disappears. Ingvar's expression is, as ever, unreadable. But there's more warmth. It's his ability to hold space for their thoughts.

"You shouldn't be that angry with yourself," he tells her. "My mother doesn't get many visitors." When he takes her in, still sniffling, something in him softens. "Did you love your grandfather very much?"

Would you still love me, if it were true?

"I—" she begins. She could say, *I did.* But when she speaks, what comes out is, "I don't even know why I'm here."

Part Two

INTERLUDE

February 8, 1979

I hope you can forgive me, in time, for what I've done.

Marie sits back from the kitchen table and considers the letter in front of her. She's spent hours—days—trying to plan what she'd write. She drops the pen to the table and massages her hand. What she's done is unforgivable. It's almost pointless to put it all into words. But she has to do something. She can't keep living this way. She supposes something inside her, some hidden, twisting, strange part of her, had wanted to hurt Einar. She'd wanted to punish him, perhaps, for taking her so far away from everything she's known. For never once acknowledging what she's done for him, for their family. For still, even nine years later, making fun of her pronunciation. *Let's hear your Danish again, country boy,* she'd say, and he wouldn't talk to her for hours.

But now that she's actually hurt her husband, she realizes how much she wants him. Just him.

She looks away from the letter, down to the bundle of blankets on the floor. Agnes, sleeping. She sleeps only on hard surfaces these days. She's already taking after her brother, the feral boy.

Where is Marie's feral boy?

It's close to sunset. The house is still empty. Magnús knows the rules. In winter, he has to be home by dark. But Marie supposes she hasn't been enforcing that rule very well recently, has she? She's hardly paid any attention to her family. All she's wanted since summer—she looks again to the bundle of blankets and thinks, privately, viciously, *Since you*—has been some peace and quiet. Time to herself.

And now that she has finally found herself alone, she can hardly breathe for the panic building in her. She paces through her empty home, her heart breaking when she thinks about Magnús. When was the last time she saw him? This morning? Had she even said goodbye to him? Had she tucked him into bed last night? Or had she just called out good night to him from across the hall, like a stranger?

She feels, suddenly, like she's been on a long trip, and she's trying, desperately, to come home. But there is no home to be found. It's vanished into thin air.

Where is Magnús?

Marie opens the back door and shouts for her boy. She can't imagine he will hear her over the roar of the rushing river, but she screams all the same.

When nothing moves, nothing but the changing light in the sky and the water racing toward the ocean, she returns to the kitchen. To the phone. She has no other option, not if she wants to see her son.

She calls Júlía. Even though she'd told herself she would never speak to the woman again, even though she can feel the woman's judgment oozing on her skin like oil, she calls Júlía because if Magnús isn't here, then he's probably there. With his nicer mommy.

It isn't Júlía who picks up the phone, though. It's Karl.

"'Lo?" he answers, his voice gruff.

Marie doesn't announce herself. "Is my boy with you?"

"Which one?" Karl jokes. "Ingvar or Magnús?"

"Magnús," she says, and suddenly the whole arrangement makes her sick. What has she been doing? She's known from the very beginning that it was a mistake. Many mistakes, rolled into one. What's wrong with her, that she can't stop?

"I don't know," Karl says. "I just walked in and picked up the phone. It's good to hear you calling, Marie. It's been a while since I've seen you. Have you gone into hiding?"

"Magnús," she repeats, pressing the receiver into her skin until it hurts. "Is he there? Can you look?"

There's the sound of a sigh. Then the man's voice calling into his house. "No one's here but me," he reports back. "Would you like to come over and help me look?"

"Are you sure he's not there?"

Magnús has taken to roaming. She doesn't know how to help her son. Her childhood had never been so lonely as his. She'd grown up in the apartment blocks in Copenhagen, playing with the big groups of kids like they were her family. Her fellow soldiers. They played at war, a group of marauders pillaging the other neighboring kids' camps. By the time she was Magnús's age, she could've shouted out her kitchen window and heard ten other children returning the battle cry. Marie tells her son to go play, and he goes, dutifully. But he plays by himself.

Next time, she will go with him. If he can't find anyone to play with, it will be her. It should be her. What more is there to life? What could be more fun than spending time with your own son?

"Marie?" It's Karl. She'd forgotten about him. "Is everything okay?"

Marie considers her daughter, her little body curled in the blankets like a pastry. Marie has never felt so lonely. "Fine," she says. She clears her throat. "Where is everyone?"

"Júlía should be back from Borgarnes soon," Karl tells her. "Do you want me to send her over to you? Help you look for Magnús?"

"No," she says sharply. "I don't want her here."

The sting of their last conversation hasn't faded. In fact, it's gained strength. *You're making a fool out of yourself.*

If only Júlía knew how much of a fool Marie has been.

"Why don't I come over?" Karl suggests. "It seems like we should talk."

The baby scrunches up her face, tightening her little features into an angry ball. Her fat fists gather at the sides of her head, her curved legs springing up to her stomach. She twists and fusses. She's coming awake. The crying will start again.

"No," Marie says, and she hangs up the phone without another word.

She reaches for her baby. Her beautiful daughter. Agnes. Beautiful only in sleep. In wakefulness, she rages. She rages at her mother, her father, and she rages at her life. Marie loves her daughter. She feels it inside her, the love populating every cell of her body. But sometimes, in the late hours of the night, she finds herself thinking what terrible luck it was to have her. What terrible luck Marie has had in her life. Meeting Einar, letting him convince her to marry him, to move all the way here, to have Magnús, all when she was young, so young. In these dark, sleepless nights, she tells herself it was all out of her control. Fate.

But what she's done now, that's not fate. It's her own mistake. She'd sought out that man. She'd asked him to kiss her. She'd taken him to her bed. She'd started a relationship with him, hoping for what? To hurt Einar? To prove that she could choose for herself?

Her daughter stares unseeingly up to the ceiling. Her cloudy blue eyes glimmer for a moment, and her gaze touches, briefly, on her mother. Then the rage begins. The screaming, twisting, unholy rage.

Marie gathers her daughter into her arms, and she paces the length of the kitchen. She holds her baby tight to her chest and she feels herself crying, too. The truth is, she has chosen this life for herself, every part of it. Her husband. Her daughter. Her son. Her lover.

In the living room, she bounces her daughter in her arms while she looks at her wedding pictures on the wall. Marie is so young in these pictures. A child. But, she sees now, so is Einar. She touches a hand to the record player she and Einar had bought for Magnús. She doesn't even know what his favorite record is. She's made a mess of things. It's time to come home. Time to make everything right again. Starting with her son, who needs her the most. Marie feels something raw and exhilarating tear through her. Something like strength.

She hears the door open. It's not the front door. Marie can see the front door from where she stands, and it's closed.

The gust of wind, the momentary rumble of the river, tells her it's the back door.

Magnús.

Marie's so relieved she feels her legs buckling. "Maggi," she says, calling out high above the baby's rages. "Come here."

She wants to touch her son's hair. The fine white-blond silk, so much like her own father's. She'll tell him she'll go out and play with him. She will swallow her pride, she will crawl on her hands and knees if she has to, and give Agnes to Júlía for an afternoon, so it can be the two of them. Maggi and Marie. Playing marauders in the snow.

But the voice that calls back to her isn't her son's. It's a man's.

Marie tightens her hold on her baby, and for once, the screaming stops. As though Agnes, too, can sense the danger.

"Marie," the man says. His voice is so soft in the sudden silence. "We have to talk."

CHAPTER THIRTY

February 8, 2019

When Nora returns that evening, Agnes has created a mess of her research papers in the living room. Folders splayed open, papers strewn
in every direction. She's hidden the crime scene photos, but there are
others. Geological surveys of the land. Maps. She had been searching
for something and it had, unfortunately, been at the bottom of the pile.

"What," Nora asks, frozen in place, "are you doing?"

"Did you talk to Óskar?" Agnes asks. She has lived entire lifetimes
in this one day. She has no time for pleasantries.

"He wasn't there."

"Was he with the police?"

Nora shakes her head, her eyes tracking all the papers on the floor.
"He apparently has driven down to Reykjavík already, for his show
tomorrow. Can you explain what's going on?"

"I know something," Agnes tells her. She's shocked to hear how
steady her voice is. She has an idea, and she hopes, prays, that she's
right.

"What's that?" Nora asks. She folds herself onto the couch oppo-site Agnes, hands braced on her knees.

"Thor Senior," Agnes says from the floor. She holds up the photo-graph she'd been searching for. "The first-generation Thor." A portrait of a middle-aged man, all high cheekbones and thin eyes. The larger version of the son. "He and my grandfather shared an ancestor, or whatever you call it. Right? The two sides of the family split this land up, but they fought over it. They hated each other."

"From what I've learned," Nora says, "it wasn't like the Hatfields and the McCoys. The two neighboring families in West Virginia, the blood feud? No? Well, this wasn't a violent rivalry. It was more like, Thor's people wanted to buy the land back from your family and con-solidate the wealth. Your side said no, until the murders."

"What if," Agnes says, "what if Thor Senior killed them to get the land?"

Nora plays along. "Why not just kill Einar?"

"Because that's too obvious."

"All murder is obvious."

"If he killed Einar," Agnes presses on, "Marie and the kids would stay in the house, right? She'd probably remarry and someone else would take over. Maybe he wanted to run Einar out of town." It's a wild, desperate idea. But she clings to it, hard, like a life raft.

"Or kill Einar and marry Marie himself," Nora says.

"Yeah." They're close to the truth. Agnes wonders, suddenly, if Nora knows some of this already. If she's just keeping her cards close to her chest.

"That's diabolical," Nora says. "Sociopathic."

"Maybe he was. Thor Junior told me his father was a horrible man. He moved out of here when he could, and he only came back when his father left."

"When did he tell you that?"

"Today." Agnes tells her about their walk across the river.

Nora doesn't speak.

"What?" Agnes asks. "Did I do something wrong?"

"No," Nora says, a touch too quickly. "It's just—you've done a lot today. Good job. I've arranged a dinner for us with Thor Junior when we get back from Reykjavík. We can ask him more about his father then."

"There's something else," Agnes says. The phone's already on the coffee table between them. She hands it to Nora. "It's Ása's."

Nora doesn't move. She doesn't even appear to be breathing.

"Lilja," Agnes says. She does her best to explain, about inviting her in for a coffee, about the party, about Ása's drunken journey home. She doesn't tell Nora about their plans for later. The fact of their texts. But she tells her about the two phones. When she's finished, she says, all too aware of the symmetry of the gesture, "Take it. Give it to the police. You know them."

Nora holds it strangely, like she's never before held a phone. "She just gave this to you?" she repeats.

"Yeah. Not right away. But she wanted to get rid of it, I guess."

"Why did she give this to you?"

Agnes's mouth dries up. *Because there's an undercurrent of something else happening between us, Nora, because I think she's as attracted to me as I am to her, and she's terrified and lonely and so am I, and if you're swept up in a river and drowning and you spot a point of safety, you don't think about it, you just swim for it.* But that's impossible to say. Impossible to vocalize for this woman whose entire life is held secret. Agnes doesn't know much about Nora, but she likes her. She thinks they could be friends, genuine friends, outside of this podcast. But that doesn't remove the fact that she feels she knows more about Lilja, a woman she's spent all of two hours with, than the woman sitting across from her. Nora's a glacier. There's so much underneath the surface, stuff she doesn't want to share. And that's fine. Agnes doesn't blame her. In fact, she likes her more for it.

But that doesn't mean she's entitled to all of Agnes's secrets, when she's shared nothing of herself.

"Lilja's lonely," Agnes says carefully. "Sometimes you need a friend to talk to. I think I gave that to her."

"Why not hand it over to the police? Did she say?"

"She's dug herself into a hole," Agnes says. "She lied to the police, before she knew it was serious. The night of the party, Ása pushed her away. It sounds like she'd been pushing her away for weeks. Lilja was hurt. She thought Ása was with her boyfriend. She kept her friend's secrets, and then, when she realized what was going on, she couldn't figure out a way to tell the police the truth, not without looking even more suspicious. Sometimes, you lie for stupid reasons, and then it gets out of your control. It becomes bigger than you, you know?"

Nora rotates the phone in her hands. Examines every smooth edge. "There are a lot of reasons to lie." She comes to standing. "Okay," she says. "I have to think about this. Thanks."

"What are you going to do?"

"Think," Nora tells her. "And make us some dinner." She stows the phone in her bedroom, somewhere hidden now, not in the pile of papers that Agnes has riffled through. Nora returns to the kitchen, heading straight for the alcohol. She pours Agnes a generous glass of wine and a healthy dose of gin for herself, before she starts to cook.

Nora taps her glass against Agnes's. "It's nice to have a partner in crime. You're better than Hildur—who, by the way, is *desperate* to talk to you. I told her we'll arrange something, but she's probably just going to show up soon, if we don't arrange a time for you two to talk."

"Maybe I don't want to talk to her."

Nora ignores this and throws herself into preparing their risotto. The smell of food still turns Agnes's stomach, so she focuses on her wine. By the time Nora's doling out their portions, they've both blown past tipsy to something close to drunk. It's still early, but the sun had vanished from the sky hours ago, leaving them in complete and total darkness. Nora has set the lights low to make the fire in the center of the room the brightest source of light.

She joins Agnes at the cluttered dining table with a sigh. "So you hate Hildur, is what I've gathered. Any particular reason why, other than some bluntness?"

"You don't like her, either," Agnes says. "Be honest."

Nora barks out a laugh. "Am I that obvious?" She sips her drink. "It's not that I don't like her. She's been so helpful, getting me in the right rooms, making introductions. She's everything you'd hope for, in a situation like this."

"But . . ." Agnes prompts.

"But for every reason she's great, she's a hindrance. She helped act as a bridge at the beginning, but now she's a reminder of the town to everyone we speak to. People here are so connected. They know each other in so many ways that you and I can't even fathom. Hildur's an authority figure to Óskar and Lilja, she and Thor went to school together, I'm sure they all know each other's parents and cousins and they've all seen everything there is to see of each other. Sometimes, this kind of connection helps establish a sense of ease in an interview. But most of the time, she's like a fact-checker. Part of the reason why people share so much with me is because I'm an outsider. I don't have a bias. They can editorialize and narrate their own lives however it suits them, and it doesn't matter because I'm a traveling circus. Their sins leave with me."

"But their sins are recorded," Agnes says. "And then you release them on a very popular podcast."

Nora tops up their drinks. "Does that bother you?"

"Would you understand if it did?"

"Yes and no. It's your life." Nora swallows down more gin than risotto. Agnes has hardly touched her own plate. "It's your family. You've got an uphill battle, because clearly your father does *not* want me to do this. And he has good reason, of course he does. So it's tough on a personal level, I get that. But in the grander view, it's not as though you'll be persecuted. You're in the sweet spot. You're so connected, but you aren't. And, frankly, you're not really telling me any sins, are you?" In the dim light, Nora's pink frames seem to glow in the dark. "Unless there's something you're not telling me."

Agnes rubs at her bottom lip, feeling the raw, chapped skin. She hadn't wanted to tell Nora what she's learned. What she's suspected. But the words spill out of her now, almost against her will.

"What if," she says, unaware of the tremor in her voice, "I learned something today? What if I—What if he—" She falters.

There's a hand covering hers on the table. "Take a deep breath," Nora instructs her. "What is your biggest fear, in all this? It's not the public's reaction to my podcast, or you wouldn't be here at all. It's something else."

"You know what it is," Agnes says.

"It helps if you say it. I don't like guessing."

"If you—" Agnes begins, stumbling over the words. She steadies herself with another sip of wine. She forces herself to say it all: "If we keep going down this road, Nora, I think we're going to find out that my grandfather was a killer. And that's unbearable."

Nora tightens her grip on Agnes's hand. "What did you learn today? What's changed your mind like this?"

It requires so much effort to explain. Agnes hears herself telling Nora everything about her time with Júlía, as though she were talking about someone separate from her. An acquaintance who learned about Marie's possible affair with Thor Senior and passed it along to Agnes.

"What would you say, then?" Agnes asks Nora. "Einar found out his wife was sleeping with another man. His neighbor. His cousin, or whatever. What would you say happened?"

Nora pushes herself to standing and makes her way to Agnes, quickly. She wraps her up in an awkward hug.

Agnes pushes her away, and not gently. "What then?" she asks. "What about this affair? What happens when you put all the pieces together, everything that Júlía told me? He and Marie are arguing all the time, he hates the baby, then one day they're both killed. Maybe he finds out his wife has been sleeping with the neighbor, the neighbor who he also hates, and maybe he thinks the child isn't his, and then—What, then?"

"I'd say," Nora says, returning to her seat, "that I need to talk to Thor Senior."

This pulls Agnes up short. "What?"

"Thor Junior said his father left," Nora says. "Not that he died. I'll find him, and I'll talk to him. That's how this job works, Agnes. You follow the threads. You don't find one and say it's all over, that explains everything. Not until you reach the end of it all."

"Don't you realize," Agnes says, speaking through a lump of unshed tears, "that if you do this, if we keep following this thread, you're taking away the one person who loved me?"

"Then you get to join the club," Nora says, her voice unbelievably tired. "I've been a member of it since I was ten." The shadow of a smile, humorless and grim, passes over her face. "Don't look so confused.

"I don't talk about it," Nora says, "so I can't really blame you for not knowing, but I wonder how you can spend all this time with me and think that I have no idea what you're going through. I grew up with an older sister. I told you about her. I worshipped her. It was just us and our mom, who had to work all the time to keep us alive, so I spent more time with Chloe than I did with my own mother. For the first ten years of my life, Chloe was my mother, my sister, my whole world. And then she disappeared."

Now Agnes is the one reaching out to grab Nora's hand. It remains limp in her grip.

"Chloe dropped me off at school," Nora continues. "It was on the way to her high school. She went to her morning classes, and then she left at lunch. She didn't tell anyone where she was going. They never found her. Not even a trace of where she went, after she left the school grounds. I don't know . . . if she's alive. If something terrible happened to her. But that's what I have to think. Something terrible happened to her.

"A man happened to her.

"I went to school to become a public defender. I was one, for a while. Then my divorce happened, and I was alone again. And I couldn't stop thinking about Chloe. I started this podcast as a way to help the families of missing girls. So no one has to go through the torture of not knowing. So you have to believe me when I say I know what you're going through. But you need to recognize just how lucky you are."

"Lucky," Agnes echoes, stunned. "Lucky for *what?*"

"You know where they are," Nora says. "And the world knows who they are. There are books about your family. Theories. Songs. No one's written anything for my sister. I know you're afraid of finding out your grandfather was a killer. But you had twenty-six years with him, twenty-six years of him loving you. Twenty-six years of ignorance. You're so lucky, and you don't even realize it."

Nora doesn't give Agnes any room to respond. "I'm going to regret saying all this in the morning," she says with a sigh. "But I'm driving down to Reykjavík tomorrow. If you still want to join me, then great. I'll be up at seven. If not, I understand." Without waiting for an answer, she takes her glass and the bottle of gin, and leaves the room.

Agnes lets Nora go, feeling a deep sense of loss. How sad it is, she thinks, to compare personal tragedies and to lose.

CHAPTER THIRTY-ONE

February 8, 2019

Agnes listens for Nora's shower to come on. Then she's up and out the front door. She stumbles through the snow and then she's in the rental car, cranking the heat and watching the windshield fog over. She checks her phone, its signal straining to reach the Wi-Fi. By the time the whiteness clears, she knows where she's going. She nudges the car out of the snowbank, along the tight circle of the driveway, and then she's following the headlights through the tunnel of trees.

She wipes her eyes. There's no moisture there, but she can't seem to bring anything into focus. It doesn't matter, though. The road is empty. She might as well be the last person on earth.

When she reaches the slick pavement of the highway, she flattens her foot on the accelerator, savoring the sense of freedom, of losing control, of moving beyond the point of thought. Where there is only survival.

In a matter of seconds, there's the turnoff to town. She steers the car over, through the small streets. She parks in front of Ása's building and imagines Ása there, drunk and hurt and lonely, an echo of her now. Agnes has never had any trouble understanding a suicide, has never quite believed it when someone said, *I don't know why they would do that.* It's a miracle when someone reaches the edge and doesn't jump. It's a feat of untold strength. The edge is the call of something wild and free and dark and promising. There is nothing inhuman, nothing mystical about following it.

She wishes she could have met Ása. Wishes she could have helped her. She could have told her that no matter how promising the edge is, how satisfying it is to answer its call, there's nothing, too. She's sorry the woman chose to do it, chose to go, and that it happened when she was alone.

Agnes counts the buildings down the deserted street. There are lights in the windows, warm, glowing lives, but no one is outside at this hour, in this cold. Only Agnes, stalking the slippery pavement, searching for the correct building and then, when she finds it, the right apartment number. She buzzes. The door unlocks, fast, as though she'd unlocked it herself.

She doesn't have to climb any stairs. The apartment is on the ground floor. The door opens for her before she even steps inside the hallway.

CHAPTER THIRTY-TWO

February 8, 2019

Lilja looks like she's been crying.

"Are you okay?" Agnes asks.

Lilja's place is so much smaller than Ása's, but far cozier. There are stacks of books along the walls, an enormous desk that's piled high with legal textbooks and art supplies. The bed, covered in a haphazard pile of pillows and quilts, is in the farthest corner of the room.

"I don't know," Lilja says. "No. Do you want something to drink?"

"No."

There's a beat of silence. The black eyes snap to hers. Beseeching and understanding, all at once. Agnes savors the moment, the pause before the leap.

"Can I kiss you?" she asks.

Lilja's there. Agnes can feel her breath on her cheek. Then there's nothing but the nearly unbearable heat of Lilja's mouth on her own, the tightness of her arms on her back, her head. It's a lifetime of pleasure, and yet not enough. She comes up for air and realizes Lilja's brought them to the bed, their bodies teetering over the edge. Then there's the weight, the blessed weight, of Lilja pressing her down to the mattress.

Lilja unbuckles Agnes's jeans, and time shudders to a stop. There's a hand on Agnes's bare thigh. Another on the denim, dragging the material down, revealing her skin to the air.

Revealing her scars.

She freezes.

"What's wrong?" Lilja asks. She leans back, her hands sliding away.

It gives Agnes one brief, final glimpse of the room around her. The art supplies, the pile of legal textbooks. There's the woman with the short hair and black eyes. The woman who needs Agnes just as much as Agnes needs her. This is the moment when she must decide if she will show Lilja her new body. The room around her is unfamiliar, the woman straddling her legs a stranger who will never know what she looked like before. This version of Agnes, broken and taped back together, is all that Lilja will know of her. She's nowhere near to home, nowhere near to the woman she once was.

"I have scars," she tells Lilja, "on my left leg. It's my first time—since."

Lilja runs a hand down the length of her leg. It sends a shiver through Agnes. "Do you want to stop?"

"No," Agnes says. She lifts her hips, helping Lilja to pull her jeans all the way off. She feels the goose bumps puckering the exposed skin. Let Lilja see. Let her know. Let Agnes be new. "I want more."

CHAPTER THIRTY-THREE

February 8, 2019

Lilja's head is on her shoulder, and Agnes thinks the weight of it is the only thing keeping her pinned to the earth. She smooths her palm over Lilja's bare back, enjoying the silky texture of her skin. Lilja's talking about a graphic novel she's working on. It's the only thing, other than Ása, that's helped her remain sane during her studies.

"What's it about?" Agnes asks. She can't imagine Lilja as a lawyer, can only picture her now hunched over that desk, drawing, bringing new worlds to life.

"I'm not really a writer," Lilja says. "I've been sketching out images, things I want to include. You're going to laugh at me, but it's mostly about trolls."

"Trolls?" Agnes asks. "Like the kind that live under a bridge?"

"No," Lilja says. "The ones in our legends. They say the trolls lived in total darkness and turned to stone in sunlight. I like the idea of this entire landscape, all these black rocks, being trolls. Living things, sleeping like they're under a fairy-tale spell. There are other, less fun stories of them getting drunk and stealing bad children, but I'm not drawing that."

"So these beautiful fields," Agnes says, "this entire island, basically, is just a troll graveyard."

"Basically."

"Why would I laugh at that?" Agnes asks. "It's lovely. What's the story?"

She feels Lilja's sigh at the base of her spine. "That's as far as I've gotten. I want to write about one specific troll. The *last* troll. She tends to all the others, cultivating their moss, making sure they're all still there. She's trying to find a way to bring them back, is what I'm thinking. But there are volcanos here, you know, the shifting magma. She's lonely, like me."

Agnes pulls Lilja in tighter. "What does she do, when she realizes they're turning into magma?"

"She's going to leave."

"Do you want to leave?"

"No," Lilja says. "I don't know. I want to move to Reykjavík. I don't want to be here any longer than I have to." Restless, she rolls away from Agnes, stretching and finding a new position in the sheets. "Ása wanted to leave, too. Sometimes I can tell myself she's just in the city, living with her boyfriend and forgetting us."

"Is that possible?" It's a nice thought.

"No. She's on the news. Her face is everywhere. She wouldn't be able to hide long."

Agnes says, "I'm going to the city tomorrow. Nora wants to see Óskar's show. Will you be there?"

Lilja turns back to her. "I wasn't going to go." The soft gaze, hovering somewhere above Agnes's cheek. "Maybe I will, if you'll be there."

Agnes reaches for her. Outside of this room is Nora Carver and her grandfather's sordid history and every other responsibility waiting to crush her. Right now, in this bed, with this woman, she feels quiet. At peace.

CHAPTER THIRTY-FOUR

February 9, 2019

Agnes makes the drive back early in the morning, when Lilja is still asleep and when Nora is hopefully still asleep, too. She's bleary-eyed and hungover, but happy. She sneaks in the front door and manages to shower before she hears Nora calling for her, her voice booming against the concrete and glass walls.

"The road keeps closing," Nora's saying. "It's open now, so we have to hurry."

Agnes drags her suitcase to the truck, behind Nora. Apparently they'll be staying in Reykjavík, too, after they watch Óskar's show. Nora's booked them both hotel rooms. Agnes hasn't had time to pick and choose what to bring with her to Reykjavík, so she's just bringing everything. It's not much, anyway.

When they reach the highway, Nora finally asks, "Are we okay?"

You're so lucky, and you don't even realize it.

Agnes tells Nora yes, because they are.

"No," Nora insists. "I mean it. Are we good? I can be a mean drunk sometimes—a gift from my mother—and I don't want that to affect our relationship."

"Nora," Agnes says, feeling generous because she's spent the evening with Lilja, because she feels closer, too, to her, now that she knows about her sister, "we're good."

"Okay," Nora says, clearly relieved. "Because I have a surprise for you. I found Thor Senior. He lives in a nursing home in a suburb outside of Reykjavík. We can talk to him on our way in."

"Did you get his son's permission?"

"He's not Hannibal Lecter. He's living in a low-care senior facility. He can have visitors."

The drive into Reykjavík is a blur. Agnes disappears at first into the ragged drops of volcanic rock falling into the gray sea, but then she disappears into sleep, head nodding with the rhythms of the road. She wakes when Nora guides them off the highway. Agnes catches a view of Reykjavík, of the storybook buildings, before they turn completely away. Here, though, there's actual sunshine. A brief wash of blue in the sky, surrounded by a threatening ring of dark clouds. Nora navigates them to something that looks like the university campus back at Bifröst. There are long, squat buildings, all done in the same modern style, white stucco paint and black window trim.

Nora, carrying her recording equipment, leads them to one of the wings. "From what I can tell, this should be our building."

In the lobby, there's a single security guard before the elevator bank. Nora introduces herself. The man makes a call up to Thor Senior's room. They receive their instructions: second floor, room 201. Upstairs, there's a nurse's station at one end of the hall, but the facility could otherwise be any normal apartment building.

Nora knocks on 201, shooting Agnes a half smile. "Ready?" she asks in a whisper.

There's no time to answer. The man was waiting for them, evidently, because the door jerks open instantly after Nora's knock. Thor Senior is a large man, taken down to reasonable height by time. Great shoulders, wide and square like a linebacker's, curl inward. The lantern jaw, sagging, and the hard glitter in the eyes so like his son's speak of a man handsome not from aesthetics but sheer force of will.

"Hello, sir," Nora says, and Agnes wonders if she's even aware of calling the man "sir," or if that just came naturally, because he very much is a "sir." "My name's Nora Carver, and I am the host of—"

"Come in," Thor Senior interrupts her. He shuffles back and swings one long crooked arm into the room. "It's impolite to talk in doorways."

They file in, quickly and obediently. Agnes smells the man's early lunch on his breath when she passes him, and it's pungent, a mixture of blue cheese and fish. He shuts the door behind them and leads the way to his sitting room. The apartment is hardly larger than Lilja's studio. Thor reclaims his reclining chair by a window overlooking the parking lot and he indicates for them to take the narrow couch.

"As I was saying," Nora begins, "I am the host of a show that researches and documents cold cases. I'm here in Iceland to cover a case that you might remember. I was hoping to talk to you about it, for my show."

Thor Senior has no patience for explanations. He's holding a release form he's been asked to review and sign, and while Nora explains all his options for participation, he isn't looking at the form. He's looking at Nora. Memorizing every detail of the woman's compact body. It doesn't seem as though it matters what Nora's saying—though, Agnes notes, Nora's purposefully avoiding mentioning Marie, Einar, or even Bifröst.

Nora's also neglected to introduce Agnes, calling her "my associate," and nothing more. As in, "My associate here is just going to observe, if that's all right with you." When Thor Senior can tear his gaze away from Nora, he frowns at Agnes. Confused, like he can't quite place her. She doesn't shy away from him, but she doesn't announce herself, either. She's decided, very quickly, she doesn't like the old man, doesn't appreciate the way he looks at Nora. And besides, this is Nora's show. Let her use Agnes's identity when she deems it necessary.

Nora hands Thor Senior a pen.

"I will tell you whatever you want," he says, a grin creasing his cheeks. He scrawls a tight signature at the bottom of the release form and hands it back, eyes traveling over Nora's wild hair, the neon-pink glasses, the red lips. "Ask me whatever you wish, my dear."

Agnes flinches at the term of endearment, but Nora is unflappable as ever. In fact, if Agnes had to guess, she'd say Nora is hamming it up for the man. She's taking extra care in setting up the microphone, smiling wide and bright, asking Thor Senior if he's comfortable. While Nora prepares the scene, Agnes melts into the background, choosing a seat far from the camcorder. In a way, she's surprised he doesn't recognize her, but perhaps that's a relief. She's had enough. This, right here, is almost too much for her.

Nora dives right in. "First," she says, "can you tell me about yourself? Where did you live, before you came here? What brought you here?"

"I am here," Thor Senior says, thunderclouds gathering on his great forehead, "because my son put me here. I was born in Bifröst, in the house where my mother was born, where her father was born. That was *my home*. Do you understand what that means? I am meant to die there, too. But my son convinced a doctor to declare me unwell, so here I am."

"A horrible lie," Nora says to Thor Senior, "right? If you don't mind me saying so, you seem more than capable of taking care of yourself."

This earns her another lecherous grin. Agnes marvels at Nora's bravery. Waltzing into a stranger's home without even a moment's hesitation. Thor Senior, though old, is certainly not feeble. And he's volatile. Because the pleasure vanishes quickly, to be replaced once more with gathering fury. "I am healthy," he insists. "My son brought me here to die in a chicken coop."

"Why?"

"He's greedy. He wants the home to himself."

"I imagine that the land is worth a lot of money."

"Yes." Thor's effusion shutters, an instinctive closing of the ranks. Just because it's no longer his doesn't mean anyone else can have it.

"So you wouldn't say you're close with your son," Nora says.

"Not close," Thor Senior scoffs. "I should have drowned him like a kitten in a river. I would have, if we had had any more."

Nora doesn't falter. "Why do you say that?"

"He is not a good man."

Agnes spares a moment's pity for Thor Junior, for having this man as his father. She would have left home as soon as she could, too.

"A good man protects his family," Thor Senior continues. "He doesn't take from his family, or his neighbors. He doesn't break windows. He doesn't steal his neighbors' jewelry. My wife left, because of that boy. He took everything from me. My wife, my home, my history. I am left with nothing but my own death in an anonymous hellhole."

He leaves them in a stunned silence. Agnes is struck, yet again, by the ease with which someone will spill their secrets with strangers. Thor Senior's never met Nora before, he doesn't even know why she's interviewing him, but he's venting out years of private anger and frustration as though she were a therapist. A trusted friend. Is he that desperate to be heard? Or is this, to him, not private? Something worth sharing, as loud as he possibly can?

She supposes, though, she's shared, too. With Lilja. With Nora. With Ingvar, even.

"When did your wife leave you?" Nora asks Thor Senior.

"In 1977."

Two years before the murders.

"Was your son a problem for the entire town?"

"No," Thor Senior says, bristling. "We keep our business to ourselves."

"It's been my experience that in small towns, it's next to impossible to keep secrets."

"There were no problems."

"What about the neighbor's jewelry? You said he took it? Surely they had to notice that."

"He stole the earrings out of her house. He put them back the same way. She never knew." There's an unconscious flex of the man's hand. "I made sure."

"Which neighbor was this? Marie or Júlia?"

"Marie."

"How much," Nora says, "did you know about your neighbors?"

"I knew only what they wished me to know."

"Were you close with them?"

"We knew to say hello," Thor says, unbothered.

"I have to confess," Nora says, "I did some digging. My research shows that you and Einar, your neighbor, were related. There was some argument over the land. Can you tell me more about that?"

"There was no argument."

Nora acts surprised. "Are you sure? I've heard—"

"There was no argument." Thor is firm. "The land was split. I wanted to buy it. Páll said no. That is not an argument. Páll wanted to provide for his family, so he didn't sell."

"Páll? Einar's father?"

"Yes."

"Tell me more about him."

The creases in the old man's skin deepen. "He was a good man. When I was young, I pitied him for his son. Einar left. And now I am the same as Páll. I will die alone, like him. But it is worse, because my son isn't patient. He isn't waiting for me to die to claim his inheritance. He took without waiting."

"Einar came back after his father's death with a young Danish bride. Marie. Tell me more about them."

The question finally comes. "Why are you here? What are you wanting?"

"I'm researching the 1979 murders of your neighbors, Marie and her child, Agnes." Nora tells him everything. About her podcast, her work on the Lopez case, her time spent in Bifröst. When she finishes her introductions, she doesn't continue with her line of questioning. She holds the man's gaze. Expectant.

Thor Senior says, finally, "Einar killed them. What more is there to say?"

"I'm just not understanding why everyone is so certain," Nora says. "He was never formally charged with the murders. Nor is there any evidence, as it stands, that points to him. But no one else was treated like a suspect. Once Einar and his son left for America, the investigation seemed to stall out. As someone who does a lot of research into cold cases, I find that conclusion worrying. Don't you?"

Thor Senior doesn't seem to register this as an actual question.

"If that were my cousin," Nora continues, "or even my neighbor, I wouldn't be happy with a rumor. I would want to know what happened to them."

"I can't help you," he tells her. "I'm not God. I only know my life."

"You don't need to be God," she assures him. "You just need to tell me about them. I wasn't there. I can only go off photographs, records, and memories. Memories are the most precious."

Thor Senior considers Nora carefully, no longer lecherous, but hard. Intimidating. Nora waits, placidly. With a hearty sniff, he says, "Einar thought he was better than Bifröst, because he went to Copenhagen. I do not mind. But he comes to me after murdering his wife and child and he asks me for money. He was *spoiled*."

"He came to you to sell his property," Nora says, "right? You accepted in the end, and you bought the property. That valuable land. You got what you wanted."

There's a ghost of a smile. "Yes."

"Tell me about his Danish wife. Marie."

"She was a silly girl," he says.

"Everyone I have spoken with has said that Marie was a beautiful woman. Charming. Everyone was halfway in love with her, from all accounts."

"Is there a question?"

"Were you in love with her? Did you find her beautiful?"

"I don't fall in love with every beautiful woman with long legs," Thor says. He leers at Nora. "Some exceptions can be made, of course. But I noticed she was beautiful, yes. She wanted everyone to notice, so I noticed."

"Did she and Einar have a happy marriage?"

"I don't know." The same exasperation. *I'm not God. I only know my life.*

"Was she faithful to her husband?"

"I don't know," Thor says, "but it wouldn't surprise me if she wasn't."

"Why do you say that?"

He doesn't answer.

"I'm asking," Nora says, "because I happen to agree with you. It wouldn't shock me to learn that she'd been having an affair. From everything that I've gathered, Marie may have been taking time to herself, away from her children, away from her husband. She was a young, beautiful woman, alone in the countryside, far away from her own home. I've heard comments about her accent, her adjustment to the language. In moments of stress and isolation, we search for an outlet for relief. Some people choose to devote themselves to their work, like Einar, and some people choose to find happiness in someone else. She needed someone. You were right there. Alone, just like her. You were a young man, forty-nine. I've seen the photos. You looked like a movie star."

The flattery doesn't affect Thor. The only indication that he's even listening is the way his eyes follow Nora's body when she leans in close to him.

"I've spoken to your neighbors," she tells him. "Your life wasn't as secret as you thought."

"I have nothing to hide."

"It isn't hidden," Nora says. "It's right there. Out in the open. If one person knows, everyone knows. You were having an affair with Marie."

"Who told you?"

"Júlía," Nora says, easily. "She was Marie's confidante. She warned her not to get involved with you. But she did. You did. Didn't you?"

Thor holds up a hand. "I am finished."

For one brief, wild moment, Agnes misinterprets the meaning of his words. That he's confessing, like a cowboy in a spaghetti western— *You caught me, I'm done for.* But then the anger follows, and his meaning becomes clear.

"Go," he says. "I do not speak to liars."

"I'm not lying," Nora insists. "I'm relaying what I've heard. What other people have told me. I'm not accusing you of murder. What I am asking you now, though, is why this didn't come up at all during the investigation. Even just as a motive for Einar's actions. A controlling husband catching his beloved wife in an affair, it's understandable—"

"You will not accuse me," Thor says, his voice rising to fill the room, to drown them in it. "I have spoken with the police. They have heard my story. My neighbor slaughtered his wife and his child, like animals. There is no *why*. There is no affair. There is only the dead."

CHAPTER THIRTY-FIVE

February 9, 2019

The hotel Nora has chosen for them is on the main street in downtown Reykjavík, just a few blocks away from where Agnes bought her jacket and boots. She's gotten them adjoining rooms and left the door connecting them open. Nora perches on the edge of her bed, scribbling away in her notebook. Agnes leans against the wall in Nora's room and tries to pretend, for the moment, that she's not about to scratch her way out of her skin.

Nora's speaking, but Agnes hasn't heard her.

"I'm sorry," Agnes says. "What?"

"I said you can take the night off if you want to," Nora tells her, concern etched into the lines of her face. "Óskar's band is playing at ten, at that whisky bar two doors down. I'll be there. But feel free to do your own thing tonight. Rest. It's been a lot of—well, just, a lot. I'd love to share a drink with you tonight, to commemorate the anniversary, but I understand if you'd prefer to do something on your own."

Agnes pushes away from the wall, checking the date on her phone. "It's the ninth."

"Forty years ago today," Nora says, "your grandmother and aunt were reported missing. If you don't make it to the show, let's meet back here in the morning. We have to talk to Thor Senior again, before we head back up to Bifröst."

"Do you really think he'll talk to you again?" Agnes asks, her lips cracking at the edges. When was the last time she had a sip of water? "He shouted at you."

Nora laughs. "I've gotten worse before, believe me. And I have to try. He's holding something back. I can taste it."

And there it is. The reason why Agnes wants to run. Wants to leap from a high spot, wants to feel the fear and the adrenaline overtake her, obliterate the last bit of sanity she has left, until she's nothing.

"This is the proof you were looking for," she hears herself say. "Einar killed his wife because she was having an affair."

Nora shakes her head. "That's a huge intuitive leap. I'm just following a thread."

"It makes sense," Agnes insists. Because it does. It's a complete picture. Marie, a young mother, in a small town, isolated in that house, taken away from her home, her language. Left alone for long stretches, and there's her handsome neighbor, the one who makes her feel not like a mother, not like a wife, but a beautiful woman with long legs.

And there's Einar. The possessive husband who once told another neighbor that he wants nothing in this life except his work and her. He finds out. Of course he does. How could Thor and Marie hide? The emptiness of the land seduces you into believing that you are alone, you are anonymous, when in fact it only makes you that much more exposed.

Einar finds out and he, the man who expects everyone to follow his lead, starts to wonder—How long has it been going on? Is this child, the one that screams at night, the one that is so different from Magnús, even his? Then the rage. Quickly followed by regret.

Agnes's father had known. And he'd let her get close to Einar. Let her love him. Let Einar raise her.

I had to trust him, Agnes, because he was all I had left.

"You're making enormous leaps," she hears Nora say. "Thor's acting like he has something to hide, but it could be something entirely different. People *lie.* They do it all the time. They withhold or they exaggerate. It's really easy to shape someone's testimony into whatever narrative you want. Your brain wants to impose a pattern onto everything. That doesn't mean that that's the only interpretation. We're going to talk to him again, and I will probably tell him who you are, so he can remember Marie as she was when he knew her. Which is a lot, again, but please, take a breath. All we've gotten out of this is a confirmation that Thor held some sort of financial power over Einar—I'm assuming he paid Einar a pittance for the land—and that he *may* have had a relationship with Marie. I overplayed my hand. I wanted to get his reaction. It came out wonky. That's it. Okay?"

Agnes nods. She wants to believe Nora, and a small, rational part of her mind agrees with her. More than that, though, she wants to leave. Now.

She stops in the lobby, just long enough to check her phone on the Wi-Fi. There are texts from Lilja.

I'm in Reykjavík. I missed you.

Lilja's sent Agnes another address. Where she's staying.

Agnes sends a quick text back. Then she's outside, in the fresh air, disappearing into the crowds.

CHAPTER THIRTY-SIX

February 9, 2019

They're standing in front of a frozen pond. It came out of nowhere. Lilja's been leading Agnes through the city, pointing out different shops and points of interest along the main street and they followed it down, down, down with the flow of the foot traffic, until suddenly they reached an open space. The air is brisk, the sky dark. Lilja's fingers are laced through hers. Agnes keeps stealing looks at Lilja and finds her doing the same.

The city echoes with shouts of laughter and many overlapping babbling voices. Couples beckoning to each other. They're walking on the frozen water, farther and farther out, their footsteps light on the ice. Agnes watches a child racing into the exact center of the pond. Her heart crawls into her throat, picturing the sudden drop. Imagining she can hear the screams as they all fall into the frigid water.

But the screams are victorious, mischievous. They're all having fun.

"Do you want to try it?" Lilja asks her.

They choose a spot with heavy foot traffic, where the ice has been proven to be able to support the weight of an adult woman's body.

Under Lilja's guidance, Agnes slides one foot forward, then another. There's no noticeable difference that she can tell, through the soles of her boots, from the solid earth to the solid water. She grips Lilja's hand tighter, feels the returning squeeze as though it were a blessing. Agnes should be used to this. The shock that life goes on, that miracles are not found in otherworldly feats but in moments of connection. She's walking on water. She used to do this on her board, with her grandfather. Now she's doing it on borrowed legs, with Lilja.

Lilja pulls her farther out, to the center of the pond. They hold each other and stare out at the city lights surrounding them. Lilja tells Agnes where she hopes to live, one day, when she moves here, and Agnes can see it all so clearly. Lilja will find another room to sleep in, another room to fill with more art supplies and legal textbooks and another woman to share it all with.

They find a restaurant nearby for dinner, then a bar for drinks. They wait out the night, both reluctant to reenter the world. They don't talk about Ása or the past. They talk only of themselves. Agnes doesn't feel like the granddaughter of an infamous murderer, and she doesn't feel like a series of broken ligaments and hearts, either.

"I should go," Lilja says, finally, her head in her hands. "Óskar's holding an after-party. He says it's a tribute to Ása. I should be there."

Agnes leaves with her. The city glows with leftover Christmas decorations, the streetlamps radiating bubbles of light every few feet, and Agnes can't help but think of bog lights, the supernatural lanterns that would lead travelers farther into the muck, to a horrible wet death. She tries to shake away the ominous feeling, the self-pity, now that her day with Lilja, alone, is over, now that they're walking back into reality, but it's too powerful.

She sneaks another glance at Lilja. The light washes over her face, hollowing her broad cheeks and dyeing her skin a lurid orange. Agnes should be sick of her by now. But she isn't. She wants more time with her.

The bonfire is easy to find, once they reach the beach. Against the backdrop of the black water, lined in the middle distance with the street-lights of faraway roads and buildings, the massive bucket of flames sears Agnes's retinas. Lilja nods hello to a few of the stragglers. She presses close to Agnes, diving upward to kiss her cheek and to whisper in her ear, "I have to talk to Óskar." Then she's hurrying ahead.

Agnes heads straight to the flames.

She scans the faces of those around her, but she can't find Nora. Nora must be here, right? Agnes worries she didn't get the invitation, yet again, to the party. Then she reaches the bonfire, and she's distracted by the warmth.

There, on the other side of the flames, stands Óskar. He's different this evening, looser. Lilja's beside him, arms wrapped around herself again, like she's holding herself together, but barely. Agnes can only make out the tone of their voices. Lilja, low and gentle compared with Óskar's hoarse bites. Óskar leans into Lilja's space, speaking into her ear, almost into her mouth.

Jealousy kindles somewhere deep in Agnes's bones. She has no logi-cal right to it. She's wandered into someone else's life, with no intention of staying long. But it's there, building, and there's no talking herself out of it.

She starts at the touch on her shoulder.

Behind her, finally, is Nora. "Got a minute?"

"Now?"

In answer, Nora points a gloved thumb in the direction of the city, away from the group, away from the warmth of the flames. Agnes com-plies, stumbling behind Nora's nimble footsteps. They stop when they can only hear the vibrations of the group's many jumbled conversa-tions. Nora waits for Agnes to catch up, turning her body at an angle so Agnes can only see the profile of her face. The glint of the neon-pink glasses.

"What's going on?" Agnes asks.

"This is a delicate question," Nora says, "but I have no time to be delicate."

Nora looks to Agnes significantly, as though expecting Agnes to speak up. Agnes has no idea what she's talking about.

"What's going on with you and Lilja?" Nora asks.

Immediately embarrassed and immediately defensive, Agnes counters, "What does it matter to you?"

Nora tilts her chin upward, the realization dawning on her physically. "You're sleeping with her."

"How is that any of your business?"

Nora barks out a harsh laugh. "Are you kidding? This isn't just some random person off the street. This is someone deeply, deeply connected to what I'm researching. Of course it's my business. Of course it's my place to ask. And of course you shouldn't be sleeping with her. Jesus, Agnes, you *just met*—"

"No," Agnes says, temper flaring, hot and fast, "this isn't any of your business. You have no right to tell me who I can or cannot see. You've said it yourself. You aren't a detective. You aren't even a journalist. You're just asking questions. You have zero say in who I talk to."

Hands grab Agnes's shoulders, hard enough to hurt. There's a single, tough shake. "Agnes," Nora says. "Listen to me. I'm not—"

"Don't touch me." Agnes pushes her away. "Please don't put your hands on me when you're calling me a whore."

"Okay." Nora runs a hand through her wild hair, regaining her composure. "I'm going about this all wrong," she says. "I'm not slut-shaming you, Agnes, and I'm not trying to dictate who you can or cannot sleep with. It's just—Lilja is *so close* to this. Don't you get that? Don't you see her, right there, with Óskar? She had Ása's phone. She gave you her phone! She lied to the police. How do you know she isn't lying to you? I'm not a detective, no, but if I were, those two would be my primary suspects. I'm sorry you think I'm being high-handed here, but I think it's within my rights to *mention* that."

"Why?" Agnes asks.

"Why what?"

"Why do you have to mention it? Because you're concerned for me? Or because you want to know if Lilja's told me anything more about Ása?"

This catches Nora by surprise. Frustration gives way to humor. "If I say 'both,' will that offend you?"

"You're ridiculous," Agnes says, but she feels her own anger draining away. She sighs. "She didn't say anything you don't already know. Ása was unhappy. Okay?"

"Sleeping with Lilja crosses a line, Agnes."

"For you it would. But you've made it clear that I'm not part of the show, not in that capacity. I'm just me. I'm entitled to sleep with whoever I want."

Nora puts her back to Agnes, puts her back to the entire crowd. She's staring out into the glowing city. Agnes would like to cave, to smooth things over, to protect the fragile bud of friendship that has been growing between them.

But she doesn't.

"All right," Nora says, turning to face Agnes again. "I *am* sorry. For this and for my outburst last night. I'm not this way with many other people, believe it or not. I think sometimes you remind me of my sister. Chloe. Not the way you look, but the way you hold yourself. Chloe couldn't connect very easily with other people. She used to tell me she was a freak because she could only understand me. It was like everyone else was speaking another language, and only I could speak English . . . Sometimes, when I look at you, I see her. And that makes me . . ." She casts about for the right words. She finds only "this." Then: "We're okay, right?"

Agnes says, "We are," but wonders, truly, if they are. Since when did she become a Rorschach test? How many people have projected the image of her grandmother onto her these past few days? And now

Nora's sister? Since when did she become something that *happens* to people?

"I like Lilja," Agnes tells Nora. "You don't get to take her away from me."

Nora's opening her mouth to answer when a tremendous yell cuts through the air. It silences all conversations as completely as a gunshot. It's Óskar, body slanted like a boomerang, arm raised in a salute. The bonfire's glow flickers over him, lighting his red hair into a blaze. He lifts his rough, tired voice to cover the beach as he rattles off a long monologue in Icelandic. Even from a distance, Agnes is shocked by the force of emotion in his voice, his features. It contorts him, the rage and the adrenaline and the sorrow, into something other than human. He stops, suddenly, choking on his last words.

He takes a moment to collect himself.

"Ása," he says finally. He repeats the name like an incantation. Raises his drink again into the night air. "Our Ása."

CHAPTER THIRTY-SEVEN

February 10, 2019

Nora eases the truck into the senior center's parking lot. Even the weather feels hungover. The morning sky is a steely, uniform gray, with no hint of yesterday's sun. Dark rings line Nora's eyes, but she otherwise appears alert. Caffeinated and ready to start in again on Thor Senior.

"We'll stop for more coffee," Nora tells Agnes, who isn't nearly as alert, "when we leave here, okay? I've invited Thor Junior to dinner tonight. I want to compare and contrast father and son."

Agnes agrees. Her tongue feels like something dead and rotting in her mouth. At the bonfire, Lilja had told Agnes that she had to stay with Óskar. *It's easier this way*, she'd said. *We have to talk.* In the moment, Agnes hadn't argued. It hadn't felt like her place to ask for more. But Agnes only has so many nights here, and this is one less now. She'd spent most of the night in her hotel bed, awake, overloaded with spiraling thoughts, about Einar, Lilja, Óskar, Ása, and Nora, a swirling mass of half-finished connections and strange feelings, and she seems to have reached morning with nothing left.

On the way in, Nora asks her one more time, "Are we good?"

"Yeah," Agnes croaks. She can tell this doesn't satisfy Nora. "Honestly, if I seem like . . . this . . . it's not about you. You get that, right?"

Those hazel eyes miss nothing. "Okay."

Agnes trails behind her while they go through the same choreography as yesterday's visit. Talk to the security guard. Go up the elevator. Knock on 201.

Thor Senior appears at the door. "You," he says to Nora, one innocuous word becoming an indictment.

"Good morning, sir," Nora says. "I understand how you must be feeling about me right now. It's why I'm here to apologize. May I come in?"

Thor Senior doesn't step aside.

"It was not my intention to accuse you of anything," Nora continues. "You see, I care a lot about the women I document on my show. That tends to make me aggressive at times, when I shouldn't be. I can lose sight of who I'm talking to, and I know that isn't an excuse, but I felt—maybe I should have said before—I feel a particular connection to Marie. Because I grew up with her story, her tragedy. And because I know her granddaughter." She indicates Agnes. "We didn't properly introduce you yesterday. I'm sorry for this, too. Another example of how I can get carried away. This is Agnes, Einar and Marie's granddaughter."

The old man stares at Agnes, his expression wiped clean of any emotion.

"Hi," Agnes says, resigned.

Thor Senior steps back into the shadows of his home. Agnes prays that he will slam the door shut behind him, blocking them out. But then he reappears, his face slack with shock. "You are her," he says. "I didn't—I thought—Magnús?"

"Yes," she says. "My father."

He allows them inside his home. Agnes sits on the edge of the couch, the farthest from Thor Senior's chair. He falls into it with a grunt.

Nora comes in last. She's removing her bulbous microphone, her camcorder, before she's even seated.

"Where is Einar now?" Thor Senior asks Agnes.

"Dead," she says. "He passed away a year ago. My father and I live in California."

"I never knew where he went."

Agnes doesn't speak. Nora takes the lead again. "Like I said yesterday, you are an invaluable resource. I'm sure the police must have spoken with you many times, as Einar's closest neighbor. As a family member, however distant. I—"

Thor Senior holds up a hand, cutting her off. "I thought about what you said." He resettles his long, aching bones in the recliner, the better to face Nora. "I have thought about this. I have something to say, and then you will leave. No more talking, from anyone." He casts a wary glance at Agnes, as though checking to see she's still there, not a nightmare his mind conjured up for him.

"I did not like Einar," he continues, "but I cared for his father, Páll. I was there when he died. Not Einar. Páll died without his family. So I was there. Páll asked me to help his son, if he needed it. Help him, because we are family. On his deathbed, he holds me and he asks for my help. So I say yes. So I did.

"That is why I did not tell the police what I knew. Because of my promise. But he is dead now, and my promise is complete. He was protected.

"I know Einar killed his wife and his child because I saw him, walking on my property. With blood on his hands."

Agnes wants to go home. But no, that's not right. Not where the memories of her grandfather live. She wants something, anything that isn't this. But Thor's still speaking, in that measured, calm voice, the truth coming in relentless, inescapable waves.

"It was the morning," he's saying, "before she goes missing. I see him walking by the river. His mouth open, hollow. I call to him. 'Einar!' I want to know if he's hurt. But he keeps walking. And I let him go. I did not know it was serious, not until they found Marie. And then I knew.

"I did not tell," he says, "because of my promise."

CHAPTER THIRTY-EIGHT

February 10, 2019

Thor Senior holds firm. He will not tell them more. He is finished. Nora packs up her equipment and makes her way to the front door, but Agnes remains sitting, just as Thor does.

"Give me a minute," she tells Nora, without looking away from the man in front of her.

She expects Thor to tell her to leave, but perhaps he's curious. Perhaps he has more to say to her. She hears the door close, and she takes a breath. It feels like the first one in a long time.

"I have said everything," Thor insists, "that I wish to."

"I'm not wearing a microphone," she tells him. "I'm not recording this. Whatever we say, it's just us."

The yellowing skin around his eyes. The pitiless gaze. The long nose. She can see every detail, every line and pore of his face, and she feels nothing. She will feel more, she knows there's a mountain of more, somewhere inside her, but for now, she is a pipe. Open on both ends, things sliding through.

"You had an affair with Marie," she says, and there's the rage, roiling through the black. "You slept with her, and my grandfather found out."

"I will not—"

"Please." She's got her hand on something sharp, and she realizes it's his knee. When had she gotten closer to him?

"You should be careful," he tells her. "Asking these questions. There is danger."

"Are you threatening me?"

He's a big man. Those bones aren't frail beneath her grip. Neither are the muscles surrounding them. She realizes, distantly, that she should be afraid of him. But she would welcome the opportunity to hit him, even though she's never hit anyone in her life. She'd like to try. She'd like for him to try, too.

"Go," he tells her. He leans back, away from her. There's something pathetic in the swipe of his hand. "You're hurting me. Go."

CHAPTER THIRTY-NINE

February 10, 2019

They arrive back in time to prepare for Thor Junior. Agnes stands in the snow, watching Nora unpacking her equipment, their two suitcases. She doesn't move to help her. She doesn't feel like she can move at all. She hears her name. But she is not there.

She's able to connect to the Wi-Fi. Messages from Lilja pile up on the screen. Lilja, only Lilja.

"We should go inside," Nora tells her.

There is the wind. There's the general overwhelming chill of this place. But Agnes doesn't mind. For once, she welcomes the pain of it. "You go ahead," she tells Nora.

"I know that was a lot," Nora says, her voice impossibly gentle. "Do you want to talk about it?"

"I'm fine."

"Okay," Nora says. "But just so we're clear: we don't know if what Thor Senior said is true. He could be lying. He explained why he didn't bring this information to the police all those years ago, but I don't fully understand why he'd tell us this now. Not after keeping the secret for forty years. Do you see the danger of this whole line of work? I ask people to narrate their lives for me. They're going to editorialize."

"Nora," Agnes says, feeling heavy. Like she were filled with lead and she's slowly sinking through the icy ground, cracking the earth into eggshell shards. "I get it."

"But you believe him."

"Why do you care what I believe?" Agnes asks, sinking further.

"Because I care about you. I genuinely do. And it's okay to not be fine, Agnes. It's okay to grieve your grandfather, to reckon with the idea that maybe, just maybe, he wasn't the man you thought he was."

Agnes's stomach twists. *I care about you.* It's exactly what she needs to hear, and it isn't. It's not enough, certainly, to stop the hurt from spilling out of her. "You don't know who he was to me," she says. "You don't know what I thought."

"You thought he was innocent," Nora says softly. "I'm not trying to win any points here. And I know it's not my place, but if I can give you some advice . . . don't let this taint your memory of him. He's your second father. Something horrible happened in his past. It sounds like, if he did commit those acts of violence, he wasn't that person with you. That's all that matters."

Lilja's messages are brief, letting Agnes know when she'll be back in Bifröst. There's an attachment, though. A portrait of Agnes. It's quick, done in pencil and what looks like scrap paper, but it captures her. The tilt of her nose, the sweep of her hair. Her thin lips, caught in a smile. A real smile.

Agnes presses the phone to her chest, gripping it hard enough to hurt.

"Agnes," Nora presses.

"I'm okay," Agnes tells her, and it's not quite a lie. "Thank you. I appreciate what you're saying. Really." She doesn't have to finish the rest of the sentence: *But you can't help me. Not with this.*

Nora hears it anyway. "I'm going to get dinner started," she says with a sigh. "Thor Junior will be here soon."

Agnes lets her go. Nora leaves Agnes's suitcase behind, as though she knows how much Agnes wants to run away, and she's accepted it. Agnes could throw the suitcase into the trunk of the rental car and rocket out of here. But she doesn't know where she'd go. Home is so complicated, so far away. She's in the middle of the ocean. She could go in either direction and find land, but she's frozen in indecision. Not even in indecision. Indecision implies options, well thought-out choices. No, she's frozen in blankness.

It's the thought of Lilja that compels her to stay. To abandon her suitcase in the gathering wind, and to walk.

She doesn't want to go inside. Not where Nora is. Nora, who sees her, who understands her, who cares about her.

She follows the path of the driveway blindly, not paying attention to where she goes, so long as she is out, away. She walks, she limps, she embraces the grinding pain in her leg. For once, she doesn't even crave a pill.

She believes Thor Senior. He confessed only after he knew Einar was dead, that his promise to Einar's father would not be broken. She believes her father.

Her grandfather, the man who raised her, murdered his wife and child.

That's the truth.

And then there's Ása.

It shouldn't bother Agnes, the disappearance of a woman she's never met. But it does. There are two options in Agnes's mind: someone, probably Óskar, hurt Ása and buried her, likely in the river, or Ása met her death on her own terms, also likely in the river.

Agnes fights the wind, the slip and slide of the snow, and she lets herself articulate what has unsettled her the most. What has begun to haunt her. Despite what she has told herself, she actually, truly, wholeheartedly hopes that it was someone who hurt Ása. It's a terrible wish to cast out to the universe, but the alternative, that the woman crossed the finish line on her own, is devastating.

Agnes doesn't deserve to feel this way. She's the one who has spent the past year courting death, dipping her toe over the line, waiting to see what will come for her. She's resented her life.

When she sees what Ása has done, though, it all feels so hollow.

She should have fought.

Agnes emerges from the protection of the trees, out into the open air where there's nothing but the snow and the empty highway. She grips the metal gate separating her grandfather's land from the rest of the world with one ungloved hand. The wind gouges at the exposed skin of her face and her hands and her joints howl. She pushes past the gate. She's walking blindly toward the road, feeling nothing, seeing nothing, except the pain. But somewhere underneath, there's something else.

Release.

It catches her by surprise. The sobs fight their way out of her chest. She cries for herself, and she cries for Ása, until the two women blend into one. The impulse and the action.

Agnes doesn't notice the cars whipping past, just beyond her. Or when they both come around, moments later, parking in the shoulder of the highway across from her.

She notices only when the doors open. When the voices, harsh, carry over the wind to reach her, and when the owners of the voices follow.

CHAPTER FORTY

February 10, 2019

She should have expected this. Not that she'd run into Lilja on a bare stretch of highway in the middle of nowhere, but that she'd run into someone she knows after she's been crying so hard her eyes are swollen. She wipes at her runny nose, drags both hands along her pillowy eyelids. She knows it's useless. She'll look like she's been crying because she has been. There's no covering it up.

But there's more than Lilja here.

There's Óskar, too.

Lilja's leading the charge across the road, with Óskar at her heels. When she catches sight of Agnes, Lilja pulls ahead. Or perhaps Óskar hangs back. He slows to a stop, his expression closing into his resting smirk.

"Agnes," Lilja says. "What's wrong?"

Agnes can only shake her head. She wraps her arms around Lilja, pulling her into her body.

"Lilja." It's Óskar. "Get away from her."

Lilja responds in Icelandic. Whatever she says, it sounds harsh, but it has no effect on the man.

"You," he says to Agnes. Stopping short of their embrace. "You're everywhere. Einar Pálsson's child. Why are you crying, murderer's child?"

"Go," Agnes says, "away."

Óskar doesn't move. It's Lilja who pulls away. Now Agnes is standing alone in the whipping air and snow.

"What do you want?" Agnes asks.

He shrugs. "I want nothing from you. I just don't think Lilja should be around you. You shouldn't be here. The town is worse for having you here."

"Are you accusing me of something?" Agnes asks, taking a step closer to him. There's no chance she will intimidate him, not with her limp or her shaky voice. But this is the second time today someone has told her to leave Bifröst. It doesn't matter that she'd considered running away, that not a few minutes ago she'd thought she didn't belong here. That is her prerogative to decide. Not his.

Óskar drags his gaze up and down Agnes's form and raises his eyebrows as if he's seen all of her and isn't impressed. "No," he says again, more slowly. "I'm telling you to go."

"Enough." Lilja's voice cuts in between them. "Go home, Óskar. I'll talk to you later."

Óskar holds his ground. Agnes wonders what she'll do if he stays. If he insists on separating them. Exhaustion washes through her at the thought, as brutally as the wind wraps around her body.

"You aren't my keeper." Lilja's frustration has transformed into something softer. Something much more intimate, a call to their friendship that only they know. It isolates Agnes from her with more totality than if they had spoken in Icelandic.

Óskar, too, softens. But when he says, "She isn't Ása," Lilja flinches as though he's hit her.

She recovers slowly. "Go," she says, and this time, finally, he listens.

He reaches his car quickly, but he doesn't get in. Instead he stands by the passenger door, watching them.

Lilja sighs. She turns to Agnes, takes her in almost for the first time. "Are you out here alone? No car? Wearing this?" She gestures to Agnes's jacket. Agnes hadn't dressed for the cold. Compared with Lilja and her expert layering, Agnes looks like she's naked.

"I needed to think," Agnes says.

"Come on." Lilja leads her to her car. They ignore Óskar. "I'll drive you home."

Agnes climbs into the passenger seat, skin prickling at the sudden warmth, and she fixates on Lilja's hands at the wheel, the variations in her grip, the length of her fingers, the assured touch. She remembers a boy in her middle school art class asking her and her friend why girls were so attracted to hands. She hadn't been able to articulate it then, and she can't articulate it now. Her friend, however, had said, "Well, of course you don't understand. Look at your hands, *ewww*."

Lilja maneuvers her car through the gate. Agnes instructs her to follow the makeshift snow road, and they dip down and up through the lunar craters, the tunnel of trees.

"Out on the road, I thought you were Ása," Lilja says, not even bothering to deny what they were both thinking. She steers them along the rim of another crater. "From far away, you looked like her."

Agnes wipes at another tear. She's horrified to hear herself sniffle.

"Why are you crying?" Lilja asks. Her tone is matter-of-fact, not pitying, not overly gentle, as Nora's had been. Simply asking. She isn't acting like Agnes's mood is something to be fixed.

"My grandfather," Agnes says. "Everyone thinks he's a murderer. And I think they're right." She doesn't elaborate. She can't handle it. "And Ása," she says, because she might as well be honest.

Lilja stops the car. They haven't reached the house. They might as well be the last two people on earth. "What about her?"

Agnes knows what's going to come out of her mouth is a mistake, but she can't stop it. She needs to say it, just as much as Lilja needs to hear it. "She's dead," she says. "I didn't know her, but I've heard so much about her life. She was in pain, wasn't she? All the time, she was in pain. You have to start dealing with the fact that she might not come back. She didn't want to. I know you love her. And I know it looks like I don't know what I'm talking about. But trust me. She chose this. I'm sorry if she did. But I think she did. And that's getting to me."

Lilja squeezes her eyes shut. "You're trying to hurt me."

"No," Agnes says. "I'm really not. I'm—"

"You are," Lilja insists. "And I don't know why." She opens her eyes. Starts the car again. "I'll take you home."

"Lilja—"

"No," Lilja cuts her off. "Enough. Don't lecture me on what you don't understand, and I will do the same. Okay?"

Agnes sits back and watches the house come closer. Her lone suitcase, encrusted in snow now, like powdered sugar. "I'm sorry," she says, and she really, truly means it.

"I know." Lilja pulls up in front of the house, bringing the car as close as physically possible to the door so Agnes won't have to limp far.

The kindness of this simple, unspoken gesture is too much for Agnes. She waits until Lilja's brought the car to a complete stop, then she reaches for her. She drags Lilja's mouth to her own, begging her to understand. She feels Lilja's response against her own skin. It's complicated. There's so much left unsaid. But there's safety, too.

CHAPTER FORTY-ONE

February 10, 2019

When Agnes emerges from the bathroom, hair dripping from her shower, Thor Junior is there, in the living room, sipping a glass of red wine on the couch and pointing to the different details of the house. "I have dreamt of a home like this," he says, winking at Agnes, "my entire life."

To his right is Hildur. They're on one of the couches, sitting shoulder to shoulder. Agnes isn't surprised. Isn't anything except tired.

"You built it yourself?" Nora calls out from the kitchen. "I could never."

"I am an architect," Thor says. "It would have been the greatest shame to bring someone else into my own house. I suppose I did have *help*, but this is mine. Much as the farmhouse will be."

"That amazes me," Nora says. "I tried to hang a painting in my office, and I somehow tore off a chunk of drywall."

Everything is picture perfect. The blizzard surrounding them, the warm food, everyone in sweaters. Like a commercial. Agnes accepts a glass of wine from Nora and tries to imagine a world in which she belongs in such a scene. She chooses a seat on the couch across from

Thor and Hildur. They could be an old married couple. Or siblings, with their matching hair and eyes. But where Hildur's grin is so sharp it's almost predatory, Thor simply seems pleased to see Agnes.

Agnes downs half her glass of wine in one swallow and resists the urge to chug the rest. She hadn't been able to resist a couple more pills, just before the shower, to take the edge off the evening. Too much wine will make her drowsy. But as she tells herself to slow down, she's already taking another sip. It's hard to care about temperance right now.

"Is it weird for you," Agnes asks Thor, wiping her mouth, "having us here in your home? Cooking for you? Sleeping in your bed?"

This is her first time seeing him in regular clothes. Underneath his snow suit, he's a lean form with a bubble around his gut. He stretches his long legs from the couch, wearing wool slacks and a turtleneck. He is the next doll down in the Matryoshka set from his father. More suited to soccer than football.

"It's like having friends over," he says expansively. "And I do rent this out many times a year, so it comes easily. It is odd, though, that this evening, I will not be sleeping in my own bed."

"I would say you're welcome to it," Nora says, now fussing with the serving dishes at the kitchen island, "but that room is too incredible."

"Soon," Hildur says, "there will be space for all of you. Thor's reconstructing your grandfather's house, Agnes, so there will be three homes here. One for each of you, when you visit. More, hopefully."

Thor shifts uncomfortably in his seat. "Yes. I have been wanting to discuss this with you, Agnes."

"Nora told me," she says. She tries to recall her previous outrage at the idea of her family's ancestral home becoming a tourist attraction. At this point, she'd rather burn it all down. "You're going to turn it into another vacation rental, right?"

"It was my idea," Hildur says. "When I saw what Thor could do . . . With his gift, he can transform the town. We have the university, sure, but we should have more visitors."

"Have you lived here your whole life?" Agnes asks, certain already of the answer.

"I was born here," Hildur says, "and I will die here. I didn't leave. I never will. Unlike some of us." She pulls Thor in for a hug—or a wrestling move, Agnes can't tell which.

Thor pulls himself out of Hildur's grip, cheeks red. "I came back."

"Did you grow up together?" Agnes asks. It's as though she's caught in the middle of a fight between siblings.

"I don't remember a time we weren't together," Hildur says.

Nora invites them to sit for dinner, indulgently listing out their feast. The salad bowl filled to the brim with greens and colorful vegetables, large slabs of baked fish, piles of steaming white rice. Nora waves away their compliments. "Don't be too impressed," she says. "Dessert is grocery store candy."

Agnes negotiates her way to a seat that has some distance from Hildur. It doesn't resolve much—at opposite ends of the table, Hildur can and does watch her every move—but at least she can't engage her in conversation. This lands Agnes beside Thor, however, and across from Nora. Nora, she realizes, who has spent the day driving and cooking and cleaning. Her equipment, normally scattered across the table, is gone. Agnes feels a curious pang of guilt. She could have helped Nora. Nora, who has helped her so much. Who has tried to help her, anyway. It's not Nora's fault, Agnes supposes, that she's ruined her.

Thor doles the fish out to each woman's plate. "I am the only man in a room full of women," he says. "My favorite kind of party."

"Is this a dream come true for you, Thor?" Hildur asks.

"I must have had this dream a thousand times," he says, grinning. "But it probably won't end the way I'm hoping." This earns him a guffaw from Hildur. Thor turns to Agnes. "So how are you liking your return home? Do you feel your soul calling to this place? Or is it the other way? Do you feel this place calling to your soul?"

Despite everything, Agnes feels herself smiling. This is his field of wild strawberries. "Part of me does," she says. "But I don't feel like I belong."

"It's the language," Hildur says, knowingly. "You shouldn't let that stop you. You can learn."

"Yeah," Agnes says, thinking of Thor Senior and Óskar. *Go. Leave.* "That's probably it."

"But it's in you," Thor insists. "The language. The place. This is where you should be. This is where you were made."

"If you were a piece of clothing," Nora jokes, "your label would say MADE IN ICELAND."

Cheeks burning, Agnes swallows more of her wine. She doesn't love the spotlight. Doesn't love the feeling like she's being analyzed and teased, even if it's all meant kindly.

"Are you two related?" she asks Thor and Hildur. They look so similar, it's not a ridiculous question. And it takes the spotlight off her, in an instant, as though the lightbulb had exploded.

Hildur chokes on her food. She thumps a hand against her chest, waving away Nora's help.

"No," Thor answers for her. "What I told you before was a joke. Not everyone is so closely related here."

Hildur clears her throat. "That would have been disgusting."

"You two dated?" Nora asks. She's the only one drinking gin. Agnes is in no position to judge, but she wonders, suddenly, at the amount of alcohol she's seen Nora consume, every night she's been here. It's not insubstantial. *I'm a mean drunk,* she'd said. "Or," Nora says now, delighted, "are you two dating?"

"Once upon a time." Hildur shoots Thor a speculative look. "I thought I was in love with him. You should have seen him. So handsome, without that belly he has now. All the girls followed him around, but he was so respectful. I was the most persistent. But—"

"But I broke her heart moving away," Thor concludes. He pats Hildur's hand. "I'm sorry I ruined you for all men."

246 / *Melissa Larsen*

Hildur switches to Icelandic with a laugh. It's a rapid-fire exchange that mystifies the two Americans, but the banter is easy enough to follow in tone. The mock outrage, the playful apologies.

In English, Thor says, "Hildur's boyfriend is a prince among men." He flexes one biceps. "Bigger than us all, handsomer, nicer. She's done well for herself."

The conversation shifts over to Nora's work. The glories and responsibilities of being a true crime podcast host who actually managed to solve a case. Agnes focuses on her wine and tunes the rest out. For once, she realizes, she has an appetite. She avoids the fish, but she shovels the rest in, because she needs it, and because it keeps her from having to talk.

When the meal is finished, Nora instructs everyone to sit in the living room while she clears up. She waves away all offers of help. "I'll be with you in a second," she says. "Please. You're my guests."

Thor turns to Hildur, suddenly serious. They speak again in their shared language, only this time, the tone is much less decipherable. In the end, Hildur announces, in English, that she must get going.

"You and me," she says to Agnes. "We have to speak soon."

Agnes lifts her glass in a mock salute. "Fine." She'll be out of here soon enough.

When the front door shuts behind Hildur, Thor drops into the couch cushions beside Agnes with a sigh. "I asked her to leave," he tells her, pitching his voice low so Nora won't hear. "You forget when you leave home, how much baggage there is. I became another person in Denmark, and then I come back and no one lets me be that person."

"I've been living at home for a while, too," Agnes says. "I regressed so fast."

"Regressed," he repeats. "That's exactly it. I am eighteen once more. Only in a slightly, *slightly* older body." He pats his stomach and Agnes laughs.

Nora sets up the microphone on the coffee table in front of Thor.

Agnes takes this as her cue to find another seat. She chooses the kitchen island, where she has access to the candy and wine. This is such a different setup from all the other interviews Nora's given. They've been drinking and socializing like friends. There isn't much professional distance.

Thor underlines this dynamic by clinking glasses with Nora. "You've been here two months," he says, "yes? Does your husband mind? That is a long time to be away from home."

Nora takes her seat across the couch from him. "I don't have a husband anymore," she says. "I have no strings, Pinocchio."

"Strings?"

"No partner, no pets, no plants, even," she says. "Mark took a lot in the divorce. So I'm now responsible for no one but myself. And my podcast, of course. I'm a pirate captain. Married to the sea."

This makes Thor smile. "What does that feel like?"

"Free," Nora says simply. "Aren't you the same? I've heard through the grapevine that you're single, too. Divorced, right?"

"Yes," he says, unbothered. "As of a year ago, yes. I guess I'm free like you in that way. But I have so much responsibility for this town, I don't feel free."

"You've lived here your whole life," Nora says. "Now it's my turn to ask: what does that feel like?"

"No. I was born here. I left when I was eighteen, and I didn't return until three years ago. If you count the years, I've spent more of my life in Denmark than Iceland. But this place has a hold over me. It's in my body. When I was in Denmark, I wasn't the same man. I had to become the person who lived there. Now that I'm back, I see how much I missed being *this* person."

"Why did you move to Copenhagen?" Nora asks. "Why become someone else?"

"I came for the schooling, and then I came for the women." Thor laughs at his own crude joke. He's the only one. "That was ugly, sorry.

I wanted to leave. I wanted to see who else I could be. I wasn't done with school. Here, we have a different system from yours, we call it *menntaskóli*, and we don't finish until age nineteen or twenty. But my mother was gone and I was miserable. I couldn't survive living alone with my father for another two years. I chose Denmark almost at random. I finished my studies, I got a job, I got married, and the next thing, I realize I'm not who I want to be. Sometimes your life takes on its own shape, without your guidance, or even your knowledge. I'm trying to fix that."

Agnes feels a sudden, strong sense of kinship with him. She knows she's made choices. No one's forced her. But she'd never understood how those choices would lead her here.

"What brought this on?" Nora asks. "This change of heart?"

"My father could no longer live on his own," Thor says. "I set him up in a facility in the city. And then . . ." He spreads his hands, indicating the rest.

"I'm sorry."

"Why?" Thor takes a sip of his wine. Agnes has lost count of how many they've all had, but she knows he's had more than her. And yet he looks absolutely fine.

"It's a lot of loss in a short span of time. Realizing your parent needs care like that is its own type of loss. The beginning of the end. Then a divorce . . . even the most amicable divorce is a tremendous loss."

"I'm used to it," Thor says breezily.

"How so?"

"My mother left my father when I was young. Which meant leaving me, too. She couldn't take me with her, she told me, because she didn't want my father knowing where she was. I heard, only after I came back three years ago, that my mother had died a decade before. Parkinson's. My father . . . it's good to have him out of here. Good for me, good for the town. He didn't hit my mother, if that's what you're thinking. It wasn't so easy as that. For a long time, I didn't understand what it was that drove her away. My father was not a kind man. Far from it. But he saved most of his anger for me." Thor takes a long swallow of his wine. "I thought about it, though, after, and I realized, he didn't have to hit her to make her afraid of him."

"What did he do?" Nora asks.

"Sometimes," Thor says, playing with his wineglass, "I think of Ingvar. How he is the only one of us out here who has a good father. Hildur—well, you'll have to ask her. But Ingvar and Karl. That was a kind father. It explains why Ingvar is so popular now with women. Out of all of us, he was loved, and loved well."

"Popular with women?"

"I have seen you," Thor tells her. "You love him. All the girls do. Marie did, even when he was a baby. He has the ability to make women love him." The raw envy in his voice surprises Agnes. Between the two of them, Thor and Ingvar, she'd have called Thor the ladies' man. But she supposes Ingvar's charm is more subtle, more accessible. Thor is quicker, more prone to dominate the conversation. She likes them both. They're just different.

"What do you mean, 'us'?" Nora asks. "Who else had a bad father?"

"Magnús," Thor says. "Surely you have heard the stories of Einar as a father."

"Tell me."

"Why do you think he spent so much time outside? With Júlía and Karl? He was afraid, as I was. My father used to tell me he could do whatever he wanted to me. No one would ever know. My mother and I both left when we could. I used to resent my mother for doing it. I see now that she had to keep herself alive. No matter the cost."

"It cost you a lot."

"In some ways, yes. But I am older now. I accept what has happened. You have to move on. Leave the past where it is buried."

"That's admirable," Nora says. "But it would be understandable if you couldn't forgive her, or your father."

"I didn't say I forgive my mother," Thor corrects her. "I accept it. Forgiveness means it's okay. I don't forgive either of my parents. But I have moved past it. I am nearly sixty. It is time to stop being eighteen." The message is clear: I don't want to talk about this anymore.

Nora persists, "How did your father react to your mother leaving him? I can't imagine a man like that would take it well."

Thor's demeanor doesn't change, but something about him sharpens. Agnes wonders if Nora can sense it, too, can feel the edge of the man's patience. There's a silence that stretches on long enough for Agnes to consider speaking up, to ask Nora to change the subject, to please free them from this awkward prison. Finally, at her breaking point, Thor says, "You talked to my father. You know how he reacted. Why don't you ask me the real question?"

Agnes feels the same crackle of adrenaline that comes before her surfboard would catch the wave's current, when she fought the pull, the breathless yank upward. Trying to maintain control on the surface of something beyond control.

Nora doesn't falter. "What's the real question?"

"My father is a brute," Thor says, as though she hasn't spoken. "The world will be better once he is dead. But he is an old man, and you shouldn't confuse him, dragging up these memories."

The board slips from beneath Agnes, leaving her in that drop to the water, to the rag doll spiral through its spin cycle as it races toward shore, to deposit her on the sand, half-dead and disoriented. Here it comes. Once again.

"What's the real question I should ask you?" Nora repeats.

"Was my father sleeping with Marie? Did Einar know? Yes."

When Agnes had hit the sand that shattered her ankle, that halved her kneecap, that tore her ligaments, that subsequently changed the entire course of her life thus far, at the very least it had knocked her out, too. It had only been for a moment, so she's been told. But that brief lightning bolt of pain, of her leg crumbling to pieces beneath her, had been so overwhelming it had short-circuited her system. She woke in a state of shock that smothered the pain.

This moment in Thor's home offers no such relief.

How was she the only one who didn't know the truth?

Nora clears her throat. "How do you know?"

"I saw them together. There is so much space here, but there is nowhere to hide. Nowhere to go but to each other. I was home at the wrong time. There they were. If I saw this, then Einar saw. If I knew, then Einar knew. Why do you think they were fighting all the time?"

"And you believe Einar killed Marie, because of the affair."

"No," Thor says again. "I know. My father is not a liar. He saw Einar with the blood on his hands."

"Did Einar confront your father?"

"No." Thor finishes his wine. "He knew what he did. He needed a way out, and my father gave it to him. That is the best thing he has done, and the worst. Letting the murderer go."

Agnes should never have come here. She made a mistake. So many mistakes, she now realizes.

"Why not go to the police?" Nora asks Thor. "If your father has this evidence. If Einar killed the woman your father was sleeping with. Why would he let her murderer go free?"

Thor wipes at his mouth. "That is his business."

"Why wouldn't *you* go to the police?"

"You can't understand," Thor tells her. His voice is so gentle Agnes can almost pretend like she can't hear him. "You say you have nothing, and you feel free. No family, no responsibilities. You don't understand what it's like to have these things and then lose them. There is no freedom, there is only what you once had. The police don't bring them back. Einar got to leave, and he got to live. But he had to live with what he did. That is punishment enough."

CHAPTER FORTY-TWO

February 10, 2019

Thor tells them he'll walk home. "It's not far," he says, zipping himself up into his snowsuit and pulling out a flashlight. Without a goodbye, he disappears into the woods. Agnes watches his distant beam of light get smaller and smaller, until it's nothing more than a ghost image on her retinas.

Agnes lingers in the doorway, her toes going numb in her untied boots. Nora's giving her space, she supposes. Or maybe she's forgotten about her, too lost in her own enormous discovery. Once again, Nora has broken a new lead in a cold case. She's found, finally, the motive for the murders, with testimonies to back it up.

Slowly, carefully, Agnes folds at the waist to tie the laces of her boots. She doesn't think about what she's doing much more than the simple desire to move forward. She slides her jacket over her shoulders. Nora's flashlight is still in her pocket. Then she's following her old tire tracks, her old footprints, in the snow. It's difficult work. Her eyes narrow into slits when the snow pelts her face, freezing her cheeks. By the time she reaches the highway, she's out of breath and dizzy and ruined, but at least she's going.

Crossing the highway is a terrifying limping jog. Agnes knows that she'd get enough warning from any oncoming cars with their headlights, but still, it's a relief to find herself on the other side. To what she believes is the start of Ingvar's driveway.

In her car, the road to Ingvar's house had not felt steep. Just a long, meandering curl around a hill. On foot, it's almost impossible. Agnes has to dig her heels into the hard snow, her body bent double. She's practically crawling. She takes breaks to catch her breath, to let her left leg rest. When she finally reaches flat ground again, her entire body is one solid, aching cramp.

She knocks on Ingvar's front door and fights the urge to vomit.

While she's calculating the likelihood of getting that over with before anyone sees, Ingvar opens the door. He stares down at her in disbelief.

The house beyond him lies quiet. Dark. There's no sound of his mother. No lights on other than the ones he obviously turned on for his journey to the front door.

"I woke you up," Agnes says, panting.

Ingvar looks around. "Did you walk here?" He ushers her inside. In the light, she can see the piles of snow that have accumulated on her jacket, soaking her jeans, her hair. "What's happened? Are you okay?"

What Agnes wants to say is *I came here because I found out my grandfather really did murder his wife and daughter and I need a friend. I need a friend and Lilja's already seen too much of my mess today.* But she can't say that. What she says instead is, "Can I come inside?"

She's inside, but she means farther, to somewhere she can sit.

Ingvar nods and, after watching her remove her boots, which is next to impossible to do with her frozen fingers, he leads her not into the sitting room, but down the hall, to what is clearly his office. The light is already on, so perhaps she didn't wake him after all. Perhaps she just disturbed some late-night work. There's a desk pressed up against the wall, facing out some windows, an office chair, and a low armchair with a cozy reading lamp hanging over its middle. Ingvar indicates with his uninjured hand for Agnes to take the armchair. The injured hand, the one in the cast, hangs limply at his side.

He asks her if she needs something. "Tea, water?"

She shakes her head. He says he does, and he disappears. When he returns, his good hand holds a glass of whisky. The other has a scratchy wool blanket draped over the forearm. He drops the blanket, awkwardly, onto her lap.

Then he takes the office chair at his desk and turns to face her.

"Nora," she begins, overwhelmed, "she's done it. She's got proof. Or a motive. Whatever." She has to say it. She has to confront the truth. It's better to do that here, with Ingvar, with someone who doesn't know her all that well, someone who cares, but who ultimately doesn't matter. She's afraid of what she'd do, if she were alone with herself right now.

Agnes jolts at the touch on her knee. Without her realizing it, Ingvar has rolled his chair toward her. Agnes stares into his eyes, so bright, so steady.

"Marie was having an affair," she says. "With Thor's father." She tells Ingvar about her morning with Thor Senior, the story of Einar walking away, covered in blood. Thor Junior's confirmation. When she's finished, Ingvar offers her a sip of the whisky, which she takes, gratefully.

"Thor," he says. He's said it many times already.

"Yes. They—your mother. She knew. Did you know?"

"She doesn't talk about that time," Ingvar says. "But she's been struggling. Since you visited. She told me, after you left, that she regrets her mistake. 'I never helped her,' she said. 'Instead, I helped Einar.'"

I told him to take his boy and run.

Agnes stares down at her frozen fingers. Is this really her body? She tests it, flexes a finger. It obeys the impulse. Is this really her life? She feels a new touch on her shoulder. Ingvar again. Trying to get her back into her body, into the present.

"I'm sorry," he's saying.

"For what?" Agnes asks.

Ingvar doesn't answer.

"Can I tell you something?" she asks him. She registers the tilt of his head and assumes it's a yes, but she's in California. She can see the curvature of the earth on the misty horizon, and she's at the edge. Feeling the rush and suck of the air as the tide attacks the rocks below. She breathes with their rhythm. "A year ago," she says, "I tried to kill myself."

It's a relief to say it. The words are there, and they aren't. Ingvar is there, and he isn't.

"When I hear about this missing woman," she says, "when I hear about her life, I know, for certain, that she made the same choice. And it's been messing with my head. It makes me feel so guilty, because she had more reason to. Whoever she was with, they wanted something from her. When people talk about her, they say, 'Everyone loves her,' but the only person that everyone loves is someone like Marie. Someone who gives themselves entirely to the other person. Who isn't allowed their own secrets. Ása had all these reasons to do it. At the time, I didn't really think I had a reason to do it. She *wanted* to. And I thought I didn't."

This, more than anything, is what has haunted her ever since. The lack of premeditation. She hadn't been depressed, had never even considered it before. The decision, in the middle of the day, had been some dark impulse taking hold of the steering wheel. One intrusive thought and one split second's mistake.

Or so she'd thought, at the time.

"My grandfather died," Agnes says. "And I tried to talk to my dad, but he—he didn't want to talk about it. They weren't close. And my girlfriend, she couldn't get it. My grandfather used to take me swimming in this small beach town, Bolinas. After he died, I went to our old spot. I wanted to feel close to him. And I don't know how to describe it, but I was happy. I was so happy that day. And then I got out of the water. I was in this inlet, where you can hike up the cliffs. If you're careful, there are places to sit. So that's what I did. One minute, I was sitting. The next, I was up again. Looking down. And I—I fell."

She hears Ingvar's intake of breath, and she waits. But there's nothing more.

"I was lucky," she says. "Everyone told me so. I only shattered my leg. Some people found me and they got me to the emergency room. I told everyone it was an accident. Because it was, and it wasn't. Does that make sense?"

Ingvar seems startled that it's an actual question. "I think so."

"But now," Agnes says, her voice breaking, "now I know it wasn't an accident. Of course it wasn't. I did it because I missed my grandfather. And my life, after that? Ruined. Everything, gone. I haven't been the same person since that day. And now I know that that man, my grandfather, lied to me. He killed his wife. His own child. He was a murderer, and I loved him so much."

You're empty, Ingvar's mother had said.

And Agnes is. Not like Marie or Ása, empty because everyone wanted something from her, because she gave it all away. She's empty because there's something missing. There is nothing for her to give. She had sensed this about herself, but she hadn't known where that feeling came from. And now she does. It was being raised with a lie.

"You're okay," Ingvar tells her. He's trying to comfort her.

"No," she says. "I'm not."

"Einar loved you," he says, "and that's something—"

"I should go," she tells him, cutting him off. She doesn't need to hear it. In fact, she can't.

Ingvar doesn't argue with her. He offers to drive her home.

She accepts the kindness, even though she doesn't deserve it.

Part Three

INTERLUDE

February 3, 2019

The fourth-floor window, the one with the warm salt lamp and the figurine of a rocket ship on the windowsill, comes alive with light.

She's finally home.

There are shadows on the visible slice of the ceiling. Silhouettes of the people inside, dancing and shrinking and changing shape. Like the games children play in the comfort of their beds, toying with the dark, manipulating its form with their fingers, pretending like they aren't frightened of it.

The air inside the truck is frigid and stale. There's no heat on, because that requires the car to run. That would be an announcement. *Here I am.* The driver sits at the wheel, waiting, watching the frost creeping up the glass, relishing the burn of the winter freeze. There's no reason to rush. This night feels like it could go on forever. This night is the world at its best. Vicious, black, and cold.

In Ása's window, there's the briefest flash of a face. The boy.

He's my friend, she'd insisted. *We're close. It's not like you think.*

The lying whore.

In time, the silhouettes disappear. The light turns off. There's nothing left in the window but the glow of the salt lamp. Like a taxi's light. Open for business.

But still, there's no reason to rush.

The girl falls out the front door. She's unsteady, and she's alone. No boy with her this time. Did he stay inside, with Ása?

The girl turns left. She's halfway down the street when she stops. She looks back, to the fourth-floor window. She, like the driver, feels the draw of that salt lamp. Something in the girl breaks. There's a sound, audible from across the street. A sound like crying. Then she's walking again, weaving her way to her own building.

Finally, there's nothing left but the salt lamp and the truck. The key's already in the ignition. It's the work of a moment to turn the engine on. The headlights are dazzling. The truck idles, while the driver decides what to do. There is no plan. There is only the rage, turning the body to stone.

The imprint of a hand appears in Ása's window.

One flick of the driver's fingers, one flicker of the headlights.

The imprint fades.

The driver waits.

The front door opens again. Ása walks outside, wearing nothing but her thin shirt, leggings, and boots. She stumbles on the ice. The driver doesn't move to help her. Too mesmerized by her, even now, even in the grip of fury. Ása's breath billows out of her mouth in a white cloud, floating around her white-blond hair like a halo. The night here is a wonder. Vicious, black, and cold.

Ása makes it to the truck. To the open window.

"What's wrong with you?" she asks. Her face is a mask of hatred. It's so ugly, and so beautiful. "Why can't you leave me alone?"

"I don't know," the driver tells her, "but I'm so sorry." There is no plan, but the words spill out so easily. "I read your message, Ása, and I agree with you. I will leave you alone. I will do anything you want me to. Please, can you get in the car? You're shivering. I just need to talk to you. Then I will leave you alone forever. I promise."

CHAPTER FORTY-THREE

February 11, 2019

The snow is no longer actively falling, but there are dark, heavy clouds hanging above the house, weighted and bulbous like a pregnant woman's belly reaching the end. Nora and Agnes spend the morning in the living room, both on their own respective couch, speaking, officially, for the podcast. Agnes recounts memories of her childhood with Einar, as though she weren't really the one speaking. She focuses on the distant past, and when Nora presses for more recent memories, Agnes shakes her head, wordless.

Nora concludes the interview with a hug. "You did great," she says. Then, stretching and assessing the weather outside, she tells Agnes she's going to head into town. "Ideally I'd like to speak with Júlía again," Nora says, "but if that fails, I'll find Óskar again. I can't lose the thread."

"It's better if I stay behind," Agnes says. "I confuse Júlía too much."

She can't face Ingvar. Not now. Not after what she told him last night.

Nora understands, as she always does. "Hey," she says from the front hallway, "what time is your flight on the fifteenth? It's coming up, fast."

Agnes says, "In the evening, I think," even though she still doesn't have a ticket. She'd forgotten about this lie, but she supposes she should get one now. Other than Lilja, there's nothing left for her here except more misery.

Nora leaves with only a vague promise to check in with her in a couple of hours.

Alone now, Agnes pulls up her phone. She supposes she should call her father. Tell him what she's learned, before the show comes out. It's the right thing to do. But she can't bring herself to do it.

Why do you think we left, Agnes?

He already knows.

And she can't talk to him. He lied to her. Her whole life, he lied to her. He let her love Einar, and be loved in return. He let her find the truth, out here, all on her own.

She taps to her text exchange with Lilja. This morning, Lilja had sent her an apology. Busy today. Tomorrow? When do you leave? How long do I have you here?

Agnes replies, Not sure, actually. Let's do tomorrow. Please.

She paces the living room. The fireplace, the couches, the kitchen. She tries to talk herself out of it. *Don't look for more. You know too much already.* But when has she ever listened to that rational voice in her head?

Nora's room is magnificent. There's a view of the mountain, the river. A massive bed. Stacks of papers. Agnes has already looked through those, when she'd searched for information on Thor Senior. What else does Nora have tucked away in her room? Agnes pulls open the dresser drawers. Clothes. Folded with expert precision, of course.

Agnes reaches for a photograph on the nightstand, thinking it will be a photograph of Thor and his ex-wife.

It's a photograph of two young girls. The smaller one has a mass of wild, tangled hair and a button nose, and she's wearing a too-big Mickey Mouse sweatshirt and too-small pants. Hand-me-downs, most likely. She's holding the hand of a preteen girl, pint-sized, awkward in her posing. She isn't smiling. She's wearing checkered flannel and motorcycle boots, the uniform of an angry teenage girl.

They're outside, skin overexposed in the brilliant sunshine. Surrounded by tall pines. In the far distance, a rocky outcropping thrusts into the blue sky. Agnes brings the photograph closer. It looks like Half Dome in Yosemite. She camped there, once.

This must be Nora and her sister. Chloe. The girl who introduced Nora to the Frozen Madonna. The girl who disappeared.

Agnes isn't aware of sitting on the edge of Nora's bed, or of the way she clutches the frame so possessively. Has Nora ever used her prodigious skills to find out more about Chloe's disappearance? What is she doing here, in Bifröst, worrying about Agnes's family, when she could be in California, looking for her sister?

Agnes replaces the frame in its original position, on the nightstand, where Chloe can watch over her little sister.

Then she opens the drawer beneath the photograph. It's empty but for a phone. Agnes reaches for it, her stomach sinking. She recognizes that phone. She picks it up, and the screen lights up at her touch.

There're Ása and Lilja, their heads tipped toward each other.

Ása's phone.

It's almost out of battery. The little icon in the top corner of the screen flashes the dangerously thin sliver of red in its outline.

Why hasn't Nora taken this to the police yet?

Did she forget about it? It has been an eventful couple of days, sure, but isn't this important?

Agnes taps the home button. There's still a security lock. Either Nora hasn't figured it out yet, or she's memorized the code. It's an older Samsung, many iterations behind the current models. Agnes's old coworkers used to trade notes on how to hack into smartphones. For this model, she thinks there's a security flaw in the software. Agnes doesn't think about it. It's a matter of a few taps and then she's bypassed the security lock.

There are no new messages, no emails. The phone has service here, so the messages should load, but nothing comes through. No one has called Ása, or even texted her. Yet more proof that this isn't her primary phone.

Agnes knows she should call the police now. While she still has some plausible deniability. She and Nora have been holding on to the missing woman's phone, to sensitive information that could very well change the course of the investigation, for days.

But she can't help herself. She opens the messages app. There's only one conversation to choose from. There's no assigned contact name.

The last messages were sent by Ása. A long paragraph of text, followed by one sentence, sent later in the night. Agnes types the words of the last text into her own phone to translate. It's slow going, particularly with the different characters used in the Icelandic alphabet. But, finally, it comes clear.

I hope I haunt you.

Ása's last words.

There's no reply.

In fact, there are hardly any texts from the other number. Most recently, there are only one-word texts. Yes or no, to a proposed date and time.

Agnes hunches over the two phones and types the rest of the long paragraph into Google Translate.

> *I'm done. I can't do this anymore. I can't be responsible for you anymore. Not for your happiness, or your anger. I can't be your savior. Think about who you are, because it is sick. You are sick. Take your anger and choke on it. I hope you understand what*

you have done. You've lost me. I hope this hurts you, the way it has hurt me.

Then, hours later. *I hope I haunt you.*

Agnes clicks into the conversation itself. Earlier on, there are links, sent back and forth. Songs.

To the photographs. Sunsets. Vista of the town. Mostly, though, there are selfies of Ása. Body shots. Her breasts pressed together. The curve of her hip, against the soft fabric of her bedspread.

Nothing from the other person.

Agnes squeezes her eyes shut. She shouldn't have seen any of this. Not the pictures, not the texts. Not the phone itself.

She turns off the phone to conserve the battery, and to keep the images locked away.

Why wouldn't Nora give this to the police? Does she really believe, after the Lopez case, she is a real investigator, better than the actual detectives?

That has to be the reason, right?

Nora isn't the person who fell in love with a young, vulnerable student. She isn't the one who gave the student a secret phone for them to communicate with, the high-tech equivalent of a walkie-talkie. She isn't the one who received those nudes but never sent her own, because she knew, deep down, that those could be used against her.

Right?

I'm nothing, she'd said. *Married to the sea.*

Divorced. All she has is this podcast.

Agnes can feel panic building through her body. The shallow way her chest moves with her breathing. *Notice things,* Dr. Lee would say. But she can see only Nora's face, tending to her over the toilet. *This might sound twisted, but I kind of like taking care of you.*

The knocking causes Agnes to leap, briefly, out of her skin. She looks around, wildly. The knocking has to come again, for her to understand what's happening.

There's someone at the front door.

Agnes stows the missing woman's phone in her jacket pocket. Let Nora come find it, if she discovers it missing. Let her explain why she wants it back.

CHAPTER FORTY-FOUR

February 11, 2019

"Just the woman I hoped to see," Thor Junior says. "May I come inside?"

Agnes hesitates in the threshold. "Could we go somewhere else? A walk, maybe? I've been inside all day."

Thor looks delighted. "Would you like to see my other home?"

Anything to get outside. Agnes drags her jacket over her shoulders and shoves her feet into her boots. She hasn't properly layered up for a walk outside—she's still wearing the leggings she'd slept in—but she doesn't want to be here anymore.

Thor leads them to the right, through the trees on the other end of the driveway. It's a short walk. The two houses are closer than she'd thought. Thor's childhood home is the opposite of the building she's staying in. This structure is old, traditional. The exterior is some kind of corrugated metal, painted a mild mint green. There are patches of rust eating away the paint. This long, low bungalow has only a few windows interrupting the green.

Thor leads Agnes inside, apologizing for the state of the house.

"This is my childhood home," he says, without an ounce of affection in his voice. "When I am finished with your family's house, I will tear this down."

"You don't like it?" she asks. It's old-fashioned, but if he replaced the furnishings, like the hallway rug that's lost its pattern to thousands of footsteps, it would be nice.

"It's a shrine to unhappiness," Thor says. "It shouldn't exist."

Agnes imagines his father would have something to say to that, but she doesn't blame him. She follows him down the hallway, to the sitting room. There's an old misshapen couch in one corner, a narrow upright piano in the other.

"Do you play?" she asks.

"No," he says. "My mother."

Agnes takes a seat on the couch, suddenly aware of what she's wearing. Her leggings and a hoodie. She hadn't even put on a bra.

Thor sits beside her. "I owe you an apology," he says. "I saw how much I hurt you last night."

He waits for Agnes to speak. To confirm that yes, he did hurt her. Or perhaps for her to say, *No, you didn't hurt me. I'm fine. It was a shock to hear that my grandfather did, in fact, kill his wife and daughter, but that's not your fault.* She has no voice to say either. She still doesn't know what led her to this moment. Was it the split-second decision, on that cliff's edge, when she saw the water and she thought of her grandfather, gone, and she decided to jump, to see what was on that other side, only to discover it was more life, more pain, more grief?

Or was it the day her surgeon prescribed her fifty tablets of oxycodone and told her to take the pills before she even felt pain, so she could stay on top of it? Was it the day she ran out of the refills, when she spoke to the same surgeon and asked for yet another prescription and he finally, finally said no?

Or was it forty years ago, when her grandfather took the knife to his wife's throat, when he held his infant underwater until neither of them existed?

Thor mistakes her silence for anger.

"I'm so sorry," he tells her. "You didn't believe it." Then: "Are you afraid of your father?"

The question startles her. "No," she says. Her father intimidates her, but he doesn't frighten her. He never has.

"Your mother?"

"No." Her mother is sea glass. The hardship of her life didn't destroy her. It rubbed her into a new, edgeless shape.

"Brother? Sister? Bully at school?"

Agnes says no to them all. No siblings. No bullies. She went to small progressive schools in the Bay Area. The worst she got was loneliness.

"Good for you," Thor says. "Truly, you have lived a wonderful life. Not easy, of course. But you don't know what shaped me. You can't understand the fear in your head. You can only feel it in your gut. That's where it lives." He wants her to understand something, but she can't figure out what. "I didn't help," he explains. "I didn't help Marie. I didn't help the baby. I didn't do anything, because I knew my father was guilty."

He's apologizing, she realizes, for not speaking up. It's an apology to the wrong person. The apology should go to her grandmother, not her.

"You cannot imagine the way I lived," Thor tells her, "when I was a child. How much I hated my father, for driving away my mother. He took her away. Please don't hate me for what he's done."

"It's okay," Agnes says, more to get Thor to stop talking than because it's true. She's said this phrase so many times in the past few days, about so many things that were not, were never, could never be okay. "I appreciate what you're saying. But you have nothing to apologize to me for. What I'm dealing with is . . . something else. I grew up with my family's story as just that—a story. It never felt real to me. And I never believed it. Learning all these secrets, hearing the truth, it's like I've lost my grandfather, all over again. That's what I'm dealing with. Not you."

She watches the relief wash over him. "We all have secrets," Thor says. "Some more terrible than others. You must have secrets that you would protect, too."

Agnes nods. Her hands are shaking because she hasn't swallowed a few of her secrets today. She's limping on a secret.

"I want you to know," Thor says, "I know. And it is fantastic, Agnes."

"I'm sorry, what?"

"Your girlfriend."

Lilja? But—"What's wrong with that?" she asks, more dumbfounded than confrontational.

"Nothing," Thor says quickly. "I hope I'm not putting my foot in my mouth. When I was walking to dinner last night, I saw you in the car. Kissing your girlfriend, yes? You're a lesbian, yes?"

"Sort of," she says, still confused. "But why is that a secret?"

"Well, I don't know," he says. He flounders in his embarrassment. "She didn't come to dinner. Some people don't know how other cultures will react to these things. You shouldn't feel ashamed, though, or like you have to hide her. This is a very accepting place in general and I myself—I think it's great. What a wonderful woman you are. I never had children. I would have loved to have a daughter like you. You are who I pictured, always."

"Thank you," Agnes says. She pushes herself to standing. "I should go."

Thor stands with her. "Did I put my foot in my mouth?"

"No," she lies. "I just have to go." What else is she supposed to say?

"I will walk you home."

"No," she says again. Not too quickly. Not too forcefully. Softly, to be kind. "I like to think while I walk."

He accepts this, but not gracefully. She stares at anything but him on the way out. Thor helps her into her puffy jacket, asking if she's sure.

She is. He points her in the right direction, hovering close enough to be useful.

"Thank you for what you've said," she tells him, and she means it, even if it's made her uncomfortable.

Agnes retraces the path of their footsteps, back to the house. She needs to get a flight home. She'll see Lilja again, and then she'll get out of here. This is enough now.

She stops short at the driveway. Parked behind her rental car is a new car. Empty. No one's standing at the front door, waiting for her.

Agnes hadn't locked the front door when she'd left. With a grit of her teeth, she limps the rest of the way to the entrance. She hears the voice calling to her from the trees, but she doesn't stop, not until she has her hand on the doorknob.

"Hello!" It's Hildur. Pink-faced and grinning, dressed in a sweater and jeans, on the path leading to the farmhouse. She reaches Agnes quickly. "Is now a good time to talk?"

"Not really. What were you doing?"

"I came to see you. Nora tells me you are leaving in a few days, so it really is now or never for you and me. When you weren't here, though, I thought I would visit the Murder House, say goodbye before Thor changes it completely. Were you on a walk? Alone? That seems risky."

Agnes opens the front door. "Nora isn't here."

"I know." Hildur follows her in without an invitation. She starts down the hallway, but Agnes stops her with a hand on her arm. The muscles underneath her grip flex, and they surprise Agnes with their rigidity, their bulk. Beneath her elegant sweaters, Hildur's hiding a serious physique.

"This isn't a good time," Agnes tells her. It's nothing personal—or maybe some of it is. It's the way Hildur looks at her. Like she's a celebrity, not a person. She's objectified Agnes.

"Listen," Hildur says, resting a hand over Agnes's, "I didn't know Marie well, but I did know Einar. He was very kind. He helped me, did you know? He was friendly with my parents. They begged him to help me with my mathematics. I was awful. I didn't understand any of it. He gave me lessons. I wrote my book, after, to understand what he did. I couldn't believe that the man who was so kind to me could do something like that. He brought Marie's cookies to every session. He told me I should associate learning with happiness. I didn't want to think of him as a monster. But—" She doesn't finish the sentence. *But he was.* "We are not only one thing. Monster or man. You knew him, as I did. The man. Not the monster. And I have always wondered, what was his life like in California? What did he do, when he left? Who was he, after the killings?"

Agnes reaches for the doorknob again. "I'm glad to hear that you cared about him," she says, pulling the front door open once more. "I appreciate your words. But I can't handle this right now. I really can't."

CHAPTER FORTY-FIVE

February 11, 2019

Agnes waits for Hildur's car to clear the driveway, then she sends two texts. One to Nora. The other to Lilja.

> I don't have a return ticket. I'll find a flight that leaves in the next few days, I promise. I'll see you later.

> I know you're busy, but can I come over? Please.

CHAPTER FORTY-SIX

February 12, 2019

In the morning, Agnes pulls into the driveway to find Nora packing up her truck. She brings the rental car to a stop and climbs out, her body both stiff and supple, the smell of Lilja's shampoo wafting through her wet hair.

"Hey," she says.

Nora doesn't turn around. She's sliding her bags in the trunk, one after another, grunting with the effort.

"Where are you going?"

Still no answer.

"Are we good?" Agnes asks, parroting Nora's favorite question.

This gets her attention. Nora turns in place, color high in her cheeks. "No," she says, "we're not good."

"I didn't get a return ticket because I didn't know how I was going to feel," Agnes says. She'd thought she'd gotten her defense planned, but all the carefully crafted explanations fall out of her head the moment her temper rises. "I didn't want to make any decisions, until I got here. And then, now, it's—"

Nora cuts her off. "Do you honestly think I would've cared if you had said you didn't buy a return ticket? I'm not loving the fact that you've been lying to me, but I get it. What I'm upset about is you turning off your phone and disappearing for the night. I've been *worried*, Agnes."

"I didn't have service," Agnes says lamely.

"Right," Nora says. "And you spent the night where? With Lilja? Look, I know we talked about this, but I have to tell you, once and for all: this makes me uncomfortable. There are gray areas with this kind of thing. You said it yourself, I'm not a journalist, not in every respect, but I do try to live by some of the ethics of it, you know. And while you aren't one—at all—you're here, with me, under my umbrella. You said you're entitled to see whoever you want and sure, you're right about that, but do you ever stop to think about what an insult this is to me? How you're undermining my work here?"

Agnes digs her hands into her jacket pockets, fisting her cold fingers into her palms. She touches two phones.

Her own.

And Ása's.

What kind of journalist keeps a missing woman's phone in their bedside drawer?

"I hadn't thought about that," Agnes says. "Where are you going?"

"Reykjavík," Nora says. "To talk to Thor Senior again. I was going to invite you to join me, but you weren't here and you weren't answering your phone. The weather is so crazy, I don't have time to wait for you to get your stuff. I have to leave before they close the roads again."

Agnes tightens her grip around the two phones. She doesn't know what to think. She's lost some intrinsic faith in Nora. But still, she hears herself apologizing. "I didn't realize you'd be worried about me."

Nora laughs, but it's exasperated. "How many times do I have to tell you? I care about you." She tosses her hair back, frowning but relenting. "Do you want to come with me?"

"No," Agnes says. She's touched. But no. "I need to get my ticket home."

There's not enough time to argue. Nora sighs. "I'll text you some numbers. Hildur, Ingvar, and Thor Junior. In case you need anything. Hildur's far away, but she's reliable."

Agnes tells Nora she'll be fine, and she doesn't wait to watch the other woman leave. Instead, she closes the front door behind her and locks it.

CHAPTER FORTY-SEVEN

February 12, 2019

Agnes finds herself in the kitchen with a full glass of wine in front of her on the counter. Untouched, for now. Beside it, her bottle of pills. Unopened, for now.

She knows there are better things to do. Like, for instance, finding herself a flight home. What she wants to do, though, is swallow the first two pills with the first sip of wine. Finish the glass while she's alert. Start the next with two more pills. Enjoy the feeling of consuming and being consumed.

There's nothing holding her back from doing this. No more Nora. No more Einar. Just Agnes. Alone again. Even more alone than ever before.

Except there's Lilja now. It's the thought of her, the smell of her freshly washed sheets and clean skin, that holds Agnes back from the bottle. She doesn't want Lilja to know that she's the type of person who spends her days dipping her toes into absolute oblivion because she can't think of anything she'd rather be doing. Lilja isn't here right now, but somehow it feels like she is. The memory of her is so strong, Agnes is certain she could conjure her into the living room, if she could just concentrate hard enough.

Lilja, tucking her head into the crook of Agnes's neck. Her breathing slowing as they slipped closer to sleep.

Lilja had whispered the words against her skin, *I don't want to spend my whole life missing Ása.*

Agnes leaves the wine and pills on the counter and makes for the foyer, to her jacket. She slides the two phones from its pockets. Her iPhone. Ása's old Samsung.

She returns to Ása's texts. She'd translated Ása's last messages to her mystery boyfriend. There hadn't been any identifiable information in those final texts, but maybe there's something more in their earlier exchanges. She scrolls farther back. There are long stretches of conversations. It'll be tough with Google Translate, but what else is she going to do?

The bottle of pills calls to her on the counter.

She's hesitating, torn between curiosity and temptation, when the phone in her hands signals low battery. The screen goes dark.

The bottle of pills shouts louder.

Agnes has to go now, before she gives in. She stows the phone back into the pocket of her puffy jacket, then she throws it over her shoulders. She steps outside into what she'd call a blizzard. The snow she's seen here so far has come down in gentle, clumsy currents. Thick slices of frozen water drifting down like feathers onto her skin. But this is closer to rain, to heavy sheets of ice thumping against the ground like they've been thrown, hard, from the sky.

She doesn't turn back. She just weaves, blearily, through the trees, head down to protect her eyes.

I would have loved to have a daughter like you, Thor had told her yesterday. And she'd looked away, embarrassed. She hadn't been able to meet his eye, not until she was on his front doorstep. Instead, she'd scanned the room. Eyes snagging on the many strange details of someone's life. Old pictures, knickknacks, scuffs on the sideboards. Just as she'd been leaving, she'd seen something. The black cord of an old phone charger. She knows from experience that her iPhone charger isn't compatible with Ása's phone.

But Thor has one. She can borrow it, charge Ása's phone, and find the secret boyfriend.

The green metal house emerges from the white in a matter of minutes. She must have been moving quickly, but she'd taken the wrong way. She's at the rear of the house, near the kitchen. When Thor had escorted her, they'd landed at the front drive. She stomps through the piles of snow, hoping he doesn't choose this moment to look outside his window and find her hurrying past. The lights are on, so she pushes herself to go faster, not wanting to frighten him.

Reaching the front door, she knocks once, hard.

She waits.

Knocks again.

When no answer comes, she watches her hand try the doorknob as though it were disconnected from her. Watches the door swing in. Unlatched. It's easy, she supposes, to get used to keeping your doors unlocked out here, in the anonymity of the woods.

The air inside is blessedly warm. Agnes takes a step in, and then another. She doesn't remove her shoes. She hesitates at the threshold, listening for Thor. No one calls out. There are no sounds of human life in here, no bodies moving through the space. No breathing but her own.

"Hello?" she calls. "Thor?"

Nothing but the rush of the wind over the roof. The heavy beats of the snow landing on the metal.

Agnes wanders into the sitting room, where they had spoken

yesterday. She's here, she might as well take the charger. She searches the corners of the room, every surface. No black cords. She returns to the hallway. Checks around the entrance. Then she finds herself in the kitchen. It's bare, similar to the one in the farmhouse. Except there are a few takeout containers here, splayed open on the countertops, their contents congealing into unrecognizable lumps.

Still no charger.

The next room is a bedroom. Thor's room. It, too, is bare, but for the necessary bed, the desk and chair in the corner, a small ward-robe. The bed catches Agnes's attention. It's small, a twin, built for someone much smaller than Thor. No wonder he wants to go back to his new house. The bed in there is three times larger. And no wonder he's regressed. He's sleeping on what looks to be his childhood mat-tress. It would be impossible not to feel infantilized by that.

She slides her gaze to the nightstand. There's the black charger, coiled up into a bundle next to a phone. An old Samsung. No case. She's seen Thor's cell phone, peeking out of his pocket. That one has a case. Thick, clear plastic. The type to protect it from a great fall.

Why would he take his phone out of the case to charge it?

Agnes checks over her shoulder, half expecting to find him hanging over her. Waiting for her to notice before he shouts *Boo!* But there's just the empty hallway.

She picks up the phone to disconnect the charger, and the screen lights up.

A sense of déjà vu washes over her.

The phone is so familiar because she's held one like it recently. Ac-tually has its twin in her jacket pocket. She swipes this one open. Like Ása's phone, there are no notifications in any of the apps. Nothing beyond the bare minimum of a home screen.

Agnes taps on the messages icon.

There's only one conversation on this phone, too.

She enters the chat and there's the wall of text, followed later by a single line. Agnes can decipher it, even if she doesn't speak the language. She'd already translated it once, after all.

I hope I haunt you.

CHAPTER FORTY-EIGHT

February 12, 2019

The sounds terrify her. The push and pull. She wants to tell the woman to shut up, to let her think for a minute. And then she remembers that she's alone. It's her. It's her breathing that she's hearing. She has to slow herself down. She's getting dizzy.

She's found Ása's secret boyfriend.

They've been seeing each other for months. Then something went wrong. *Take your anger and choke on it,* Ása had said.

She breaks up with him.

Then she disappears.

Thor hasn't said anything. Hasn't told anyone about his relationship with this young woman. Why hide it?

She puts the phone back onto the nightstand. She doesn't want to touch it.

A single thought consumes her:

She has to get out of here.

Now.

CHAPTER FORTY-NINE

February 12, 2019

Back in the wind, Agnes bends her head to the current, as though she were at the bottom of the ocean, pushing herself against a relentless tide. She sticks out an ungloved hand to check that she won't walk straight into a tree. She'll get back to the Wi-Fi, then she'll call Nora. Nora will know what to do.

Agnes should have taken the phone with her. But she couldn't have risked it, could she? Not right now. Not alone. Nora will believe her. Agnes just has to get to the house, then she'll call her.

But, Agnes realizes with dawning horror, she can't go to Thor's house. It's *his house.* He'll have a key.

She has to go somewhere safe. To Ingvar. He'll help her.

Her boot slips painfully over a buried rock and for a moment Agnes nearly pitches forward into the snow. She rights herself with an effort, checking her bearings.

She can't think properly. She could scream.

He lied.

Thor lied.

He lied about his relationship with Ása.

Why lie, if there's nothing to hide?

Is it the age difference?

Agnes stops in place. The house is in front of her, but once again she's veered off the path. She's managed to make it to the side of the house, to Nora's room. There are glass walls here, too. She can see the big bed. The chairs.

And a light on, that she hadn't put on.

She's trying to think if there's any chance she could have done this by mistake. There are so many different light switches in the house, and it's not like she's lived there long enough to know them all. She could have turned it on, accidentally, when she was turning on the hallway light. She thinks she had left the house in darkness, but she hadn't checked Nora's room. Why would she?

But that's when she sees the movement inside. The figure crossing the hallway beyond Nora's open door.

Heart pounding, Agnes ducks out of sight, hurrying as best as she can to the cover of the trees. She's making noises with her breathing, can't stop them from coming, can only listen as they transform into words. Words like *god oh god what do I do.*

Someone is inside.

And it had looked like he was going into her room.

She leans against the tree, praying he doesn't step into Nora's room. She hadn't been able to see him clearly, only the dark silhouette of his body, but she knows who it is. Who it must be.

Thor.

What does he want from her?

I would have loved to have a daughter like you.

He wouldn't hurt her.

She knows that, rationally.

But she can't get her feet to move. To take her inside, to speak to him as though she doesn't know about his relationship with a woman thirty years younger than him who disappeared after breaking up with him over text.

Ása broke up with Thor and he reacted. Reacted in the same way her own grandfather did, forty years ago. The certainty of it solidifies within her.

She knows what she has to do. First, she needs to get somewhere warm. Even with her jacket on, she's cold. Some people die from being this cold. A lot of people do, actually. Exposure is what they call it. She's never appreciated this fact until now, that she could die from this feeling.

She can't go into the house. Not with Thor there.

She can't go to the rental car. The keys are in her room, thrown carelessly on her bedside table.

Ingvar. That's where she'll go.

But her body is still sore from the hike she'd made to his home the other night. She pictures that long, steep driveway. The endless curve around the hill. She'd hardly been able to manage it then. Today, in this weather, she doesn't trust she'd make it. Not when she's starting to vibrate, bodily, from the shivers.

There's only one other place she can go. Not to stay. Not for long. Just to think.

Agnes crouches as low as she can and she hurries across the driveway, careful to keep her body beneath the porthole of her bedroom. Her body protests every step. The joints in her left leg scrape against their bearings, their frozen ligaments and cobbled together bone fragments. She can't slow down, though, she can't wait to see if she's been caught.

When she's in the trees, she straightens and pushes herself into an all-out run. She can't hear anything behind her, no door opening, no following footsteps. Nothing but the wind pressing against her, the crunch of her own footfalls, the pounding of her heartbeat. This is the first time she's tried anything faster than a halting quick-step since the surgery. And it doesn't last long. She doesn't know if it's her body or something she's stepped on, but her knee buckles at an odd angle, and suddenly Agnes is tumbling forward into the snow, and she doesn't have time to catch herself. She lands in the snow in a breathless heap.

Sparks of electricity radiate up her left leg. Did she twist her knee? Sprain her ankle? She can't pinpoint where the pain is coming from. It's just—everywhere. Agnes doesn't know how long it takes her to recover enough to come to standing, but she knows she's wasted a lot of time. Her hands burn from the snow, the skin of her fingers turning almost neon yellow with cold.

Standing, shaking, she attempts a step. Her knee buckles again, but she's ready for it this time. She falls forward into a tree.

No, she thinks, she would never have made it to Ingvar's.

She'll be lucky to get to the farmhouse.

It's an endless shuffle to the house, and a fight to get to the front door. By the time she's reaching for the doorknob, she's breathing heavily through her mouth in harsh, desperate heaves. Sweat drips down the length of her face.

She hobbles inside. The relief from the wind is enough to make her cry. But the reprieve doesn't last long. It's cold in here, too. Despite her sweat and the exertion getting here, she feels the shivers on the edge of her body, threatening to consume her again.

She doesn't need to stay here long. Just long enough to call Ingvar for help. For him to drive here and pick her up.

Treading carefully, haltingly, she threads her way up the rickety staircase. In her father's room, there are old sweaters. His old bed, relatively okay. She will likely have to share it with a nest of rodents, but she can't afford to care about that right now.

Wind pounds at the walls. She stops at the top of the stairs, icy water trickling down the sides of her arms. Pivoting in place, she stares down the staircase, expecting to see Thor's silhouette at the bottom. Knocking on the wall to let her know he's there.

But there's no one. Only the repetitive pounding against the walls. A tree branch, thrown against the stones by the storm.

Agnes forces herself onward. There's not much else she can do.

She gathers up everything from her father's displaced wardrobe, everything he left behind. It doesn't amount to much, but it's something. Hesitantly, her left leg crooked and screaming, she lowers herself onto the small mattress. There's no movement underneath her, no bodies writhing, desperately searching for air, so she relaxes a bit more, draping the old threadbare clothes on her legs. The wood of the bed-frame creaks and moans. She fights the hysterical urge to shush it.

There's that pounding. The knocking of the tree branches.

And there's her breathing.

Nothing else.

She's safe.

What must Thor think she's doing? Had they somehow missed each other on their walks through the woods? Had he seen her rental car, still in the driveway, and assumed she left with Nora?

She wrestles her phone out of her jacket pocket, her hand bare and stinging from the cold. She enters the passcode, her fingers clumsy and not cooperating. She switches off airplane mode, but her phone can't seem to find a signal. The bars keep loading, back and forth, like piano keys trilling. When it finds service, she'll call Ingvar. Then Nora. Then the police.

On-screen, the bars disappear.

No service.

Agnes resists the urge to throw the useless device across the room. Instead, she digs again in her pockets. She finds Ása's phone, presses her thumb against the power button, and prays. If she has to go back out into the wind, she doesn't know if she'll make it back to the house.

The phone screen blinks on. There's an icon of a dead battery. And then it goes dark.

"*Fuck*," she shouts.

Now what?

She stows the two phones in her pockets, crosses her arms over her chest, and leans forward over her legs, as though this tiny bit of scrunching will warm her up. She doesn't want to die, not like this, cowering in a cold room. She's been so close this past year. She leapt from the rocks. Suddenly, though, it feels like she never jumped at all. That in fact she'd slipped and lost her footing on life. Dropped and caught herself just by her fingers on the ledge. And for the past year, slowly, agonizingly, she's lifted one finger off at a time, until she's down to one hand. Now that she's here, now that she's faced with it, with death coming for her, racing toward her, not her meeting it. She wants to live.

She stands, joints grinding. Her father's moth-eaten sweaters fall to the floor. She starts out of the room. There's no other choice.

It's either go to Thor or stay here and die.

She steps onto the top stair. Ingvar's voice calls to her, again and again. *In this cold, even in there, you can lose consciousness from hypothermia.* She takes another trembling step, her knee buckling under her weight. *And then you're not waking up.*

There's a crack underneath her. The loud *bang* of a spring exploding from its coil. And then the staircase opens up beneath her, gravity welcoming her downward. She doesn't have time to scream.

CHAPTER FIFTY

February 12, 2019

She hears the pounding footsteps. Feels the cold rush of water on her skin. Sand everywhere. In her hair. On her face. In her teeth. She coughs through it. Blinks her eyes open, expecting to see the beach in Bolinas, the white spray of the tide coming toward her. The hands on her body, the surfers asking if she's okay. Fighting with each other. *Of course she's not okay,* the woman had said. *Look at her.*

But she's not in California. She's in Iceland. This isn't sand gritting her teeth, but dust. At least forty years' worth of decaying wood. It isn't near noon. There is no sun in the sky. There is only the dark ceiling of her grandfather's farmhouse.

There's no one to save her. No one to pick her up, gently cradling her neck. No one to administer the painkillers she so obviously needs.

Her father is thousands of miles away. Nora and Ingvar, they might as well be, too.

She lifts her head and the world spins off-kilter. Nauseated, her head falls back with a hard jolt against a plank of wood. She doesn't know how long she lies there, waiting for the dizziness to subside, but it's all-consuming. There's a groan, and she assumes it's from her.

Taking a deep breath, she tries to move again. Smaller attempts. She twitches her fingers. They respond. She counts each finger, tapping them to the wood shards. Then her toes. It's painful. But she can wiggle them.

She slides her arms back, rattling the debris around her, and props herself up on her elbows. Dust and splinters coat her body, muting her once luridly red jacket. For a moment, the floor lurches to the side and she thinks she's going to die from the nausea. If she had to vomit right now, which is what she thinks her body wants to do, could she even survive it?

But then, in bits and pieces, the floor rights itself. She breathes in through her mouth and coughs around the dust. She's alive. She's going to get up. And she's going to go back to the house.

To call Ingvar. Then Nora. Then the police.

Maybe the police first, for an ambulance.

Whining in the back of her throat, Agnes gets herself farther upright, so she's sitting. She takes stock of her body's injuries. She's in shock. That must be why nothing hurts, other than the nausea. Or did she miraculously survive the fall with nothing more than a dizzy head?

She pushes herself up, laboriously, to standing, only to crumple back down to the floor, helplessly, like a rag doll. Now she calls out, unable to stop the scream of pain. It's her knee. Her knee falls apart, giving out quick and fast, like someone's blown it apart. She catches herself on her hands, but that doesn't halt her momentum, and she can't see anything but stars when her chin connects with the hardwood. She pulls her throbbing face out from the dust. She has to breathe. *Breathe through this.*

A line of spit falls to the floor underneath her. She probably broke everything all over again. Probably shattered the tenuously healing joints.

She's going to die. Out here, in the dark and the cold. She's going to die like her grandmother. She's going to be found, days later. Frozen. A memorial to pain, to a young life cut tragically short.

No.

She thinks she speaks the word aloud.

She's not going to die like this.

She drags her left leg back underneath her, bending at the knee. The bones grind together, and it feels—it feels twisted. Like she's pulling on the last remaining threads connecting that part of her skeleton. Her kneecap pops in an explosion of fire.

But there's relief. She brings her right knee in beside it. Then she steps, carefully, onto her right foot. Leans all her body weight into that one point of contact and lifts herself up to standing, only allowing the toes of her left foot to touch the ground for balance. Like she did for all those months after surgery. She can do this. She's up. She's standing. She holds back a battle cry. It'll be slow, but she'll get back to the house.

Agnes peers down at the broken boards of the staircase and selects the longest, sturdiest piece of wood. A makeshift cane. Propping her weight onto it, she attempts a step. It's going to be a horrific, ugly shamble back to the house, but the adrenaline will get her there.

There's the knocking again. The rush of wind, yes, but the knocking is so much closer now. And it's not coming from outside.

Agnes feels the vibration under her feet.

There's more.

Something like a scream.

Agnes strains her ears. It's the wind. It has to be the wind whistling through the house, the secret hidden places that only wind or water can find. But it sounds like a woman. Is it Nora? Had she come back and found Agnes missing?

Knocking again. Turning around, Agnes wonders if she's gone crazy. If this is what she's become. She's left her living world behind and has entered some new dream state she can't escape. But she thinks someone's there.

She tries to tune out everything but the present moment. Everything but this small section of the earth.

She sees it. Puffs of dust unsettling from the floor with each pounding knock.

Agnes lowers herself haltingly back to her hands and knees, keeping her left leg out of the way. She brushes the shards of wood away from her, clawing at the new floor. The knocking is coming from underneath the floorboards.

Scrambling now, Agnes makes her way forward, until she finds a latch. It's covered. Easily overlooked in the shadows of an exposed staircase in an abandoned farmhouse only partying students frequent. And this latch, too, is new. The metal of the ring shines.

Threading her hands through the ring, she pulls, but the floor doesn't budge. She tugs harder, but it holds firm.

She hears another round of knocking and she says, her voice wretched with pain and desperation, *"I'm trying."*

The ring twists in the opposite direction and then she feels it wrench free. Forcing her broken body to stand once more, Agnes drags the heavy door open.

What she sees first is the eyes. Hollow, wide.

Then there's the hair, white and stringy with oil. The cloth tied around her mouth. Hands, also bound, bleeding. Reaching above her head. The cellar around her black and molding and claustrophobically small.

"Ása," Agnes says. That's all she can say. "Ása."

CHAPTER FIFTY-ONE

February 12, 2019

With numb fingers, Agnes unties the knot at the back of the woman's skull. When it comes free, the woman tilts her head forward, yanking the cloth out of her mouth. She coughs, swearing in another language.

"Do you speak English?" Agnes asks, feeling the heavy sense of unreality unfolding around her. Distantly, she knows there's a ticking clock. That at any moment, Thor could show up. They're both cold, exposed, and weak. But she's stunned. Ása's alive.

Ása stares up at her, her expression wild and fearful. She can't seem to bring Agnes into focus. How long has she been down here? Luckily, Agnes thinks, she's wearing a snowsuit. Thick pants and thick jacket. They hang on her frame, as though they don't belong to her, but to a bigger man.

"Help me," Ása says, her voice nothing more than a croak.

"I will," Agnes promises. She reaches for the woman's hands. She tries to untie the knot there. The plastic rope digs into the woman's skin, leaving it red and raw. Agnes struggles with it, but her fingers bend against the binding. "We'll have to cut that off you," she says, "when we get back."

"Get me out of here," Ása says. "Please."

Agnes looks around her. There are no steps into the cellar. No step-ladder, either. While she catalogs her options, Ása sways unsteadily on her feet, threatening to pitch backward, farther into the cellar.

"Come here," Agnes beckons.

There's something wrong with the woman's pupils. She's spent time in absolute darkness, and this room isn't exactly bright. Her pupils shouldn't be this small.

"He's been drugging you," Agnes says.

The woman nods. It sets her off-balance again.

Agnes grabs for her arm. She tugs Ása closer to the edge of the cellar. Tells her to jump. "Try to land on your elbows, then I'll pull you," Agnes says, aware of her own limitations.

Ása jumps, but it's a pitiful hop. She lands wrong and falls to the side. She tells Agnes, "Sorry."

If Agnes's skin weren't crawling, if she weren't waiting, every heartbeat, for the door to open, for Thor to walk in and discover them, she would cry. Instead, she tells the woman to try again. "I've got you," she says, forcing her body into a crouching position that crushes the broken bones and overstretches the frayed cartilage in her leg. She clamps both hands into the woman's armpits and leans back on her heels, left heel quaking beneath her and making her whole body shake. She counts to three and the woman hops again. When Agnes feels Ása's body lift from the floor, she throws her weight backward, a scream tearing through her as though splitting her open.

Her knee comes undone. *This is it*, she thinks. *It's ruined. Shot.*

And there's the heavy weight on top of her. The smell of an unwashed body. Animalistic terror. The dank stench of deep earth.

The woman rolls off her, and she's all elbows and sharp corners, scrambling. Agnes slides back to give her space, breathing hard, but she can see the woman's problem. Ása's ankles have been tied together, too.

"Stop," she says. She reaches for the woman's legs. The knot, nestled between the legs, is big enough for Agnes to struggle it loose. It takes far too long. Agnes feels sweat pouring down her temples, her teeth grinding, but finally, the rope falls to the floor.

"Takk," Ása says.

Agnes pushes herself to standing. The makeshift cane trembles beneath her. Her left leg shakes and jolts, weight on it or not. "We have to go," she says. "Can you walk?"

"I will." Ása pushes herself awkwardly to standing. She can't find her feet, and she seems close to fainting, but she stays upright. "No other choice," she says.

They shuffle forward, down the hallway, and it's slow, but it's going.

There's no room for thought. No room for feeling.

If there were, though. If Agnes had the space to think about it, to name the emotions coiling around her. She'd call it desperate. Terrified.

She'd call it relief, too.

She found Ása.

She's alive.

CHAPTER FIFTY-TWO

February 12, 2019

It's not an easy walk. Agnes can hardly see for all the snow pelting into her eyes, can hardly hold her left leg up, away from the ice. Ása's trying her best, but she's been drugged, been held captive, has probably not eaten properly, if anything, for days. She can't move in a steady line.

"He'll kill me," Ása says. Her lips are on their way to blue. "And you."

"He won't," Agnes says. She digs her makeshift cane into the snow in front of her. Forces all her weight into that one point of contact with the earth. Hops forward on her right foot. Rinse. Repeat. "I won't let him."

It sounds like empty bravado, but Agnes is angry enough to tear Thor apart. He's a monster. This woman beside her, trembling and broken, he's ravaged her. He's felt entitled to take everything from her, to hurt her, to terrorize her. If she could, Agnes would kill him. Now.

There's nowhere else to go but back to his house. Just to grab the car keys, Agnes tells Ása. She's repeating the phrase like a mantra. First the car keys, then the drive to Ingvar's. She's sorry to bring Ása back to

Thor's home, but it'll only be for a moment. And Thor can't be there still, can he? If he is there—Agnes can't think about it. She'll do what she can to protect Ása. To protect herself.

Maybe it's just the desperation driving them both forward, but the house appears out of the haze quicker than Agnes had expected. The last steps across the driveway bring her to a new height of pain. Her left leg won't bend—but that ability was lost so long ago now. It's agony to lift it the few inches into the air that she must to get herself forward. It's become a sandbag, dragging underneath her. She throws herself into the front door.

Agnes calls out, her voice hoarse, "Hello?"

There's no answer.

She waits another beat. No other voices, no other footsteps. No other heartbeats in this house but her own. Nothing except the roar of the wind outside. Lights—left on by Thor—flicker with every new gust. At a particularly strong one, the house turns into an underground club, the strobe light thumping to the beat of some unheard house mix.

Agnes beckons Ása inside. "It's okay," she says. "We're safe."

Ása hesitates at the threshold. She takes in the dark hallway with wide, rolling eyes. "Why did you bring me here?"

"Just to get the car keys," Agnes assures her again. "I need your help grabbing them. Then we're leaving."

Stepping inside, Ása visibly reins in her fear. She manages to close the door behind her with her bound hands.

"Thank you," Agnes says, and she means it.

Limping, she leads them into the kitchen. When she reaches the counter, she drops her cane and leans her body weight against the cool marble. Her hands are like claws, frozen in a white-knuckle grip. She digs through the drawers, grabbing for the scissors. Ása comes up behind her, questioning. Agnes doesn't answer, just hacks at the woman's bonds. When the rope comes loose, dropping to the floor with a pathetic clatter, Ása lets out a cry. Of pain, of joy, it's all the same thing now. Her first act of freedom is to drop her head into the sink, sucking at the running water.

Agnes reaches for the bottle of pills, unopened, on the counter. She's at the end of her sanity. She needs a couple, so she can manage through the next few hours of her life, so she can think. When the cap finally releases, though, the bottle falls from her hands and the pills scatter everywhere but on the counter.

She lets out a hoarse curse.

The faucet turns off with a squeak. Ása, flinching away from her.

"I'm sorry," Agnes says, her face contorting from the effort not to cry. She can't bend over again. Not like this. She can't reach. "It's just—I'm in so much pain—"

She cuts herself off. Ása bends over for her. Unsteady, but making it look easy. Her fingers, still swollen and stiff, covered in blood, swipe at the pills, pushing them around rather than picking them up. Finally, though, she gathers a few in her hands. She drops them onto the counter, the color drained from her face.

Agnes swallows them all immediately. "Thanks."

The pills stick to the back of her throat. She muscles them down. Will they be able to muffle some of this pain? Make Agnes forget, even for a moment, the sight of Ása, tied up in the complete darkness of a cellar?

"Who are you?" Ása asks. "Why are you here?"

"I'm Agnes," she says. "It's a long story. But we're getting out." They're going to get in the car and drive themselves to Ingvar's home. "The car keys are in the bedroom there." She directs Ása to the right one. "Can you get them for me?"

Watching Ása hurry down the hall, the adrenaline that has propelled Agnes so far drains out of her system. She deflates against the counter. She knows this isn't over. But she's warm, and the opioid bleeds into her limbs in a trail of heat so pleasant it's almost sexual. It can't cover the throbbing from her leg, but it can soften everything else.

"There are no keys," Ása tells her. When had she come back?

"On the bedside table," Agnes hears herself say. "In the second bedroom?"

"There are no keys," Ása insists. "I checked."

Agnes straightens against the counter, reaching for the cane. It's possible that she'd put the car key somewhere else. She asks Ása to check her bag in her room. Then she forces herself to follow the woman down the hallway.

When Agnes stops moving, a long slow wave of nausea courses over her, setting her in a swing like a carousel. She waits for the vomit to force its way out, but nothing happens. She scans the room. There are no keys on the bedside table, as Ása had said. The quilt on her bed is still knotted how she left it. She wouldn't put her key there. She leans her weight on the mattress, one hand free to dig through the bedside table's drawers.

No key.

She asks Ása if she found it.

The lights snap off. For a long moment, Agnes can only see the ghost image of the woman's silhouette, crouched in the corner of the room, searching her backpack. Then, with an effort, the lights flick back on. It's the storm, gaining strength. Disrupting their power.

"No." There's a tremor in Ása's voice. A warning that she's close to losing it. Agnes can't blame her, but there's no time. She asks the woman to look under the bed. Maybe Agnes knocked them to the floor, kicked them under without feeling it. Ása complies, bloody hands groping in the dark. She pulls back. "Nothing," she says.

Now the panic climbs up Agnes's spine. She hadn't taken the keys out of this room. They're not in her jacket pockets. She empties their contents on the bed to be sure. Two phones. A tube of lip balm. The flag-bearer figurine from her father's room. No keys. She's usually pretty good about keeping track of these things. She thinks she would have left the keys on her bedside table, as always. Easy to grab.

That's when she remembers.

Thor. She'd seen him cross the hallway, into this room. Had he taken the keys?

To trap her?

Why?

Ása asks, accusation threading through every word, "Why do you have my phone?"

Agnes can hardly breathe, let alone answer. They're stuck here. Stranded.

"What do you want from me?" Ása asks. "Are you helping him?"

Agnes's phone isn't out of battery. She takes it from the bed. Hustles out of the room, aware that Ása's following, aware that she has to answer, but everything can wait until they call Ingvar. Her fingers fumble on the screen.

"You are," Ása says, her voice rising to a hysterical pitch. "Oh my god, you're helping him."

She's about to lose it. Lose it and not get it back.

"Lilja gave me your phone," Agnes says, loud and firm. "She said Óskar found it. It's all so convoluted, Ása, I can't think right now. Please, just trust me. Lilja got it from Óskar and she gave it to me. She was worried the police would think that she hurt you. But she didn't, right? You sent that text and you left the party. She and Óskar took you back to your place. And then something else happened."

If Agnes's knowledge of her life frightens her, Ása doesn't show it. Perhaps she, too, has reached the limit of her own emotions.

"I was crying," Ása says, "and I saw"—she shakes her head—"I saw the headlights outside. He was in his truck, waiting for me. I got so angry, I didn't think. We'd been fighting. I ended it. But he was there. I went outside to tell him to leave me alone. He asked me to talk. He wanted to apologize and then he promised me he would leave me alone." Ása watches Agnes carefully, waiting for the accusation. The inevitable *You should have known better.* But Agnes feels nothing but sadness. Anger, too, but it's a distant roll of thunder on the horizon. "I agreed. He took me here and gave me some wine and it—I woke up in the dark. I don't know for how long."

"You've been gone for nine days," Agnes says. The horror of it threatens to consume her.

Ása nods to herself, absorbing this information somewhere deep inside. Agnes wants to admire her for her strength, but she suspects most of her stoicism is due to shock. To whatever drugs lace her system. Later—if there is a later—she will have time to fall apart, when she lets everything that's happened sink in. Hopefully she'll be able to put herself back together.

"He brought me food and juice," Ása says. "I knew it had something in it making me sleep. But I had to—I was so thirsty."

All this time, she's been fighting to survive. Agnes wants to tell her she's safe now. But she can't promise that, can she?

Ingvar.

Agnes unlocks her phone and dials Ingvar's number. It rings through to voicemail.

She hangs up.

Dials again, furious with herself, with everyone. This time, she waits for the beep, and then she leaves a frantic message. "We need help. I found Ása. She's here. We're—Thor's dangerous. We're stuck. I'm hurt. I can't drive. Please, come. *Please.*"

All the while, Ása's staring at her.

"What?" Agnes asks, trying not to snap. She's doing the best she can, and she's aware that it's not nearly enough.

"I kept waiting for him to kill me. But every time, I would wake up. Now I don't think that's happened. I think I've died."

"Stop it," Agnes says. "That's not happening." She crosses the last distance to one of the couches and descends with a jolt that sends a spear of hot metal through her body, like she's been branded from the inside out. She leans back, resting her leg on the pillows. Already she can see the swelling against her jeans. She allows herself one whimper of helplessness. Then she digs the heels of her palms into her eyes, trying to clear her head.

The police.

She asks Ása for the emergency number. Dials 112 with a shaky finger. *I've found Ása Gunnarsdóttir,* she'll say. *She didn't run away. She didn't commit suicide. She was kidnapped by Thor Thorsson. And he's still here. And my leg is shattered. Come quick.*

The phone rings. She hears the pick-up, hears the sound of a woman's voice on the other end, polite and urgent, and then everything goes black.

The lights have flickered out again. The phone beeps a small, pathetic rhythm to let Agnes know that the call has disconnected. She waits, holding her breath, begging the electricity to please, *please* come back on. But there's nothing. Just the darkness. The scant illumination of the snow outside.

"We've lost power," Agnes says, her voice coming from far away. "And my phone—" She glances down. No Wi-Fi. No bars. Ása's phone is dead. Her charger is in her kidnapper's other home. "Can you get to Ingvar?"

"What?"

Agnes tells her how to find the driveway across the road. The long incline to his house. Ása nods like she knows this already.

"You have to go," Agnes says.

"What about you?"

"My leg," she says. "I can't." It's all she can say about it. "Go. The power is out. He might come here to check on me. You need to go. Get help."

Ása hesitates.

"Go!" Agnes shouts.

Ása flinches, which breaks Agnes's heart, but she can't waste any more time. Ása makes for the front door, weaving and catching her balance against the walls. Agnes listens to the door slamming behind her and falls into the couch cushions.

She's in the black. Wounded and waiting.

CHAPTER FIFTY-THREE

February 12, 2019

Her eyes roll in her head when she hears the knocking. She doesn't know where she is. She'd been in a half sleep, back home in California, listening to her father's footsteps on the old wood floors. He'd been calling her for dinner, and she'd been disoriented, too stoned to be able to do anything but drowse.

Then comes the man's voice and it isn't her father's. "Hello?" Thor calls. "Did you lose electricity, too?"

And she's back in Iceland. Back on the big couch, back in the dark, back in the hellhole of Thor's making. Her entire left leg, she can feel from its throbbing, is swollen now. She wonders, briefly, what they'll be able to do to fix it, if she takes it to a doctor. What can they do?

All thought deserts her. There's Thor, hanging above her. "What a storm!" he exclaims. "Have I disturbed you?" Then, with alarm: "What's happened to you?"

"I fell," she croaks. When did her throat start to swell, too? She attempts a swallow, but it doesn't quite make it all the way through. "Broke my leg."

"How?" he asks, and she feels a hand on her thigh. It sends a shower of sparks behind her eyes that nearly blinds her. She tastes the edges of a blackout. The hand reappears on her forehead. She welcomes the cool touch. "How did you do this?"

"Ambulance," she manages to say. "I need a hospital."

"Of course," he says. The cushion beside her dips. He's sitting next to her, his face so close it's all she can see. "What's happened? You look—" He doesn't finish that sentence. He brushes his hand on her puffy jacket. Her hair. He stares at his fingertips.

"Fell," she repeats. "Ambulance."

"Yes," he says. He drags more dust from her jacket. "Are they coming?"

"No power."

"I see," he says, and she realizes her mistake, slowly, in stages. She should have said yes. The authorities are on their way. Let him run away while she waits for Ása and Ingvar. That is, if Ása has made it to Ingvar's. Reality comes crashing through the doorway her pain had tried to shut. She's sent Ása, drugged and traumatized and disoriented, into a snowstorm, to find a place she's never been to before. Up a long, steep hill Agnes could hardly manage herself. And now she is alone with Ása's kidnapper.

"It's okay," Thor tells her. "I'll help. What happened? Where did you fall? Why are you covered in—" He shows her the dust on his fingertips. "Were you in the farmhouse? I told you, it's dangerous while I work on it."

Agnes wonders if this is really happening. If she'd actually found Ása and freed her, or if she fell in the farmhouse and she's still there. Hallucinating.

"This storm," Thor's saying, "it's too dangerous to take you to a hospital. We will wait it out. You will be okay, I promise. I will take care of you." He pushes himself to standing. "I will get you some water."

The world sets back to spinning while she waits for her water. But there's no sound of the tap running. There's only a shocked noise. A "What's this?" and then dead silence.

Agnes buries a hand underneath the layers of her jacket and hoodie and shirt and digs her fingernails into the soft flesh of her stomach. This is real. This is actually happening to her. She can't drift away. She starts to push herself up to sitting, but stops.

There's Thor again, standing at the edge of the couch. Holding the length of the rope that had once bound Ása's hands.

"Agnes," he says, and there's no smile, no paternal twinkle in his eyes, "what have you done?"

CHAPTER FIFTY-FOUR

February 12, 2019

"She's gone," Agnes says. She drags her body backward on the couch. The leg is useless, but the rest of her, she can move. "She's safe."

"What are you talking about?" Thor asks. Still that rope, hanging from one hand.

"Ása," she says. "I found her."

Thor looks around them. "Where is she?"

"Not here," Agnes rasps. "I got her away from you."

Frowning, Thor steps out of the living room, making his way down the hallway. Agnes can hear doors opening and closing. "Is she okay?" he asks, calling from the master bedroom. "Is that how you hurt yourself?"

She's not sure if it's the shock of everything that's happened today, the cold or the pill making her so slow, but she can't keep up. What does he mean, *Is she okay?* He's had Ása locked in a cellar for nine days. Now he's worried for her safety?

Thor returns to the living room. "Tell me what happened," he says, more urgent now. He resumes his seat on the couch beside Agnes. "You were at the farmhouse, weren't you? You're covered in dust. You hurt your leg. You found her there? Is she still there?"

Agnes shakes her head.

He doesn't believe her. "I will be right back," he says. "Stay here."

She has no other choice but to watch him open the sliding glass doors and disappear into the churning snow. She drops her head back to the cushions, trying to stop the spinning from overwhelming her again. This isn't what she expected. Does she have it wrong? How is that possible? She found the phone on Thor's bedside table. She found Ása trapped in the cellar of the abandoned farmhouse on his property. But, Agnes realizes with a growing sense of horror, did Ása ever actually say that it had been Thor? Everything has become a blur of pain, of trying to survive.

She feels herself slipping into a sort of fever dream. Exhaustion washes over her in waves, and she feels like she's being dragged under. Hands on her body, wrapping around her shoulders, her legs, pulling her under the surface, down where there's no air, nothing but the deep.

She's halfway to oblivion when she hears the sliding door open again. When she hears the puffing breaths, the footsteps racing toward her. The pressure on her body. Shaking her back to the present moment. Forcing her to look into those thin gray eyes.

"Where is she?" Thor asks her.

CHAPTER FIFTY-FIVE

February 12, 2019

Agnes babbles through her panic. "I found her," she's saying, and she can't stop herself. "I got her out of the cellar, and I brought her here. The power went out. I couldn't walk. So she—she's gone. She's somewhere safe. Somewhere far away and safe." She repeats the last words, as though she could assure herself of this fact. But Ása isn't safe, is she? She's walking through a blizzard looking for help.

Thor doesn't seem to be listening to Agnes, though. He's staring out at the storm, somewhere else entirely.

"What—" Agnes begins, but she's not brave enough to finish the question. *What are you going to do to me?*

This one word, though, is enough to call him back to her. Thor drags a hand down his face, giving her a brief glimpse at the gaudy pink flesh protecting his eyes. Suddenly, he seems ten years older, haggard and strange.

"Agnes," he says with a heavy sigh. "Why did you do this? You hurt yourself," he says, more to himself, it seems, than her. He rests his hand on what used to be her knee. Even the lightest touch feels like he's dragging a fishhook through her chest, down the line of her body, to her groin. Everything loses focus. "You found Ása."

He eases up. Still, she can't recover.

"You say she's gone," he says. "Car's still here. If someone picked her up, they would take you, too. Did you make her *walk*? Where? To Ingvar? Oh, Agnes."

He squeezes her knee, and she wonders if this is it. This is what it's like to die. To be hauled into it. She wants, more than anything, her dad. She wants to be home in Berkeley. She wants to be a kid again, safe in her dad's bed, listening to him flipping the pages of his book, feeling his hand on her hair. *Agnes and Magnús, two sides of the same coin.*

But she's here.

She can't wish her way home.

Thor's eyes seem to look straight through her. "She wouldn't make it to the road," he tells her. "You killed her."

"No," she says, knowing it's useless. Knowing, in that moment, exactly what is coming for her. "How could you do it?" she asks. "You took her. You drugged her." She tries to push herself upright onto her elbows, but Thor's there in an instant, and he stops her easily with the pressure of one hand on her chest.

"Settle down," he tells her.

"You put her in a cellar," she says. She takes big gulping breaths. "You kept her underground."

The hand pressing on her chest digs deeper. "You are the one who sent her out into the snow."

"You're a monster," Agnes chokes out.

"Did she tell you," he asks, emotion raising the volume of his voice to a near shout, "what she did? No? Six months, we are together. She tells me she loves me, we have something special. She's never felt this way before. And then something changes. She stops answering my calls. She doesn't want to see me. I beg her to talk to me. To tell me what it is I've done. Is it someone else? She tells me no. It's no one else. She tells me she was pregnant. With my baby. And she killed it. She wasn't answering her phone, she wasn't here, because she was in Reykjavík, killing my child."

His rage threatens to tear him into two. He drags himself away from Agnes and paces the length of the living room while he speaks. "She tells me this and she expects me to be calm. She expects me to accept what she's done. Then she's sending me these texts, telling me I am too angry. She killed my baby, and *I'm the monster?*"

"You're insane," she says. It comes out unbidden. But that's what this is. That's what's sharing the room with her: insanity.

"You don't understand," he says. "You've never had children and lost them. You've never dealt with this pain before, have you? You don't know what I feel. You can't even imagine it, and you don't want to. I know you. You feel so much, but you're selfish with it. You're like Marie. Selfish."

"Like Marie," Agnes says. Something bubbles up underneath the surface of her panic. She can't grab hold of it. She's hardly able to hold onto her own sanity now. She suspects if she blacks out now, though, she'll wake up in the cellar. And then there will be no escape.

"Marie killed my baby, too," he says.

The final pieces of the puzzle fall into place. Thor had been eighteen when Marie, age twenty-six, was killed. As old as Marie had been when she'd met Einar. Too young, far too young, but old enough.

"It wasn't your father," she hears herself say. "It was you."

"I loved her so much," Thor says. The smile he sends her, so sad, chills her blood. "And she loved me."

CHAPTER FIFTY-SIX

February 12, 2019

"I had no one," Thor says. "My mother left without telling me where she was going. She didn't want my father to find her. She was there one day, and then the next, *gone*. She left me alone with him. I had no one. And then, one day, by the river, I see Marie. She's holding a postcard and she's crying. I ask her what's wrong and she says it's a letter from her mother. She was crying like a baby, missing her home. I tell her I understand. I miss my mother, too. And then she's holding me, and we're both crying." He marvels to himself, as though even now the memory comforts him.

"We sit out here." Thor points to the small patch of land outside, overlooking the river. It's hardly discernible in this storm. "She tells me about her home. I still don't know how it happened, but we fell in love. She started leaving me gifts out here, where I could find them. Secret messages. One of her earrings. She would wear one and I would wear the other, and we would always be thinking of the other. My father saw it and took it out. He took everything from me.

"She grows with child," Thor says, and he stops. He reaches into his jacket, pulls out a folded sheet of paper. Unfurls it, stares down at it, his expression unfathomable and strange. Then he's showing Agnes the paper, shoving it into her face so she can see. It's the printout Nora had given her, the family portrait. "Look at her," he says. "My baby."

He snatches the paper away, restoring it to his jacket pocket.

"But you kept meeting," Agnes says. "She had Ingvar watch the baby, so she could spend time with you. Right?"

"In the warm months, we have picnics out here. I want to spend time with the baby—*my* baby. But she can't. Little Ingvar is there. He tells everyone how he is Marie's best friend. He would have told everyone he saw me. We had to be careful. But that was my child."

The world slips a notch to the side. Agnes isn't in pain anymore because she isn't here. Not all the way. "Did she tell you it was?"

"She tells me it's Einar's, but I know the truth."

"What happened?" Agnes asks. She thinks she knows. She doesn't want to hear it, but she will, regardless. "How did Einar find out?"

"I go to her house," Thor says, his hands flexing at his sides. Opening and closing into fists. "In winter, it's difficult for us to see each other. Magnús is home. But for once, Magnús isn't there. No Ingvar. And she's got the baby in her arms, and they're both crying. They're both there, my family. When she sees me, though, it's like—she acts like she is afraid. She tells me I shouldn't be there.

"'He knows,' she says.

"I ask her, 'He knows what?'

"'Einar,' she says, 'he knows about us.' I try to hold her, and she pushes me away. She tells me she doesn't want to be with me. She wants Einar. If he'll forgive her. That's all she wants.

"I don't believe her. She tells me to leave. She takes me outside, even though it's cold and it makes the baby angry. I take the baby. She's mine. I deserve to hold her.

"She's so precious, and she's mine.

"But Marie tells me to give her back. She loves her husband. She loves her baby. She loves her son. She doesn't want to lose them. I tell her *I* love her. And she loves me. Doesn't she love me?" It's a cry of self-pity, of insatiable need. "And she says—she tries to take my baby from me—and she says, 'Not enough.'"

There's no light in the room anymore. The blizzard's claimed the sky, painting it in a wash of static.

"And I won't let her have my baby," Thor says. "She tells me I am too young to understand. She has taken advantage of me, and she's sorry. I tell her to stop. I know that I love her. But she keeps saying she doesn't love me. She says I frighten her."

Agnes grips her fingernails into her stomach again. Whatever's coming, it's coming fast now.

"I show her the baby," Thor says, "and I'm telling her this is us. This is our love. She shouts at me. She tells me it's Einar's child. It will always be his child. Just like she will always be his."

Thor looks down at his open palms. Then back up, to Agnes. There are tears in his eyes.

"You can't imagine my regret," he tells her. His voice breaks. "You have no idea the pain I felt. I didn't know what I was doing, until I had done it. I am holding my baby, and then my hands are cold. So cold. The baby's not crying anymore. She's quiet in my arms. But someone is fighting me. Attacking me. I turn around and it's Marie. She's like a wild animal. And I feel this hatred. Then she's underneath me, too, and there's all this blood in the water. You have to believe me, Agnes, I didn't know what I was doing until it was done."

He's lying. Somewhere in there, he's lying. They were outside when he drowned the baby. But he'd cut Marie's throat. Where had the knife come from? Had he left Marie, weeping over her murdered child, to go to the kitchen to retrieve the weapon? Had rage propelled him that far?

"I believe you," Agnes says, horror somehow keeping her calm. Present. "After you killed them. What did you do?"

"When I saw what I'd done," Thor says, sinking down next to her, hands clasped together as though asking her for forgiveness, "I ran home. I took off my bloody clothes, and I put them into bags. My father walks in. I try to make him leave. I beg him to leave. But he forces me to say it. He tells me he will kill me. But he doesn't do anything. Not until that night. He tells me I will have to be the one to leave. 'I will help you,' he says, 'but you must never come back.'"

A good man sacrifices for his family.

"He protected you," Agnes says.

I didn't tell, because of my promise.

"There is not a day," Thor says, "that I have not missed her. That I have not seen her face in every girl I pass. That I have not wondered how my life has gotten here. I have lived with this regret for so long. Agnes. My baby. My sweet girl. Later, my wife, she couldn't have children. We tried for so many years, but nothing. And I thought that that was my penance. I was paying for that mistake, by not having children. I will be left to live out my days knowing what I could have had. Then I met Ása, and I thought my punishment was not over. I tried to fix it, but I should have known it wasn't over. I should have known, too, that it wasn't Ása punishing me. It was you. The daughter I should have had. You are my punishment."

Thor rubs a hand over his mouth, and Agnes can see his fingers trembling. "I'm sorry," he tells her, and he sounds genuinely devastated. "I'm so sorry it had to be you."

Agnes understands, again, all at once. He's made a decision. They've reached the end.

CHAPTER FIFTY-SEVEN

February 12, 2019

Agnes shoves herself backward on the couch, trying to gain some distance from the man, bringing her one good knee into her chest. Thor is too quick, and he has the luxury of two working legs. He's up in a flash, reaching for the length of rope that had once been Ása's prison. Now it's going to be hers.

Kicking out desperately, Agnes aims for his head. But it's like fighting in a dream. Nothing moves the way you want it to. She hardly connects with any force. Instead, she only jolts her other leg. And she's wasted precious time, she understands in the instant she's lost that moment, she should have used trying to get off the couch. She's scrambling, trying to summon her strength, when he lands on top of her.

The arms on her shoulders. The burn of the rope on her skin, connecting with her windpipe.

"Stop struggling," he says.

She chokes on the pressure.

"You're making me do this," he tells her. "Stop struggling, and it will be easier."

She reaches up with both hands. Aims for his eyes. One thumb actually slips into the gooey flesh of an eyeball, but then he's jerked himself away. She manages to scramble off the couch, landing with a terrible jolt on the floor, her leg hitting hard enough for her to heave from the pain. She's at Thor's feet. She crawls, ignoring everything except the desire to get away from him, but she can't move fast enough.

A hand curls around her left ankle, dragging her away from the relative safety of the coffee table, out into the open. She had thought, somewhere in the attempt to rescue Ása, that she had surpassed her pain threshold, that there was nothing else that could hurt more on this earth. She'd been wrong. She's not herself. She's not a person. She's a hurricane of agony, of mortal terror.

She's stopped. Thor's left her underneath him. But still she feels like she's moving, like she's sliding down the cliff into the dark void.

"Don't make this worse," she hears him say. "Please. Don't force me to make this worse."

It's everything she can do to breathe. She savors each new rush of air, wondering when she will reach the point when she can no longer take it in.

Then he's gone. Walking away from her. Agnes twists her head to the side and watches as Thor stoops down to collect the pills she'd scattered on the floor a lifetime ago. "How much have you been taking?" he asks her. He wanders through the kitchen, as casually as if he were in search of a snack. He uncorks the wine bottle next to her already full glass. He fills it to the brim. He gathers the pills into the bottle.

Haltingly, Agnes props herself up on one elbow and reaches for her makeshift cane. This isn't how it goes. This isn't how she dies, prone and obedient. Making it easy for him.

"You hurt your leg," he says. "You take more pills to soften the pain. Only, you take too much. And you don't wake up. It's a tragedy. It really is."

"Ása's safe," she tells him. "No matter what you do to me—" Her voice falls apart. She balances on her right leg, holding the makeshift cane in one hand. "She's out there telling everyone what you did. You're going to get caught. Killing me does nothing."

"She's frozen in the snow," he says. "*You* are responsible for her death. I was only trying to make her stay."

He comes within reach, walking toward her with the wine, the pills. Raising the cane, the only weapon left at her disposal, Agnes aims for his head. He blocks her easily, and he retaliates, sweeping one leg to knock at her left knee. Through a howl of pain, she grabs at him, dragging him down with her. They land in a horrible twisting heap, because he's trying to muscle his way out of her grip and she won't let go. She can't. There's the shatter of the wineglass, a splash of the acidic liquid exploding across her face, and the wind has been knocked out of her, but for the moment, she's winning. She's fighting for her life.

An elbow rams into her stomach and she rakes her fingernails over every exposed piece of flesh. The world spins out from underneath her and there he is, looming over her, his face an unearthly shade of red. He shifts his hold to lock one hand over her throat, and she becomes a live wire.

She hears his grunt of effort. Feels the strength of his body clamping around her. But she can't give up. She's going to get out of this. And she's going to kill him.

Bucking. Reaching. Searching for anything. A hot line of fire drags along her right palm, and she grabs for it. A shard from the broken wineglass. Gripping it, despite the searing burn of it tearing into her skin, she rams her fist upward.

The glass finds purchase in his cheek.

It's a sensation unlike anything she has ever experienced before, the brief resistance of his flesh, then the jolt when the glass sinks in. The grisly satisfaction she feels when it penetrates. When he shrieks, when he rips himself away, rending a longer split of his cheek, she aims again, for anything, catching his hands when they fly upward to protect his mouth.

And then everything moves so quickly she can't keep track of it. She hears a roar, and she sees a blur of movement, and then the man on top of her disappears. There's a sickening, dull sound of a body being hit, and the unmistakable crack of a skull ricocheting off a hard surface.

Then there are hands on her. Everywhere the hands. On her face, swiping at the wine, the blood, clawing at her jacket, checking her legs. She whimpers at the touch, and she hears a "Sorry, oh, I'm sorry."

There, above her, face frantic and more beautiful than she could ever put words to, is Ingvar.

CHAPTER FIFTY-EIGHT

February 12, 2019

There's so much warmth. Agnes's head lolls on the car seat. She's sitting sideways in the back, her torn hand gripping a towel, left leg stretched out in front of her, useless and throbbing, and she just wants to sleep, to fall back into oblivion, but they won't let her.

"Keep your hand above your heart," Ingvar reminds her.

She tries to get it up higher, but her body isn't cooperating, and they're rocketing so fast down the slick highway, the truck won't stop swerving, rattling her, that she can't quite raise the arm. She settles for resting the hand against her chest.

A thick line of wind and sleet crashes against the side of the truck and Ingvar, swearing with the effort, his bandaged hand grappling at the wheel, fights against the current pushing them side to side. "Where," Agnes says, her tongue swollen in her mouth, making her sound like someone completely new, "are we going?"

"Reykjavík," Ingvar says. "Hospital."

Agnes tries to keep her eyes open. To watch as the world outside, tumultuous and terrifying, attacks the truck and as Ingvar attacks back. As though observing it will help, will keep the dangers at bay. But she's so tired.

Her eyes close. Her head rocks forward, dangling in the air. She hears, distantly, Ingvar's voice commanding her to stay awake.

It's an effort, more than she thought herself capable of, more demanding than stabbing a man, to bring her head back up.

There's a pressure on her good leg. It's a hand. Ása's hand. Agnes would know it anywhere. Those swollen fingers will haunt her forever. She follows the thin arm upward to the hollow eyes. Ása's twisted around in the passenger seat, body swaying with the movements of the truck.

"It won't be long," Ása tells her. "But you can't sleep. It helps to talk." Her voice breaks. "That's what I did."

The truck fishtails around a curve, but Ingvar doesn't slow down. There's only moving forward.

"What about Thor?" Agnes asks. She had caught a glimpse of the man's inert body on the floor, moaning, but then Ingvar had gathered her up in his arms and she'd blacked out. Had woken up here, tucked in the backseat. "Did you leave him alone?"

There's a flash of blue eyes in the rearview mirror, then they're gone. "I called the police. They'll get him."

Ása's hand snakes its way into Agnes's free one. She squeezes. Agnes returns the pressure.

The truck bounces over a rise. Pebbles spray over its metal shell. Then they're tilting downward, skating the edges of the coast. She doesn't know how long they've been driving for, or how much longer it'll take them to get to the hospital. She can think only of the present moment, of time passing by in nearly imperceptible increments. Or— that's what she'd like to think. But there's the man. The man who took everything from her family. Who kidnapped Ása. Who tried to kill her.

While they race through the storm, Agnes starts to speak. She tells them everything, about finding the phone, finding Ása, about Thor and Marie and the baby. And it feels like bleeding.

CHAPTER FIFTY-NINE

February 16, 2019

The nurse coaxes Agnes to cross the length of the hallway. She leans heavily on the crutches they've given her, and even though it's terrifying, even though her leg still drags unsteadily beneath her, she can walk. There's more hardware, more pain. But she can move.

Standing at the exit, the final doorway separating her ward from the waiting room, is her father.

Ingvar had rushed her and Ása into the emergency room and they'd all been separated, almost instantly. Agnes had been wheeled into sterile rooms teeming with people who prodded her without introduction, who asked her to repeat what had happened. They asked her when she had last eaten. They stabbed her with needles. They took her to an X-ray. They told her they would get her ready for the operation.

She'd grabbed someone's shirt. She told them about her pills. Her tolerance to morphine.

And then she'd heard Nora Carver's voice, echoing through the hallway.

There'd been yelling. Closer. And there she was, telling one of the nurses that she was a friend. She'd felt her hand on her shoulder.

"It's okay," Agnes had said. "I'm okay."

The next day, her father arrived. Disheveled, his eyes shadowed from prolonged panic over a too-long flight, Magnús had been quiet in Agnes's hospital room when she told the police everything that had happened, everything that Thor had said. She'd been sorry for this, that this was how her father learned the truth. But it had been easier, if she had to admit it to herself, to tell him by not telling *him*.

The officers, though they had been kind and thorough, had left with a devastating parting blow. They'd found Agnes's car keys. They'd been tucked into the front pocket of an old pair of jeans, thrown carelessly into a pile of clothes on top of her suitcase.

Thor hadn't taken them from her.

Agnes had waited until she and her father were alone before she'd spoken. "I've been so stupid," she said.

Her father leaned forward and smoothed the hair away from her forehead. His hand shook, as though he were afraid she might flinch away from his touch. As though he might hurt her. "You survived," he told her. "That's all that matters."

Maybe that was true, Agnes thought. But when she closed her eyes, she could only see herself driving Ása through the pelting snow, along the curve of Ingvar's driveway. Supporting each other on the walk to his front door. The shock on his face. She could only imagine sitting in the safety of Ingvar's living room, while someone else handled Thor. While someone else heard the man's monstrous confession.

"There's something wrong," Agnes said, surprised to hear her own voice, "about what Thor told me. He said he and Marie had been arguing outside the house, right by the river. When he saw what he'd done, he ran away. Immediately. To clean up the blood. His father found him, and he confessed."

There had been something new in her father's expression. A door struggling to remain shut.

"But," she continued, "the bodies weren't found outside the farmhouse. They were found upriver. Near the Thors' place." The father and son wouldn't have gone to the trouble of moving the bodies, not when they were situated perfectly to frame the husband. Not when Thor Senior told them about Einar's bloody hands. The open-mouthed horror of a man who just buried his wife and child.

It hadn't been phrased as a question, but she let it sit as one.

Finally, when her father spoke, his voice trembled at the edges. "I was on my way home," he said. "I'd been out all afternoon. Doing I don't know what. I'm almost home when I see my father, standing over my mother. She's lying down in the water. Her body . . . it's not right. I don't know what I'm seeing at first. But then he picks her up and her head—" He stopped, breath catching.

"Her head," he tried again. But he couldn't complete the sentence.

"I see her throat," he said. "And I don't know what he's doing. He takes her away. And he comes back. And that's when—Agnes. He takes her, too. I was too afraid to ask. He acted so strange. So quiet. They'd been fighting so much . . . He told me what to say to the police. Exactly what to say. I thought he did it. All my life, I thought he'd killed them."

Agnes had wrapped her arms around her father's shoulders. She didn't ask him why he hadn't said anything to the police, back then. You can't predict how you'll react, in the face of your own soul-searing terror. But she'd wondered about her grandfather. Standing over the bodies of his murdered wife and child. She tried to understand why he hadn't called for help. Why he hadn't accused Thor. Had he known who his wife was seeing? Had he suspected?

Had he simply reacted, without thought?

She couldn't imagine her fastidious grandfather doing anything without carefully considering his options.

He had to have known how it would look. The arguments. The affair. To tell the police that his wife had been having an affair, that there was a not-insubstantial chance that his daughter wasn't his, this would have condemned him. The jealous, vengeful husband. Would anyone have believed him? That he'd stumbled upon their corpses, in his own backyard?

Her grandfather had known he was innocent. And still he'd moved the bodies. He buried them, away from the property. On Thor's land. An attempt, perhaps, to guide the police to the truth. A decision to entomb his wife and his daughter, together, in the snow. Misguided and tragic, the worst mistake.

Agnes had clutched her father tighter. She thought she heard him thank her.

"You gave me my father back," he told her.

She hadn't been able to do anything but weep. Weep for her grandmother, for her aunt. For her grandfather, for his years of silence, of guilt and suffering. But mostly, she'd wept for the child version of her father, long gone, left alone to struggle with the deaths. Left alone fearing the only family he had. Somewhere in there, too, was gratitude. That her father experienced such a great loss and it didn't destroy him, as it very easily could have.

That he kept moving forward.

Now in the hallway, considering her father's impatient form, Agnes turns instead toward a familiar voice. Crutching slowly away, she follows the growl of Óskar's voice to an open door.

There, in the bed by the window, knees curled up to her chest, sits Ása. Holding her, one arm slung around her, is Lilja. On the windowsill, watching over them like a protective rooster, is Óskar. There's no subtlety with crutches. As soon as Agnes has moved, she's announced her presence. Together, the three students turn to watch her progress.

"Hey," Agnes says, not wanting to interrupt, but not wanting to leave, either. She can't bring herself to look directly at Lilja, to meet those dark eyes. She's split her time between Agnes and Ása during visiting hours. She's sat with Agnes while she received her methadone. She's seen Agnes shivering and sweating through the worst of it. She's accepted her changing moods.

Agnes has apologized to her so many times over the past few days that the words "I'm sorry" have lost all meaning. *"I'm sorry" are weak words*, Lilja had told her yesterday, exasperated by the many apologies. *Don't thank me, either. Just accept it.*

"They finally discharged me," Agnes adds, aware that she's looking in the space between Ása and Lilja. "I guess I'm going."

Óskar hops off the windowsill. He crosses the room, fast, and before Agnes can do anything to stop him, he's enveloped her in a tight hug. She smells cologne and stale coffee.

"Thank you," he says.

She tries to accept it, as Lilja had told her. But she's uncomfortable, not just because she's being held so tightly it's making her panic, but because—"Ása did it all herself," she says.

Agnes isn't being modest, or self-deprecating. Ása saved herself. She's the one who stayed awake in that cellar, who fought to survive, who managed to find Ingvar in the snow. Agnes helped, she knows this. She knows she did what she could, and that without her falling through those stairs, Ása might never have been rescued. But when people thank her, she can't help but feel they are attributing everything to her and ignoring Ása's fight. She doesn't want to take anything more away from her.

Óskar releases her, nodding. He pats her shoulder in an awkward attempt at camaraderie. "No hard feelings," he says. "Yeah?"

"Sure," Agnes says with a half-hearted laugh.

There's a burst of Icelandic from Ása. Óskar and Lilja both seem to agree with whatever she's said. Óskar gives Agnes one more solid pat on the arm. "You did good," he tells her. "But you should have killed him." He steps out into the hallway, waiting for Lilja to join him.

Lilja stands. Agnes forces herself to meet Lilja's eye. Lilja's smiling, slightly, at her own private joke. She passes Agnes with the ghost of a touch to her hand gripping the crutches. "Find me before you go," she says. "I'll walk you out."

Then Agnes and Ása are alone again. Agnes crutches toward her bed, taking her in and feeling, finally, a sense of peace. Ása's still hollow around the eyes, but she's back on her medication. She's being taken care of.

"So you're really going," Ása says.

"I guess." Along with "I'm sorry," "I'm going" is the other phrase that has lost meaning in the past few days. What's waiting for her in California? Her bedroom, her stash of pills under the mattress? Job interviews? Finding an apartment? Starting over again?

She'd had so much time to think, lying in that hospital bed. Disturbed every few hours for new tests. She had never been alone, exactly, and she hadn't slept, no matter how much the hospital staff had been accommodating her. She'd found herself thinking about her life in a new way.

She's decided she'll talk to Emi when she gets home. She'd like to do it in the community garden, where she'd properly fallen in love with her. She doesn't want to hold on to Emi anymore.

She knows what she'll say already, even if it sounds cheesy. A quote from their favorite movie.

I'll see you in another life, when we're both cats.

"Are you going to be okay?" Agnes asks Ása. It's a ridiculous question, but she doesn't know how to talk to Ása. They've spent time together in the hospital, but they've never really spoken. They've held hands through the worst and best moments of their lives. There's too much to say.

"I don't know," Ása says honestly. "What about you?"

Agnes shrugs. "We'll see."

She has nursed a secret hope, a seed that's germinated in the dark, liminal hours of the night, when everyone is supposed to be sleeping, everyone except her and the graveyard shift. She's fed it water, she's tried to let it grow.

"When I made it to Ingvar," Ása says, reaching again for Agnes's uninjured hand, "I didn't tell him what happened. I could only think of being away. He was going to call the police when he saw your voicemail. He listened to your message. That's why it took so long. I'm sorry."

The absurdity of the apology hits Agnes in stages. She squeezes the woman's hand. "You saved me," she says, suddenly understanding Lilja's *Accept it* philosophy. She doesn't need an apology. "That's it."

They exchange their contact information. Agnes leans forward for a hug. Then she forces herself to leave. She limps out with one last look behind her.

Ása, hair luminous in sunlight, smiling.

Agnes doesn't make it far down the hallway before Lilja joins her. She walks steadily, unhurried next to her halting progress. Agnes sucks in a shaky breath, shocked at how quickly her heart started pounding, how she can feel it everywhere now, but mostly in her ears. "I'm terrible at goodbyes," she hears herself say. Her voice is rough, filled with unspoken words. "Really terrible, actually."

"Is this goodbye?" Lilja asks her. She tips those black eyes toward Agnes, and there's that seed growing. That idea blooming, wide and searing and exultant.

Agnes wrestles with the words while they find their way to the end of the hallway. Lilja stops at the door separating them from the waiting room. She puts a hand on it, but she doesn't move. "It's too soon," she says. "You shouldn't fly when you can hardly walk."

The words are there. They're filling Agnes's chest, she's a balloon about to burst. She's saying, "It's crazy, but—" when the door swings open, out of Lilja's hand.

"Ready?" Agnes's father asks her. He's already gotten her bags to the rental car. "Let's get out of here." He looks around him, cagily, as though expecting someone to stop them, physically, from leaving. When his eyes light on Lilja, they flit back to Agnes. Back to Lilja. "Oh," he says.

"One sec," Agnes tells him.

"No," Lilja says. "It's all right." She rocks forward on her tiptoes to brush her lips against Agnes's. She wraps her in a hug, but it lasts for only the time between heartbeats, and those are coming fast for Agnes. "Goodbye."

"I'll call you," Agnes says desperately, but it doesn't stop Lilja from walking away. From waving at Agnes and saying, "Okay," like they'll see each other later that afternoon. Like they have so much time, boundless, that they can be lazy with it.

Magnús clears his throat. "She seems nice," he says. "Are you two—?"

Agnes says, "Not anymore." She can sense her father wants to say more, so she sucks in another shaky breath and tries for a smile. "Let's go."

He's relieved. And he's fast. She crutches along in his wake, out the front doors to the rental car, idling near the entrance. She doesn't know if she'll have to testify at Thor's trial. She'll cross that bridge when she gets to it. For now, she's following her father's silhouette, wobbly from unshed tears.

She climbs into the backseat, much like she did in Ingvar's truck, sliding her leg straight out on the seats, and there's no more ceremony than her father starting the car and driving them out of the city, back to the airport. This time, there's no snow. There are sudden, torrential showers of rain that occasionally splatter the windshield, but the light has been turned on. She drinks in the view. Thinks, *This is the last time I will ever see this country*, and then, *Maybe not*. This can't be the last time she will ever see these black lava fields, covered in their blankets of moss, of snow, the mountains that look close enough to touch but are always jumping out of reach.

She's in outer space. She's an astronaut. And she's going back to Earth.

She's tired of the goodbyes. To Ingvar, who had been the first to meet her after her operation, who had waited all those hours to make sure she was all right before he went home to his mother. She'd been groggy, the anesthesia casting everything into a surreal shadow, but she'd been aware enough to feel the lips on her forehead. To hear him tell her she's brave. Not empty. Brave.

She will see Nora again. She's staying behind, but she's promised to find Agnes in Northern California, or Agnes will visit her in Los Angeles, when she feels ready.

Her father drops her off in front of the airport, so she can wait for him while he drives the car back to the rental company. While he handles the logistics of leaving a country behind—he's done it before. She stands in the chill breeze, leaning her weight on the crutches, and watches the world pour in and out of the building. The idea comes to her again, more urgent and vibrant than any color she's seen before.

She has to sit down on a bench to take out her phone. She sends the message before she can second-guess herself.

The answer comes almost immediately.

Yes.

CHAPTER SIXTY

June 30, 2019

She lands again in the morning, only this time, it's to the phosphorescent glow of daylight. It's early, but the sun's up high in the sky. Agnes takes her time on the highway, slow and careful, driving mostly one-handed. The stitches in her palm have long been removed and the scars themselves are fading into white lines, but she still struggles with the grip. The nerve pain when she puts pressure on that palm sometimes leaves her breathless. She loves this hand, though, sometimes even catches herself admiring the crisscrossing lines on her skin.

She leans into the turns of the road, guiding the car through the many roundabouts. She'll meet Lilja in Reykjavík. Outside her new apartment. It's small—really small—and it's in the basement of an apartment building with only a couple of windows at ground-level to let in light, but she's here. It's taken months to get to this point, to apply, interview, and accept the remote position at her old job, to file the appropriate paperwork, to let her leg waste away again while the joints started to heal, then to build the muscles back up. Nora put her in touch with a lawyer who's helped her with the visa application. On-going, but hopeful.

Despite months of treatment, Agnes still misses the pills. The taste of them. The comfort they'd once given her. But she can't take them, not anymore. Maybe soon, the cravings will release their hold on her.

She follows the signs to downtown Reykjavík. She's spent so much time staring at the map of the city, she's memorized the rest of the way, the turns and the unpronounceable street names.

And then there she is. Lilja, short hair fluttering in the summer breeze. Standing in front of the apartment building. She lifts a hand when she spots Agnes through the windshield.

"*Hæ!*" she hears Lilja shout. "Welcome home."

Agnes reaches her scarred hand toward the glass, toward Lilja beyond.

Hi.

AUTHOR'S NOTE

While I did base this story on a real town named Bifröst in Iceland, I have taken many, many artistic liberties with the town's geography and its history. All changes and mistakes are mine. All love and admiration for the place, also mine.

ACKNOWLEDGMENTS

Before I thank those who helped make this book a reality, I need to talk about its epigraph. "Devotion" is a song written and performed by Forest Erwin. I listened to this song practically on repeat, when this book was nothing more than a twinkle in my eye, when I was drafting, when I was revising—essentially, all the time. Its roots are intertwined with Agnes's roots. You can find this song and more of Forest's music on Spotify, under the artist named Stay in Touch. I hope Forest shares more of his music with us, and I hope you enjoy it as much as I do.

With that said, perhaps not surprisingly, most of the writing of this book took place in solitude. It started at the kitchen table of an apartment share in Reykjavík, and it found its shape in California, over the many months of recovery after yet another knee surgery—an injury ironically (?) incurred after I slipped on a patch of ice in Iceland. For all the hours this book and I have spent alone in various rooms, though, this hasn't been a solitary journey. There are so many people to whom I owe enormous thanks:

My editor, Hannah O'Grady, who made the book exactly how it wanted to be. Everything about working with you is a dream come true. The entire team at Minotaur, Madeline Alsup, Chris Leonowicz, Alisa Trager, Kiffin Steurer, David Rotstein, Meryl Sussman Levavi, Mac Nicholas, Stephen Erickson, Paul Hochman, and Kayla Janas.

My agent, Jamie Carr, whose excitement never wavered and who knows me far too well at this point. There's no hiding from you. My film/TV agents, Olivia Fanaro and Orly Greenberg, for your understanding and your passion. My foreign rights champion, Jenny Meyer.

My writing community. The Hardcore Berkletes, who were there with me in spirit in Iceland, who have kept me safe and sane. Mina and Leyla Hamedi, Zeynep Özakat, Jennifer Herrera, Carol Goodman, Hildur Knútsdóttir. I'm not sure there would have been a book without you all.

My hosts in Iceland, particularly Guðlaug Ýr and Júlíús Eymundsson, for opening your homes to me. Stefán Laxdal, thanks for the music.

Dr. Vincent Chow, for fixing my knee (Twice! Hopefully never again! No offense!) and for your help with Agnes.

My friends and family. My grandparents, Tracy and Charles Stephenson and Judith Strong and Frants Albert, for your friendship, your guidance, and our time spent together. Mom, for everything. Ray, for all the many times you read it. Dad, for not being Magnús, for being better than.

ABOUT THE AUTHOR

Emily Hlaváč Green

Melissa Larsen is the author of *Shutter*. She received her MFA from Columbia University and her BA from New York University. When she isn't traveling somewhere to research her next novel—and somehow hurting herself in the process—she lives in New York City and teaches creative writing.